W9-AKV-641

A Harlequin
JANET DAILEY
Collector's Edition

1 NO QUARTER ASKED
THE INDY MAN

2 BOSS MAN FROM OGALLALA
DARLING JENNY

3 DIFFICULT DECISION
ENEMY IN CAMP

4 HEART OF STONE
BIG SKY COUNTRY

5 ONE OF THE BOYS
BEWARE OF THE STRANGER

6 THE WIDOW AND THE WASTREL
SOMETHING EXTRA

Harlequin Books

TORONTO • NEW YORK • LOS ANGELES • LONDON
AMSTERDAM • PARIS • SYDNEY • HAMBURG
STOCKHOLM • ATHENS • TOKYO • MILAN

These books by Janet Dailey were originally published as follows:

THE WIDOW AND THE WASTREL
Copyright © 1977 by Janet Dailey
First published by Mills & Boon Limited in 1977
Harlequin Presents edition (#211) published June 1977

SOMETHING EXTRA
Copyright © 1975 by Janet Dailey
First published by Mills & Boon Limited in 1975
Harlequin Presents edition (#248) published August 1978

ISBN 0-373-80606-X
First edition October 1982

PRINTED IN U.S.A.

CONTENTS

THE WIDOW AND THE WASTREL

HIS KISS WAS WARM, DRUGGING HER SENSES.

"Damn," Jed muttered softly. "Liza—" She hated his calm, controlled voice.

"Please," she whispered. "I don't want to talk."

"A few minutes ago you called me contemptible and disgusting." His low voice was cynically amused. "Am I supposed to feel honored now that you want me to make love to you?"

"Don't be cruel," Elizabeth murmured, shame creeping in to steal her pleasure.

"I'm sorry, Liza," he said in a gentler yet firm tone. "I thought I'd stopped wanting you, but I haven't. The bitterness hasn't gone, either," he ended grimly.

"I don't understand," she gazed at him bewilderedly.

"I know you don't." The glint in his eyes was ruthless. "Maybe someday. . . . " He was withdrawing from her, emotionally as well as physically. "Good night, Elizabeth."

CHAPTER ONE

ELIZABETH CARREL stepped through the door of her home, a tennis racquet tucked under her arm. it was another hot August day. The heat and exertion had combined to leave her feeling drained and exhausted as she leaned tiredly against the hardwood door.

'Elizabeth, is that you?' The mature, feminine voice held an authoritative ring.

Pushing the thick, raven-black hair away from her face, Elizabeth straightened away from the door, the vulnerable look leaving as her canvas shoes carried her farther into the brick-tiled foyer.

'Yes, Rebecca," she answered, not bothering to glance into the priceless antique mirror hanging on one wall of the entryway.

At the archway into the living room, she paused, her green eyes gazing at the smart, sophisticated woman within. Perfectly styled silver-gray hair gleamed from beneath a summer hat of blue flowers, an exact match to the opaque flowered dress of pale blue, impeccably tailored to show off the slender form of the much older woman. A brooch of amethyst and sapphires was the only jewelry. A bone-colored handbag to go with the bone-colored shoes sat on an oak table.

'I thought you would have left for your luncheon by now,' Elizabeth commented.

'I would have,' Rebecca Carrel replied. The melodic smoothness of her tone carried a hint of censure. 'But I sent your daughter to her room an hour ago to get ready for her music lesson and she hasn't come down yet. Perhaps you will see what's keeping her.'

Elizabeth smiled wanly at her mother-in-law. 'I'll see.'

The stairway leading to the upper floor of the old home was in a hallway of the foyer. Her shoes made little sound on the hardwood steps, the patina of many years adding to their high polish. At the door to her daughter's room, Elizabeth paused and knocked once.

The action brought a curious smile to the full curve of her lips. It hadn't been prompted by a reluctance to enter Amy's room without permission, but by a silent demand that the formal atmosphere of the house made. After a grumbling acknowledgment from the room, she entered.

There was an understanding light in her eyes as Elizabeth looked at the sullen figure staring out the window. Rebellion was outlined in the erect frame and squared shoulders.

'Hello, Amy.'

The cap of curling brunette hair turned at her mother's voice, brown eyes snapping with displeasure. 'Mother, do I have to have my lesson today? Can't I miss it just once? If I was sick you wouldn't make me go.'

The impulse was there to agree, but Elizabeth held it

back, and walked farther into the room. Her daughter was rebellious enough as it was without adding impetus to her fight.

'I think you'd better have your lesson today. There will be other days when you'll have to miss because of some special thing that's planned,' she reasoned.

'I'll bet,' Amy pouted openly.

'Your grandmother's waiting for you downstairs.'

'I know.' The admission was made through gritted teeth. 'I just hate these lessons, Mother! Mrs. Banks keeps making me do the same thing over and over and over. And that fan keeps making horrid noises and it's so hot.'

'I thought you told me that you liked playing the piano.' Elizabeth prompted gently, a smile held in check at the vehemence in her daughter's voice.

'I like playing the piano, but I don't like lessons and practising those stupid scales!'

'In order to do one, you have to do the other.'

'Oh, Mom!' Amy sighed.

The reverting back to the less formal mode of address signalled the agreement of her daughter. This time Elizabeth didn't hold back her smile, but let the warmth of her love show through as she tilted up the downcast chin.

'You'd better get your music books and get downstairs or your grandmother will be late for her luncheon,' she ordered lightly.

'The sooner I go, the sooner I can leave,' Amy sighed again, widening her eyes with mock adult resignation.

'Such enthusiasm!' Elizabeth laughed softly and pressed a quick kiss on her daughter's forehead before pointing her in the direction of the door.

She didn't follow Amy down the stairs, but remained at the top of the landing near the door to her own room staring after the youthful form going down the steps. She was a beautiful child who would be an even more beautiful adult. Unconsciously Elizabeth marveled that this exquisite little human being had come from her flesh and blood. She had long ago ceased to remember that Amy's father had played any part in the creation.

When Elizabeth stepped into her room, the photograph on the dressing table reminded her. The man in the picture was a stranger to her. Their marriage had been of such a short duration when he was killed in an automobile accident. At the time, she hadn't even known she was carrying Amy. It was difficult to remember she had ever been married, so brief had been their interlude together.

Of course, she had been married to Jeremy Carrel or she wouldn't be living in his family's house today. And Amy resembled her father with her dark brown hair and eyes, but her attitude and personality was totally dissimilar to his. Jerry, who had never been a mother's boy, had accepted the role his family played in the community, society, business, and leadership. When Elizabeth had married him, he had been marking time and preparing for the day when he would take command of the Carrel law firm and its holdings from his father. Never once did he strain at the invisible bonds of what was socially acceptable as Amy did. He never did anything in excess except what was accepted.

Turning away from the photograph, Elizabeth saw her reflection in the full-length mirror standing freely in the corner of her room in its self-supporting oak frame. Her tennis whites accented the gleaming bronze shade of her shapely legs, slimly rounded hips curved into a slender waist, then the line curved back out to indicate the adult fullness of her breasts. She didn't need the reflection to tell her that she was a beautiful woman, hardly looking old enough to have an eight-year-old child.

Perhaps, Elizabeth decided as she turned from the mirror to remove her tennis clothes, Amy's stubborness did come from her father's unshakable determination. And from her own as well. She simply hadn't been able to steer Amy's self-will into a constructive outlet. The minor rebellions seemed to have increased in the last year. Elizabeth wondered if the lack of a male figure in her daughter's life was the cause.

Amy's grandfather, Jerry's father, had been taken from them quite suddenly with a heart attack almost two years ago. He had never spent much time with Amy even though they lived in the same house. Nor had Amy ever indicated any great affection for her grandfather, but sometimes Elizabeth found it difficult to know exactly what was on her daughter's mind.

Hesitating in front of the open door of her closet, she shrugged away the thought of dressing and reached instead for the cotton caftan. Its loose-fitting folds would be much more comfortable on this hot, stickily humid day.

Downstairs again, Elizabeth paused in the roomy, old-fashioned kitchen long enough to fix herself a cold glass of lemonade. She had already had a light lunch with her tennis partner and friend, Barbara Hopkins. Besides, with the house quiet, this was the perfect time to read through the plays the local theatre group was considering using this season.

Although there was no longer a Carrel in the business community, Rebecca Carrel had not relinquished her leadership in the other areas. Elizabeth had the impression that now that her husband was gone, her mother-in-law actually enjoyed being the sole center of attention, no longer needing to share the spotlight with her husband. It was a mean thought since Elizabeth knew at first hand how devoted Rebecca had been, always the perfect wife, the perfect helpmate and the perfect confidante to her husband, while maintaining her own social position and never allowing the two to conflict.

Rebecca Carrel was a marvel of organization and Elizabeth had learned considerably from her. Now she played an active role in the 'right' social clubs of the community. She was a Carrel, and the younger set sought her out in much the same way as her mother-in-law. Her life was full to the point that there was rarely an empty moment. Maybe that was why she never missed Jerry as much as she thought she would. In the beginning, Rebecca had not allowed her the time to grieve, although Elizabeth had felt more shock than grief. Then there had been Amy. And now — well, now there was now.

As she entered the living room, Elizabeth stopped and, with a smile, walked to the piano in the small alcove. She ran her fingers lightly over the ivory keys, remembering her own young rebellion at practising scales. Amy seemed to have an aptitude for the piano, expressing an enjoyment similar to what Elizabeth had known. Certainly she had never pushed Amy into learning.

Setting her lemonade glass down, she began experimentally picking out the melody of a song. More memories came flooding back as the nimbleness of her fingers increased. It was at the piano recital that she had met Jerry. He had come with his parents and they had been introduced for the first time at the reception that followed the recital.

Not that Elizabeth hadn't known who he was all the time. She doubted that anyone in the county hadn't known Jeremy Carrel. Nearly everyone had given up expecting that he would marry a local girl. When she had seen that admiring light in his dark eyes, she knew there was hope. If she played her cards right, Elizabeth had realized that she could catch the most eligible bachelor around — and in truth, that was exactly what she had set out to do. It had been terribly easy to let herself fall in love with Jerry.

Mary Ellen Simmons, the aunt who had raised Elizabeth after her parents had died when she was eleven, had not entirely approved of the marriage. She had insisted that at seventeen Elizabeth couldn't possibly know that she wanted to spend the rest of her life with Jerry Carrel, fearing that her niece was more impressed with his background than in love with the individual. Her suspicions were never proved one way or the other. In fact, Elizabeth hadn't given them a thought until this minute.

Curious. Her fingers slipped into a slower, more pensive tune. Why was she suddenly dwelling on what happened so many years ago? She had never questioned before whether she had truly loved Jerry or not. It was a moot question that had no definitive answer.

A surge of restlessness burst through her for no apparent reason. Her fingers clanged on the keyboard, discordant and harsh. Anger turned inward that she had wasted time with useless daydreaming that could have been better spent studying the theater's plays.

Sliding to the edge of the piano bench, Elizabeth reached for her lemonade glass. With it safely in hand, she turned to rise impatiently and froze. A figure was leaning against the wooden frame of the living room archway.

A cold chill ran down her spine at the unkempt appearance of the man; a sweat-stained shirt of light blue was half-unbuttoned to accent a masculine chest tanned teak brown. Lean hips were covered by slacks that were probably a darker blue, only they were too dust-covered to be certain. The stubble of unshaven beard darkened the chiselled angles of his face. A windbreaker was over one shoulder and a much used duffle bag was sitting on the floor beside him. Thick, tobacco brown hair had been combed away from the tanned face by the fingers of one hand. Hazel gold eyes were watching Elizabeth with lazy intentness.

'What are you doing in here?' she breathed, suddenly conscious of how isolated the house was in its country setting.

'Is the concert over?' his deep, husky voice asked.

She rose to her full five feet six inches, making her shaky voice sound icy and imperious. 'You have no right to be in here. I suggest that you leave immediately before I contact the authorities.' There was a flash of white in the beard growth as the man smiled and remained where he was. 'If you're looking for a handout, you'll get none here. The highway is a half mile down the road. I'll give you five seconds to leave and I'm phoning the police.'

With the threat voiced, she walked to the telephone and picked up the receiver. Any second she expected him to pull a gun or knife and assault her.

'I didn't expect the fatted calf,' he drawled, 'but I did think I would at least be offered a meal.'

'You'd better leave.' She dialed the first digit, ignoring his comment.

'You're going to feel like a fool, little sister. It might be interesting to see a Carrel with a red face, even one claiming the name by marriage,' he chuckled softly.

For the second time, Elizabeth froze, her green eyes swinging back to the stranger in the archway, confident, not the least bit intimidated by her threat. She didn't know him, but he seemed to know her, or at least he was aware of her connection with the Carrels.

'Who are you?' she demanded. Her fingers were still tightly clenching the receiver.

'Have I changed that much in all these years?' A brow lifted in mock inquiry. 'I would have recognized you anywhere. I like your widow's weeds. Jerry always did like you in blue.'

The receiver nearly was dropped from her hand. 'Jed?' she whispered in disbelief.

'The one and only,' he confirmed, straightening from his slouching position against the door. 'Had you given me up for dead?'

'We haven't heard from you —' Elizabeth began, then stopped. 'Jed, your father — he had a heart attack almost two years ago. He's ... he's dead.' There seemed no way to put it less bluntly.

'The house hasn't changed much,' was his comment as his tawny gold gaze swept the room, then it returned to the sympathy etched on her oval features. 'I heard about Dad.' he said finally with little emotion visible on his unshaved face. 'Mother's letter caught up with me about a year ago. There seemed little point in returning by that time.'

'Why ... why have you come back?' she asked.

His tongue clicked in mock reproval. 'It's bad manners to ask probing questions, Liza.'

'Elizabeth,' she corrected automatically, and he laughed.

'Still striving for status, I see.'

'I don't like the name Liza. It sounds —'

'Common was the adjective I believe you used'

before,' he reminded her. 'It was shortly after you became engaged to my brother and you were trying to appear the poised and sophisticated young lady to impress my mother. You became very angry when I called you that in front of them.'

'I remember.' A tautness crept into her expression as she averted her eyes from the watchfulness of his.

'Where's Mother?'

'At a luncheon in town,' Elizabeth replied.

'Of course, it's Thursday, isn't it? I had forgotten that she holds court every Thursday.' A hard smile moved over his mouth, somewhat cynical and derisive.

'If you would like to clean up, the room at the end of the stairs is empty. You can put your things there. There are fresh towels in the bathroom.'

His expression didn't change. 'Is that a subtle hint that you find my appearance less than presentable?' Jed Carrel queried mockingly. 'It was a hot, dusty walk out here.'

'Do you mean you walked from town?' She frowned at him in surprise.

He glanced down at his dust-covered shoes and slacks. 'My feet were the only transportation available. The local taxi was no doubt ferrying Mother's lady friends to their weekly luncheon with the Queen.'

'You could have waited,' Elizabeth murmured automatically.

'I was anxious to see if Thomas Wolfe was right, that you can't go home again. So far I would say he's right. My old room at the head of the stairs is in use?

'It's Amy's now.' She bristled faintly at his implication. They had met only once. They were virtually strangers, so why should he expect her to welcome him back with open arms?

'Amy?' Jed questioned with a dark brow arched in inquiry.

'My daughter.' Her chin lifted fractionally to a defiant angle.

Again there was the cynical movement of his mouth that was supposed to resemble a smile. 'Oh, yes,' he nodded. 'I remember Jerry left you with a child. Amy, that was my grandmother's name.'

'That was her namesake,' Elizabeth admitted.

'Mother must have liked that. Or was it her suggestion?'

His mocking jibe struck home, but Elizabeth wouldn't acknowledge it. 'Several names were discussed before Amy was born.' She turned away abruptly. 'Have you eaten? Would you like me to fix you a light lunch?'

'Breakfast, please,' he requested instead. 'I haven't adjusted to the time zones yet. For me, it's tomorrow morning. Omelette and toast will be fine.'

He was picking up his duffle bag and striding with catlike smoothness for the stairway door. Elizabeth stared after the lean, masculine figure. After almost nine years she couldn't be blamed for not expecting to see her husband's brother again, or for practically forgetting his existence. In the last few years, his name had only been mentioned once that she could recall, and that had been when Rebecca, his mother, had wanted to notify him of his father's death. Just once.

They had only received three cards from him that Elizabeth could remember, short little notes that had been postmarked in different foreign ports ranging from the Pacific Islands to South-east Asia. His name had almost been forbidden from the very first.

Naturally when Elizabeth had first met Jeremy, she had been aware that he had a brother, younger by little more than a year. Jed was a wild one, the gossips had said, expelled from schools and colleges, ignoring every edict and principle of social behavior that his family stood for.

Her only interest had been in Jeremy. The escapades of his brother were of little importance. If she had thought of him at all, it had only been a concern that she should approve of her as a future member of the family. She had always known in the back of her mind that if Jeremy's family didn't approve of her, there would be no marriage regardless of how much he had professed to love her.

Unconscious of her actions, Elizabeth turned to the kitchen, caught up in the memories of the past, a trip backward that had already begun before Jed's sudden arrival. Now her thoughts focused on her single meeting with him.

It had occurred only a day or two after Jeremy had proposed. She had met his parents once, briefly at a dance he had taken her to at the country club. After his proposal, she had been invited to dinner. Elizabeth had been afraid it was very significant that Jeremy had not yet given her an engagement ring.

When they had arrived here at his house, she had been a bundle of nerves, terrified that she would do or say the wrong thing. Jeremy had offered little support, growing more silent with each step they had taken toward the door. His parents and Jed had been in the living room awaiting their arrival. The hostile atmosphere had almost smothered Elizabeth. She had been certain the silent animosity was directed at her. It was quite a while before she realized their censure was directed at Jed.

Initially he had been silent, not the silence of disapproval, but of cynical amusement. Although he had never uttered a word to confirm it, Elizabeth had the distinct feeling that his parents' approval or disapproval of the girl he wanted to marry would not have affected his decision and he found it amusing that Jeremy sought it so earnestly. At the time, Elizabeth had been angered that he couldn't understand the necessity for it.

Except for an initial greeting and an odd comment at the dinner table, Jed had not addressed any conversation directly to her. Not that she had cared. In fact, she had been glad that he hadn't singled her out for attention in case his parents' anger rubbed off on to her. There had been an inner sensation that he knew she had silently taken the side against him and knew why.

After coffee had been taken in the living room, a tiny voice had suggested that this was the time to make a discreet withdrawal and give Jeremy an opportunity to speak to his parents in private. The smile of approval that had flashed across Jeremy's face when she asked to be excused to freshen up had told her that the suggestion was a wise one.

She had fussed with her hair and make-up and lingered as long as she dared before venturing into the hallway, crossing her fingers that she wasn't returning too soon. Jed was in the hallway. Something in his manner had prevented Elizabeth from walking past him.

'So you're the angel of virtue that has captured my elusive brother,' he had murmured softly, almost mockingly. 'You look more like a dark-haired witch to me.'

Her nervousness had increased with her uncertainty how to reply to his comment. It was one of those horrible moments when no suitable response came to mind.

She had smiled weakly. 'Jeremy will be wondering where I am. Excuse me.'

The light touch of his hand on her arm had stopped her. 'Doesn't it bother you that they're in there deciding whether to allow you the dubious privilege of becoming a member of the Carrel family?' He had frowned.

'I wouldn't marry Jeremy without his parents' permission,' she had answered, her expression adding that to do otherwise would be insane.

'How old are you?' Unusual hazel-gold eyes swept her oval face and slender figure, inspecting her with swift appraisal.

'Seventeen. Quite old enough to know my own

mind I'm sure,' Elizabeth had asserted defiantly.

'And you're in love with the idea of becoming Mrs. Jeremy Carrel,' Jed had mocked.

'More than anything else I want to be his wife. I love him.'

'Yet you wouldn't marry him if my parents disapproved,' he scoffed.

'Of course not,' she had answered.

'I don't believe you really love him or you'd fight tooth and nail to have him instead of passively waiting for someone else to give the verdict as to whether you'll marry him or not.'

'It's my life and my decision and none of your business!' His cutting jibe prompted a stinging retort.

'Don't marry him, Elizabeth.' There was a hard, warning note in his tone. 'Don't get caught up in the so-called glamor of the Carrel name and make a mistake you'll regret.'

'Aren't you being premature?' she had asked haughtily. 'It's possible that your parents will disapprove of me.'

'Oh, they will approve.' A corner of his mouth curled cynically upward. 'My moralistic father sees you as pure and untouched and has investigated your background sufficiently to be certain there's not a breath of scandal attached to your name. Mother is glorying in the almost worshipful attention you've been paying her. She's already deciding that she can mold you into the type of daughter-in-law she wants, as subservient to her wishes as Jeremy is.'

'That's not a very nice way to talk about your

parents.' The elation she had felt at his initial statement that they would give her permission for the marriage was taken away by his sarcastic analysis of their reason.

'The truth is often unkind, Liza.'

'My name is Elizabeth.' Her dislike of him had increased when he shortened her name. 'I don't like nicknames. They're so common.'

'And Elizabeth is filled with all sorts of royal connotations, isn't it?' Jed mocked. 'Forgive me if I don't bow.'

'Forgive me if I find it hard to believe that you and Jeremy are brothers,' Elizabeth retorted acidly.

'Don't apologize for that. That's been a puzzle almost since the day I was born. All I've heard is why can't you be more like your brother.' Jed laughed with unconcealed bitterness. 'I make too many waves, but I don't intend to change. I'm not like Jerry. I'm not content to walk in my father's shadow. I'll blaze my own trail in life.'

'So you condemn Jeremy because he is joining your father's firm,' she replied coldly.

'Not if that's what he wants.'

'Do you question that he knows?'

'The same way that I question if you know,' he replied.

'I know exactly what I want. To marry Jeremy,' Elizabeth stated without qualification.

'Do you?'

His fingers closed over her chin and tilted it up. Her green eyes rounded in surprise as she stared into the lean face bending closer to hers. The astonishment at his action was so complete that she had made not one word of protest nor attempted to draw away. Nor was she prepared for the hard, passionate possession of his kiss, the raging fire scorching through her veins. Inexperience had held her frightened by what was happening. When the bruising pressure had been lifted, Elizabeth had only been able to stare into the satisfied gleam of his gold-flecked eyes, reminiscent of a cat playing with its prey.

'I doubt that Jeremy has ever kissed you like that, Liza,' Jed had smiled mirthlessly. 'His emotions are too severely checked to permit it.'

"I certainly hope not,' Elizabeth had whispered breathlessly, a frightened pulse throbbing in her throat.

She and Jeremy had kissed many times. Warm satisfying exchanges they were, too. But never had she been left with the sensation that she was about to be seduced.

'Jerry r-respects me too much to treat me like that,' she had added in a more forceful voice that was still quivering slightly.

'Is that what you want from him? His respect and the Carrel name?' He was laughing at her youth, but she was powerless to stop it. 'He will be making love to you, you know.'

'But with gentleness and consideration.' A flush began creeping into her cheeks at his open discussion of such an intimate subject.

'I hope some day, Liza, you'll be honest enough to

tell me if that's what you really want.' He had sounded almost sorry for her.

'How dare you speak to me like this? How dare you treat me this way?' she had demanded, now angry that he thought she should be pitied.

'You've got to wake up, little Liza. Jeremy isn't the man for you,' Jed had pointed out smoothly, showing amusement at her display of temper.

'What's going on here?' Jeremy was visibly bristling at the end of the hallway, his dark eyes looking accusingly at Jed and Elizabeth.

With a guilty start, she had pulled away from the hand that was curled along the side of her neck in an obvious caress. She had been frightened that Jeremy would misunderstand and think she had invited this accidental meeting with his brother.

'I was just coming in —' she had begun to explain, but Jed broke in calmly.

'Yes, she was,' he agreed, 'but I waylaid her before she could hurry back to the safety of your side. I wanted to be the first to kiss your official bride-to-be. I didn't want her to have any doubts that I would welcome her into the house with open arms.'

The suggestive emphasis Jed placed on the last brought a stormy thundercloud into Jeremy's expression. Elizabeth had sensed that Jed was deliberately goading him into anger.

'You keep away from Elizabeth, Jed,' Jeremy had growled.

'Then congratulations are in order.' Jed turned to Elizabeth, who was still too paralyzed to move and smiled. 'The verdict is in and the sentence is about to be life. I wouldn't expect much mercy if I were you, Liza. The Carrel family isn't a forgiving lot — I know from first-hand experience.'

'Elizabeth, come here,' Jeremy ordered crisply.

As she started to walk by Jed, she read the silent message in his hazel gold eyes, repeating again that she was making a mistake. Her reply was to practically run to Jeremy's side, letting his arm circle her shoulders and draw her to him. She smiled into his face, seeing that her quick obedience had dulled the edge to most of his anger.

Then Jeremy's dark eyes had turned to his brother, standing alone several feet away, the expression in Jed's eyes shielded by half-closed eyelids.

'Mother suggested that for appearances' sake you should be the best man,' Jeremy had announced.

'I suppose I'm supposed to be honored to be included in the festivities at all. Do you think by giving me a major role that it will put me on my best behavior?' Jed had mocked.

'I've made my wishes known,' Jeremy had stated stiffly. 'I would like to have you as my best man. It's up to you to accept or refuse.'

Without answering, Jed had turned and walked away.

CHAPTER TWO

A FLASH of total recall brought vividly back to life that long-forgotten incident. Elizabeth's fingertips were unconsciously pressed against her lips. In retrospect, Jed's kiss did not seem nearly so frightening or unpleasant. The discovery was very unsettling because it was so at odds with her opinion of him.

Jed had not been best man at their wedding. In fact, a few days after her introduction to him, Jeremy told her that he had left for parts unknown. Although he had not added it, Elizabeth had sensed that Jeremy wished his brother Godspeed and a long journey. Secretly she had been surprised that his parents had endorsed the thought, but mostly she had felt relief that Jed would not be around.

In appearance, he and Jeremy had not resembled each other except for the brown hair. Jeremy had been an inch or two taller than Jed's six feet. His frame had been broader and more muscular in appearance than Jed's lean build. In Elizabeth's judgment, Jeremy had been the handsomer of the two, with a fine strong face that was youthfully manly.

At twenty-three there had been a chiseled hardness to Jed's features that the years had seemed to intensify, making him appear more cynical and rugged. Yet it had been his overpowering sense of maleness that had left Elizabeth feeling so naïvely insecure and inexperienced. She had known that she could become the kind of socially acceptable wife that Jeremy wanted, but the thought of Jed as her brother-in-law had filled her with trepidation. Then he had removed himself, taking with him her fear and uncertaintly.

Now Jed had returned. Why? It was a question without an answer, one that he had dodged successfully when she had asked him. If he had returned after Jeremy's death or his father's, Elizabeth would have understood. But there seemed little purpose for his return. She couldn't believe it was prompted by any sense of family loyalty or any driving desire to return to the home of his birth.

If it had been that, he wouldn't have returned looking like a common tramp, dirty and disheveled. No, if he had hoped to get back in good graces with his mother as the only remaining male member of the family, he would have made his homecoming in a more auspicious manner. He would have spent his last cent to look the part of a Carrel and not come walking across fields carrying a knapsack on his back, unshaven and unkempt.

'A penny for your thoughts — or is it more expensive to know what a Carrel is thinking?'

Elizabeth blinked into a pair of gold-brown eyes, catlike like the rest of Jed Carrel, always insinuating a lazy feline arrogance. She didn't have to be told it was a pose, that he could respond with catlike swiftness.

'They —' She took a deep breath to control the sudden acceleration of her pulse. 'They aren't worth a penny.'

'My omelette?' Jed prodded mockingly when she continued to stare at him.

'Right away.'

She turned quickly to the refrigerator, tearing her gaze from the transformation that had occurred in the space of a few minutes. The beard growth was gone, revealing a lean jaw and high cheekbones. The heady scent of some male aftershave lotion drifted around her nose. His tobacco brown hair gleamed a darker brown, courtesy of the shower spray, its natural waywardness even when combed properly giving him a more rakish appearance.

But again she had been struck by his maleness, her awareness awakened by the crisp, white, short-sleeved shirt only partially buttoned. The tanned skin of his bare arms rippled with sinewy muscles and the dark curling hair on his chest heightened the teak shade of his tan. His leanness made his strength seem primitively masculine. An inner sense told her that even when he was in formal clothing the impression would be just as strong.

It was difficult to work with her usual efficiency in the kitchen while his eyes watched her every move. Elizabeth forced herself to concentrate on what she was doing.

She glanced to where he sat straddling a kitchen chair to ask, 'Do you want your omelette plain or with cheese or ham?'

'Plain is fine,' Jed answered.

He waited until she had served his omelette and toast before making further conversation. 'Where's your daughter?' he asked.

'In town with Rebecca. She has a piano lesson shortly after noon.'

'Does she play as well as her mother?'

The question flustered Elizabeth. For an instant she found it difficult to assimilate that Jed was referring to her.

'Amy is just a beginner.' She reached for the coffee pot to pour herself a cup, uncaring of the hotness of the day's temperature. 'She's only been taking lessons for a little over a year. But she's quite good.'

'Does she look like you?'

Elizabeth didn't turn to the table immediately, but took her time adding a spoonful of sugar to the dark liquid. 'No, she takes after her father.'

'That's a pity,' Jed responded dryly.

'Why have you come back?' Her green eyes warily met the sliding glance of his.

'Do I have to have a reason?'

'Yes,' she breathed, letting him hold her gaze for what seemed an interminably long time before he returned his attention to the plate on the table. 'I can't believe you came back simply because this was your home.'

'Don't discount the pull of your childhood home. You can pull the roots out, but you always leave some behind,' Jed replied.

'Is that why you've come?' she asked, still not accepting the slightly ambiguous answer he'd come up with.

'That's why I've come here,' he agreed. 'But I think I returned to the States for a breath of civilization.'

'When will you be leaving?'

'Maybe tomorrow. Maybe never,' he shrugged, white teeth flashing as he bit into the slice of toast.

'I don't understand why you've come back now.' She brushed the raven hair away from her face, a tiny frown creasing her forehead.

'You probably don't even know why I left, do you?' The hard mouth moved into a wry smile.

'I know you argued with your parents,' Elizabeth hedged.

Jed pushed the empty plate towards the center of the table. 'All the time I was growing up it was one argument after another. Foolishly I kept believing that I could make my parents understand that all I wanted was to live my own life. When you and Jeremy became engaged, I'd been kicked out of three law schools. My father gave me the news that night that he had used his influence and money to get me accepted into another. He refused to accept that I didn't want to be a lawyer, that I wanted no part of the family business. A couple of days later I left.'

'I see,' she murmured.

'I doubt it.' His voice was coated with bitter mockery. It brought her head up sharply. 'Truthfully I didn't expect to find you here when I came back.'

'Where did you think I'd be?' Elizabeth laughed shortly in confusion.

'Married. You're a beautiful woman.' It was a

statement more than a compliment. 'I can't believe there haven't been offers.'

'I haven't dated all that much since Jeremy died, and not with anyone on a regular basis.' Elizabeth turned her back on him, seeking to change the subject. 'Would you like some coffee?'

'Please.' When she set the cup before him, Jed asked, 'Why have you avoided seeing anyone regularly?'

'I haven't avoided it,' she answered sharply, responding to the hint of mockery in his tone. 'I simply haven't had a great deal of free time. A person doesn't when they have children.'

'Free time can be arranged if the desire is great enough,' he observed. 'Wasn't Jerry able to arouse a great enough desire?'

His jeering question jerked her chin up. 'We were very happy together,' Elizabeth stated with a frigid anger. 'Which is probably why I haven't been interested in anyone else.'

'Do you enjoy being the beautiful Carrel widow, challenging the men you meet to win your favors?' Jed inquired with biting softness. 'Or are you afraid that some man will show you how very inadequate Jeremy was?' His gaze slid to her mouth as if to evoke the memory of his kiss.

Elizabeth pivoted sharply away from the table, walking to the counter to set her cup down. 'Jeremy was very adequate and I have a daughter to prove it. Your questions are becoming much too personal and bordering on insolence.'

'The ability to procreate is not indicative of a man's prowess to arouse a woman's desires,' he laughed arrogantly. 'Was his respect and gentleness as satisfying as you thought it would be?'

'Yes!' she flashed angrily.

'Honestly?' Jed prodded softly, and she realized he had come quietly up behind her.

'Yes, honestly,' Elizabeth declared firmly. A bitter anger rose in her throat. 'You haven't changed, Jed. I thought you were insulting and arrogant the first time I met you, and the years in between haven't altered that. You tried to turn me against Jeremy then and you're still doing it now when he isn't here to defend himself. I think that's disgusting and contemptible!'

'Seeing you again has brought back the memory of our first and only meeting, too,' he answered with serious thoughtfulness. 'You were an extraordinarily bewitching young creature, tantalizingly innocent and desirable. My mind tells me that you're mature and no longer innocent, but my eyes insist that you're still inexperienced. As a woman,' his voice became husky and caressing, 'you are even more desirable than you were as a girl.'

'Stop it!' She wanted to close her ears to his voice, but it was impossible.

'Looking back, part of the reason I left was you. That night I couldn't stop myself from kissing you, even though I knew I'd frightened you. I frighten you now, too.' His hands closed over the soft flesh of her upper arms. 'You're trembling.'

She closed her eyes to stop the quivering response at

his touch. 'From disgust,' she murmured wildly, needing to explain the reason for her disturbance.

'At least give me credit for leaving.' There was a smile in his voice. 'Had I stayed I probably wouldn't have been able to resist the temptation to make love to you, even if you were my brother's wife. Now —' Jed slid his hands down her arms, letting his fingers close around her slender wrists. Crossing her arms in front of her, he drew her shoulders back against his chest, 'Now I can hold you like this, bury my face in your silken black hair.' Elizabeth gasped in shock as he proceeded to let his action follow his words. 'And—'

'Let me go!' She tried to twist away from the sensuous nuzzling near her ear.

There was silent laughter in the warm breath that caressed her cheek and throat. Elizabeth discovered that Jed found her struggles amusing, aware that his superior strength would counter any attempt to be free.

'Elizabeth!' The startled and censorious voice came from the hallway door.

Flames of red burned her cheeks as Jed slowly released her, his tawny eyes laughing at her embarrassment as Elizabeth turned to face her mother-in-law. Jed did not turn immediately, keeping his back to his mother.

'Rebecca —' Elizabeth began, fighting to regain her composure and rid herself of the absurd sensation that she had done something to feel guilty about.

But she wasn't allowed the opportunity of identifying Jed as Rebecca Carrel broke in with haughty indignation, 'What were you thinking, carrying on like that, Elizabeth? What if Amy had come running here and seen you in the arms of this stranger? Who is this—'

'Hello, Mother.' Jed turned and spoke before she finished her slashing barrage of questions.

Rebecca's mouth snapped shut grimly, a finely drawn, charcoal eyebrow arching in something considerably less than overwhelming joy at her son's return.

'Your brother and your father have been in their graves for quite a while, Jed. Why have you bothered to come back now?' she asked shortly.

The firm line of his mouth thinned into a cold smile. 'I must have been drawn by your overwhelming motherly love,' he responded cynically. With negligent ease, he walked over and mockingly kissed her cheek.

'How long do you intend to stay? Or are you just passing through?' His mother's expression was still rigidly controlled.

'I haven't made any plans,' Jed shrugged, squarely meeting her dark gaze.

'I can believe that,' Rebecca agreed with cutting reproval. 'Your father and I did everything we could to prepare you for a decent role in life and you threw all of it aside, even the opportunity for a college education. You refused to plan, always insisting that you knew it all and refusing to listen to us. What has it gained you, Jed? You've hopped all over the Pacific and what do you have to show for it?'

The only indication Elizabeth saw which revealed

Jed's determined control of his temper was the slight clenching of his jaw. Otherwise he withstood his mother's tirade without any show of emotion.

'I haven't come back to argue whether what happened in the past was right or wrong, Mother,' he replied calmly. 'I guess I wanted to come back when I'd made my fortune.' He smiled in self-reproach. 'When I received your letter about a year after it was written and realized that Dad was gone, I knew I had too much of the same Carrel pride that I'd condemned. I've come home to make peace with you, Mother.'

Again there was the long, measured look between them. Elizabeth unconsciously held her breath, believing the sincerity in Jed's voice yet uncertain whether his mother did.

'You can have the room at the end of the stairs as long as you're here,' Rebecca said at last. 'Amy, Jeremy's daughter, has your old room.'

'Yes, Liza already offered me the use of the other room shortly after I arrived. I —' he glanced down at his fresh clothes — 'I needed to clean up after walking from town.'

'You *walked* from town!' his mother exclaimed in distressed anger. 'Did anyone see you? For heaven's sake, why didn't you take a taxi? What will people think if they saw you walking along the highway?'

'If anyone had seen me, they would probably have thought that I was on my way home,' Jed reasoned dryly.

'I wish you would be more conscious of our position

in the community,' his mother sighed rather bitterly.

At that moment, Amy appeared in the kitchen doorway having changed into an everyday outfit of shorts and top. Her gaze was immediately drawn to the stranger in their midst. Elizabeth realized it was probably the first time her daughter had seen a man in the house during the daytime since before her grandfather had passed away.

As she made her way to Elizabeth, Amy kept her curious brown eyes centered on Jed. There was no shyness in her silent appraisal, nor did she flinch from his returning look.

'Hello, Amy.' Jed's greeting was casual, not forcing any undue warmth or gladness into his voice.

Amy tilted her dark head back to look at Elizabeth. 'Who is he?' she demanded in a bold, clear voice that bordered on rudeness.

'Your manners, Amy,' Rebecca repremanded sharply.

Except for a stubborn tightening of her mouth, Amy pretended not to have heard her grandmother's reproval. Elizabeth had the fleeting thought that her daughter's slightly rebellious nature might have come from her uncle.

'This is your uncle Jed, Amy. He was your father's brother,' Elizabeth explained patiently.

Curiosity still remained the uppermost emotion as she turned her attention back to Jed. 'Hello,' she greeted him naturally. 'Did you know my father?'

'Yes, we grew up together,' Jed answered, calmly returning her intent scutiny of him.

'Did you know me when I was a baby?'

'No, I was on the other side of the world when you were born.'

His response did not impress Amy. 'I didn't know my father. He died before I was born, you know,' she informed him with marked indifference.

'I knew that,' he nodded.

'Did you like my father?'

'Oh, Amy, what a question to ask!' There was a brittle quality to the laughter Elizabeth forced through her throat, as she tossed a pleading look to Jed. 'He was your uncle's brother. Of course he liked him.'

'That's not exactly true,' he ignored her silent request to keep Jeremy's memory untarnished.

'Jed!' Elizabeth appealed to him angrily.

'He was my brother,' Jed continued with a faint smile grooving the side of his mouth. 'Because he was my brother, I loved him. But I didn't necessarily like him. Brothers tend to fight and argue a lot, Amy. Your father and I didn't agree on a lot of things.'

'What did you fight about?' Amy tilted her head interestedly to the side.

'That's enough questions, Amy,' Rebecca broke in coldly. 'Your uncle is probably very tired after his long journey and you're supposed to be practising the piano. Mrs. Banks told me you didn't do very well today, so from now on you'll practise an extra fifteen minutes at the piano every day.'

'Oh, Mother, no!' Amy made her angry protest to Elizabeth, frowning her appeal for the edict to be rescinded.

'You'd better do as your grandmother suggests,' Elizabeth answered quietly. 'If you do better at your next lesson, we'll consider eliminating the extra fifteen minutes.'

'Mrs. Banks is stupid,' Amy grumbled.

'I was going to swim in the pool after a while,' Jed inserted quietly, too quietly Elizabeth thought. 'Perhaps you can join me when you're finished with your practice, Amy.'

The frown was replaced by an immediate smile as Amy opened her mouth to heartily accept his invitation.

'I believe you've forgotten, Jed,' his mother spoke sharply, 'but in this house, there are no rewards or bribes for doing what you are supposed to do.'

With that parting shot, Rebecca Carrel pivoted around and left the kitchen. Seconds of heavy silence ticked by as Jed stared after her, yellow fire smoldering in his eyes.

'I'm sorry, Amy,' he said simply, turning back to the crestfallen child. 'Maybe another day.'

'Yes, maybe,' she sighed as if she didn't hold out much hope for that nebulous day to come. Her feet were dragging noticeably as she left the room.

'Nothing's changed,' Jed muttered bitterly beneath his breath.

Elizabeth knew the comment was not directed to her, but at his mother's insistence on strict discipline. Several times she herself had protested in Amy's behalf, but Rebecca's argument that it was for the good of the child always seemed a valid one. Besides,

Amy's spirit had never faded under the unbending rules of the house. In fact, Elizabeth was convinced it was the only way to keep her assertive personality under control. On her own she wouldn't have been as unwavering as Rebecca.

'Why are you living here, Liza?' Jed asked as she began clearing the dishes from the table. 'I'm certain the deaths of Jeremy and my father must have left you very well provided for.'

'They did,' she acknowledged, not pausing in her task as she replied. 'But this has been my home. And my name is Elizabeth.'

'What about the house you and Jeremy had? Wasn't that your home?' he countered.

'We only lived here after we were married.'

'Oh, my God!' he laughed in disbelief. 'You actually lived here — with my parents, after you were married! That must have given you a lot of privacy and time to get to know each other, with Mother for ever organizing your lives!' he jeered.

'It was only a temporary arrangement!' His mockery stung her into retorting sharply in defence. 'We had bought a house, but the whole place needed to be redecorated and furnished and the kitchen remodeled. It would have been foolish to try to live in it when it was in such a disorganized state.'

'Of course it never occurred to either of you to move into it and re-do the house in stages,' Jed offered dryly.

'Jeremy couldn't see the point in prolonging it. It was his decision to do it all at once and I agreed with him,' Elizabeth stated. 'Besides, he was working very hard for your father. It was only natural for him to want to come home to an orderly house at night.'

'What did you do all day?'

'If it's any of your business,' her chin quivered in anger, 'I was kept quite busy with the redecorating.'

'Under Mother's supervision, right?' he mocked.

Her eyes brightened with volatile temper to a more vibrant shade of green, contrasting sharply with the rich blue of her caftan.

'I was seventeen at the time and too inexperienced to handle such a formidable job on my own. I was very glad of your mother's assistance!'

'So the house was never completed?'

'Yes.' She turned away to the sink as she made the clipped response. 'We were to move into it, but Jeremy was killed in that car crash and I simply ... c-couldn't bring myself to live in the house that we were to share together.'

'So you stayed on here,' he said in a faintly accusing note.

'After I discovered I was pregnant with Amy, there was nowhere else for me to go. My aunt was in the hospital with a severe diabetes attack.'

'And Mother offered her assistance again, is that it?' Jed mocked harshly. 'When Amy was born, you were still young and inexperienced and knew nothing about babies, so you accepted her guidance again. You could have found a better teacher. In fact, you could have fumbled through on your own with the same results. A lot of women do, and without the benefit of the financial peace of mind you so luckily had.'

'You're so strong and so arrogantly confident that you know exactly what's right,' Elizabeth retaliated, 'that you probably don't know what it's like to feel lost and alone and frightened. I doubt if you know what it's like to need the support of someone else. I doubt if you know what it's like to need anyone!'

'Believe me, I need!' His voice vibrated huskily. 'If I didn't, I wouldn't have come home. Although it's some homecoming!'

'Don't blame me for that. You were the one who left! And three letters in nine years hardly sounds as if you were very homesick!'

'Do you want to know how many letters I received from my parents?' Jed flashed. 'Exactly two! One telling me of Jeremy's death and the other of my father's. My effort to keep the lines of communication open was not encouraged. I felt as if I was batting my head against a brick wall ten feet thick!'

'Then why did you come back?' she lashed out, angry that he was taking his frustration out on her.

'I've been asking myself that question ever since I arrived. I should have realized the age of miracles is over. I had thought,' the smile curving his mouth was turned inward in self-mockery, 'if I came back willing to make peace, my mother would meet me halfway, accept the way I am. The only thing she can allow herself to acknowledge is success.'

'That's a cruel accusation!' Elizabeth breathed in sharply.

His gaze glittered to her face, hard and unyielding

like a topaz sapphire. 'I love my mother deeply, but that doesn't make me blind to her faults.'

'What's wrong with being ambitious? Or wanting to better yourself?' she demanded.

'You've climbed to the top of this small social ladder. What do you think of the view? Is it what you expected it to be?' Jed countered. 'As fulfilling and rewarding as you thought?'

'Not fulfilling exactly, but that was a qualification Elizabeth made silently. 'All the activities keep me busy,' she defended. 'And I enjoy the charity work. It's very rewarding helping deserving people.'

'Deserving by whose standards? My mother's?' He punctuated the words with a short, derisive laugh.

'I think you've become harder and more cynical than she is,' Elizabeth observed.

'What about you? Are you becoming like her? Don't you think you'll ever desire the warmth and companionship of a man's love?'

'I haven't thought about it.' She was suddently wary, not liking the subject change from his mother to her.

'Don't you think you would miss not having a man's arms around you again?' Jed continued his pursuit of the subject.

Her chin was raised upward to a defiant angle. 'I doubt it,' she replied. 'I was raised by a maiden aunt. Jeremy was killed so soon after we were married that I never really became accustomed to a man's attention. I think I can get along quite well without one.'

'Do you?' responded Jed with a faint challenge.

The instant he started walking toward her, Elizabeth backed away. Her defiant bravado was driven out by the sudden fear that he might try to test her assertion.

He stopped and chuckled softly. 'I was just going to get myself another cup of coffee,' he explained, letting his amusement show. 'Did you think I was going to challenge your statement and demand physical proof?'

'Earlier —' she began to remind him, with mistrust flashing in her eyes.

'What happened earlier was a fleeting impulse.' His expression was uncompromisingly hard. 'I may have said that I found you desirable, Liza, but I don't desire you. There's a vast difference. So you don't need to fear any unwanted advance. I don't intend to touch you again.'

Jed's statement was made so emphatically that Elizabeth was forced to believe him. His rejection of her as a woman was more of a blow to her self-esteem than she had thought. She should be rejoicing, but instead a strange depression was settling in.

'Don't you feel relieved, little sister?' His soft voice insinuated itself into her astonishment.

'O-of course.' She turned away, running a nervous hand through her ebony curls, pushing them behind her ear as she sought for her cool poise. 'Immensely so.'

'That's what I thought you'd say,' he murmured.

'Help yourself to the coffee. I have some work to do.' She avoided looking directly at him as she made her exit from the kitchen, grateful that she had the excuse of reading the plays to be alone for a while.

CHAPTER THREE

'PUT the roast at the head of the table, Elizabeth,' Rebecca instructed. 'Since Jed is here, he can carve it.'

As she started to transfer the platter of meat to the opposite end of the table, Jed appeared in the dining room archway. He was wearing the same white shirt and brown slacks as before.

'I'm honored, Mother, that you've put me at the head of the table,' he commented in a faintly derogatory tone, letting them know that he had overheard their conversation from the hallway.

'The eldest male Carrel always sits at the head of the table,' Rebecca responded curtly. 'In this case, it happens to be the only male Carrel.' Her dark gaze ran over his casual attire. 'We can delay serving for a few minutes while you change. I'm sure you must have forgotten that we always dress for dinner.'

'I hadn't forgotten.' Jed continued into the room, drawing the end chair where Elizabeth stood away from the table. 'Unfortunately I couldn't fit my white tie and tails into my duffle bag.'

'Don't exaggerate,' his mother snapped. 'A simple suit is sufficient.'

'There wasn't room for one of those either. You'll have to take me the way I am,' Jed stated, reaching for the carving knife and fork that Elizabeth had placed near the platter.

Rebecca pursed her lips together in displeasure, but said nothing in response. Waving an imperious hand at Elizabeth and Amy to be seated, she took the chair at the opposite end of the table from Jed.

'By the way,' he laid a perfectly sliced cut of meat on to Amy's plate, 'where's Maggie? Is this her day off?'

Maggie Connor had been a cook-housekeeper to the Carrel family for years, an almost permanent fixture in the house when Elizabeth had married Jeremy.

'She has retired. After your father died,' his mother explained. 'We no longer entertained, so there was no point in retaining her for just the three of us. Your father provided a generous annuity for her in his will and I let her go.'

'This meal looks very tasty,' Jed observed. 'Who does the cooking now? You, Mother?'

'Elizabeth does for the most part, although I occasionally lend a helping hand.'

Only Elizabeth knew how rare that helping hand was. Not that she objected. She preferred having the kitchen to herself.

'A Carrel who cooks?' The tawny gaze slid mockingly to her, dancing over her face when she quickly averted her green eyes. 'How did you learn such a skill, Liza?'

Elizabeth found it was difficult to respond naturally. She felt on the defensive and she didn't know whether to blame his taunting mockery or the hated abbreviation of her name. Perhaps it was simply an inability to feel at ease in Jed's presence.

'Actually I learned to cook as a child,' she answered stiffly. 'My aunt thought it was essential for me to learn, so I fixed a great many of our meals. After Jeremy and I were married, I naturally helped Maggie in the kitchen so I could learn how to prepare his favorite dishes. Later I simply helped out.'

'Maggie's age was beginning to show at last,' Rebecca inserted. 'She was becoming increasingly slow and haphazard in her work. It was best that she retired when she did.'

'Wasn't Maggie a year or two younger than you, Mother?' questioned Jed, a sharp glitter in his eyes.

'I really don't have any idea,' his mother bridled visibly.

'Do you do the housework too, Elizabeth?'

The faint emphasis he placed on her proper name made it even more difficult to tolerate than the nickname. 'Not all of it, no.'

'We have a young girl come in two or three times a week to take care of the general cleaning and the washing,' Rebecca explained.

'I like Mary,' Amy spoke up, adding in a faintly adult note. 'She's very nice.'

'Do the Reisners still own the farm down the road?' Jed asked.

'Yes, they do. You went to school with Kurt, didn't you?' His mother glanced up to receive his answering nod. 'He's taken over the farm from his father and his parents have moved into town. Why?'

'I thought I would stop over to see them tonight, that is,' there was a falsely courteous inclination of his tobacco brown head toward his mother, 'if you'll let me use the car.'

'There's a set of spare keys in the china cabinet,' she agreed.

Elizabeth had to restrain herself from audibly sighing in relief. She hadn't been looking forward to an evening of stilted conversation. Despite the appearance of polite discussion, the atmosphere between mother and son was decidedly hostile. Her own inclination was to avoid Jed as much as she could. He had delved too deeply into her personal life, asking questions that were none of his business and laughing at her answers. Arm's length was not a far-enough distance.

The instant the evening meal was over, Jed excused himself and left to visit their neighbors, the Reisners. He hadn't returned by the time Elizabeth went to bed some time after ten o'clock. Although she lay awake in the double bed for nearly an hour, she didn't hear him come back.

The next morning Elizabeth discovered the coffee was already made when she entered the kitchen. Breakfast dishes for one were washed and sitting in the draining board beside the sink. Rebecca didn't get up that early in the morning, so the dishes could only be Jed's. But there was no sign of him in the house nor in the yard surrounding the house.

Not until she returned to the kitchen to fix toast and juice for herself did Elizabeth find the note he had left under the bowl of fruit on the small dinette table. Her fingers crossed in a fervent wish that Jed had decided to leave as abruptly as he had arrived. The boldly firm handwriting informed her that he would not be back for lunch, but made no mention of where he would be in the interim.

If he had gone visiting, the only logical place he could have gone at this early hour of the morning was to the Reisner farm again, Elizabeth decided. She wasn't aware that he and Kurt had been close friends, but if they had gone to school together, it was possible. The few times she had seen Kurt, he had made no mention of it, although most of the townspeople had been reluctant to introduce Jed's name into a conversation.

Even though they were neighbors, Elizabeth didn't know Kurt that well. She knew he had been married at one time, but was presently divorced. That information she had gained from his sister Freda, who was a year or two younger than herself. She had liked Freda and would have seen her more frequently socially, except she had sensed that Rebecca would have disapproved of the friendship. Looking back, it seemed a weak reason for not pursuing the relationship. Elizabeth could well imagine Jed's contempt if he ever found out.

His opinion did not matter to her in the least, she reminded herself. She wished violently that he had never returned. Life had been very smooth. Now she was seeing all kinds of chuckholes in front of her. He was a disruptive influence that she had to learn to ignore to retain her own peace of mind.

'Good morning, Elizabeth.' Rebecca entered the kitchen looking youthfully fresh in a pink satin robe, her silvery blue hair carefully styled and light make-up adding color to her face. 'Is there any fresh grapefruit this morning?'

'Yes, I'll fix it for you.' Elizabeth slid back her half-eaten toast and walked to the refrigerator.

'I see Jed isn't up yet. I suppose he'll sleep until noon,' Rebecca sniffed her disapproval of such laziness.

'Actually he's up and gone.' She sliced the grapefruit in half and began running the knife along the skin of each section.

'How do you know that?'

'He left a note saying he wouldn't be back for lunch,' Elizabeth answered. 'He was considerate enough to wash up his breakfast dishes before he left, so he must have been up quite early.'

'Good,' Rebecca declared with a wide smile of satisfaction. It took Elizabeth a second to realize that she was commenting on his planned absence that morning rather than the fact that he had cleaned up after himself. 'You're going into town this morning, aren't you?'

'Yes, I have a committee meeting to see how the ticket sales are progressing for the charity dinner at the country club,' Elizabeth acknowledged as she set the grapefruit half in front of her mother-in-law.

Rebecca slipped a manicured hand into the pocket of her robe. There was a faint rustle, then she was handing a slip of paper to Elizabeth.

'While you're in town, I want you to stop by Shaw's Men's Store. I've made a list of things that Jed needs. The sizes are listed on the right,' Rebecca stated. 'I'm sure Fred will reopen our account.'

Elizabeth stared blankly at the paper. 'But how can you be sure these are the right sizes? I mean . . . wouldn't it be better to send Jed in himself when he comes back this afternoon?' She stammered slightly.
-operate just to be obstinate. As for the sizes,' Rebecca paused, 'I've already checked to be sure they were correct.'

Glancing from the list to the woman delicately spooning out a grapefruit section, Elizabeth knew without a doubt that her mother-in-law had not questioned Jed. He would have been certain to guess the purpose.

'Do you mean,' she found the question she was about to ask distasteful, 'that you went through his things?'

'He doesn't even have a sports jacket.' Rebecca shook her head in arrogant disbelief. 'I didn't believe him last night. 'After the way he was raised, I was certain he had something decent tucked away in that disreputable bag, so I went through it last night while he was at the Reisners'. I hope he doesn't intend to get too friendly with them.'

For the first time that she could remember, Elizabeth took offence at the faintly snobbish ring in Rebecca's voice. 'They're very nice people,' she stated firmly.

Her mother-in-law's mouth opened to comment,

then she met the flashing defiance in the green eyes and appeared to change her mind. 'I suppose they are,' she agreed with marked lack of interest.

'Excuse me while I go to see what's keeping Amy,' Elizabeth murmured, moving away from the colonial style table.

'Be sure to put that list in your purse so you won't forget it,' Rebecca reminded her.

Fingertips curled around the paper, crackling it slightly. The impulse burned to hand it back to her mother-in-law with the retort to do her own dirty work, but Elizabeth held it back. The animosity in the air since Jed's return was beginning to affect her own outlook.

'I won't forget,' she promised, and walked from the room.

It was nearly noon when Elizabeth paused beside the store-front. The sign above the canopy read Shaw's Men's Clothing. She wished she hadn't left the cold lunch for Rebecca and Amy before leaving this morning. She would have welcomed an excuse to postpone this errand. Outside a few Christmas gifts for her father-in-law, she had never purchased any clothing for men. During her short marriage, Jeremy had always preferred to choose his own.

Nervously she ran her fingers along the scalloped neckline of her white sundress. Squaring her shoulders in determination, she walked to the door. A bell tingled above the door to announce her entrance.

The balding head of Fred Shaw, the owner, turned away from the customer he was helping to glance toward the door, and immediately he waved to his other male clerk to take his place as he excused himself to walk toward Elizabeth.

It flashed through her mind that this was usually the case. The owners or managers of the various stores in Carrelville invariably were the ones who waited on her, sometimes even letting other customers wait. It struck her suddenly as being very unfair.

'Good morning, Mrs. Carrel,' he greeted her. A wide, professional smile spread across his face while his eyes crinkled at the corners behind steel-rimmed glasses. 'It's going to be another hot one today, isn't it?'

'Yes, it is,' Elizabeth agreed, wondering if her vague embarrassment was revealed in her cheeks. 'If you're busy, Mr. Shaw, I don't mind waiting a few minutes.'

'Not at all, not at all,' he assured her quickly. 'I'll bet I can guess why you've called. I was just saying to my wife last night that we hadn't got around to buying tickets for your dinner. She suggested that I get a couple of extra so we can take our daughter and her husband along.'

'That's very generous of you, Mr. Shaw, but actually,' her smile faltered slightly, 'I stopped by to purchase a few items. Of course, I'll gladly sell you the tickets.'

Elizabeth knew that he was undoubtedly curious about who she was buying clothes for, but he didn't comment until the money and tickets had been exchanged.

'Now, what may I show you?' he asked, Elizabeth

took the list from her purse and handed it to him. 'This is almost a complete wardrobe.' He peered at her over the top of his glasses. 'Is the—er—rumor true that young Jed has come home?'

'Yes, Jed is back,' she admitted stiffly.

'For good?' Then as if he thought the question was too personal, Fred Shaw shrugged it aside. 'I suppose with Jed it's impossible to be certain.' He led her toward a rack of expensive dress suits. 'Craig Landers said that he thought he'd recognized Jed at the airport yesterday. The engine of Craig's small plane was being overhauled. That's why he was out there. Jed flew in, didn't he?'

Since Elizabeth hadn't asked, she could only assume that was so. 'I believe he did.'

'This is a nice one,' he suggested, removing a suit from the rack for her to examine. 'Craig mentioned that Jed looked a little worse from wear. Has he been ill?'

'Not that he mentioned.' Elizabeth guessed it was a reference to Jed's untidy appearance. 'Of course, he'd had a long journey. He was quite tired when he arrived at the house.'

'Where has he been? I heard once that he was on some South Pacific island.'

She fingered the material of a dark brown suit. 'He traveled a good deal,' she replied, remembering that the three letters had been postmarked at different places.

'What's he been doing all this time?'

That was another question that Elizabeth hadn't

thought to ask him. 'Various things,' she hedged.

'Jed never did seem the type to settle down to one thing. Never seemed the type to settle down at all.' Fred Shaw laughed as though he had made a joke. 'You probably never got to meet him. I think he'd already left by the time you became engaged to Jeremy.'

'He left shortly after our engagement was announced,' Elizabeth admitted, and tried to distract him from the subject by questioning him about the material in a particular suit.

Once he had answered that, Fred Shaw returned the conversation to Jed. 'Yes, I remember now. You and Jeremy were engaged before Jed left. We were all expecting Jed to come back for the wedding. 'Course, he never was one to follow convention. No, he wasn't dependable like his brother. Now Jeremy was a son that any parent would be proud to claim. He was a fine boy, trustworthy and a hard worker. But I guess I'm not telling you anything you didn't already know.'

'Jeremy was a very wonderful husband,' she murmured.

'His death was a real tragedy.' He shook his head and sighed. 'It's always the hardest thing to understand why somebody like Jeremy is taken. He could have done so much good for the community. Jed was always the irresponsible, reckless one with his devil-may-care attitude. I remember when he was barely in his teens he'd disappear for a day or two, then show up and claim he'd hitch-hiked to Dayton to see the Air Force Museum. Heaven only knows where he truly went. That was one boy who brought more than his share of heartache to his parents. They tried so hard to see that he had all the advantages that Jeremy had. Mr. Carrel refused to stop trying to get him a university education. Every time Jed was expelled, his father would be out looking for another place that would take him, paying whatever money was necessary. It was a shame, truly a shame.'

'That was all very long ago, Mr. Shaw,' Elizabeth said coldly.

Lost in his thoughts, as he was, it took several seconds for her reprimand to penetrate the storeowner's thoughts. By then it had lost some of its strength.

'Yes, it was a long time ago,' Fred Shaw agreed. 'After losing both Jeremy and Franklin, your mother-in-law is probably relieved to have a man around again.'

Nodding crisply in agreement, Elizabeth began selecting dress and sports outfits from the rack. She was fully aware that the instant she left the shop the news would spread all over town that Jed was back. The subtle barrage of questions she had endured led her to believe that Rebecca had sent her so that she wouldn't have to answer them initially.

Choosing quickly and unerringly, Elizabeth unconsciously picked out styles that would complement Jed's lean virility and not attempt to cloak it in formal, sophisticated designs. It was a relief when the list had been filled and the clothes carefully folded in boxes. She signed the charge ticket with a flourish, anxious to be gone before Fred Shaw's curiosity burst to the surface again.

Her car was parked at the end of the block. Elizabeth walked swiftly ahead of the male clerk who had been designated with the task of carrying the cumbersome parcels to her car. Opening the rear door on the driver's side, she stepped back to let him pass.

'Elizabeth.' A male voice spoke her name in warm surprise.

Turning, she saw Allan Marsden standing on the sidewalk in front of her car, a wide smile of pleasure directed at her. He was the administrator at the local city-county hospital and had been for the last year and a half. The townspeople were holding their breath to see how long he would stay. It was difficult to keep a man of Allan's caliber when they had to compete with larger cities that could offer him more prestigious jobs and better salaries. He was a young man, in his late thirties, which was young by their standards, and one they felt destined to go places.

'Hello, Allan.' Her greeting wasn't as warm as it usually was. Elizabeth was too anxious to be gone.

'I hadn't guessed that you would be in town over the lunch hour or I would have invited you to join me.' Sandy brown hair glistened a bronze shade, catching the sun when he inclined his head toward her with a rueful smile.

'I had a committee meeting and a few errands to run, so I was a bit pressed for time, anyway,' she assured him.

'That's all of them,' the young male clerk inserted

courteously as he closed the rear door of her car. 'Mr. Shaw wanted me to be sure to remind you that if any of the clothes didn't fit properly you were to bring them back.'

'Thank you,' Elizabeth nodded.

There was a puzzled light in Allan Marsden's eyes as he watched the clerk re-entering Shaw's Men's Shop. When his gaze swung curiously to Elizabeth, she very nearly didn't explain. But she liked Allan. She had accepted three dates with him, the last being nearly two weeks ago. He had been a pleasant, undemanding companion, although what she had told Jed was true, she didn't feel the need for a man's constant attention or companionship. With all those parcels in the back seat of the car bearing Shaw's name, it would be unfair to let Allan speculate why she should be buying men's clothes, especially considering that the news would be all over town within an hour that Jed was back.

'That was one of my more formidable tasks,' Elizabeth smiled, gesturing with her hand toward the rear of the car. 'My brother-in-law has just returned after a lengthy absence. His clothes haven't caught up with him yet, so I was appointed to buy him a few things.'

'Your brother-in-law?' His sandy brow lifted in surprise. 'Forgive me, I always assumed your late husband was an only child.'

'Jed is the younger brother, but he's been out of the country for several years.'

'Then you and Mrs. Carrel must be enjoying the reunion,' he smiled.

'Yes,' she agreed, knowing it was impossible to discuss the uneasy hostility that was tainting her life.

'I intended to call you tonight.' Allan stepped down from the curb, bringing himself closer to her. 'I purchased two tickets to your charity dinner and I was hoping that you would give me the privilege of being your escort.'

There was no reason for her not to accept, but Elizabeth found herself refusing. 'I'm sorry, Allan, but I do have to be there early to supervise the arrangements. As one of the committee chairmen, I'll have other duties throughout the evening that I'll have to see to. Perhaps it would be best if we simply planned to see each other there,' she suggested.

She sensed his objection to her alternate proposal, but he didn't express it or allow any disappointment to show. If he was interested in her and she was fairly certain of that, he seemed to have no intentions of rushing her. Perhaps it was because he didn't want to risk offending a Carrel and take the chance of having a black mark placed on his record by the family's influence in the community. That was a bitterly distasteful thought.

'The weatherman promises that Sunday is supposed to be a beautiful day. How about you and me and Amy going for a picnic? Say around two?' Allan countered.

Hesitating for a second, Elizabeth was unwilling to refuse a second invitation from him even though she was just as reluctant to accept it.

'Would you call me this evening, Allan?' she stalled.

'I'm not certain what plans Rebecca — my mother-in-law — might have made, with Jed back and all.'

'Of course I'll phone,' he smiled, 'and keep my fingers crossed.'

'I'll wait for your call,' Elizabeth promised, reaching for the handle of the driver's door. 'I really must get back now.'

'Yes, I'm due at the office, too. I'll talk to you this evening, Elizabeth.'

He was still standing on the sidewalk as she backed out of the parking place. She waved to him self-consciously, wishing she had refused the second invitation outright and wondering why she didn't want to go.

The Carrel home was two miles outside town, established many years ago by one of the ancestors who had combined his career as a judge with that of a gentleman farmer. In later years, the slight isolation from the rest of the community added to the image that they were apart from others like feudal lords of old.

Elizabeth didn't drive the car into the garage, but parked it next to the sidewalk to make it easier to unload and carry in the various packages. Amy was on the far side of the lawn under a large shade tree playing with her dolls. She waved, but didn't come over to greet her mother.

Balancing the precarious stack of packages in her arms, Elizabeth opened the front door of the house and walked in. Out of the corner of her eye, she spied her mother-in-law in the living room talking on the telephone. A pad was on the table beside her and a pencil in her hand. Rebecca glanced up and quickly, and vainly, removed the reading glasses from her nose.

Placing her hand over the receiver, she asked, 'Did you get everything on the list?'

'Yes,' Elizabeth nodded.

'You'd better take them right upstairs and hang them up before they get creased and need pressing,' Rebecca instructed. Once the order was given, she resumed her conversation with the person on the telephone.

It was tricky negotiating the stairs when the packages didn't enable her to see her feet, but Elizabeth made it to the top without incident. Walking to the end of the hallway, she found the door to Jed's bedroom ajar and she pushed it open. She paused on the threshold, reluctant to step inside.

There had always been an impersonal air that had made it just another bedroom. Now, there was something strangely different about it. Glancing about, the only thing she saw in the room that belonged to Jed was the duffle bag sitting in one corner. The bed was expertly made without a wrinkle. Considering the washed dishes in the sink, Elizabeth was certain the hand that had made it belonged to Jed and not her mother-in-law.

Entering the room, she spread the packages on the bed. Curiosity turned away from them, directing her footsteps to the adjoining bathroom. There she found neat evidence of Jed's habitation with razor, toothbrush, comb, and aftershave lotion sitting on the counter next to the wash basin, unmistakably male.

The heady fragrance of the cologned lotion touched her nose. Elizabeth decided it was this faint masculine scent that she had detected when she had entered the bedroom. With a guilty start, she realized that she was snooping and backtracked swiftly.

The trembling of her fingers surprised her as she began untying the packages and removing the clothes from the folds of the protective tissue. There was a strange curling sensation in the pit of her stomach and a faintly embarrassed warmth in her face. It was silly, she scolded herself. She had hung up men's clothes before. Why was she self-conscious about it now, she asked herself as she straightened a suit on its hanger.

Turning to walk to the closet, Elizabeth found herself staring into Jed's lean face. He was leaning against the door jamb in much the same lazy, slouching position as she had seen him yesterday, his hands stuffed in his pockets. The expression on his leanly carved face was unreadable, but there was faint amusement in the topaz-brown eyes that were studying her intently.

Her fingers closed nervously over the sleeve of the suit jacket as his gaze swept from her to the packages on the bed and back. With a poise she didn't feel, Elizabeth turned away and walked to the closet, trying to make the movement appear natural.

'Your mother thought you needed some additions to your wardrobe,' she explained off-handedly.

CHAPTER FOUR

'No doubt she discovered that when she went through my things last night.' His footsteps made no sound on the carpet, but Elizabeth could tell by the direction of his voice that he had moved to the bed. 'You have excellent taste,. Liza. I should have you pick out my clothes all the time.'

'How did you know —' She spun around in surprise.

'That it was you?' Jed finished the question for her, plainly showing amusement in his expression now. 'I couldn't imagine Mother running the town's gauntlet when she could send you in her place.'

It had occurred to Elizabeth too that she had been used as a buffer for the town's curiosity, but she wasn't about to agree with Jed. She hung the suit in the closet and carried another wire hanger back to the bed.

'I opened our old account with Shaw's,' she told him. 'If there's anything I've overlooked, you can get it there.'

'I'm certain Mother's list was as thorough as her search,' Jed responded dryly.

'What makes you so certain that I wasn't the one who went through your things?' Elizabeth asked, driven by a surprising impulse to defend Rebecca.

'I guess there's just something about you that makes it difficult for me to visualize you pawing through a man's personal clothing,' he answered.

Bending over the jacket lying on the bed, she made a pretence of straightening the lapel to conceal the color that had swept into her cheeks.

'You did have your lunch, didn't you?' she asked in an effort to direct the conversation away from herself.

'Yes, at the Reisners.'

'You were gone so early this morning that I thought you might have gone there.' Elizabeth kept moving, occupying her hands with the clothes and walking back and forth to the closet to avoid any more than a brief glance at Jed.

'Freda, Kurt's sister, seems to like you,' Jed commented idly. 'As she puts it, you're not a snob like my mother.'

'I like Freda too. She's very nice.'

'It's strange that with you two living so close, you don't see each other that much. Freda said that mostly you just bump into each other in town.'

'Well, you know how it is.' She gave a stiff, smiling shrug. 'I'm usually busy with a meeting of one kind or another. The free time that I do have, I like to spend with Amy.'

'That's commendable, but I'm sure Freda wouldn't object if you brought Amy along. She seems fond of children. As a matter of fact,' he continued with a complacent smile, 'I was invited to dinner on Sunday and Fred asked me to extend the invitation to you and your daughter. I'm to let her know if you're going.'

'That's impossible,' Elizabeth refused immediately.

'Why?' For all its softness, there was a knife-sharp thrust to his question.

'Because I've already made other plans,' she answered, suddenly glad that she hadn't refused Allan's invitation. It was a perfect excuse to avoid Jed's company.

'Really?' he mocked.

'Yes, really.' Irritation flashed in her green eyes that he should doubt she was speaking the truth. 'Amy and I have been invited to go on a picnic this Sunday.'

'Since you have a prior invitation, I'll give your apologies to Freda,' mocking skepticism was still in his tone.

'I am not making it up!' Elizabeth defended angrily. 'Allan Marsden did ask us out this Sunday. As a matter of fact, he's phoning tonight to confirm it. I thought your mother might plan something extra for your first Sunday home or I would have accepted immediately.' It was a small white lie, but one that she thought was justified under the circumstances. 'Since you aren't going to be home, there isn't any reason not to accept.'

'Allan Marsden?' Jed repeated. 'He must be new in town.'

'He's the hospital administrator.'

'Did the hospital ever raise the funds for that new clinic they were wanting?' he asked.

'No.' Suspicion loomed suddenly. 'Why?' she frowned.

'Curiosity, I suppose,' Jed shrugged disinterestedly, 'You mentioned the hospital and I wondered if they'd ever accomplished that proposed expansion.'

'If you're implying,' Elizabeth didn't believe his question had been prompted by casual curiosity, 'that Allan is seeing me in the hopes that, through me, your mother would be persuaded to make a sizeable donation, then you're wrong.'

'I'm sure I am,' he agreed smoothly.

'Allan leaves all that to his fund-raising committee.'

'Of course.'

Her lips tightened mutinously, the faint smile of mockery around his hard mouth goading her into losing her temper. His complacent tawny gold gaze studied the flashing fire of her green eyes.

'I doubt if Allan will even mention the hospital while we're on the picnic,' Elizabeth defended again, her fingers tugging impatiently at the suit jacket on the hanger.

'He wouldn't be much of a man if he did,' Jed stated with a curling suggestive smile. 'A warm summer afternoon, a shady glade, a blanket on the ground, and you as a companion on that blanket — I certainly wouldn't be thinking about my work.'

'You are impossible, Jed Carrel!' Elizabeth muttered. Walking angrily to the closet, she jammed the hanger hook on to the horizontal pole. 'You twist everything until it manages to come out cheap and sordid.'

'Do I do that?' He tipped his head to one side in laughing inquiry.

'You know very well you do.' She removed the tissue from the last box.

'I'd better offer my apologies, then.'

'Don't bother to pretend that you feel regret,' she cut in sharply. The last outfit was in the closet and she began busily gathering the boxes and tissues together, loading her arms with them. 'Now, if you'll excuse me, I have a great deal of work to do,' she flashed with biting sarcasm.

'Please accept my thanks for choosing my wardrobe, even if it was at Mother's instigation.' Again there was an underlying hint of mockery in his tone.

'It's only sheep's clothing, Jed,' Elizabeth tossed over her shoulder before leaving the room. His throaty laughter followed her down the hall.

The evening meal was routinely eaten at seven o'clock, a time that had been chosen not because Rebecca thought it fashionable, but because her late husband had always worked past the five o'clock office hours. The habit of eating at that hour had been too deeply ingrained to be changed after his death. Elizabeth had never minded it. It seemed to make the long evenings go by faster.

Allan Marsden telephoned her as he had promised, but his call came just as she was setting dinner on the table. She was on the living room extension when Jed wandered into the room. Staring at the brown suit he was wearing, one that she had chosen, she was stunned by the way it enhanced his dark virility. The suit fitted his muscular leannes so perfectly that it might have been tailor-made for him.

For a full second Elizabeth was aware only of his disturbing presence. Then she realized that Allan's voice was repeating the time of their planned outing and waiting for her acknowledgment. Forcing her clamoring senses to ignore Jed, she concentrated on the male voice on the telephone.

'Sunday at two is fine, Allan,' she agreed with false enthusiasm. 'Amy and I will be ready then. Are you certain there's nothing I can bring?'

'I've arranged for everything,' he replied. 'I didn't allow myself to consider the possibility that you might refuse. I'm glad you didn't, Elizabeth.'

'Yes, well,' she glanced apprehensively at Jed, realizing suddenly that he had no intention of leaving the room and that he was perfectly aware she was talking to Allan. He was deliberately eavesdropping. Anger flashed in her green eyes, prompting a flicker of amusement in the tawny eyes lazily watching her. 'I really have to let you go now, Allan. We were just sitting down to dinner.'

'Of course.' Allan didn't seem perturbed by her sudden desire to end the conversation. 'I'll see you Sunday.'

'Yes, Sunday,' she agreed quickly. 'Goodbye, Allan.'

She was already replacing the receiver as Allan's goodbye echoed into the room. There was an instant's hesitation as she considered commenting on Jed's bad manners at listening in before deciding such a comment would only lead to an arrogantly mocking reply.

'Dinner will be on the table in a few minutes,'

Elizabeth stated, turning away from him as she spoke.

'There's no need to hurry on my account,' Jed responded calmly.

Clamping her mouth shut, she refused to be baited into replying and walked swiftly from the room. He might not have felt the need for haste, but Elizabeth did. She wanted to get the meal over with as quickly as possible. A little voice told her that she was becoming much too conscious of him and she would be very foolish if she let him disturb the even tenor of her life.

In the middle of the meal, Elizabeth remembered that she hadn't told Rebecca of Allan Marsden's invitation. She disliked bringing it up in front of Jed, but she knew her mother-in-law had a church meeting that evening and would be leaving directly after dinner.

'Amy and I will be out this Sunday afternoon, Rebecca,' she said with false casualness. 'We've been invited —'

'Oh, are we going to the farm with Uncle Jed?' Amy burst in excitedly.

'What farm is this?' Rebecca demanded, her dark eyes centering immediately on Elizabeth, her interest not nearly as vague as it was a moment ago.

Darting a poisonous look at Jed, who appeared immune to its sting, she replied firmly, 'We aren't going to a farm. Amy and I have been invited on a picnic by Allan Marsden on Sunday.'

Amy frowned across the table, disappointment starting to cloud her face. 'Aren't we going to the farm?'

If it hadn't been for the distinct impression that Jed was deriving some sort of amused satisfaction from all this, Elizabeth's response would have been gentler.

'I just told you, Amy, that we're going for a picnic with Mr. Marsden.'

'What is all this nonsense about a farm?' Rebecca inserted, looking pointedly at her son.

'I've been invited to have Sunday dinner with the Reisners.' He nonchalantly buttered a hot crescent roll. 'Kurt suggested that perhaps Elizabeth might like to join us and bring Amy, but of course, she had a previous invitation from Mr. Marsden and had to decline.'

'I see,' was his mother's clipped response.

'But I wanted to go to the farm,' Amy declared with a defiantly pleading look.

'Well, I'm sorry, but we're going on the picnic.' Even as she spoke, Elizabeth knew she was being insensitively cold to her daughter. She should be quietly explaining that they could go to the farm another time instead of making a coldly worded order. It was Jed's fault.

'I don't want to go on your stupid old picnic!' The silverware in her daughter's hand was discarded angrily on to her plate, clanging loudly in accompaniment to her mutinous expression. 'I want to go to the farm and see the animals. I don't want to go with you!'

'That will be enough, Amy,' Elizabeth warned with firm softness.

'Maybe you can go another time,' Jed inserted, a

warm persuasive smile turning up the corners of his mouth.

'I never get to do what I want.' Her lower lip jutted out in a self-pitying pout, as Amy flashed a resentful glance at Elizabeth. 'I always have to do what *she* wants!'

Elizabeth was angered that Jed should attempt to quiet her daughter's temper. If he had not mentioned the invitation to the farm to Amy in the first place, none of this arguing would have occurred. Wrongly she directed this anger at Amy instead of the man at her right who deserved it.

'You will stop this sarcasm at once, Amy,' she ordered.

'I don't want to go on that picnic!' Tears began filling the brown eyes of her daughter.

'I think you'd better go to your room, Amy,' Elizabeth tried to speak calmly and control her own growing temper. 'When you can behave correctly at the table, you may return.'

'No, I will not go to my room!' The stiffly held back tears made Amy's voice tremble.

Although Jed might have been the instigator of the quarrel, Elizabeth recognized that she had handled it very badly. Sending Amy to her room was probably unfair punishment, but the open rebellion of her daughter at the order made it imperative that she carry it out, regardless of the knife of remorse that stabbed her heart.

Flashing Jed a speaking glance, Elizabeth rose from her chair and walked round to the opposite side of the table where Amy sat. With a downcast chin, Amy pushed her own chair away from the table. A tear slid down a round cheek as Amy refused to look at her mother, letting her sense of injustice be known.

'Come along, Amy,' Elizabeth said quietly. She touched the girl's shoulder with her hand and immediately Amy pulled away to walk rigidly toward the hall.

As Elizabeth turned to follow, she looked fully into Jed's bland expression. 'It's not her fault, Liza,' he said.

'I'm perfectly aware of that,' she snapped. 'You had no right to even mention the invitation to the farm without consulting me first. If anyone's to blame, it's you!'

Her long legs moved to follow her daughter's dragging steps. Once she was free of Jed's presence, she would explain to Amy why they were going on the picnic instead of to the farm. She would do so with the patience and understanding she should have exhibited in the first place. Yet there was the nagging memory that she had seized on Allan's invitation in order to have a plausible reason for refusing Jed's.

The large, patterned area rug cushioned the sound of the chair being pushed from the table. Not until a hand grabbed hold of Elizabeth's wrist to halt her forward movement did she realize that Jed had followed her. Her hair swirled about her face in an ebony cascade of curls as her head swung around to face him. His eyes had narrowed on to her expression of astonished outrage before they flickered briefly to

Amy, who had paused to listen near the stairwell.

'Go on up to your room, Amy,' Jed said firmly, but without anger or an ordering tone. 'I want to have a little discussion with your mother.'

Amy hesitated, then the stairway door opened and closed. Next there was the sound of her footsteps slowly carrying her up the stairs.

'I don't see that we have anything to discuss,' Elizabeth said tautly, tossing her head back to glare into his lean, carved features.

'But I do,' he answered in the same firm voice that he had used with Amy.

'Perhaps we do,' she agreed suddenly with a haughty lift of her chin. She didn't attempt to pull free of his hand. The iron grip of his fingers already told her it would be useless. 'I'd like to hear your explanation. After I'd already turned down the invitation I think you were terribly cruel to mention it to Amy and try to use her to persuade me to change my mind.'

'In the first place, I didn't tell Amy about the invitation,' Jed answered curtly.

'Do you expect me to believe that?' Elizabeth demanded. 'I hadn't even mentioned to her that we were going on the picnic Sunday, let alone tell her that we'd turned down your invitation. There's no one else who could have told her about it, except you!'

His mouth thinned dangerously narrow. 'The only conversation I had with your daughter concerned my whereabouts this morning. I *did* tell her I'd been at the Reisners' farm.'

'And that you were invited on Sunday and so were we,' she inserted.

'I did tell her that I was going there on Sunday,' he admitted tightly, 'but I didn't mention that you were invited. Or that you'd made other plans for the day.'

'Then where did she get the idea that we might visit the farm?' Elizabeth asked with cold disbelief.

'As I recall,' amber lights were flashing warning signals in his eyes, 'Amy asked if she might go over some time to see the puppies I had told her about. I said she would have to ask you.'

'That's a likely story,' she scoffed contemptuously. 'Why can't you admit that you were trying to prejudice her into influencing me?'

'Because I don't care whether you ever go to the Reisners' or not,' Jed snapped. 'I merely extended Kurt's invitation. If I wanted you to change your mind — there are other means of accomplishing it without involving a child.'

'Then why did you bring the farm up with Amy at all?' Elizabeth continued to protest angrily. 'Were you jealous of the fact that we have a warm relationship? Did you want to make it as miserable and bitter as the one between you and your mother?'

'I don't give a damn what you think!' He released her wrist abruptly, glowering fury in his face. 'If you want to paint me black, then go ahead! The only opinion that matters to me is my own.'

In the next second he was striding away and Elizabeth was staring after him in open-mouthed and angry amazement. He disappeared into the front hallway. Then the front door slammed with resounding violence.

'Elizabeth!' Rebecca Carrel's voice called to her imperiously from the dining room. 'Was that Jed who just stormed out of the door?'

'Yes,' she acknowledged, her voice trembling in indignation that he should have walked out on her like that.

'You might as well come back in here and finish your meal,' her mother-in-law ordered.

Elizabeth glanced to the dining room archway, then toward the stairway and the room at the top where Amy was waiting. She forced herself to swallow back the tight knot of anger.

'In a moment, Rebecca,' she said in a more controlled tone. 'I want to have a talk with Amy first.'

'I think it would be best if you left her alone for a while. It will give her an opportunity to consider how unforgivably rude and cheeky she was. An apology is definitely in order after her ill-mannered behavior at the table.' There was a light pause before Rebecca added in a bitter tone, 'I don't see why she doesn't take after her father.'

Instead of Jed her uncle, Elizabeth finished for the older woman. Yes, Amy's aggressively independent nature was more indicative of Jed than Jeremy. Amy was never satisfied that things were to be done in a certain way because that was proper or expected.

Breathing in deeply, she walked toward the steps. In the back of her mind, she knew that when she had explained to Amy why they were going on the picnic, she was going to find out exactly what Jed had told her about the farm. She couldn't believe that her daughter might think they would go to the farm only on the strength of what Jed had indicated that he had told her. As soon as Amy had given her the proof she needed, she intended to confront Jed with it.

The outcome of her discussion with Amy did not produce the satisfying results that Elizabeth had anticipated. She had been forced to accept the fact that Jed had told the truth. It had been Amy's imagination that made her leap to the conclusion that they were going to the farm. It was a fairly logical deduction, Elizabeth had decided silently, since it was the farm that was uppermost in Amy's mind.

As for the picnic, her daughter's lack of enthusiasm at the prospect didn't improve after their talk. She had grudgingly agreed to go, but had refused to return to the dinner table. The sulky droop to her mouth had remained despite Elizabeth's lighthearted cajoling, a portent of things to come.

Amy's boredom on the picnic couldn't have been expressed more plainly if she had spent the entire afternoon sitting on the blanket and yawning. Elizabeth had been too self-conscious and irritated by her rudeness to react naturally. The responses she made to Allan's attempts to lighten the atmosphere were stilted and false, increasing the discomfort that saturated each moment of the outing. Her embarrassment had increased when Allan had suggested they call it a day at four o'clock, a scant two hours since it had begun.

To make matters worse, Amy had mumbled an

ungracious 'thank you' and bolted from the car the minute Allan stopped it in front of their house. Elizabeth had stared after her for a full minute before turning to Allan, the wryly twisting line of his mouth marking his expression.

'I must apologize for my daughter,' she murmured self-consciously. 'Her behavior today was unforgivable. She really isn't usually this sulky and —'

'You don't need to explain,' Allan smiled understandingly, taking one of the hands that were twisted together in her lap and holding it in his own. 'Children tend to be a bit selfish about their parents, especially if they have only one.'

'It wasn't jealousy.' Elizabeth shifted uncomfortably. 'I took my anger with someone else out on her the other day, and she hasn't forgiven me for it.'

'I can't imagine you being angry. You're much too beautiful.' The smooth compliment sprang easily from his lips.

'I am human,' she smiled nervously to shrug it aside.

'That's encouraging.' His gaze swept over her wind-touseled hair, curling jet black against her lightly tanned skin, then it returned to the jade greenness of her eyes. Leaning forward, Allan pressed a warm, lingering kiss against the roundness of her lips. 'I'll see you at the dinner if not before.'

When he straightened away from her, Elizabeth reached for the door handle, then paused with the door partially ajar. 'Thank you, Allan, for — for everything,' she offered in gratitude for his understanding.

'Maybe another time the three of us can make it a more enjoyable day,' he suggested.

'Yes, another time,' she agreed uncertainly, andd stepped from the car.

Waving once as he reversed out of the drive, Elizabeth walked toward the house. Amy's behavior should not be allowed to go by without comment, but she was reluctant to lecture her about it. Sighing heavily, she opened the front door.

The sound of Amy's laughter halted her on the threshold. The entire afternoon she had barely smiled at all, now she was laughing. Elizabeth's chin lifted at the sight of her daughter standing in front of the bending form of Jed. His tawny gaze saw her first, a watchfulness in his expression despite the wide grin on his face. Then Amy glanced over her shoulder and the smile faded from her mouth. Apology flickered in her dark eyes before she dashed toward the stairs.

Jed stood upright as Elizabeth shut the door behind her. A flashfire of irritation raced through her veins, angered that he had prompted Amy's laughter when Allan had tried so hard and failed.

'I didn't expect you back so soon,' Jed commented.

'That makes two of us, because neither did I,' she retorted coldly.

'What happened?'

There was a chilling arch to her brow. 'Didn't Amy tell you? Her little sulk succeeded in making the picnic totally miserable for everyone.'

'No, she didn't mention it,' he returned evenly.

'Really? I was certain that's what the two of you were laughing about,' she said in a faintly accusing tone. It completely slipped her mind that she still had not apologized for doubting his word the other night. She had not had the opportunity to speak to him alone and she had no intention of apologizing to him in front of Rebecca or Amy.

'I wouldn't worry.' Jed tipped his head to the side as he mockingly inspected her. 'I doubt if your boyfriend will be put off by one less than satisfying afternoon.'

'He's not —' Elizabeth checked the denial that Allan was her boyfriend. It would only earn her another taunt. 'As a matter of fact,' she said coolly, 'I'll be seeing Allan at the charity dinner next Saturday night.'

'I hope you didn't agree to let him escort you there,' he observed dryly.

'What business of yours would it be if I did?' she challenged.

'It would be Mother's business, not mine,' Jed corrected. There was an indication of some secret knowledge in the wryly amused curl of his mouth.

'Rebecca doesn't dictate my social life,' Elizabeth stated firmly.

'That's one you can argue out with her.' Uninterest moved across his face as he turned away.

'What makes you think that I would need to argue with her?' she demanded, drawing an over-the-shoulder glance from Jed.

In the fleeting instant, there was the look of a rogue about him, youthful and daring. His eyes glittered with mischievous satisfaction, totally erasing the cynicism that was nearly always present in one form or another. But more, the hard look was gone, the look of a man who had seen much that was unpleasant.

'Mother has decided that I'm to make my public debut at your dinner next week,' Jed replied. 'She intends the Carrel family to attend this social function as a unit.'

'And you're going?' she murmured doubtfully.

'You've forgotten, Liza.' His gaze narrowed slightly. 'I came back to make some sort of peace. That requires compromise. So yes, I am attending your black tie banquet.'

CHAPTER FIVE

'JED has arrived with the sitter, Elizabeth. Are you ready yet?' Rebecca called.

Halting the tube of coral lipstick inches from her mouth, Elizabeth answered, 'In a minute!'

'Well, please hurry,' her mother-in-law returned impatiently. 'I don't want to be the first to arrive, but neither do I want to be the last.'

Sighing ruefully, Elizabeth looked into the mirror, wishing for the umpteenth time that she hadn't allowed Rebecca to persuade her to arrive at the dinner with Rebecca and Jed. She had thought she had the perfect excuse, the supervision of the pre-dinner arrangements. But Rebecca had adamantly insisted that as chairman, Elizabeth should appoint someone else to the task. Now she realized that she had given in because of the subconscious re-echoing of Jed's words concerning compromise and making peace. So she had compromised her own judgment by agreeing to Rebecca's demands.

The silk underlining of her white lace dress rustled as she walked toward the hallway door. Turning the doorknob, she remembered her matching shawl and evening bag were lying on the bed. She retrieved them quickly from the blue satin coverlet. Her pulse was behaving erratically and her nerves were so jittery that she was certain she hadn't been this disturbed by her first date. But her outward composure revealed none of her inner agitation.

Amy was waiting for her at the bottom of the stairs. Her brown eyes widened and her mouth rounded into a sighing, complimentary 'Oh!' A smile of genuine pleasure eased the tense muscles around Elizabeth's mouth.

'Do I look all right?' She turned slowly for her daughter's benefit.

'Oh yes, Mom, you look scrumptious!' Amy assured her in a breathy voice.

'Hello, Cindy,' Elizabeth greeted the schoolgirl standing in the hall.

'Hello, Mrs. Carrel. That's a lovely gown.' The young girl gazed almost enviously at the gently moulding long lace gown. There was a telltale glimmer of braces as she barely moved her lips to speak. Elizabeth remembered her own schoolgirl dreams of enchantment whenever she had seen adults dressed in formal attire and smiled.

'Thank you,' she nodded, wishing she could cast aside her misgivings toward the evening and catch some of the stardust that was in Cindy's eyes. 'Did my mother-in-law give you the telephone number where we can be reached if you have any problems?'

'Yes, she did, but I'm sure everything will be all right,' the girl added hastily.

'Elizabeth, Jed is waiting in the car,' Rebecca stepped into the archway of the front hallway.

Bending to kiss her daughter's cheek, Elizabeth teased, 'Be good for a change, Amy.'

Brown eyes twinkled back at her. 'I'll try,' she said as she wrinkled her nose impishly.

Following her mother-in-law to the car, Elizabeth took her place in the back seat, murmuring a polite thanks when Jed held the door open for her. The country club and adjoining golf course was only a mile or so from th e which made the journey short. But Elizabeth was conscious of Jed's faint air of preoccupation. She was almost certain his silence couldn't be blamed on the evening before them.

Silently she acknowledged that his dark evening clothes suited him. It wasn't until they had arrived at the club that she noticed it was not the suit she had picked out for him. The entrance lights fully illuminated the expertly tailored suit as he opened the car door for her, offering a hand out. Elizabeth frowned her bewilderment. The material of his suit and the white silk shirt were much more expensive than any she had seen locally.

'What's the matter?' One corner of his mouth lifted as he tossed the car keys to the parking attendant. He touched the dark lapel with his finger. 'Don't you like the suit?'

'Yes,' she answered quickly, avoiding the roguish light glittering in his eyes. She made a pretense of adjusting her rectangular shawl. 'It's just that you didn't mention that you'd bought anything when you went to Cleveland last week.'

'I wasn't aware that I needed to,' he replied, lightly

touching her elbow to guide her around the car to where Rebecca waited.

Pressing her lips tightly together, Elizabeth didn't comment. Jed had been absent most of the week, a situation that had preyed on her nerves since she had never been entirely certain when he might turn up. His explanations, even to his mother, as to where he had been were vague and uninformative. Elizabeth couldn't make up her mind whether his mysteriousness was deliberate or merely an extension of his personality.

When they reached Rebecca's side, she preceded them into the club, her head tilted regally as though she were leading a royal procession. In answer, heads turned at their approach. Curiosity was the main reaction, cloaked in the guise of greeting. The farther they walked into the small reception area where cocktails were being served, the more conscious Elizabeth became of another reaction.

Her gaze slid sideways to the man at her side. Six foot, lean, with thick, carelessly waving tobacco brown hair and rakishly carved features, Jed Carrel was a compellingly attractive man. He was not the handsomest or the tallest man in the room. And Elizabeth realized that he was not holding everyone's attention simply because he was a Carrel or because he was a Carrel who had become an outcast by his family.

Perhaps a part of it was the worldly look in his eyes, that intimation that he had seen and experienced much without ever revealing what had happened. But more, Elizabeth knew, with a certainty that it was the potent virility, his maleness that silently challenged women.

She was still making a surreptitious study of him when Jed turned his head and held her gaze. In that charged second she knew that he had been aware of her inspection all along. It was there in the laughing glitter of his eyes.

'What do you suppose they're thinking?' he murmured to her in an aside as he nodded and greeted the various people who were acknowledging them.

Elizabeth gave a quick hello to Mr. Shaw and his wife before answering Jed's question in a voice as soft as his. 'That you've grown into a fine-looking man.' The smile she gave him as she looked into his face was cool and controlled. 'No doubt the mothers are wondering if they should let their daughters near you and —' pausing for emphasis, 'whether they're too old to catch you themselves.'

His quiet chuckle touched only her ears. 'I didn't expect cynicism from you, Liza.'

The captivation in his smile caught her by surprise. She hadn't realized he could be so charming if he chose. She quickly averted her gaze, feeling the warmth rising in her neck, but bringing only an attractive pink tint to her cheeks.

'I didn't mean it to sound cynical,' she replied.

At that moment Barbara Hopkins detached herself from a younger group of adults and glided forward to meet Elizabeth. Her friend's eyes kept straying to Jed, leaving Elizabeth in little doubt as to whom she was really interested in meeting. It was only natural, she supposed. After all, Jed could be classified as an eligible bachelor and there wasn't an abundance of unattached males in Carrelville.

'Elizabeth!' Barbara called gaily, reaching out with a ringed hand in greeting. 'That's a stunning gown.'

Patiently Elizabeth returned the greeting and compliment, before introducing Jed. Barbara's coy gaze vaguely irritated Elizabeth when it was directed at Jed, but he didn't seem to find it too sweet.

'So you are Elizabeth's tennis friend?' he smiled, holding Barbara's hand longer than Elizabeth thought was necessary.

'Oh, yes, we play at least once a week. Do you play, Mr. Carrel?'

'Jed, please,' he corrected smoothly with a brief inquiring tilt of his head, 'if I may call you Barbara?' His answer was a wide, satisfied smile of agreement. 'I do play tennis, although not recently.'

'Perhaps we can arrange a game of doubles.' Barbara glanced pointedly at Elizabeth, letting her know it wasn't an idle suggestion. 'You'll have to persuade Allan to be your partner.'

The reference to Allan Marsden made Elizabeth conscious of the man standing to her left. At the mention of his name, he stepped forward, handing Elizabeth one of the drinks he held in his hand.

'Hello, Elizabeth. I've been waiting for you to come.' He smiled pleasantly as he spoke, a vague questioning light in his eyes.

Not meeting his gaze squarely, she replied, 'there was a last-minute adjustment of the schedules,' completely aware that she had put him off escorting her tonight because she was supposed to be here early.

Jed's hand shifted from her elbow to the back of her waist as he leaned around her, a faint intimacy in his touch that she found unnerving. 'You must be Allan Marsden. Elizabeth has mentioned you.' He extended his hand. 'I'm Jed Carrel.'

'Welcome home,' Allan said, shaking the hand firmly and smiling. 'I imagine that's been said to you many times.'

Tawny eyes slid to Elizabeth, mocking her quickly ricocheting look. 'Not all that many times that I've grown tired of hearing it,' Jed responded.

Her fingers tightened around the cocktail glass Allan had given her as she wondered if anyone had told Jed that before. Certainly she hadn't, and neither had his mother. It would be ironic if his first words of welcome were given by a stranger. Ironic and cruel.

'I see you've been here long enough to locate the cocktail bar,' Jed observed, glancing to the iced drink in Allan's hand.

'Let me show you where it is,' Barbara offered quickly.

Her friend was wasting no time in staking a claim on Jed, Elizabeth thought with a flash of bitterness that surprised her. Jed's gaze laughed openly at the darkening green of her eyes.

'You will excuse me, won't you, little sister?' The grooves around his mouth deepened with a suppressed smile.

'Of course,' she nodded.Her skin felt suddenly cool where his hand had warmed the back of her waist.

Some of the chill crept into her voice, tight and dull.

'He certainly isn't what I expected,' Allan commented quietly as he watched Jed being slowly led through the crowd by Barbara.

'Oh? Why not?' Elizabeth asked. Her attempt at vague interest came out frosty and defensive.

Allan glanced at her sharply, taking his time in wording his answer. 'From the rumors I've heard since his return, I suppose I expected someone more belligerent and arrogant. His self-assurance and easy charm caught me by surprise, I guess.'

'I suppose it would.' Elizabeth didn't want to discuss Jed, averting her gaze from his hypnotic form still discernible on the far side of the room.

'Was your husband like him?'

'They were very nearly total opposites,' she answered curtly. Then with an abrupt change of subject, she inserted, 'I want to apologize for the mixup this evening. I hope you didn't arrive too early thinking to find me here.'

'No, I didn't.' Allan followed her lead.

But it was impossible to completely avoid the topic of Jed. Nearly everyone she and Allan talked to had some comment or question about him. And her sensitive radar never lost track of where he was located in the room. No matter how casually she glanced around the room, her gaze invariably homed in on Jed. She couldn't avoid noticing that he had that ability to hold himself apart from others while appearing to join in with their laughter and conversation.

At the long dinner table, Elizabeth and Allan were

seated on the opposite side of the table from Jed and ever-constant Barbara. Fortunately they were several chairs down the table. Yet Elizabeth couldn't avoid seeing him whenever she glanced in that direction.

As the meal progressed, she found herself becoming sickened by her girlfriend's actions. The way Barbara kept leaning confidentially toward him and accidentally brushing against him robbed her appetite. The boldness of the flirtation left little to the imagination of the onlookers, and they were many. Jed did not rebuff Barbara's advances. In fact, Elizabeth was certain that the amused interest in his eyes was meant to encourage.

By the time the last course was served, anger was smouldering inside her, igniting into hot flames whenever her eyes wavered toward Jed, which was becoming increasingly often. The merry sound of Barbara's laughter drew her gaze again, and this time it was met and held by Jed's. As his mouth quirked in lazy amusement at one corner, Elizabeth realized her eyes were revealing her distaste and disgust for their conduct.

Then Barbara's hand was touching the sleeve of his suit jacket in light possession, drawing his attention back to her. Elizabeth stared at her untouched dessert plate, her nerves so taut that she felt at any moment they would snap. Smiling stiffly at Allan, she excused herself from the table. She cursed silently at the way she was drawing attention to herself, but she didn't care. She had to get away from the table to regain her perspective.

In the powder room, she waved aside the administrations of the attendant, taking deep, calming breaths and willing herself to relax the tense cords in her neck. Turning on the cold water tap, she let the chilling liquid stream over the insides of her wrists to cool the feverish heat in her veins.

When she left the powder room, Elizabeth still didn't feel sufficiently in control to return to the table. Luckily her role as chairman of the dinner committee allowed her to enter the kitchens without a questioning look as to her motives. She deliberately took her time waiting until the moment when the guests were leaving the dining area to return to the reception room where a small dance band had been engaged to play.

Unfortunately Allan was standing with Jed and Barbara. Elizabeth hesitated for an instant, about to change direction, when Jed saw her. Fixing a smile on her face, she tried to pretend that she had just that moment seen them, but she didn't think Jed was fooled.

'Is everything in order?' Allan inquired with a welcoming smile.

'It seems to be,' she answered in what she hoped sounded like a satisfied sigh.

'I'm glad my only responsibility was in selling tickets,' said Barbara, her hand resting on the inside of Jed's arm. 'Now I can simply enjoy the party.'

'How astute of Elizabeth to select you to sell tickets,' Jed murmured, glancing at the blonde. 'I doubt that there was a man in town who refused to buy one from you, unless his wife was around.'

'Jed Carrel!' Barbara sounded properly shocked, but it was only a pose.

Elizabeth moistened her lips and turned to Allan. 'I hear the band is very good,' she said.

As if on cue, the band struck the opening chord of the first song. A hand lightly touched her arm. Elizabeth stared at its owner, unable to keep the disdain from glittering viridescently in her eyes at Jed's touch.

'It's only fitting,' he said quietly, a mocking challenge in his gaze, 'that since a Carrel is mainly responsible for this evening, we should lead the first dance.'

If she hadn't been so certain that it was what Jed expected, she would have refused. Instead she inclined her head in agreement and allowed him to take her hand. She sensed that neither Allan nor Barbara approved, but there wasn't any way they could protest.

Two couples had started on to the empty dance floor at the band's prelude to 'Beautiful Ohio'. They stepped near the edge when they saw Jed leading Elizabeth on to the floor. In the center of the floor, he turned her into his arms and stopped. His eyes swept over her almost grimly unenthusiastic expression with a lazily relaxed study.

'I feel as if I'm holding a cold fish. Loosen up, Liza,' Jed chided softly. 'And smile. You're not going to an execution.'

'I'm not?' But she smiled sweetly, forcing her muscles to become pliant under his gliding touch as he led her into the first step.

The firm pressure of the hand at her back made it easy for her to follow his lead. With each step she became more fluid, the rigidity lessening as if answering the challenge of his natural grace. From the first he had held her gaze. Now Elizabeth found herself becoming fascinated by the darkening amber hues. They glided twice around the floor before the first couple joined them.Jed slowed their steps and confined their route to a smaller area of the floor.

'Isn't it better to have these duty dances over in the beginning?' The spell of the dreamy, sentimental tune was broken by his faintly sarcastic tone.

Breaking free of his compelling features, Elizabeth stared at the contrast of the white shirt collar against the dark tan of his throat. Her own throat felt dry and parched, caused no doubt by the heat that was emanating from the hand spread on her back and the rock-firm muscles of his thighs.

'Yes, much better,' Elizabeth agreed huskily, straining slightly against his arm so she wouldn't be held too closely against his hips.

'Now everyone is saying how very well we dance together.' From her side vision she could see that his eyes never left her face, although her own made a quick sweep of the room to affirm his statement. They were the object of much interested scrutiny. 'Had I not danced with you, they would have been wondering all night why.'

'Would you have cared?' she challenged.

Jed grinned. 'I wonder what the townspeople would say if they knew how easily sarcasm slips from the alluring mouth of the young and beautiful widow Carrel. That's what they call you, you know — the young widow Carrel.' The line of his firm mouth became crooked with derision. 'They regard you as a courageous figure, rising above the tragedy that befell you so young, always behaving with the utmost decorum, and faithful to the loving memory of your husband. Perhaps you should apply for sainthood?'

A betraying crimson flush raged across her face. 'Must you make it sound as if it's something I should be ashamed of?'

'Blushing — another rare commodity.' There was the sensation of an invisible shrug. 'I've always been skeptical of the "goody two-shoes" in the world, maybe because very early in life I became tired of being reminded what a good boy Jeremy was when I knew all along that he wasn't any different from me. I took the blame for some of his pranks too many times.'

'Must we discuss Jerry?' Elizabeth demanded uneasily. There was the sickening knowledge that she couldn't visualize her husband's face without the benefit of his picture.

'Is the memory too painful?' Jed taunted, his eyes narrowing on her averted profile.

Ebony dark curls touched the bareness of her back as she tilted her head to direct the flaring resentment in her green eyes up to his face. She longed to startle him with the admission that her recollection of those brief moments as Jeremy's wife was hazy, that she had almost forgotten he had ever existed until Jed returned. The memory of her first meeting with Jed was clearer and more vivid than her wedding night with her husband, his brother. She obeyed the inner caution that checked the admission.

'Think what you like,' she replied bitterly. 'You will anyway, regardless of what I say.'

'Do you know what I'm thinking?' he murmured with piercing softness. 'I'm curious why you're so defensive every time I mention his name.'

'Maybe it's because you are so offensive,' she retorted.

The song ended and she moved as swiftly as possible out of his arms. Her legs were treacherously unsteady. She realized that they had been all along, but the firmness of Jed's supporting hold had blinded her to it. His rangy stride had him at her side almost instantly, an arm circling the back of her waist as he guided her off the dance floor.

'Out of condition?' he mocked in an undertone.

'I believe it's the immense relief I feel that I don't have to dance with you again,' Elizabeth muttered savagely beneath her breath.

'Ah, there's your adoring Allan,' Jed smiled wickedly, 'waiting patiently for me to return you to him. Do you know, he reminds me of Jerry?'

'He doesn't look at all like him,' she answered sharply, secure in that statement since Alan was light-complected and Jeremy had been dark.

'Not in looks,' he chuckled, 'in temperament. Your Allan will never make waves. He'd be too concerned he'd upset the boat he was in.'

'What's the matter, Jed?' Her temper flared. 'Are you jealous because Allan has made a success of his life while you've come home a failure?'

'Oh, Liza!' Anger trembled in the sighing way Jed spoke her name despite the tight control in his voice. He breathed in deeply, caution lights flashing in his narrowed look. 'You make waves, too, don't you?'

Elizabeth almost ran the last few steps to Allan, intimidated more than she cared to admit by the anger she had provoked. There was the frightening knowledge that she had been making waves and the last one had nearly swamped her boat. Allan was the lifeline and she clung to his hand tightly.

Barbara had been waiting with Allan and she stepped forward quickly to meet Jed. He smiled at her as if in answer to the silent promise in her eyes. The same feeling of distaste began to tie Elizabeth's stomach into knots again.

'I'm in need of a drink, Barbara,' Jed stated, sliding a still smouldering look to Elizabeth. 'Why don't you lead me to the bar again?'

'Would you like a cocktail?' Allan offered.

Elizabeth felt in need of a burning jolt of alcohol, but not for anything did she want to follow Jed and Barbara. She refused firmly, the vigorous shake of her head trying to dispel the warning voices that kept whispering to her.

The evening had been hopelessly ruined, but she fought against it, determined to have as much fun as Jed. Allan was most attentive and her smiles and laughter encouraged him even more. It was unkind and unfair to focus her green eyes on him whenever Jed's shadow fell on her. No matter how hard she tried, Elizabeth was unable to ignore him.

Despite Barbara's attempt to monopolize him, Elizabeth noticed when he danced with others. More duty dances, she had thought viciously. Resentment seethed behind her smiles. It exploded into disgust and hatred every time she saw Jed and Barbara on the dance floor.

By midnight her head was pounding from the tension of constantly suppressing her emotions. She was certain she could not endure another minute without screaming. Her nerves were raw. Her stomach churned with nauseating constancy. She nearly cried with relief when she saw Rebecca approaching her.

'I think it's time we should leave, Elizabeth,' her mother-in-law stated after smiling politely to Allan. We promised the sitter we wouldn't be late.'

Inwardly Elizabeth recognized that Rebecca was not motivated by any consideration of the schoolgirl watching Amy. Just as her mother-in-law didn't like to be the first to arrive, she didn't like to be the last to leave. Besides, it wouldn't be proper for a Carrel to be too fond of parties.

The idea was forming in Allan's expression to offer to take Elizabeth home. She knew that once outside the walls of the club, she would not be pleasant company. Considering the way she had behaved toward him all evening, he would find her changed attitude puzzling and totally unlike her. Before he could speak, she did.

'I'm ready whenever you are, Rebecca,' she agreed quickly, dredging into her reserves to turn to Allan and smile. 'Perhaps we can get together for lunch one day this week.'

'Yes —' he hesitated slightly before resigning himself to her half promise. 'Yes, we'll do that.'

A brief exchange of goodbyes and Elizabeth and Rebecca were walking toward the exit. 'Did you get the keys from Jed?' Elizabeth inquired, clicking open her evening bag to see if by chance she had a spare set for the car.

'Jed is having the car brought around now,' Rebecca frowned. 'Where did you think he was?'

Elizabeth glanced back toward the group, surprised to see Barbara smiling and dancing with someone else. 'I supposed he was going to stay for a while,' she murmured.

'He is leaving with us,' was the firm response, as if any other action was unthinkable.

The car was at the door when they walked out, the parking attendant holding both side doors open. Jed was behind the wheel with the motor running. He didn't seem at all surprised that Elizabeth was returning with them and not with Allan. The instant the doors were closed, he put the car in gear and turned it down the lane.

'It's such a relief to be away from that noise,' Rebecca sighed. 'It does get on a person's nerves after a while.'

Elizabeth's throbbing temples echoed the sentiment, but she didn't place all the blame on the noisy gaiety of the party. It had only been an irritant. In the concealment of the darkness, she cast daggers at the strong profile of the driver.

'I was talking to Clive Bennet tonight,' her mother-in-law continued. 'He's one of the directors of the country club. The position of club manager will be vacant the first of September. I sounded him out on the possibility of you taking it on, Jed. The club pretty well runs itself. The golf pro manages the greens and the restaurant manager sees to both the food and drink. Yours would be a strictly supervisory role.'

'Thanks, Mother, but no, thanks,' Jed refused evenly.

'What exactly is it that you intend to do?' Impatience sharpened Rebecca's voice to a cutting edge.

'What I've been doing.'

'Which is nothing,' she retorted.

He smiled thinly. 'I know you were motivated by the best of intentions to make the inquiry on my behalf, Mother, but I believe I can decide for myself what I want.'

'I swear you'll be a wastrel the rest of your life,' Rebecca muttered.

'But then it is my life, isn't it, Mother?' His gaze slid to her briefly before returning to the highway illuminated by the car's headlights.

He was so arrogantly certain that he knew what was right, Elizabeth seethed. She saw him glance at her reflection in the mirror and directed her gaze out the side window. If only he would leave, she wished silently, and stop disrupting the quiet pattern of her life.

CHAPTER SIX

'DID Amy behave herself?' Elizabeth removed the required amount of money from her purse and handed it to the young girl.

'I didn't have any trouble at all,' Cindy assured her, stifling a yawn as she stuffed the money in her shoulder bag.

'I hope we didn't keep you too late,' Elizabeth smiled stiffly, brushing back a strand of black hair, aware of Jed watching them near the front door waiting to take the baby-sitter home. 'I wouldn't want your parents to be worried.'

'Oh, no, Mrs. Carrel, I'm sure they're not worried. I explained that you were going out to a dance tonight and they don't expect me back until much later.'

Nodding, Elizabeth turned to make the polite request of Jed that he take Cindy home, but he was already straightening away from the door, smiling at the schoolgirl self-consciously returning his look.

'If you aren't expected home right away, then that means we can take the long way home, doesn't it?' he winked.

It was an innocently teasing remark, but Elizabeth's fingers curled into her palm. A scarlet blush was enveloping the girl's face. Her own teenage years were not so far behind that Elizabeth didn't recognize the symptoms of a schoolgirl crush. At that age it didn't matter that the suggestion had been made in jest. What mattered was that Jed had noticed her at all.

It wasn't the first time that evening that Elizabeth had seen such a reaction. Women in their sixties had blossomed just as quickly under the attention of his charm. It seemed every female was vulnerable to his considerable masculine force. The knowledge irritated her, more so perhaps because there was a certain vulnerability within herself.

'Goodnight, Cindy.' There was a faintly clipped edge to her voice that arched Jed's brow in mockery.

'Goodnight, Mrs. Carrel,' Cindy returned, glancing swiftly at Jed through the tips of her lashes as he held the door open for her.

A tiny smile that bordered on the flirtatious turned up the corners of the girl's mouth as she started through the door. The smile wasn't wide enough to reveal the corrective braces on her teeth, and thus remind Jed of her immaturity. Elizabeth whirled away in anger before the door closed behind them.

The impetus of it carried her swiftly up the stairs to her room, but there was no relief in the solitude of the room. The screaming tautness of her nerves did not relax within the security of the four walls. If anything, the pain in her head throbbed more furiously than before. She paced the room restlessly for several minutes, wishing for a warm glass of milk to soothe her tension, but reluctant to go back downstairs to get it. Rebecca would be sure to hear her and come to find out what was wrong, and a conversation with her mother-in-law was the last thing Elizabeth wanted.

With impatient movements, she stripped off the lace evening gown. Tears of frustration filled her eyes when she poked a finger through her nylon pantyhose, ruining them beyond use. After slipping her pale green nightgown over her head, she donned the matching silk robe, securing the sash around her waist, and walked into the adjoining bathroom. Hurriedly she swallowed two aspirins, washing them down with a glassful of water and praying they would work quickly.

Her hands shook traitorously as she creamed the make-up from her face. Without the cosmetic mask, she lost her air of sophistication. There was a vaguely yearning light in her green eyes. It reminded Elizabeth of something. Then the answer flashed through her mind. It was the same wishful look that she had seen in Cindy's eyes. She slammed the jar of cleansing cream on to the shelf in disgust.

Swiftly she returned to the bedroom. Glancing at the small clock near her bed, she quickly worked out that Jed would have already left Cindy at her home and be en route to — where? Her lips compressed into a thin line. He would no doubt be returning to the country club and Barbara's waiting arms. Yes, she thought grimly, that was exactly what he would do. He had willingly left to bring her and Rebecca home so he wouldn't be encumbered with them later. He and Barbara would have the night free to — She left the thought uncompleted as a nauseating shudder trembled through her. She didn't want to think. Her imagination was becoming too vivid. She needed to rid her mouth of its bitter taste. Forcing a silent fluidness into her legs, Elizabeth stepped into the hallway, quietly turned the doorknob to her daughter's room and walked in.

Standing beside the bed, she stared at the small sleeping figure, the dark hair against the white pillow appearing black in the dim light. The covers were half thrown off and Elizabeth pulled them back over her daughter. A serene joy filled her heart during moments like this, a contentment in knowing that, God willing, she would always be there to look after her daughter.

Sighing wistfully, she turned away from the bed. If only she had someone of her own to look after her and protect her from — again she halted in mid-thought. Protect her from what? What was it that suddenly made her feel frightened? It was absurd. She shook her head firmly. She was being nonsensical, she scolded herself. There was nothing threatening her.

As she turned to close the door behind her, the sound of footsteps on the stairs penetrated her consciousness. The door clicked shut and Elizabeth froze; the footsteps halted as well. Jed was midway up the stairs, a hand on the partially unknotted tie around his throat, the dark evening jacket swinging open. His tawny gaze held her captive and she felt threatened by the virility closing around her with suffocating strength.

Then Jed was pulling the tie the rest of the way free, letting it swing from his hand as he mounted the rest of the stairs. Elizabeth still didn't move, watching the unconscious grace of his movements. Not until she was again looking into his eyes, tilting her chin slightly upward now that he had reached the hallway, was she aware that she had waited for him and not retreated as she should have done.

His implacable gaze swung from her to the door she was standing in front of. 'Is Amy all right?'

'Yes.' Her answer was short and frayed. She was confused that she had waited. 'She's sleeping.'

Her fingers closed around the neckline of her robe, a defensive action although there had been no outward move from Jed to warrant it. A watchfulness crept into his lean, cynical features as he remained standing in front of her, making no move to continue down the hall to his room.

'What is it, Liza?' There was a drawling laziness to his voice, but it was a thin veil that concealed its sharpness. His eyes narrowed dangerously as she warily averted her gaze.

'I don't know what you're talking about,' she answered stiltedly, turning completely away in the direction of her room.

'Something's on your mind,' Jed prodded deliberately.

'If anything at all,' she kept her voice low so as not to disturb her sleeping daughter and worked to put chilling indifference in it, 'it's surprise to see you back so soon. I didn't expect you to be back until the morning.'

'Where did you think I'd be?' He drew in a deep,

impatient breath and exhaled it slowly in challenge as he spoke.

Hauteur made icicles in her voice. 'I didn't attempt to speculate what out-of-the-way place you and Barbara might choose.'

'I thought Barbara was your friend,' he drawled.

Irritation seethed in the flash of her accusing green eyes. 'She is,' Elizabeth snapped.

'Then why are you so indignant because I was friendly to her?' he mocked with harsh cynicism.

'Friendly?' she challenged coldly. 'You were very nearly making love to her on the dance floor. I'm not the only one who noticed.'

'What's it to you if I was?' He made no attempt to deny her accusation, a fact that further incensed Elizabeth.

'Because it was disgusting and contemptible to behave that way in public!' she retorted shrilly, then caught back the faintly hysterical tone in her voice. Lowering her head, she took a deep, calming breath. 'I found it extremely embarrassing. Your behavior was despicable.'

'And Barbara?' What about her behavior?' A cold smile was directed at her. 'She was hardly an innocent victim of unwanted advances,' he jeered.

Elizabeth refused to admit that much of the blame was Barbara's. 'I don't condone her behavior either.'

'What gives you the right to judge?' A contemptuous sound came from his throat and Elizabeth started toward her door. Jed jerked her around sharply, wrapping the tie around her neck and holding it beneath her chin with one hand. 'I can't make up my mind if you're frigid or just a prude.'

'Let go of me!' she ordered, her fingers closing around his wrist. The steel of his grip resisted her efforts to be free.

There was wild palpitation of her heart as Jed used the tie to draw her easily closer to him. The savage glitter in his gaze drove out the last of her poise. Her breath came in uneven gulps as he let his gaze dwell on her lips.

'I think it's time I found out,' he commented with analytical coolness.

The imprint of his hips was already making itself felt through the silkiness of her peignoir as Elizabeth arched herself away, pushing her hands against the solid wall of his chest. A frenzied sob of despair tore at her throat.

'You said you didn't want to touch me,' she reminded him frantically, as the tie bit into the back of her neck and pulled her inexplorably closer.

A thin smile twisted the hard line of his mouth. 'And that made you feel secure, didn't it? You felt safe in provoking me.' His male features taunted her foolishness. 'Did you forget who I am? I'm Jed, the worthless one, the black sheep. Haven't you learned that I'm not to be trusted?'

'No,' she pleaded weakly.

The tie around her neck and the hand under her chin wouldn't allow her to escape and his mouth covered hers in a series of slow, drugging kisses. Had he been bruising and fierce, she might have resisted, but his sensual possession was her undoing. She responded.

At some point the tie was discarded and his hands moulded the feminine softness of her form more fully aggainst the male hardness of his. The tidal wave of desire that carried her to dizzying heights exposed the raging core of passion within herself that not even she had known existed.

Her arms slipped beneath his jacket, circling the sinewy waist, the thin material of his white shirt like a second skin. The caress of his hands began an intimate exploration, too, that left her weak from the completeness of her response. She whimpered softly in protest when she felt the beginning withdrawal of his lips and clung to him more tightly.

'Damn,' Jed muttered softly in self-reproach, and she understood the reason. She had not wanted to feel this way about him either.

As he cupped her face in his hands and held her away, her lashes fluttered open to reveal luminous green eyes that were frightened by the depth of her desire for him and at the same time asking him to make the possession complete. Gold fires blazed in his eyes as he read the message in hers.

'Liza —' She hated the calm control that had entered his voice.

'Please,' she closed her eyes again, melting against him and nuzzling her cheek against the palm of his hand as a cat would prod the hand that had stopped stroking it, 'I don't want to talk.'

He allowed her to cuddle into his chest, his hands unconsciously caressing her shoulders and back. She had always guessed at the extent of his worldly expertise.

'A few minutes ago, you called me contemptible and disgusting.' His low voice taunted her with its cynical amusement. 'Am I supposed to feel honored now that you want me to make love to you?'

There was a stifled gasp of pain. 'Please!' An agonizing bubble in her throat choked off the rest of her protest.

'Please what?' His mouth moved along her temples. 'Please understand? Please forget all the insults? Please make love to me? What?' Jed prodded unmercifully.

'Don't be cruel,' Elizabeth murmured, a shame creeping in to steal her pleasure.

'I'm sorry, I feel cruel tonight,' he said harshly. 'I can't help it.'

His hands dug into her arms and pushed her away. It wasn't a genuine rejection because she knew he wanted her. She was not an inexperienced girl. She was a woman and she knew when she had aroused a man's desires. Still it hurt.

A tear quivered on the edge of her lash. Jed touched it, his forefinger catching it as it fell. Pride kept her gaze fixed on his impenetrable features, an aching need still pulsing through her body.

'I'm sorry, Liza,' he said again in a gentler yet just as firm tone. 'There really is such a thing as the right place and the right time. I thought I'd stopped wanting you, but I haven't.'

'Then why —' she started to ask huskily, but his finger touched her lips to silence them.

'Then why don't I take you?' He smiled wryly and sighed. As crimson heat colored her cheeks, he folded her gently into his arms. There was too much restraint in his embrace for her to draw any comfort or warmth. His voice vibrated with charged emotion near her ear. 'Because overriding my desire is a bitter violence,' he stated grimly.

'I don't understand.' Elizabeth had buried her face against his neck, now she raised it to gaze at him, bewilderedly.

'I know you don't.' The heady smile he bestowed on her didn't change the ruthless glint in his eyes. 'Maybe some day —' Jed hesitated. She felt him withdrawing from her, emotionally as well as physically, detaching himself from her arms with an impatient firmness. 'Good night, Elizabeth.'

Turning, he walked down the hall, not looking back once, not even when he walked through the door of his own room and closed it behind him. Empty and cold, Elizabeth stood where he had left her, wanting to follow him and frightened by the vague warning he had given her. Finally she went back to her own room and crawled into bed, her ears straining for some sound from his, but the walls of the old house were too thick.

She hadn't been certain what his attitude would be the following morning. He was such an enigma to her that she hadn't been able to guess whether he would silently mock the way she had thrown herself at him or pretend that it had never happened. She was uncertain what her own attitude should be.

Her own emotional upheaval was difficult to understand. She couldn't make up her mind whether she had been carried away by a wave of love or the backwash of sexual abstinence. In the end, she adopted a wait-and-see attitude and let Jed take the first step.

The first day there had been the crushing sensation that he was completely indifferent to her, aloofly so. The way he had of holding himself apart from others in their presence was more pronounced than ever. Then, that evening, she had felt his gaze dwelling on her with thoughtful, almost brooding intensity. He rarely addressed any comment to her, keeping the main flow of conversation with his mother, but neither did he subject her to any taunting jibes or mocking looks.

The waiting game was a difficult one for Elizabeth to play. Hope would alternately rise and fall until she felt she needed a barometer to record the erratic fluctuations. The physical attraction Jed held for her was undeniable. The most accidental contact had her senses leaping in immediate response. And she guessed that he had only to take her in his arms and she would be his for the asking.

Five days she went through the tortues of Tantalus. Jed's previous routine didn't vary much; he spent most of the day away from the house and some evenings. Yet there was never any pretense on his part that nothing had happened.The very second she thought there was, Jed would send her a look that was meant to remind her.

How much longer was this going to go on? Elizabeth

sighed to herself. Painstakingly she trimmed off the crust of the bread, varying the design of each slice from circles to squares to triangles. Flaky cherry tarts were cooling on the counter, the tarts and the canapés she was making were refreshments for Rebecca's Literary Club women. Their monthly meeting was being held here this time and Elizabeth had naturally been requested to take on the task of fixing the light refreshments.

'Can I help, Mom?' Elbows propped on the table, chin cradled in her hands, Amy glanced up at Elizabeth.

'May I help,' she corrected automatically. She pushed the small bowls of egg salad, ham salad and tuna salad to her daughter along with a knife. 'You can help me with the sandwiches.'

'*May* help,' Amy corrected her mother with impish humor.

A slow smile spread across Elizabeth's face as she ruefully nodded an acknowledgement of her own grammatical error. Cooking and preparing foods was another interest of Elizabeth's that Amy appeared to be beginning to share.

'How long are those ladies going to be here?' Amy asked in a less than enthusiastic tone.

'Probably until after four,' Elizabeth answered. At her daughter's grimace, she added, 'It would be best if you stayed in your room until it's time for the refreshments.'

'I suppose Mrs. Cargmore is going to be here,' Amy

grumbled, then adopted a mimicking voice. ' "Children should be seen and not heard." '

'At least not too often,' Jed added in conclusion.

The bread knife clattered to the floor, narrowly missing Elizabeth's foot as she spun around to face him. She tried to cover her confusion by bending to the floor to retrieve the knife, but in the next second Jed was kneeling beside her, handing her the knife. For all the amused mockery in his smile, his eyes were golden warm in her face.

'Someone should teach you to be careful with knives or you're going to end up chopping off your toe,' he scolded gently.

Her pulse was accelerating at an alarming pace. She straightened quickly, trying to hide the flow that brought an emerald brilliance to her eyes.

'You startled me,' she breathed in defense.

'Is that what I did?' Jed asked with a questing arch to one brow.

Bouncing her gaze away from his face, Elizabeth realized that he knew the way he disturbed her. He made a lazy, sweeping appraisal of her from head to toe, his eyes twinkling merrily when they returned to her face. She caught her breath at the change in his manner. The aloofness was gone, but what did it signify?

'All of this can't be for our consumption. Are we having a party?' Jed shifted his attention to the sandwiches Amy was stacking neatly on the plate.

'Not exactly,' Amy explained. 'Mom and I are doing the refreshments for Grandmother's Literary Club meeting.'

'Looks like I'll have to change my plans for the afternoon. I had thought I'd spend it around here, but not if we're about to be invaded.' The tobacco brown head made a definite negative shake.

'It isn't that bad,' Elizabeth murmured, her heart sinking slightly as she wished she knew if there was a particular reason why Jed had intended to spend the afternoon here — possibly with her? Was that what he had intended?

'Well, I sure wish I had somewhere else to go.' Amy licked the salad off her fingers and picked up another slice of bread.

'Amy, you shouldn't do that. Now wash your hands,' Elizabeth looked her reproval.

There was a disgruntled sigh as Amy replaced the knife and bread and walked to the sink. Jed was leaning against the counter, smiling faintly at Amy.

'So you've been condemned to spending the afternoon here?' he teased.

'In my room,' Amy answered with an expressive widening of her brown eyes. 'Isn't that exciting?'

'Well, you can always sit and count how many times Mrs. Garth sneezes,' he suggested dryly. 'That's what we used to do. Her record was twenty-four times as I recall.'

'Did you really count?' Amy giggled.

'Must you encourage her, Jed?' Elizabeth sighed, but with humor. 'Your mother already thinks she's disrespectful of her elders.'

'On second thoughts,' a smile played with the edges of his mouth, 'why don't you come with me this afternoon? I thought I'd visit Maggie.'

'Could we stop by the farm and see the puppies, too?'

'Amy, you —' The quick words of reproval were interrupted.

'Perhaps you should ask your mother if you can go,' Jed suggested.

Amy rebounded to Elizabeth, not allowing her time to bask in the faintly intimate smile he had turned to her. 'Please, Mom?'

'If Jed is sure he wants to take you, I don't object,' Elizabeth agreed. Her gaze was drawn back to the leanly carved face, less cynical now with its expression of patient indulgence, but no less compelling.

'Oh, he's sure, aren't you, Uncle Jed?' Amy hastened to have the invitation affirmed.

Jed straightened from the counter, the muscular length of him achieving his full height. Elizabeth felt the force of his masculinity drawing her to him even with the width of the table separating them.

'Yes, I'm sure,' he nodded. The grooves around his mouth deepened as he ruffled the top of Amy's head. 'I think we'd better be leaving before your grandmother discovers what we're up to and changes us into a couple of bookworms!'

Amy was already giggling and racing for the back door. Silently Elizabeth observed that her daughter seemed as anxious for Jed's company as she was. If only she could react that naturally and with such obvious pleasure instead of being plagued by uncertainty and caution!

'I'll look after her,' he said quietly, misinterpreting the slight frown.

'Of course,' Elizabeth smiled wanly. 'Thank you ... for asking her.'

Jed seemed to examine her words, his gaze running over her with disruptive thoroughness. Elizabeth was certain that her inner agitation must be apparent. Her shaky poise felt completely destroyed, assaulted by too many days of uncertaintly and doubt. But he made no comment regarding her stilted expression.

'We'll be back later this afternoon, with luck after the dragons have left,' he said, and followed the path Amy had blazed out of the door.

Staring after the lean figure, wide shoulders tapering to a slim waist and hips, Elizabeth wished they had asked her to come along. She couldn't have gone, of course, she acknowledged with a sigh, reverting her gaze to the bread slices on the cutting board. But she wished Jed had asked her for her company.

Luckily she didn't have to take part in the afternoon's meeting. As a silent participant, she was not required to concentrate on the book reviews being given. Once the meeting was over and the refreshments served, the women seemed to intend to linger indefinitely, exchanging local gossip. Mrs. Garth sneezed again and Elizabeth contained a smile.

This would never do, she told herself sternly. One more time and she would surely laugh aloud when she saw Mrs. Garth raising the embroidered handkerchief to her nose. As unobtrusively as possible, Elizabeth excused herself from the two ladies she had been sitting beside, guessing they would not miss her since she had added so little to the conversation, and began gathering together the dishes and carrying them to the kitchen.

On the third trip, she found Jed and Amy seated at the colonial kitchen table. Amy raised a conspiratorial finger of silence to her lips.

'Ssh!' she whispered. 'We don't want Grandmother to know we're back yet. Did she say anything?'

'Only that she hoped you'd behave yourself,' Elizabeth answered softly, not commenting on Rebecca's initial surprise and wary doubt on the advisability of letting Amy go with Jed. 'Did you have a nice time?'

'Oh, yes. Maggie was so glad to see me,' Amy asserted proudly. 'And Uncle Jed, too. And you should see the puppies, Mom! Freda said I could have one when they're old enough to leave their mother.'

'We'll see about that.' It was difficult to keep her gaze from straying too often to Jed. An odd breathlessness had claimed her lungs from the moment she had entered the room and encountered his tawny gaze. She carefully stacked the dishes in the sink, trying to control her schoolgirl reaction to his presence. 'There are some cherry tarts left. Would you two like some?'

'Yes, please,' Amy accepted eagerly, while Jed only nodded.

Just as Elizabeth set the plates with the tarts on the table in front of them, a sneeze echoed into the room.

Jed darted Amy a knowing look and smiled at her.

'There goes Mrs. Garth again,' he observed dryly.

Amy suppressed a giggle with her hand. 'How many times do you suppose that is?' she whispered gleefully.

'Sevent—' Elizabeth bit quickly into her lip, suddenly and guiltily aware that she had been counting. Red flags of embarrassment ran up her cheeks at the mocking light in Jed's eyes.

'You've been counting!' Amy's brown eyes rounded in astonishment.

'Nonsense, I —' Her protest was defensively automatic, but the expressions on both their faces mirrored their disbelief.

'How many times, Liza?' Jed prompted softly.

Flustered for a second, Elizabeth turned back to the counter; their infectious humor was beginning to replace her chagrin. A smile hovered near the surface.

'Make her tell, Uncle Jed.' Checked laughter rippled through Amy's voice. 'I knew she was counting!'

At the scrape of the chair leg, Elizabeth glanced over her shoulder. At the sight of Jed's deliberate approach, her heart pattered wildly against her ribs.

'We shouldn't be making fun of Mrs. Garth this way,' she protested again. For too many years, her life had been ruled by strict courtesy for Elizabeth to succumb easily to their amused, yet innocent mockery. 'She can't help it.'

'How many, Liza?' A wide smile was daring her to continue to withhold the information.

Elizabeth pivoted to face him, her fingers closing over the hard counter top pushing into her back. 'It isn't polite.' Good judgment and discretion were rapidly being overtaken by the onslaught of his amused gaze.

'How many?' Jed persisted.

He was in front of her now; his nearness weakened her resistance. A smile started to break through and Elizabeth pressed her lips tightly together, glancing wildly at her daughter. But he had seen the laughter glittering in her green eyes. The touch of his hands on her shoulders brought it bubbling to the surface in soft giggles.

'Jed, Please!' It was a half-hearted protest through her laughter that acknowledged she was about to give in. Her palms spread across his chest in an effort to keep his intoxicating length at a safe distance.

Tilting back his head, he chuckled quietly in victory and drew her closer, locking his arms around her waist. 'You can't escape, Liza, until you tell us.'

'Seventeen.' Her answer was immediate and breathless.

Another sneeze was heard and they all broke into open laughter. Tears filled Elizabeth's eyes and she couldn't remember the last time she had laughed this hard. It was a wonderful, joyous sensation, especially since she was sharing it. Gradually it lessened into deep breaths for control. She found herself nestled under the crook of his arm, her head resting weakly against his shoulder.

Curving his hand under her chin, Jed raised it to inspect her face, and Elizabeth was much too contented and happy to do any more than gaze at his compellingly masculine features as he grinned at her.

'I've never seen you look more beautiful,' he murmured huskily, the gold light in his eyes burning over her face. 'You should laugh like that more often.'

'Really?' she whispered, basking in the fiery warmth, unable to decide whether the heat racing over her skin came from contact with him or was born inside herself.

'Yes, really.' Although there was mocking amusement in his voice, it wasn't the message she saw written in his gaze as he slowly turned her into his arms, his hands moving in an arousing caress down her shoulders and spine to mold her closer against him.

A tiny sound from the table reminded Elizabeth suddenly that they were not alone. Amy was watching them with obvious interest. Quickly she averted her head from Jed's descending mouth, gasping slightly as he settled on the lobe of her ear.

'Jed, please,' she whispered with a self-conscious glance at her round-eyed daughter. 'N-not in front of Amy.'

He lifted his head a few inches from hers in seeming discretion, a crooked smile twisting the sensually male lips. The glitter of his eyes never left her face.

'Amy, do I have your permission to kiss your mother?' he asked quietly. The grooves around his mouth deepened at the rush of pink in Elizabeth's cheeks.

'Yes,' Amy answered quickly with a broad, conspiring look, and settled into her chair to watch.

'You see?' he mocked.

This time he didn't take any chances that Elizabeth might avoid his kiss, but held her chin firmly until he had taken possession of her mouth. At his masterful touch, she surrendered to the whirl of inevitability, letting the waves break over her head and become submerged in the superior force of his attraction.

A horrified gasp broke through the ardency that was about to carry Elizabeth completely away. As she broke away from the addictive pressure of his lips, her startled gaze encountered the shocked faces of three members of the Literary Club. At her twisting turn, Jed partially released her from their embrace, keeping one hand firmly around her waist and in plain view of the ladies. Before he glanced at the trio, his gaze mocked Elizabeth's crimsoning complexion.

'Was there something you ladies wanted?' he inquired with unbelievable calm.

'We were just leaving,' one of them sniffed.

'We thought we should see Elizabeth and offer our goodbye,' a second responded, a brow arching at Elizabeth in disapproval.

The third woman merely looked from Elizabeth to the gleaming Amy and back to Elizabeth. Her indignant shock was more condemning in its silence than the rest. Stiffly Elizabeth thanked them for coming.

The three women were barely out of the kitchen before the rapid exchange of their voices could be heard, no doubt comparing reactions. Only then did Jed remove his hand from her waist, lighting a cigarette from his picket and letting his contemplative gaze dwell on the uncomfortable warmth still reddening her face.

'Does it bother you that you're going to be the subject of a lot of talk?' His tone challenged despite the softness of his question.

'Yes,' Elizabeth swallowed. 'It does a little.'

'Jeremy was always the apple of the town's eye, not me. Are you ashamed to be seen with me?'

Her gaze bounced away from the harshness in his otherwise calm expression. 'Not ashamed,' she hedged. 'I would have been self-conscious with anyone.'

Jed studied her face for a long moment. The expression in his own masculine features was unrelenting. Then he turned to walk away.

'Jed.' Her whispered plea called for his understanding.

Without glancing back, he paused beside her daughter's chair, and Elizabeth noted the faint softening of his profile as he gazed into Amy's curious and concerned expression.

'Your mother is a prude, Amy,' he smiled crookedly.

'Is that bad?' Amy breathed.

There was a resigned shrug of his shoulders that was hardly encouraging as it accompanied the negative shake of his head. 'No, it isn't bad.' Then glancing briefly at Elizabeth he added, 'I'll be back for dinner,' and left from the rear door of the kitchen.

CHAPTER SEVEN

'IS that everything, Mrs. Carrel?' The woman clerk paused before ringing up the total on the cash register.

'Yes, thank you,' Elizabeth responded, absently glancing to be certain that Amy was still at her side.

'It's quite a chore getting children ready for school these days. The list of things they need keeps getting longer and longer,' the woman sighed. 'With five of my own in school, I ought to be an expert on it.'

'I think this completes Amy's list.' Elizabeth smiled as she took the smaller of the two parcels and handed it to her daughter, juggling the larger into a comfortable position with her two previous purchases.

'Are you ready for school to start?' The clerk smiled down at Amy.

'I suppose so,' she shrugged.

'I thought you were looking forward to the first day of school?' Elizabeth tilted her ebony dark head in curious surprise.

'Not since Unce Jed came back. It's much more fun at home now that he's there,' Amy observed.

'Uncles usually are more fun than school,' the clerk agreed, darting an amused look at Elizabeth.

'Jed is fun. He even makes Mom laugh,' asserted Amy.

Another customer approached the check-out counter and Elizabeth was relieved to direct her talkative daughter toward the door. The clerk's look of amusement ha d been tinged by speculation after Amy's last comment. There was little doubt in Elizabeth's mind that the incident witnessed by the three members of the Literary Club had been transmitted all over town.

A faint sigh of frustration slipped from her throat as she and Amy stepped outside. Truthfully she had expected Jed to seek her out again, but over the weekend not once had he indicated that he wanted to be alone with her. He had been charming and amusing, as Amy had pointed out, but he had also avoided any opportunity to be alone with her.

'Good morning, Elizabeth. We seemed destined to meet on the sidewalks of Carrelville. Good morning, Amy.'

Focusing her gaze on the man who had stopped in front of them, Elizabeth realized that she hadn't even noticed Allan approaching them.

'Hello, Allan. How are you?' Her words of greeting were falsely warm to cover the initial blank look she had given him.

'Fine,' he nodded. 'Looks like you've been doing a little shopping.'

'We've been getting Amy's things for school,' she explained.

'It's getting close to that time,' Allan agreed. He addressed the observation to Amy, but she was gazing about them with obvious lack of interest toward the man now talking to her mother. There was a hint of firmness in the smile he turned to Elizabeth and she knew he was irritated by Amy's attitude, one that she echoed at this minute but was too polite to let show. 'I was just on my way to the restaurant for morning coffee. Would you two care to join me?'

'I'm not old enough to drink coffee.' Amy scuffed the toe of her shoe on the sidewalk before turning cold brown eyes toward his face.

'How about milk and doughnuts, then?' Allan suggested with thinning patience.

Elizabeth's own polite words of refusal were checked. She was no more enthusiastic about having coffee with Allan than Amy was, but her daughter's churlishness had been cuttingly rude. Allan had always been kind and considerate. He didn't deserve that kind of treatment.

'That sounds like an excellent idea,' she accepted warmly, sending a warning look to Amy, whose mouth was opening in protest. Her mouth went grimly shut as she tucked her chin into her neck and glowered at the sidewalk. 'Our car is just across the street. We'll put our packages in there and join you.'

'Let me help you carry some of that,' Allan offered.

'They're not at all heavy,' Elizabeth assured him as he fell into step beside them as if to make sure they didn't change their mind once they were at their car. 'Besides, I have them balanced in such a manner that if you took one, they would all fall.'

At the intersection, they waited for the light to change. Elizabeth made a polite inquiry about the hospital and half listened to his reply. Across the street a set of broad shoulders looked achingly familiar. A second later, the man turned away from the shop window and the sharply etched profile confirmed it was Jed. Another second later, Elizabeth recognized Barbara, curling her arms through Jed's and hugging close to him as they started down the street toward the same intersection she was waiting to cross.

Pain gnawed at her stomach walls. Jealousy had always been an alien emotion. Now she felt its tortuous grip and its sickening side effects. She tried to swallow back the nauseating lump in her throat, without success.

Do you see? a malicious voice whispered in her ear. Do you see the way he's accepting the attention as if it was his due? That's what he wants from you. He'd like to add you to his string of conquests. Once he's got you to fall in love with him, do you think he'll marry you? He's not the marrying kind, the hideous voice reminded her.

'Look, Mom!' Amy cried excitedly. 'There's Uncle Jed!' And she waved the paper sack in her hand to attract Jed's attention.

Glancing away from the blonde molded to his side, Jed saw them. A frown of displeasure darkened his face, the lean hard features still compellingly handsome. Tears of irritation and pride blurred Elizabeth's vision. She had just as much right as he had to be in town, she told herself bitterly.

The light at the intersection changed. With a proud toss of her head she started across, but the watery collection of tears in her green eyes had affected her perception. She misjudged the distance from the curb to the pavement and stumbled. The packages spewed from her arms as she released them to try to check her fall. She wasn't even aware that she had cried out nor saw Allan's arms reaching out to try to catch her.

Winded and stunned, she lay unmoving on the pavement for a few seconds to try to collect her wits. She smiled weakly at Allan as he bent anxiously beside her and pushed herself into a sitting position.

'Are you all right?' he frowned, making a quick examination of the graze on her elbow.

Elizabeth nodded, unable to speak, partly from shock and partly from humiliation. Her fall had drawn everyone's attention and they were gathered in a tight circle around her.

'Stand back. Give her some room,' a familiar voice was ordering crisply, and the people were obeying as Jed pushed his way through. Elizabeth studiously brushed the dust from her cranberry skirt, avoiding the gold sharpness of his eyes. Her heartbeat became erratic when he knelt beside her. 'Are you hurt, Liza?'

'I — I'm all right,' Elizabeth murmured, trying to withdraw her grazed elbow from Jed's hold.

'She fell down,' Amy explained.

'So I noticed,' Jed murmured dryly, completely ignoring Allan who hovered to one side, his position usurped by the firm authority that had accompanied Jed's arrival. 'Is your middle name Grace?'

The pink intensified in her cheeks. 'I simply misjudged the step.'

'Did you twist your ankle?' His fingers scorched an inquisitive trail along her shinbone to her ankle.

'I may not be a practising physician, but I am a doctor,' Allan inserted sharply, trying to reassert his position as Elizabeth's rescuer.

'And I've probably treated more injuries and illnesses than you have,' Jed snapped. Evidently satisfied that there was no indication of a sprain, he slipped a supporting arm around her waist. 'Let's get you on your feet.'

'I'm all right,' Elizabeth repeated.

'Heavens, Jed, there isn't anything wrong with her,' Barbara cut in. 'Allan can take care of her.'

The blonde's comment wasn't even acknowledged as Jed lifted Elizabeth to her feet. She didn't know whether to blame the light headedness on the fall or the steel band holding her so close to his lean, muscular hips and thighs. The malevolent dislike in Barbara's cold blue eyes did make her reel instinctively toward Jed in search of protection. His arms tightened around her.

'I'll carry you to the car,' he stated, sliding his other arm under the back of her legs and easily swinging her off her feet.

Unfortunately for the man standing toward the back of the crowd, the faint buzz of concerned voices stopped just as he murmured to a friend, 'I bet he's carried her to far more intimate and comfortable places than that!"

A rigid stillness entered Jed's features as dangerous cat-gold eyes narrowed unerringly on the man who had made the jeering comment. The ruthless set of his jaw was intimidating. Elizabeth shivered uncontrollably when he slowly lowered her to her feet.

'I believe you owe the lady an apology, Mick.' Jed spoke with ominous softness.

'I didn't mean anything by it, Jed.' The man named Mick shifted uncomfortably, as the crowd parted between the two men.

The air crackled, invisible electricity snapping at coiled nerves. The arm Jed had kept around her waist was a suffocating iron band. Elizabeth knew he wasn't aware of the force he was applying. She also knew Jed wouldn't relent from his stand until the man had apologized for his slighting remark.

'Please.' Jed paid no notice to her request for his attention, so Elizabeth turned to Mick. 'There's no need for you to apologize,' she insisted with quiet pride. 'You were only voicing the suspicions of everyone here in this town. I can't expect you to be the only one to apologize.'

'I'm sorry, Mrs. Carrel.' His gaze skittered across her face to Jed's and fell away.

'Here's your packages, Mrs. Carrel.' Another one of the group stepped forward to hand her the packages that had fallen to the street.

Jed took them before Elizabeth had a chance, giving one to Amy. 'You're big enough to carry this.' The other he retained while keeping an arm firmly circling Elizabeth's waist. She couldn't very well protest without causing more comment. Besides, she partially welcomed his strong support.

'Elizabeth, let me take you to the hospital,' Allan offered quietly. 'You should have those grazes cleaned and disinfected.'

The crowd had begun to thin, the excitement over. The sting in her scraped elbows was becoming more pronounced, but Elizabeth's only wish was to leave — as quickly as possible.

'It's really not necessary,' she refused with a weakly polite smile.

'They should be taken care of,' he reiterated.

'I'll see to it,' Jed said firmly.His jaw was still clenched, the savage anger not yet fully abated.

'What about me?' Barbara demanded.

'I'll see you later.' The light had changed again and Jed was pushing Amy to start across the street to the car, not at all concerned or interested in Barbara's indignant outburst.

'I might be busy,' she retorted haughtily.

Except for a cynical twist of his mouth, there was no reaction from Jed as he began half carrying, half guiding Elizabeth across the street. Secretly Elizabeth thought he was mocking Barbara's boldly false statement that she might reject him. It was disturbing to acknowledge that he was right. There were very few women who wouldn't take him back. And she had the dreadful feeling she was among them, and it was a severe blow to her pride.

'Well, you've done it now, little miss diplomat,' Jed snapped as he slammed the car door shut. 'Where are the keys?'

Elizabeth fumbled nervously through her bag and

handed them to him. Huddling next to the door, she heard the motor spring to life, growling with all the suppressed power of its driver.

'I didn't do anything wrong. Unless you call avoiding a fight wrong?' she challenged defensively.

'Whether you like it or not, you've been labeled as *my* property.' As they left the city limits, he accelerated until the car was whizzing by the telephone poles at an alarming rate.

'What does that mean?' Amy leaned forward over Elizabeth's seat.

But Elizabeth chose to ignore the question. 'If I have, it's due just as much to your actions,' she retorted.

'Because I chose to take offence on your behalf at that man's remarks?' Jed mocked, quirking a brow briefly in her direction. 'Did it ever occur to you that I might have been defending your "good name," ' there was a definite sarcasm in the last, 'as my sister-in-law and not as —' He glanced in the back seat to Amy's expression of round-eyed interest and didn't finish the sentence.

'What does it mean, Momma? How can you be Uncle Jed's property? I thought you couldn't own people?' Amy persisted, taking advantage of the slight lull in the conversation.

'You can't own people,' Elizabeth replied with brittle patience.

'Then what does it mean?'

'It's like going steady, Amy,' Jed answered this time with the same controlled tone. 'We aren't supposed to date anyone else but each other. That's what I mean."

'Mom can't go out with anyone but you? Not even Mr. Marsden?'

'That's right,' Jed clipped.

'Good!' Amy declared with one vigorous nod of satisfaction. 'I don't like him very much.'

'Amy!' Elizabeth's outcry was automatic.

But Jed had thrown his head back and was laughing. The deep, hearty sound was contagious. It played with the corners of Elizabeth's mouth until she too began laughing.

'Oh, Amy!' Jed shook his head with a sobering sigh as he turned the car into the house lane. 'You're a treasure. Let's get your mother's arm fixed up, then see if we can persuade your grandmother to let us have lunch outside.'

'Like a picnic? Terrific!' Amy agreed. 'But Grandmother hates to eat outside. There's too many bugs.

'No worry,' Elizabeth was still smiling. 'Your grandmother won't be here for lunch today. It's—' An expression of dismay swept across her face. 'Oh, Amy, it's Thursday! Your piano lesson.'

'Oh, Mom, no!' Amy wailed.

'Come on, Liza.' Jed switched the motor off and turned to her. 'What's one piano lesson in a lifetime of piano lessons?' he chided gently. 'Call her teacher and tell her the car won't start.'

'Please, Mom,' Amy echoed, adding her persuasions to those of her advocate.

'What if we eat later after your piano lesson?' Elizabeth suggested. 'You can skip practising this time and we'll still have our lunch outdoors, if you like."

'Instead of that,' Jed countered, 'why don't you let Amy practise for half an hour while you're getting lunch and skip the lesson?'

'Wouldn't that be just as good, Mom, please?'

'Well, all right,' Elizabeth agreed finally, glowing a bit under the admiring wink Jed bestowed on her. Amy's shriek of gladness forced her to add a cautioning note, 'But only if you practise for half an hour.'

'I will!' her daughter promised fervently, pushing open the door and hopping out of the car. 'I'll start right now.'

She was ready to race for the house when Jed whistled her to a stop. 'Don't go in empty-handed,' he told her. 'Take one of the packages.'

Grabbing one of the packages from the back seat, Amy was careering toward the front door again, not waiting for Jed and Elizabeth. He tucked the remaining two packages under his arm and stepped from the car when Elizabeth did.

'You would have thought I'd given her the moon,' she smiled ruefully after her daughter.

'Playing hookey is always fun, even if you have permission.' His lazy smile was captivating as he fell into step beside her.

'I've heard you were an expert at playing hookey,' she teased.

'I probably was absent as much as I was present,' he admitted with a twinkle. "Absolutely incorrigible" was the way the truant officer described me. I'm not exactly proud of it, but I probably learned earlier than most how to apply what school had taught me to the realities of living.'

'I remember,' Elizabeth murmured with a flash of recall, 'your father once said that you had a very analytical and logical mind and that you could have been a brilliant lawyer if you weren't so —' she hesitated.

'Incorrigible,' he supplied mockingly. 'When did he make that concession that I might possibly have some brains?'

'Shortly after Jeremy was killed.' He held the front door open for her. 'I think he was really hoping you would come back then.'

'To his way of life.' There was a bitter, downward twist to his mouth. 'Come on, let's get your arm cleaned.'

'I'm sure he only wanted what he thought was best for you,' she murmured.

'I have no doubt he meant well.' Jed motioned her toward a kitchen chair and walked to the cabinet where the first-aid kit was kept. 'I forgave him for his intentions a long time ago. The trouble is he never forgave me for choosing my own style of life.'

In the next instant, antiseptic was burning the scrape on her elbow. Her quickly drawn gasp of pain brought an apologetic smile, but Jed continued until it was clean. By then the conversation was forgotten and Amy was faithfully at the piano practising.

While Jed disappeared to wash, Elizabeth telephoned Mrs. Banks, Amy's piano teacher. Thankfully the woman accepted her explanation. Elizabeth hadn't pretended any car trouble, merely stating that Amy wouldn't be keeping her lesson today.

Working in the kitchen had always been satisfying to her, but she discovered there was a special contentment within as she set about fixing the noon meal for just the three of them. When she spied Jed standing on the patio, she realized it was the way she wanted it to be for always.

The depth of her love for the lean, virile man standing out there frightened her. She knew she had jumped into very deep water. For the present Jed was holding on to her. But what would she do if he ever let go? With Jeremy, she had only been playing in the shallows. Now she was in over her head.

Elizabeth turned from the window, fighting back the panic that nearly sent her racing to Jed's arms seeking some reassurance that he cared with more than just physical passion. The agonizing pain of the morning was vividly recalled, that twisting, sickening jealousy when she had seen him with Barbara. And Barbara expected to see him again today.

It was difficult to regain the sensation of contentment. Tensely Elizabeth waited all through lunch for the moment Jed would say he was going. While she cleared the table, Amy persuaded him to play a game of croquet. Elizabeth sensed that behind his laughter and his teasing conversation with her daughter, his mind was thinking of something or someone else. It was difficult to know if it was her imagination.

The game was over with Jed the winner when Elizabeth finished washing up the lunch dishes. She brought a fresh pitcher of lemonade with her as she returned to the patio. Jed was just leaning back in one of the lounge chairs when he saw her.

'You read my mind,' he smiled lazily. 'We'll drink that whole pitcherful before this afternoon is over. It's going to be hot.'

She steadied her shaking hand as she poured him a glass. 'What about Barbara?' Elizabeth tried to sound nonchalant.

'What about her?' After wiping the beads of perspiration from his forehead, he took the glass, sipping it appreciatively.

'Isn't she expecting you this afternoon?'

He ran an amused eye over her face, as if sensing the underlying urgency in her question. 'It wasn't anything definite.' He leaned his head back against the cushion, running the ice-cold glass along his temple. 'Besides, it's too hot to play tennis this afternoon.'

'Is that what you were going to do?' Elizabeth murmured.

'What did you think?' Jed mocked, examining her downcast gaze over the brim of his glass.

'I didn't think,' she answered, looking anywhere but at him. She didn't actually believe Barbara planned to play tennis all afternoon and certainly not if she had Jed all to herself.

'Liar,' he taunted. 'I think I detected a tint of jealous green in your eyes just then.'

'You . . . you must have been imagining it.'

'That's a pity.' Jed closed his eyes against the sun, amusement teasing the corners of his mouth. 'Since I made my preference for the company of the young widow Carrel and her daughter instead of the pleasures of her friend so obvious, I foolishly hoped she might unbend from her straightlaced ways enough to admit that she wanted mine.'

The gaze she had kept averted swung to him sharply, afraid he might be mocking her again and praying that he was speaking the truth. With his eyes still closed, Jed reached out with his hand and found the fingers that were clutching the arm of her chair. Slowly, the brown curling lashes were raised and the enigmatic gold lights in his eyes were focused on her wary face.

'It's true, Liza,' he said evenly and naturally.

Her heart quickened at his touch. 'Why?' she asked breathlessly, still questioning whether he was playing with her emotions.

'Why do you think?' There was a husky seductive quality to his countering question that sent fire through her veins.

'Let's play another game of croquet!' Amy came bounding between the two chairs, breaking the magic spell that Jed had been casting over her.

'It's too hot,' he smiled his protest.

'Come on,' Amy pleaded, taking both their hands and tugging to get them to rise to their feet.

'One game,' Jed surrendered.

Amy was delighted to have both her uncle and her

mother apparently at her disposal for the entire afternoon. Her constant presence negated any opportunity for the conversation to return to its former personal note, a fact that Elizabeth didn't know whether to be thankful for or regret. An inner perception told her that she would never find out more than Jed wanted her to know. While she — was she being blatantly transparent about her own feelings?

Under the present circumstances of uncertainty, it was ironic how innocently confident she had been when she had set out to capture Jeremy. From the first time she had met him, she had been determined to marry him. Had it ever been love? When the accident had taken him, it had been shock rather than grief she had felt. She had been an immature young girl seeking the fantasy of love. Now she was a mature woman and the eyes with which she beheld Jed were those of a woman in the thralls of a mature, profound love.

She was allowing her imagination to carry her away, she scolded herself sternly. It was a beautiful day. She should be enjoying it and stop looking around every corner for some impending disaster.

'What's the frown for?' Jed tilted his head inquiringly, his thick brown hair gleaming in the afternoon sun. Before Elizabeth had a chance to answer him, he glanced toward the house. 'Ah, Mother's home,' he sighed. 'She does inhibit people.'

Elizabeth turned as Rebecca stepped through the French doors from the living room. 'There you are. It's terribly hot out here, isn't it?' she greeted them, her dark gaze swept over the three of them, nodding briefly in response to the greetings.

'It is a bit warm,' Elizabeth agreed.

Rebecca Carrel's attention focused on her. 'I heard you had a slight accident today, Elizabeth.'

For an instant Elizabeth held her breath. She hadn't dreamed today's episode would be relayed to her mother-in-law so quickly.

'A scrape on the elbow. Nothing serious,' she shrugged.

'How convenient Jed was there to take care of you,' Rebecca murmured, swinging her sharp gaze to her son.

The cat-gold glitter returned in answer to the silent challenge of her eyes. "If I hadn't been there, there were plenty of volunteers who would have seen to it that Elizabeth was all right.'

'Well, at least you look none the worse for this mishap.' The saccharine smile did little to soften the haughty features. 'Was there anything you would like me to help you cook for dinner this evening?'

'No,' Elizabeth refused stiffly. 'I was going to put a roast in the oven. I . . . I think I'll start it now.'

She was nearly to the french doors when she heard footsteps behind her, strong quiet strides that belonged to Jed. She turned, trying to fight away the awkwardness Rebecca's arrival had induced.

'I meant to tell you earlier,' Jed stopped beside her, drawing the french doors shut behind him, 'I won't be home for dinner this evening.'

'Of course,' her frozen voice acknowledged, chilled by the cold hand that gripped her heart. He hadn't seen Barbara this afternoon because he intended to see her tonight.

'Of course?' A curious, amused frown creased his forehead. 'Why do you say, "of course"?'

'There was no special significance,' she lied. 'It was merely an acknowledgment.'

'Have it your way, Liza,' he smiled mockingly, and walked toward the stairway.

How she despised Barbara at that moment! She could have cheerfully clawed her eyes out if she had been there. Jealousy was an ugly thing.

CHAPTER EIGHT

IT was the second cup of coffee she had stared at until it got cold, Elizabeth thought resentfully as she poured it down the sink. If she wasn't so angry at herself for being so foolish to believe that Jed might care about her, she would be crying.

Yesterday afternoon he had said that he wouldn't be home for supper. She had lain awake in her bed until well after midnight, feeling miserably sorry for herself before drifting off to restless sleep with out having heard Jed return. With good reason! He hadn't returned!

After the first angrily jealous shock had receded, fear had set in. There could have been an accident. She had frantically dialled the police to see if an accident had been reported, terror filling her heart that she might have lost Jed as she had Jeremy. But none had. Nor had he been admitted to the local hospital. That left only one place for him to be — with Barbara.

Tears scalded her cheeks and she scrubbed them away with her hand. She was not going to cry because of her own stupidity. She should have had more sense than to fall in love with someone like Jed. The bitter taste of her love nearly gagged her.

The front doorbell rang. Who could that possibly be at this hour of the morning, she thought angrily. She was in no mood to entertain any visitor for Rebecca. The coffee cup clattered against the side of the porcelain sink as the doorbell sounded impatiently again.

Smoothing her hair away from her face and breathing deeply, Elizabeth walked through the kitchen into the hall, her nerves stretched to screaming pitch. She wanted to release their tension when the doorbell rang again. The smile on her face was less than welcoming as she opened the door.

'Freda?' She identified the young woman standing outside in surprise. 'What are you doing here?'

Freda Reisner's hands twisted nervously in front of her. 'Jed —' she began hesitantly.

Elizabeth immediately stiffened. 'I'm sorry, he isn't here this morning.'

'I . . . I know he isn't,' Freda faltered under the chilling coldness that underlined Elizabeth's reply. 'He's at our farm.'

'At your farm?' Elizabeth repeated bewilderedly. 'I thought he was — Is he hurt? Has there been an accident?'

'There wasn't an accident.' Freda shook her dark blonde head quickly to banish that fear. 'But I'm afriad he's ill.'

'Oh, my God!' Elizabeth whispered, covering her trembling mouth and chin with her hand.

'He had supper with us last night and fell asleep on the couch. Then later . . . he was ill,' Freda explained. 'He made Kurt promise not to tell you.'

'Have you called a doctor?'

'Yes, before I came over, but Jed refused to go to the hospital. Maybe he'll listen to you,' Freda sighed.

'May I drive over with you?' Elizabeth requested anxiously. 'Of course.' Freda Reisner turned away from the door, hurrying down the sidewalk to her waiting pick-up truck.

'Amy! Amy!' Elizabeth called to her daughter playing in the back of the house. She had barely explained to her the cause for her alarm before she was hurrying into the truck and Freda was reversing out of the drive.

The doctor's car was already at the Reisner farm when they arrived. Elizabeth recognized it as belonging to their family doctor which probably accounted for the fact that Freda was able to get him to come out.

'Where is he?' Elizabeth glanced at Freda, unwilling to blindly follow the sound of muttering male voices.

'In the downstairs bedroom, second door on the right in the hall,' Freda pointed.

'Stay here with Freda, Amy,' Elizabeth requested, and pivoted in the direction Freda had indicated.

Pausing in the open doorway, she stared at the man lying in the double bed, a fist pressed against her stomach. There was a sickly sallow color making itself seen beneath the darkness of Jed's tanned face. Perspiration gleamed on his forehead and above his upper lip. The tawny-colored eyes were closed, but she guessed from weakness rather than sleep. Her gaze swung to the tall, stoop-shouldered man who had just taken Jed's pulse.

'How is he?' Apprehension made her voice one degree above a whisper.

'Ah, Elizabeth,' the doctor smiled. 'Kurt said you and Rebecca were probably on your way over.'

At the sound of her voice, Jed moved slightly, lashes fluttering open to focus on Elizabeth. Resentment filtered through the glaze of fever dominating his gold-flecked eyes when he glanced at the second man standing near his bedside.

'Rebecca didn't come,' Elizabeth murmured, trying to return the smile of encouragment Kurt Reisner was giving her. 'She's in town at a meeting of some sort.' Her mother-in-law's whereabouts were of little concern to her at the moment. Each beat of her heart was for a previously vital man lying so listlessly on the bed. 'Jed — what's wrong — with him?'

The doctor cast a faintly amused glance at Jed before moving slowly toward Elizabeth. 'This is one case where I'm accepting the patient's diagnosis.' Again there was the reassuring smile that there was no need for alarm. 'He picked up a fever in the tropics, and he tells me that he has had recurring bouts of it before. A couple of days and it'll run its course. In the meantime, he'll be a sick man, but he assures me there are no lasting effects.'

'Shouldn't he go to the hospital?' she suggested anxiously, not as convinced as the doctor that there was no cause for alarm.

'No.' The hoarsely weak and angry protest came from Jed.

The doctor chuckled softly. 'As you can see, he's very much against that. The hospital is a bit cramped for space right now and a s long as his temperature stays at a manageable level, I see no reason to admit him.'

'Can he be moved?' Another strangled protest came

from the bed, but Elizabeth ignored it. 'I'd like to take him home if it's all right.'

'He's more than welcome to stay here,' Kurt spoke up. 'He won't be that much of a burden for a few days. If he is,' there was a darting look of amusement at Jed, 'we'll simply throw him out.'

It was the doctor's opinion that mattered. Elizabeth wanted Jed home where she could look after him.

'It probably wouldn't hurt him to be moved,' the doctor hesitated, glancing from Elizabeth to Jed and back. 'If the Reisners are willing to take care of him, it would be best if he stayed here. No sense running the risk of any outside complications.'

'Of course,' Elizabeth accepted his verdict grudgingly.

'I'd better be getting to the hospital.' The doctor pushed back the sleeve of his jacket to look at his watch. 'I still have my rounds to make.' Glancing at Kurt, he asked, 'You have that prescription I gave you?'

Kurt touched the pocket of his shirt. 'Yes.' He glanced briefly at Elizabeth, then walked to the doctor's side. 'I'll show you to the door.'

Discreetly left alone in the room with Jed, Elizabeth found herself uncertain what to say or do next. His eyes were closed again. Awkwardly she moved closer to the bed, wanting to touch him, to reassure herself that her fear was unwarranted, but she was loath to disturb him.

A bowl of water and a cloth were on the table beside the bed. As quietly as possible, Elizabeth moistened the cloth, folded it into a swuare and gently placed it on his forehead. There was a tightness in the region of her heart as she gazed at his lean features, in repose yet finely drawn into taut lines. Her green eyes mirrored the suffering that she sensed was concealed behind the controlled impassivity of his expression. When she removed the cloth to moisten it again with the cool water, she saw his eyes open. She tried to camouflage her inner anxiety with brisk movements.

'It's the young widow Carrel, soothing my fevered brow,' he mocked weakly.

'Be quiet,' she commanded softly, watching his eyes close as she placed the damp cloth on his forehead.

'Go home, Elizabeth,' Jed mumbled coldly. 'I don't need you.' He pushed her hand away, but not with his former strength. There's no one to see you. There's no need to keep up any appearances.'

Calmly Elizabeth returned the cloth to his forehead as if to pretend that his cutting words hadn't sliced deeply. She made no reply, persevering in her attempt to do something to relieve his discomfort, and Jed uttered no more protests, but slipped into a troubled sleep.

Quiet footsteps entered the room. Their feminine lightness made it easy for Elizabeth to identify them as belonging to Freda before she turned around.

'Is he sleeping?' Freda asked.

'I think it's something in between.' The corners of her mouth turned upward in a weak example of a smile as she placed the cloth on the side of the bowl.

'I've just made a fresh pot of coffee. Would you like a cup?'

Casting one last look at Jed, Elizabeth nodded. 'Yes, I would.'

There was no sign of Amy in the kitchen. Freda read

the question forming in Elizabeth's eyes and answered, 'Amy's outside playing with the puppies.'

'I'm —' Elizabeth ran a hand nervously through the side of her hair, the black locks curling about her fingers. 'I'm sorry we've put you to so much trouble, Freda.'

'It isn't any trouble,' the dark blonde assured her, setting a mug of coffee on the table for each of them. 'Jed has been like a second brother to Kurt and me ever since I can remember. My mother swore that he spent more time at our place than he ever did at home, but I don't think his parents knew that.'

'Yes, well,' Elizabeth sighed heavily, 'I'm afraid he'll be here for a few more days. Doctor Miles didn't think it was a good idea to move him, at least for the time being. Jed didn't seem anxious to leave either.'

'Nor would anyone if they were ill,' Freda defended him gently.

'Still, I wish —' Elizabeth glanced toward the hallway and the hidden bedroom door, but she couldn't put into words the compelling need to be the one who took care of him. 'It's such an inconvenience for you,' she murmured instead.

'Elizabeth —' Freda began, then hesitated, giving undue interest to the coffee in her mug. 'If you would like to stay and lend a hand, I would appreciate it. I mean, I do have the house to take care of and the meals to cook for Kurt and there's a lot of work in the garden to be done. You could sleep in the spare room unless you'd rather not.'

'Are you sure you wouldn't object?' Elizabeth held

her breath, wanting to stay with Jed more than anything.

'It would be a tremendous help,' Fred promised.

'I would like to stay.' Elizabeth's smile was genuine this time, a mixture of happiness and relief.

'The spare room has twin beds. There's no reason Amy can't stay , too. I know your mother-in-law,' Freda seemed to choose her words carefully, 'is quite busy with her meetings and all. It would save you from having to find a sitter and constantly rushing back and forth between our two places. And she isn't any trouble.'

'Oh, Freda, are you sure you want us Carrels to invade you this way?' Elizabeth laughed.

'I'm sure,' Freda nodded with a beaming smile. 'As soon as Kurt comes back in from the field at noon, I'll have him drive you over to the house to get your things. It's a perfect arrangement.'

The only one who disapproved of the arrangement was Rebecca. It was her opinion that if Jed was ill enough to require Elizabeth's attention, he was ill enought to be in hospital. For once, Elizabeth didn't allow herself to be talked out of her plans, not even when her mother-in-law insisted that Amy should remain at home with her. The tiny wedge that had been driven between them since Jed's arrival had placed a severe strain on the relationship between the two women. Elizabeth found that she didn't look up to her mother-in-law as much as she once had. In fact there were several things about her that she didn't like.

Amy was delighted at the prospect of possibly spending several days on the Reisner farm. She was genuinely concerned that her uncle was ill, but it didn't diminish her delight. The farm was a new world to her, an exciting world that she was determined to explore.

When Kurt had heard his sister's suggestion, he immediately added his second to the invitation, adding that he knew Freda would enjoy the company of someone her own age. And Elizabeth discovered how very warm and friendly her neighbors truly were. She felt ashamed that she hadn't followed her instinct and got to know them better before now. But Rebecca had never been in favor of Elizabeth becoming too closely acquainted with them.

Although she could ignore her mother-in-law's disapproval, Jed's displeasure at having her there was not so easy to overlook. Several times during the first day, Elizabeth sat with him. He had been aware that someone was with him, but in his semiconscious state, the identity of the person was of secondary importance to the cooling compress on his fever-flushed face. Not until that evening when she brought him in some chicken broth Freda had prepared did Jed recognize her.

His verbal abuse left her in little doubt that if he had the strength, he would have thrown her out of the house. Elizabeth accepted his sarcasm with forced silence, telling her bleeding heart that it was the result of the fever. She only partially believed it. He didn't want her there and she was a fool to stay, but she did.

There were moments in the succeeding two days when he was completely lucid and others when he succumbed to bouts of delirium, mumbling things that made no sense to Elizabeth. Sometimes she guessed that it had to do with his childhood, but mostly he seemed to refer to the time he had spent in the Pacific and South-east Asia.

Once he had called her name. She had slipped her hand over his, feeling his fingers tighten so she couldn't pull free.

'I'm here, Jed,' she had said in an aching whisper of love.

'You shouldn't be,' he had murmured huskily, trying to open the fever-weighted lids of his eyes. 'Why won't you go away?'

'Sssh, you must rest.' Elizabeth had bit into her lip to hold back the sob of despair.

'Leave me alone,' Jed had sighed, turning his head away from her on the pillow, but not relinquishing his grip on her hand. Stirring restlessly, he exclaimed with unexpected forcefulness, 'It's so damned hot! Doesn't anybody on this damned island own a fan?' And Elizabeth realized he was delirious again.

'He's out of it again, is he?' Kurt's voice had claimed Elizabeth's attention. He was standing in the doorway with Freda, fresh linen in her arms. 'I thought I'd give you two girls a hand changing the sheets.'

'I'll warn you, Kurt, Jed isn't very co-operative,' Elizabeth had cautioned with a sigh, twisting her hand free from Jed.

And he hadn't been co-operative, fighting the hands that removed the sweat-stained sheets from beneath him to replace them with dry, hurling profanities at them indiscriminately. Finally when they had him tucked back in, he had seemed to collapse with exhaustion.

'He's hardly the model patient, is he?' Freda had breathed in deeply.

'I'm sorry,' Elizabeth had shaken her head wearily as they went out of the room.

'Don't be sorry,' Kurt had insisted. 'You certainly could never have managed him on your own, and I don't think Mrs. Carrel would have been of much help to you.'

Elizabeth had smiled, acknowledging silently the truth of his words. She doubted if she would have been able to manhandle Jed even in his weakened condition. Assistance from her mother-in-law would have been minimal at best. She had a very low tolerance of sick people, making her duty visits as she had done with Jed, but never staying any longer than propriety dictated.

'How about some iced tea on the porch before we turn in?' Kurt had suggested.

'It's a grand idea,' Freda had agreed. 'There's a pitcher full in the refrigerator. Would you fix a glass for Liza and me?' She had begun using Jed's nickname for Elizabeth. Without the faintly mocking undertones, Elizabeth hadn't objected.

'For my sister, anything,' Kurt had agreed laughingly, leaving the two girls to make their own way to the porch.

Leaning against one of the wooden porch-roof supports, Elizabeth had gazed at the evening stars sprinkled over the night sky. 'How long do you think it will last, Freda? Doctor Miles said only a few days, but it's already been three days.'

'His fever should be breaking soon.' Freda had curled on to the porch swing, tucking her legs beneath her. 'You love him very much, don't you?'

Elizabeth had swung around, a denial forming on her lips. Then she had sighed. 'Yes,' she had answered simply.

Freda hadn't offered any words of hope or confided anything that Jed might have said to her or Kurt. If she had, Elizabeth doubted if she would have believed her. She didn't think anyone knew what Jed felt, nor was he the type to let something slip.

There was an invisible clasping of hands between Elizabeth and Freda, cementing the friendship that had been steadily growing each hour they had spent together. Elizabeth had not realized how much she had missed the nonsensical talk with another girl, the exchanging of ideas whether on cooking or clothes or world politics without any attempt to impress the other with their intellectual prowess. If she had gained nothing else, she knew she had acquired a true friend.

Staring at the ceiling above her bed, Elizabeth waited for sleep to steal upon her, but her mind refused to stop reliving the happenings of the past three days. Restlessly, she thumped her pillow to relieve the tension, turning on her side and this time gazing at the sleeping figure of her daughter in the next bed. It was no use, she thought dejectedly. She simply was not going to fall asleep as long as her mind kept racing about with thoughts of Jed.

A quilted housecoat lay at the foot of her bed. Slipping quietly from beneath the covers so as not to disturb Amy, Elizabeth slid her feet into the slippers at her bedside and picked up the housecoat. She would take a couple of minutes to check on Jed, she decided, then warm some milk in the kitchen. Wasn't that the old-fashioned cure-all for insomnia? she smiled at herself.

The yard light streamed through Jed's window, illuminating his tossing and turning figure. The blankets were thrown off, exposing the naked expanse of his bronzed chest. His pajama bottoms looked a paler blue in the dim light as Elizabeth hurried quietly into the room to draw the covers around him again. His skin was burning to the touch. Taking the ever-present cloth from the wash basin, she wiped the streaming perspiration from his unconsciously frowning face.

The fever was peaking. Cradling his head in her arms, Elizabeth pressed the water glass to his dry lips, letting the liquid trickle into his mouth. Directed by instinct, she kept repeating the procedure, first wiping the perspiration away, then giving him small swallows of water. Her heart cried out at her inability to do more to ease his discomfort as he continued to moan and toss. Her arms began to ache, her muscles throbbed with the constant repetition of her actions. She lost all perception of the minutes ticking by. It never once occurred to her to waken Freda.

Elizabeth didn't notice the exact moment when his fever broke. Suddenly she realized the frown had left his face and the restless turnings had ceased. His lean cheeks were still warm but without the fiery heat that had burned her hand. It was over. Jed was actually sleeping. With a trembling sound that was both a sigh and a sob, she collapsed wearily in the rocking chair beside his bed. She would sit here for a few minutes, she told herself, and let her aching muscles relax. It was for certain she wouldn't need any milk now, she decided with a wry smile. That was the last thing she remembered.

The next thing was the shooting pains in her neck. When she tried to move, they travelled down her spine. She frowned in protest, not wanting to move again, but the stiffness of her muscles demanded it. Slowly, unwillingly, Elizabeth opened her eyes, as the awareness of her surroundings gradually sank in and she awoke.

The sun was well up in the sky with no traces of the golden pink of dawn. Jed was sleeping peacefully, the stubble of a three-day beard growth darkening the lean jaw. The sallow look was gone from his face and there was no gleam of perspiration on his forehead. He was all right. A faint smile of relief touched her lips.

Arching her back to flex away the rigidity, Elizabeth began to gently rub the crook in her neck, the painful result of sleeping in the rocking chair the better part of the night. She still felt tired, but there was little point in going to bed at this hour. As she pushed herself out of the chair, her gaze shifted to the bed. Jed was watching her. The glaze of fever was gone, his eyes cat-gold and piercingly thorough in their appraisal.

'Didn't anyone ever tell you that chairs weren't made to sleep in?' His mouth quirked cynically at the corners.

Elizabeth opened her mouth to protest, her heart skipping beats, but the bedroom door was opened, effectively silencing her words. Freda stuck her head inside, glancing in surprise at Elizabeth, then to Jed. A smile spread across her face.

'Well, I see you've made it back to the land of reality.' Genuine welcome warmed her face. 'You must be starving, Jed. I'll bring you a tray.'

'Don't bother.' He rolled on to his back, his lazily alert gaze releasing Elizabeth to focus on his hostess. 'Elizabeth will be out shortly. She can fix it.'

The other girl raised a curious eyebrow, looked briefly at Elizabeth's astonished expression, then shrugged her agreement. The closing of the door brought an end to her initial confusion.

'I had planned to shower and change,' she told him tartly, resenting his autocratic command that she should wait on him when she had stayed up half the night taking care of him.

The complacent expression on his face didn't vary. 'I thought you were enjoying your role as the angel of mercy.' With disconcerting ease, Jed switched from mockery. 'How long have I been out?'

'Three days.'

'Three days?' He rubbed his hand over his chin, his beard scraping the palm. 'I hope I didn't bore you with recollections of my lurid past.' He smiled ruefully.

'You mumbled too much,'' Elizabeth replied quietly and honestly. 'When we could understand your rambling, it didn't make any sense.'

His hooded glance had a measuring look about it, as if he was judging the truthfulness of her answer. She met it squarely without flinching, knowing how she would dislike having the privacy of her thoughts paraded before others without being aware of it.

'I remember telling you to leave. Why didn't you?'

Her love for him made that question difficult to answer honestly, so she settled for a half-truth. 'It wouldn't have been fair to let Freda and Kurt shoulder the entire responsibility of caring for you. They had their own work to do.'

'So a sense of duty compelled you to stay. Very commendable,' he murmured dryly.

'I was worried about you!' Elizabeth declared in despairing anger.

'I'm touched,' Jed mocked, reaching for the pitcher of water on the bedside table and nearly knocking it over when he tried to turn it around to grasp the handle.

'Let me do that,' she sighed, taking the pitcher from him and filling the glass with water. Automatically she sat on the edge of the bed, cupping the back of his head with her hand and raising the glass to his mouth. She didn't consider he no longer needed her help. 'The next time you get one of these attacks,' she flashed, still smarting from his amused sarcasm that jeered her nursing efforts, 'remind me to hire some thick-skinned nurse to take care of you. This is the last time I'll sit up half the night and be rewarded with abuse and ingratitude from you!'

The glass was jerked from his lips the instant he indicated he was satisfied. Before she could rise angrily to her feet, his arm circled her waist to keep her at his side.

'I'm sorry.' His tawny eyes were sparkling over the mutinous set of her mouth. 'I didn't say thank you, did I?'

'No, you didn't,' she retorted, her stomach churning in reaction to his touch. Her hands were unable to remove his pinning arm.

'There you go again, becoming all haughty and disdainful, just like you did the first day I came back.' The grooves around his mouth deepened mockingly. 'I often wondered whether you were more afraid I would steal the family valuables or you.'

'You looked like a tramp. How was I supposed to react?' Elizabeth challenged coolly.

'You were all cool and sophisticated then, too,'' Jed continued with thoughtful amusement. 'Snapping out orders and warnings with all the arrogant pride of a true Carrel. The beautiful, fragile creature with the green eyes seemed to have disappeared, the one I remember as being intimidated by the Carrel name and frightened that she might not be good enough for the favorite son. That's probably why I kept scratching the surface to see if any traces remained of the girl I remembered. Your veneer of sophistication is very thin, Liza.'

'Jed,' she gulped out her protest as he drew her down to the pillow, 'you've been ill.'

His face was only tantalizing inches from hers. 'I don't feel ill.' He smiled at the shaky breath she drew. 'Perhaps in view of my weakened condition you should humor me.'

His hand traced the outline of her face, his thumb lightly brushing her lips before his hand settled on the curve of her neck. At the moment, Elizabeth was certain that she was the one in the weakened condition. Her resistance, what little there was, was melting as swiftly as the wax beneath a candlewick.

'I know a man isn't supposed to ask, but do you object if I kiss you?' Jed moved his head closer to hers, hesitating a breath away from her lips.

'No.' It was almost a moan.

'You've objected all the other times,' he murmured against her mouth. 'This time I wanted you to want it as much as I do.'

Still he teased with feathery light kisses until her lips throbbed with the need for his possession. She wound her arms around his neck, trying to draw him down to her, but he held himself away easily.

'I don't understand you,' Elizabeth whispered achingly.

His beard scraped her cheek, then her throat, as he nuzzled the sensitive area of her neck, sending shivers of tortuous bliss down her spine. He slid his hand into her robe, letting it caress her waist and hips through the thin material of her nightgown.

'Please, Jed,' she begged shamelessly. 'Don't torment me this way.' Her eyes filled with longing.

'I wonder if you know the meaning of the word,' he muttered, nipping sharply at her ear lobe and drawing a gasp of pain mixed with pleasure.

But her plea succeeded as his head raised, his darkening hazel-gold eyes focusing on her trembling lips. The seconds stretched together again while he deliberately waited. The moan that escaped her lips when he finally claimed them was involuntary, an unwilling admission of the completeness of her surrender.The kiss was thorough and complete, his sensual technique without fault. The wildfire raging through her blood made any other man's touch seem like a tiny match flame by comparison.

Yet her hunger for his embrace was insatiable. She arched toward him when he pulled away. He stayed just tantalizing out of her reach, teasing her relentlessly. His heart was thudding as madly as hers. She could feel it beneath the palm of her hand resting against his chest.

'Were you worried about me?' he demanded huskily.

'You know I was,' she whispered.

'Why?' He pushed her back against the pillow, pinning her there with the weight of his body. 'Why should you care?'

'Because,' lamely evading his question.

'Why?' Jed persisted gruffly, aware of the way his touch was destroying her inhibitions. When she didn't answer, his fingers dug into her shoulder bone. 'Say it!' he snapped.

Gazing into his eyes, Elizabeth saw that the flecks were not malleable gold. Only the color was there to conceal his iron control, metallic and unyielding. Her viridescent eyes glistened with the tears she knew she would eventually shed.

'Because,' her voice quivered uncontrollably, 'I love you, Jed. I love you.'

There was a gleam of triumph in his eyes before his mouth obliterated all conscious thought with a hungry passion. Before she had only felt his virile surface warmth. Now she was consumed by the fiery urgency of his kiss. Not even when she had guessed how deeply Jed affected her had she ever dreamed that she would know this exploding joy.

CHAPTER NINE

'WOULD it be an understatement to say that you've recovered, Jed?'

The sarcastically contemptuous voice was the hiss of the serpent in the garden. The spitting tongue brought an abrupt end to the kiss that had been progressively leading to more than a passionate embrace. Elizabeth struggled red-faced to her feet, quickly knotting the sash of her robe, while Jed rolled on to his back, barely perturbed by the interruption.

'You have a lousy sense of timing, Mother,' he murmured dryly.

The smoldering outrage was evident in the disdainful set of Rebecca Carrel's features, but her control was as strong as her son's. She flicked a cutting glance at Elizabeth, showing disgust for her abandoned behavior.

'That is a matter of opinion, Jed,' his mother responded coldly. 'You appear quite healthy to me. I don't see that you'll require Elizabeth's presence any longer. We can put an end to this nursing nonsense.'

'She was about to fix my breakfast,' he said with a crooked, humorous smile.

'She is not a servant!' Rebecca snapped. 'Have that farm girl get your meal.'

Elizabeth stiffened resentfully. 'Freda is busy. If you'll excuse me, I'll get the breakfast.' The nervous smoothing of her mussed black curls stopped as she moved past her mother-in-law to the door.

'While you're gone, you'd better check on your child,' was the waspish response. 'When I came in, she was playing with those dirty puppies, letting them paw and climb all over her. She looked as filthy as a beggar child!'

'A little dirt won't harm her,' Elizabeth retorted.

'Perhaps you have forgotten she has a piano lesson this morning. It may have also slipped your mind that she missed the last one for' — there was a deliberate pause in the condescending reminder — unexplained reasons.'

'The reasons were personal.' The tilt of Elizabeth's chin dared Rebecca to inquire further. 'And I will decide if it's essential that she keep this one.'

'I don't know what possible excuse you can offer Mrs. Banks. Not now that Jed has recovered.'

'Since I'm paying for the lessons, I wasn't aware that I needed an excuse!' Elizabeth was shaking with uncontrollable anger as she stepped into the hall, slamming the bedroom door behind her.

She took her time in the shower and dressed with equal slowness. She couldn't recall a time that she had talked back to her mother-in-law, and certainly never so rudely. The only twinge of remorse she felt was for losing her temper, not for the things she had said. She didn't venture out of her room until she heard Rebecca's car start up in the drive.

Freda had left a note on the kitchen table telling Elizabeth that she was out in the garden. Amy was in the porch swing, crooning to a sleeping puppy in her lap. Doubting that Jed's stomach could take a sudden jolt of solid food, Elizabeth prepared a bowl of hot cereal, toast and cocoa and carried it into his room on a tray.

Setting the tray across his lap, she walked silently to the window. It seemed incredible that a short time ago she had been in his arms, pledging her love with each breath she drew. Jed had barely glanced at her when she entered the room, remote again, withdrawn into that aloofness she had never been able to penetrate.

'You're very quiet all of a sudden,' he commented.

'There's nothing left for me to say,' Elizabeth shrugged, letting the curtain fall and turning toward him, her look unconsciously reminding him that it was his turn.

'You should have time to pack your things before Amy's lesson. Freda can drive you to the house or take you on into town if you'd rather.' He was sipping his cocoa with crushing unconcern.

'Is that what you want? For me to leave?' she asked in a choked voice that was both stiff and proud.

He held her gaze for a long moment. 'It isn't what I want, but it's what I'm willing to settle for,' he replied evenly.

'What do you want?' Elizabeth stared at the fingers twisting and untwisting in front of her, surprised to discover that they belonged to her.

'I thought I'd made that plain.' He tilted his head

curiously to one side, studying her intently. 'I want you.'

Not 'I love you' or 'I want to marry you,' but simply 'I want you,' as if she were a possession that he had coveted for a long time and intended to own.

'I'll start packing now.' Dispiritedly she turned away, her eyes downcast to conceal the gathering tears.

'Liza? What's the matter?' Jed demanded as she started towards the door. 'Liza!' he called to her again, angrily this time when she continued to ignore him. 'Dammit! Answer me!'

She hesitated in the doorway. 'I'm tired, Jed.' It was true. She felt emotionally drained.

The tears slipping from her lashes were a defense mechanism against the tension that had been building since last night. She didn't actually cry, but it took her a long time to pack her and Amy's things. The steady stream of tears kept blurring her vision.

Later Freda apologized for not warning Elizabeth of Rebecca's arrival, but Elizabeth dismissed it. 'There was no harm done. She didn't interrupt anything.' At least, nothing that didn't need to be interrupted, but she found she couldn't confide that to Freda.

Her fragile composure wouldn't survive another visit to Jed's room, so she left it to Freda to let him know that she had actually gone. Only a few grumbles were sounded from Amy's quarters, not any more than she usually offered on the days of her piano lesson. Elizabeth chose not have Freda take her own car. Too much time in her friend's company would loosen her tongue, and until she had time to think things through on her own, that was something she didn't want.

The instant they returned from Amy's lesson and stepped into the entrance hall, Elizabeth recognized the cause for the cloud of dread that had been following her. Rebecca was waiting for her, looking every inch the sophisticated matron of society with her perfectly coiffed silver hair and dusty-rose dress. This morning's incident was not going to escape without comment.

'There are cookies and milk in the kitchen for you, Amy. You may practise after you have eaten,' Rebecca smiled amiably at her granddaughter. Elizabeth started to counter her orders out of sheer stubbornness until she met the coal-hard chips of her mother-in-law's eyes. The confrontation was to occur now, she realized. It was better that it did not begin in front of Amy. 'I've put the coffee service in Franklin's study so we won't disturb Amy,' the older woman informed her when Amy had left them.

The sarcastic brittleness of this morning was absent from Rebecca's voice, but Elizabeth wasn't deceived by the pleasant tone. Tight-lipped, she walked to the closed study door. Postponing this moment would be futile. Silently she endured her mother-in-law's quiet courtesy, accepting the cup of coffee that was handed her, aware all the while that the stage had been set by Rebecca for this meeting. The calmness of her voice, the coffee, and the privacy of the study was calculated to inspire trust and confidence.

A tray of ladyfingers was offered to Elizabeth, but she waved it aside, setting the untouched cup of coffee onto the tray. 'Please, Rebecca,' she said evenly, 'let's dispense with the niceties. Say whatever it is that you brought me in here to say.'

Rebecca set her own cup down, folding her hands primly in her lap and falsely hesitating for an instant. Her head was tipped downward as if to study the clear polish on her nails.

'First of all,' the silver-gray head was raised to meet the impassive greennesss of Elizabeth's gaze, 'I want to apologize for my behavior this morning. I was shocked. It was never my intention to interfere in your personal life or usurp your authority with Amy. I spoke in haste and without thinking, and I'm sorry.'

'Was that all?' Elizabeth knew the stiffness of her attitude and her failure to soften in response to the apology disconcerted Rebecca, but she concealed it admirably.

'No.' Rebecca rose to her feet, walking away from Elizabeth as if plagued by an uncertainty how to proceed. 'I have heard the rumors that — that you and Jed were interested in each other. For the most part I discounted it as idle gossip. I never doubted for an instant that Jed would make advances toward you. He has always pursued the opposite sex and with considerable success.

She glanced over her shoulder to see the effect her comments were making, but Elizabeth deliberately kept her face devoid of any expression and waited for Rebecca to continue.

'I have never understood why the wastrels of this world hold so much appeal for women,' her mother-in-law sighed, then smiled. 'Perhaps it is because at birth they were endowed with virile looks and charm so that intelligence and ambition were wasted on them. They have no need for them. They can get what they want without them. Jed is like that — he exudes an aura of danger and excitement that make women feel deliciously sinful. His father and I recognized that early in his teenage years. It was a source of constant concern.'

Rebecca resumed her chair opposite Elizabeth, leaning forward in an earnest, confiding manner, anxiety darkening her brown eyes further. Her hands were clasped in front of her in a plea for understanding.

'Now, my concern is for you, Elizabeth,' she murmured fervidly. 'I foolishly never warned you about Jed. I should have given thought to the fact that you are young and in need of physical gratification.'

The way Rebecca was speaking made Elizabeth feel unclean. She could maintain her silence no longer, she must speak.

'It's not lust I feel for Jed, Rebecca. 'It's love,' she said quietly. 'I did not intend to fall in love with him. I tried to pretend myself that it was only physical attraction, but it wasn't. I love him, and I'm not ashamed of it.'

Surprisingly there wasn't any disapproving outburst, simply a softly spoken question. 'Does Jed know this?'

'Yes.'

'I see.' Rebecca didn't appear surprised by the admission. 'And what are your plans?'

'There are no plans,' Elizabeth answered. The faint I-thought-as-much expression forced her to add in defense, 'Jed has been ill.'

'He will ask you to go away with him.' It was a statement made with assurance, not a question.

'Did he say that?' The wary question was out before Elizabeth could stop it.

'No.' Rebecca studied her hands. 'It's more of a guess on my part, an accurate one, I believe. When he does,' she glanced up, forcing Elizabeth to meet her gaze, 'what will you do?'

'I'll go with him. I love him, Rebecca,' Elizabeth said firmly.

Her mother-in-law sighed and leaned back in her chair. 'I won't pretend that I have any right to tell you what to do. You're quite old enough to make your own decisions. But I feel compelled to point out some things to you. Jed is thirty-two years old. He doesn't have a career or a job. He doesn't live anywhere, so he has no house or apartment, not even a car. Only a token sum was left to him in Franklin's will, so he has no money either. I don't mean to imply that these things are important if you love someone,' Rebecca hastened to add in response to the seething anger tightening the line of Elizabeth's mouth. 'I'm asking you to consider these things for Amy's sake, for her future. It's true that you do receive a monthly sum from her trust fund, but it would never support a household. However much you may believe you love Jed, you must consider her welfare. Think about what I've said. Please, Elizabeth.'

With a gentle smile, Rebecca rose and left the room. Elizabeth sat silently. She had made no response because there was none to make. There was little consolation in recognizing that the speech and its delivery had been carefully rehearsed to achieve the reaction she was now experiencing. The request had been logical and reasonable and impossible to argue against. Elizabeth's vulnerable spot was Amy. Rebecca hadn't wasted time with meaningless slashes but had gone straight for the jugular vein.

Blindly Elizabeth had never looked ahead — perhaps because she wasn't convinced that Jed wanted her in more than a physical sense. If he did, what would she do then? It was so impossible to cross bridges when they hadn't been reached.

Late that afternoon, she telephoned the farm to see how Jed was. Secretly she was hoping that he would be up and she would have a chance to talk to him. The shadows of uncertainty were becoming too much. Freda answered the phone.

'How's Jed?' Elizabeth inquired with what she hoped was the right tone of interest.

'Fine. He had a big lunch and went to sleep. I think he intends to sleep the clock round. It's probably the best thing for him,' Freda answered brightly.

'Yes, you're probably right,' Elizabeth agreed reluctantly.

'Will you be coming over this evening?'

'I don't think so. I only wanted to be sure he was all right.' There was no point in going over. As always, it seemed to be Jed's move. 'I have some things to catch up here at the house.'

'I'll tell him you called.'

'Yes, Goodbye, Freda.' Slowly Elizabeth replaced the receiver.

Strangely, the hours passed swiftly. It was something of a start when Elizabeth realized that two full days and the morning of a third had gone by since her leaving the Reisner farm. The tension had increased rather than eased. Uncertainty and indecision trailed her wherever she went.

Jed was recovering quickly, or so Freda told her. Elizabeth hadn't heard a word from him. He hadn't given Freda any indication when he would be returning home, which didn't surprise Elizabeth. Something told her she could rely on Jed to come home when she least expected him.

Stepping to the raised kitchen window, she glanced out, spying Amy beside the patio table where her play cups and saucers were spread out.

'It's almost time for lunch, Amy. You'd better get washed up,' she called. 'We'll have it in the kitchen since your grandmother isn't here.'

Absently Elizabeth heard the french doors open and close and the sound of water running in the downstairs bathroom wash basin. She ladled the soup into bowls and uncovered the plate of sandwiches and set it on the table.

A carton of milk was in her hand when a deep voice

asked, 'Will lunch stretch to three?' She started.

Quickly she sat the carton on the counter before she dropped it, boundless joy surging through her veins. She didn't need to turn around to know that Ned had come back, when she had least expected him. Commanding her hands to stop trembling, she took a third glass from the cupboard and filled it with milk.

'Of course it will, Jed,' she responded warmly, sliding a glance behind her as he approached. 'You're looking fine.'

"'Completely recovered.' He stopped beside her, tawny gold eyes regarding her intently.

Hypnotically she returned the look. There was nothing about him to suggest that he had been ill. His vigorously masculine features showed no signs of tiredness or strain. Vitality abounded in his watchful stillness.

'You look wonderful.' There was a breathless catch in her voice.

His eyebrow raised mockingly. 'So do you,' he murmured.

'Oh, boy!' Tomato soup, my favorite!' Amy announced, sliding on to one of the chairs.

Jed smiled. 'I think someone is hungry! I suppose we should eat.'

Elizabeth swallowed and nodded. 'Sit down. I'll get another place setting for myself.'

Food was the last thing on her mind. Inwardly she crossed her fingers that Jed had been implying the same thing. It did little good to tell herself to remain calm, that all the unknowns hadn't vanished simply because Jed was back. She went through the motions of eating her soup and nibbling at a sandwich.

'Amy tells me she has a birthday party to go to this afternoon,' Jed commented.

Elizabeth frowned bewilderedly. 'When did she tell you that?'

'Out on the patio.'

'I didn't see you there,' she breathed.

'I know.' The grooves around his mouth deepened in silent amusement. 'What are you doing this afternoon?'

'I have a meeting.' There was no attempt to disguise the disappointment in her voice as she stared unseeingly at her soup. 'I'm the secretary. I have to attend.'

'I see,' he answered evenly, not trying to dissuade her as he switched the topic to the birthday party, asking Amy about her friends.

While Elizabeth cleared the table of the luncheon dishes, she sent Amy upstairs to dress for her party, reminding her to take her swimming suit and towel since part of the activities included a visit to the public swimming pool. Jed disappeared into another part of the house. There was no sign of him when she went upstairs to change for her meeting. But he was in the front hallway with Amy when she came back downstairs.

'Do you have any objections if I act as chauffeur?' he asked.

'None at all.' Elizabeth shook her head. Rebecca had the other car, which only left hers to provide him transportation. Obviously he had somewhere to go.

Conversation was minimal during the drive into town. Most of it was Amy's chatter about the party. No matter how many glances Elizabeth stole at Jed's profile, there was nothing in his impassive expression to indicate that he felt her disappointment.

The old familiar depression settled around her shoulders. Fortunately Amy was too excited about her party to notice the sadness in her mother's smile when they left her at the house of the birthday girl. Elizabeth stared out the window, wondering what she could say to end the silence.

'Turn left at the next corner. The Hansons' house is the third one on the right-hand side.' The directions were given reluctantly.

But Jed drove straight through the intersection without stopping.

'I meant that corner,' Elizabeth pointed behind them. 'You'll have to go around the block.'

'I know which corner you mean.' Jed glanced at her briefly and continued through the second intersection that would have taken them back in a round-about way.

'I have to go to the meeting,' she reminded him with a frown.

Slowing the car, he turned it into the curbside of the street, stopping it but not switching off the engine as he twisted in the seat to look at her.

'Which would you rather do? Go to that stupid meeting or come with me?' he asked with thinning patience.

'I'd rather come with you —' Elizabeth began sighing in frustration.

'That settles it, then.' He put the car in gear and pulled back into the street.

'But, Jed —'

'I don't know about you, but I don't want to wait until tonight,' he said firmly. 'We've postponed our talk long enough. Don't you agree?'

'Yes,' Elizabeth surrendered, not caring one whit about the meeting she was supposed to attend.

His slow smile seemed to reach and almost physically touch her. It was a heady sensation and very enjoyable. That bridge she was worried about was coming closer. She still didn't know whether she was going to cross it or not, but she had to see it. She would never be able to come to a decision until she did.

CHAPTER TEN

AFTER Jed had expressed a desire to talk, there was silence in the car. He continued driving through town and into the outskirts. It wasn't the road that would take them back to the house. Elizabeth couldn't guess what destination he had in mind. The last place she would have thought of was the small municipal airport outside town, but that was where Jed turned.

'What are we doing here?' She glanced curiously at Jed as he pulled in beside the three cars parked outside the flight office and switched off the engine.

'You might say this is my old stamping grounds.' He opened the door and stepped out, walking around to her side, smiling at her slightly bewildered expression. 'I spent more time here than I ever did in school or at home, outside of Kurt's.'

Elizabeth silently digested that piece of information, studying the happy and contented look about him as he gazed at the few buildings that constituted the Carrelville airport. A little puff of breeze was trying to fill the orange windsock.

'Do you mean' — she asked hesitantly — 'that you used to fly?'

Jed glanced down, the contented smile curving his mouth. His arm circled her shoulders as he turned her in the direction of the flight office. She was surprised.

'Come one, I'll show you,' he said. Entering the flight office, he lifted the counter and led Elizabeth into the hall leading to the back, private offices. Her puzzled frown deepened at his easy familiarity. He opened one of the doors leading off the hall. 'This is where Sam hangs up his shirt-tails.'

'Shirt-tails?' she repeated, as she walked in ahead of him.

'It's a ceremony that all prospective pilots go through,' Jed explained. 'After a student makes his first solo flight, his instructor cuts off his shirt-tail and hangs it up. It's referred to as "clipping his tail feathers." ' He led her to the wall that was patchworked with strips of cloth of every pattern and color. Those are mine,' he pointed.

On a strip of pale blue material was scrawled Jed's name and the date. Elizabeth made a swift mental calculation and looked at him in surprise.

'You were only sixteen!' she breathed.

Jed chuckled softly. 'I had the devil's own time persuading Sam to teach me without my parent's permission. He knew if there was any accident, Dad would come down on him like a ton of bricks.'

'You mean they don't know?'

'Eventually they found out. Somebody from town saw me landing a plan and mentioned it to Dad. I was only a few hours away from getting my license when Dad stopped my allowance. Fortunately Sam let me work out the rest of the money. In college, I wanted to major in aerodynamics, but Dad wouldn't hear of it.

As long as he was paying the tuition, he insisted I had to take up law, like all the rest of the Carrels. His mouth twisted bitterly before he shook away the memory. 'Come on, let's walk.'

From the flight office, they wandered into the hangar area. In one of the sheds, a man in overalls was working on a plane. When he spotted them, he cupped his hands to his mouth and called out:

'Do you want me to roll out the twin for you, Jed?'

'Not today, Sam,' Jed waved the offer aside.

Elizabeth was nestled under the crook of his arm. She tilted her head back to gaze into his face, her heart singing a bit at the warmth with which his tawny eyes returned her look.

'Have you been out here often since you came back?' she asked.

'You surely didn't think I spent all that time at the Reisner farm, did you?' he grinned.

'I didn't know where you were or who you were with.' A faint pink of self-consciousness glowed in her cheeks as she averted her gaze.

'But you were imagining,' Jed teased, tightening his arm around her shoulders as they ducked beneath the wing of a tied-down plane. 'If I disappear on you some day after we're married, don't check the golf course. Just go to the nearest airport and I'll probably be there.'

Elizabeth stopped abruptly, her gaze freezing on his face and her heart nearly stopping altogether. The light breeze lifted the tobacco brown hair that fell over his forehead, revealing his puzzled frown.

'What's wrong?' he asked.

'What — What did you just say?' she murmured.

'I said —' Then Jed stopped and laughed softly at himself. 'I didn't intend to propose to you in just that way.'

'Do you mean you want to marry me?' Elizabeth whispered, not quite believing it yet.

'What did you think I wanted?' Jed smiled gently as he turned her into his arms, locking his hands behind her back.

Closing her eyes, she leaned her head against his chest, feeling his lips moving in a tender caress against her hair. 'I was afraid to think.' Her voice trembled. 'There was always the chance that all you wanted was an affair.'

He lifted her chin with his finger. 'Would you have settled for that?'

'If that was all I could have,' she answered truthfully, the love in her heart pouring out of her glistening eyes.

Possession marked the kiss that bruised her lips. It was a hard, short kiss as if to punish her for doubting the depth of his emotion. There was a determined glitter in his eyes when he lifted his head.

'Now you know I mean to have you for ever,' Jed saif firmly. 'I knew you belonged to me that night Jeremy brought you home.'

At this moment, Elizabeth didn't want to think, only feel. She wanted this moment to stretch out for an eternity of time, to glory in his love for the rest of her life. But she wouldn't do that. Not yet, anyway.

'What . . . about Amy?' She stared at his open shirt collar for an instant before lifting anxious eyes to his face.

A bemused smile spread across his mouth. 'Amy is a part of you. What did you think I was going to do? Tell you to get rid of her?' he laughed with a trace of bewilderment.

'I . . . wasn't sure,' Elizabeth faltered again.

'Now you know,' he answered patiently, lifting her chin when she would have averted her head. 'You haven't said whether you'll marry me, Liza.'

'Yes, but —'

Jed stiffened. 'The answer is never "yes" when there's a "but" attached to it. The watchful and withdrawn look removed the warmth from his gaze as he studied her guilty expression intently. 'What's bothering you?'

There was no resistance when she pulled away from his embrace. 'Jed, if it was only me that was involved, I'd . . . I'd marry you in a minute.' Nervously she brushed the hair away from her face. 'I wouldn't care if we lived in the back room of some airport or a grass hut on a beach as long as I'd be with you. But I have to consider Amy's welfare.'

'What are you asking? Whether I can keep you in the style you've become accustomed to?' Jed demanded tightly.

'No,' she protested.

'What is it then? Do you measure the amount of faith you can have in a man by the size of his bank balance?'

Elizabeth's stomach churned at the bitterness in his expression. 'What kind of a mother would I be, Jed, if I wasn't concerned how our marriage might affect Amy?' she asked quietly, lowering her chin so she wouldn't have to meet his accusing gaze.

'You might have sufficient trust in me to know that I would take care of you both,' he answered grimly.

'I understand why you feel hurt,' she replied in a choked voice. 'You have every right to feel that way. But please understand the way I feel. I trust you with my life, Jed. And Amy trusts me with hers.'

He turned away from her, raking his fingers through the thick brownness of his hair. A controlled fury darkened his eyes when he glanced at her.

'What will it take to make you decide whether you'll marry me or not?' he snapped.

'Just a little time,' Elizabeth murmured. 'I didn't expect you to propose. I'd . . . I'd like to think it over. Oh, Jed, I love you desperately — you must believe that.' Her chin quivered. 'I just don't want to give you an answer now that we both might regret.'

'I'll never regret loving you.' He stared into the cloudless blue sky, his hands shoved deep in his pockets. 'If it's time you want, you have it.' He pulled a hand from his pocket and stretched it toward her, keys jingled from his fingers. 'Here, I'll find my own way home.'

'Jed —'

'I'd like to be alone, Elizabeth,' he interrupted sharply. 'I have a few things to think over, too.'

'I do love you,' she murmured achingly, unable to

shake the feeling that she had betrayed him as she clutched the keys tightly against her stomach.

His narrowed gaze slid to her. 'If I didn't believe that, I don't think I'd let you go.'

Slowly she turned and retraced her steps toward the car. The one time she had looked back she saw him walking in the opposite direction away from her. She felt miserable and sick inside.

At the car, she stopped and started to turn back. Her answer was yes. There was no other answer that she could possibly make. Without Jed, she would be an empty shell. She had already given him her heart and she couldn't take it back. Maybe Amy wouldn't have some of the material things that Elizabeth could give her now, but Amy would be a part of the happiness and love that she and Jed would share. And that was a priceless thing.

But she didn't run back to Jed as she wanted to. He had asked to be alone, and it was a request she felt she should respect. Besides, she didn't want him to think that her decision had been prompted by any sense of guilt. She would give him her answer the minute he arrived home. All she could do now was pray that he would accept the fact that she loved him and trusted him implicitly in everything.

Two hours later, Elizabeth was sitting at the piano picking out the tune of a popular love ballad. A gentle breeze dancing through the open French doors. The front door opened and closed. With her fingers resting soundlessly on the keys, she turned a nervously expectant smile toward the hall, lovelight glistening through the anxious green of her eyes. It was Rebecca who appeared in the archway.

'So this is where you are,' her mother-in-law said sharply. 'Mrs. Hanson said you weren't at the meeting today and that you didn't even bother to notify her that you wouldn't come. She said she phoned here but no one answered.'

'I wasn't here.' Elizabeth turned back to the piano. 'I was with Jed.'

There was an instant of alert silence before Rebecca murmured, 'I see.' She walked slowly into the room. 'Where is he now?'

Elizabeth's fingers absently began playing a soft melody to ease the tension that suddenly enveloped the room. 'At the airport.'

'He's leaving?' There was surprised disbelief in the question.

'No. No, he'll be back later,' Elizabeth assured her firmly, a faint smile touching the corners of her mouth.

'You sound very certain.'

'He has asked me to marry him. I told him I wanted to think it over.'

'That was very wise of you, my dear. I knew you were much too sensible to let your head be turned by a charming wastrel like my son. If you wish to remarry, you can certainly find a more suitable partner,' Rebecca declared complacently.

'I don't think you understood me. I didn't refuse Jed.' Elizabeth felt serenely calm as she met her mother-in-law's raised eyebrows. 'It's the things in life you don't do that you regret. In fact, I have decided to marry him. If I didn't marry Jed, I would regret it the rest of my life.'

'But what about Amy?'

'Amy will be well taken care of. We'll both see to that,' Elizabeth answered confidently.

'You can't live on love!' Rebecca declared. 'How on earth will he support the two of you when he doesn't have a job or money?'

'That's our concern, Rebecca.'

'You're being foolish! You can't —'

The telephone interrupted her with a shrill ring. Rebecca glared at it angrily before giving in to its summons and walking to answer it. Elizabeth smiled at the barely disguised impatience in her mother-in-law's voice when she picked up the receiver. Her decision was unshakable. There was nothing Rebecca could say that would make her change her mind.

'Long-distance? No, he isn't here,' Rebecca spoke sharply into the receiver. 'I do expect him later.'' — 'He has been ill for a few days. Perhaps that's why you weren't able to reach him.' — Elizabeth had been listening absently, curious who it was that was calling Jed long-distance, but not really paying too close attention until she heard the note of sharpened interest in her mother-in-law's voice. 'May I take a message for him?' — 'I am his mother.' — Quickly she began scribbling a message on the paper that was always kept beside the telephone, squinting at her writing without taking the time to get her glasses from her purse. 'The offer was from whom?' —'Yes, I have the amount.' —

'I will give him the message the minute he comes in.' Slowly Rebecca replaced the receiver on the hook, staring at the paper in front of her.

'Who was it?' Elizabeth asked, becoming more curious at her mother-in-law's puzzling behavior.

'It was from Jed's attorney in Honolulu. Jed's attorney,' she repeated as if she couldn't accept what she was saying. 'Some firm has just made an offer to buy his airline.'

'I don't understand,' Elizabeth frowned.

'I don't think I do either.' There was a short, disbelieving laugh from Rebecca. 'It seems Jed owns this company that flies cargo to the different islands in the Pacific and parts of the Asian mainland. Why didn't he tell us? Did you know?

'No, I had no idea.'

'He's,' Rebecca held out the paper as proof, 'a wealthy man. Oh, Elizabeth!' A smile broke across her face as she hurried quickly to take her daughter-in-law's hands in her own. 'Of course you must accept his proposal. I'll take care of all the arrangements for the wedding. It'll be a small affair, not too many —'

'I believe you have a message for me, Mother.' Jed's quiet voice slashed the air with the deadly silence of a rapier thrust.

The astonishment that had been on Elizabeth's face changed to horror as she whirled to see him standing in the French doors. The hardened look about his lean features confirmed her guess that he had overheard their conversation. The cat-gold eyes held her motionless, ignoring the gushings of his mother as she proclaimed how proud she was of him and how delighted she was about his engagement to Elizabeth.

A sob bubbled into Elizabeth's throat. He would never believe her now. She could never convince him that she had been willing to marry him before she found out that he more than had the means to support her and Amy. No matter what she said, he would always think that the phone call had influenced her decision.

With a muffled cry of pain, she broke free of his gaze, tears scalding her eyes and cheeks as she raced from the room. She heard him call her name, but it only increased her desire to flee. She loved him too deeply to endure the sting of his mockery at this moment. Fumbling with the front doorknob, she jerked it open, not bothering to close the door as she hurried down the sidewalk.

Before she could reach the car Rebecca had left in the driveway in front of the garage, a hand was biting into the soft flesh of her arm, bringing her flight to an abrupt halt and spinning her around so that her other arm was captured also. She struggled against the punishing grip.

'Let me go! Please, Jed, let me go,' she begged, twisting and turning her head so he couldn't see the tears streaming down her face.

But he was oblivious to her protests, pulling her rigid body against his and forcing her head back to receive his long, hard kiss. He kept on kissing her until she stopped resisting him and the love she couldn't deny. Only then did he release her lips, allowing her to bury her face in his chest. She felt utterly miserable.

'I know you'll never believe me.' Her sobs were muffled by his shirt. 'But I swear I'd decided to marry you before that phone call. At the airport, I started to go back to tell you, but you'd said you wanted to be alone and — Oh, you'll never believe me now!'

'Stop crying.' He shook her gently as he scolded her with mock gruffiness. 'I was on the patio.'

'I know you were.' Her voice throbbed with pain. 'And I know what you must think of me.'

'You don't understand.' Forcing her head up, he tenderly wiped the tears from her cheek. 'I heard everything. I was on the patio listening to you play the piano before Mother came home. You told her before the phone rang that you were going to marry me. I was on my way in to make you tell me that. I never guessed the call would be for me.I'd left Sam's number for my attorney, but unfortunately he forgot to give me the message. So you see, darling, I know you're telling the truth, that you're willing to marry me for richer, for poorer.'

'Oh, Jed,' Elizabeth gasped, her lashes fluttering shut for a second. 'I was so afraid —'

'I know, darling.' He folded her more tightly into his arm. 'Now I have to ask you to forgive me. I wasn't being fair when I kept the truth from you and demanded that you make a decision without knowing what kind of future, if any, I could offer you.'

'Why didn't you let anyone know?' she asked softly, her hands lovingly caressing his face. 'You should have been proud of your success.'

'It was foolish Carrel pride,' he smiled crookedly. 'I wanted to be welcomed for myself, not for my accomplishments. Kurt and Sam, my friends, were the only ones who could do that. And you, my lovely enchanting Liza.' He kissed her lightly. 'It seems I shall have some business to take care of in Hawaii. Would you object to spending our honeymoon there?'

'No,' she smiled happily.

'It'll be a month or more before we can come back.'

'Here?' Elizabeth frowned. 'With your mother?'

'Good lord, no!' Jed laughed. 'I may care for her, but I could never live in the same house with her.' His expression became more serious. 'We'll find a place of our own, ours and Amy's. Not too far away, because Mother needs us. She hasn't anything, darling, and we have so much. She needs our love.' He lowered his head to her lips. 'And I need yours.'

SOMETHING EXTRA

"HAVE YOU DECIDED YOU CAN TRUST ME?"

His face was turned away from her, but he had been completely aware of her scrutiny.

"I think—" Jolie fought back the briefly rising flush of embarrassment "—that if you put a gold ring in your ear, you would make an excellent pirate."

"From some women that might be a compliment." Now he turned to study her. "What a pity I'm only a poor plantation owner."

"The best things in life are free," Jolie quipped, seeking a lighter topic.

"Don't you believe it!" His laugh was cynical. "You pay dearly for everything in one way or another."

"And what is the price for love?" she asked.

"The most precious thing a man has—his freedom." His eyes were harsh and piercing as he glanced over at her. "Tell me, what is love?"

CHAPTER ONE

THE pinto, a tobiano of chestnut and white, reluctantly submitted to the pressure of the reins and turned away from the rich grasses of his pasture. His head bobbed rhythmically from side to side as he plodded down the rutted lane. Fifteen summers had been seen by his soft brown eyes. He no longer pranced and tossed his brown and white mane, nor tugged at the bit between his teeth. Through the years he had grown fat and lazy, saving his energy to swish away flies and tear at the long green grass so that he would have the strength to see another South Dakota winter sweep by.

The horse didn't need to look at a calendar to see the month of September preparing to make way for October. He had only to look at the trees and their green leaves that were dotted with gold and orange, or to raise his brown eyes to the blue skies and see the gathering of birds who were ready to begin the migration to the south at the first sign of cold. The waving fields of wheat next to his pasture had ripened and their grains of gold hung heavily on their slender stalks. The days were still warm, but the nights held a chill. The pinto had already begun growing his shaggy coat to ward off the cold northwest winds.

A heel dug firmly into his side, and he snorted his

dislike before amiably breaking into a rocking canter. The weight on his back was light and the hands holding his reins were gentle. The pinto's dark ears pricked forward as a brightly plumed rooster pheasant took wing ahead of them. But there was not the slightest break in his stride. A hand touched the side of his neck in praise, followed by a checking of the reins. The ageing pinto gladly settled back into a shuffling trot and finally to his plodding walk.

The girl astride his bare back sighed deeply, letting the circled reins drop in front of her while placing her hands on her hips. Her bare legs dangled from his fat sides as she balanced herself easily on his broad back. She squinted her own soft brown eyes at the sun's glare, feeling its warmth on the skin not covered by the white halter top or the blue shorts. If she had looked for them, she would have seen all the signs of autumn that the horse did. But her gaze flitted over them all, looking but not seeing.

Her figure was adequate, not over-curvaceous nor over-slender, just somewhere in the middle. In her bare feet, she stood five feet four, an average height for an average build. Her hair was the same warm brown shade as her eyes, thick and cropped in a feathery boy-cut that allowed its thickness and natural wave to frame her oval face. Again her features were average, not possessing any startling beauty, only a pleasing wholesomeness.

When she was younger, Jolie Antoinette Smith used to moan about her lack of glamorous beauty. Her father always used to gather her in his arms in one of his giant bear hugs and in his laughing voice teased her.

'You have a pair of very nice eyes to see with; a nose to breathe and smell with; nice, generous lips to frame a mouth that talks and eats with its full set of white teeth.' Then he would lift her downcast chin with his hand and study her face closely. His voice would become very serious. 'And by my latest count, you have two thousand, four hundred and thirty-seven freckles, which you ought to thank the Good Lord for, because he's the one who sprinkled gold dust all over your face.'

She would be scowling by that time at the faint freckles that were there and not there, so light were they. Her father would then tickle the corner of her mouth, forcing her to smile.

'And he also gave you a matching set of dimples!' he ended triumphantly. Even though Jolie knew he was prejudiced in her favour, she always felt better after one of those sessions. It was only as she grew older that she realized he had been trying to make her content with the way she was, with the things she couldn't change. Yes, she had long ceased to curse the fact that she had been endowed with both freckles and dimples, too, and learned to endure the good-natured teasing that they always brought.

Even though Jolie seldom rated a second glance when she was walking down a street, the men who did become acquainted with her found that she was an excellent listener, had a ready smile, and could carry on a conversation without giggling. She was the kind of girl that got invited home to meet Mother while her girl-friends were invited to parties. After hearing tales of what went on at some of the parties, Jolie wasn't sure she would have liked it, but she never got to find out for herself.

She was home now after a little more than three years in which she had crammed a four-year college course. She had finished her education and obtained her degree, but now what? What came next? Inside Jolie felt that surge of restlessness, that heightening sense of dissatisfaction.

She had come home and all was different while it remained the same. Home. A three hundred and sixty acre tract of land sixty miles from Yankton, South Dakota, where for the entire twenty-one years of her life, Jolie's parents had farmed. It had been a good life, and a hard life at times, the difference dictated by the weather and its effect on the crops. But it was her parents' life and not hers.

The pinto paused to munch on a tempting clump of grass until Jolie raised herself out of her indifference to lift his head away.

'If you eat any more, Scout, your sides will burst,' she admonished. Dutifully the horse plodded on. 'Poor old Scout,' Jolie sighed, 'you've changed, too, just like me. Whoever said "You can't go home again" was right.'

Her parents had lived by themselves for the last three years and had grown accustomed to it. They no longer knew how to treat Jolie. She was not a child any more, but to them she would never be quite an adult. Madelaine, her older sister by one year, was married and already had two children as well as a life completely separate from Jolie's. Change was the only constancy. And that included John Talbot.

Jolie saw his pick-up truck parked on the field turnoff of the country road. His tall, sunburned figure was standing on the edge of a wheat field, the muscles in his arms gleaming in the late morning sunlight. A stalk of wheat was between his teeth as he lifted an arm in greeting. Without any effort his long stride carried him to the edge of the field as Jolie drew level atop her pinto. His large hands encircled her waist and lifted her to the ground. There John lowered his head and with the ease of habit claimed her mouth in a kiss. Jolie responded just as naturally, liking the warmth and the closeness of his body next to hers.

'Hi.' The gleam of quiet affection in his tawny gold eyes was comfortably pleasing, as was the slow smile. 'It's been a long time since you've come out to visit me in the fields.'

Snuggling against his shoulder, his muscular arm firmly holding her there, Jolie nodded agreement as she slipped her arm behind his back and around his waist. The pinto contentedly began grazing on the grasses near the lane, ignoring the couple walking slowly towards the lone cottonwood that stood on the edge of the wheat field.

'Dad says your wheat is ready for harvest.' Jolie easily fell into the main topic of conversation in the area. It was a safe subject that steered clear of her restlessness.

John plucked another stalk of wheat before sinking down on the ground beneath the shade tree. He stripped the golden grain from its head, tossing two into his mouth.

'Still a little too much moisture,' he decreed.

'Another day or two of sun like this and it'll be ready.' He pushed the straw hat back on his light brown head and gazed out over the golden sea of grain. 'It's going to be a good harvest.'

'Dad's shoulder is bothering him, which means rain before tomorrow night.' The blade of grass in her hand split down the middle at the nervous pressure of her fingers. She tossed it from her in disgust.

'You can tell him for me that he can hold it off for another couple of days,' John smiled, and drew Jolie into his arms.

She turned her head just as he was about to kiss her and his lips instead found her cheek. But he wasn't deterred, letting his mouth wander over her neck and the lobe of her ear half-covered by her brown hair. For Jolie, there was nothing soothing in his caress and her lack of response made her feel uncomfortable. She wriggled free, plucking another blade of grass and studying it intently. His measuring eyes were on her. Jolie could feel them trail over her face and she tried to appear undisturbed.

'What's wrong, Jo?' he asked quietly. If he was angered or hurt, there was nothing in his voice to reveal it.

'I don't know,' she sighed. She glanced back at him hesitantly, letting him glimpse the melancholy expression in her eyes that silently apologized.

'You've been home a week now. No calls on any of your job applications?'

'I haven't applied anywhere.' His eyebrows raised briefly at her statement, but his face remained impassive otherwise. Jolie inhaled deeply as she averted her eyes from his face. He always knew so much more of what she was thinking and she couldn't even begin to guess what was going on in his mind. 'I've got my diploma and I don't even know what I want to do with it.'

'Home economics graduates make good wives,' John stated.

Although there was a light, teasing air about his words, Jolie knew it was a testing statement. But how could she possibly tell John that she didn't love him, or at least not the way she wanted to love the man she would marry. What was worse, she felt so guilty for not loving him.

John Talbot was a girl's dream. Not only was he good-looking, extremely so, but he was also solid and dependable. Just looking at his tanned features, so clean-cut and handsome, made Jolie wonder if she wasn't out of her mind for not snatching up this man who had waited faithfully the last five years for her. She didn't deny that John had a magnetism that attracted her to him, but nothing happened—no bells rang, her heart didn't beat any faster—when he held her in his arms. It wouldn't be fair to marry him when she knew this.

'Did you ever wonder why I didn't give you a ring while you were at college?' the quiet baritone voice asked her.

Jolie nodded, too full of her own feelings of guilt to reply vocally.

'I knew you liked me, even loved me, but I knew you weren't in love with me.' Jolie grimaced and John lifted her chin that was threatening to sink into her chest. 'You were eighteen and I was twenty-four. I decided it was only fair for you to wait until you had graduated. But, to trade on an old cliché, absence hasn't made the heart grow fonder, has it?'

'I feel like the lowest beast on earth, John,' Jolie whispered, 'but I'm not really in love with you. I care about you more than anyone I've ever met. In my way, I do love you.'

For just a moment his fingers dug in her shoulders, revealing the pain that his face didn't show. Then he had released her and was lying back against the tree trunk.

'The way you feel wouldn't satisfy either one of us for long.' His smile was slow and regretful with only the barest traces of bitterness around the corners of his mouth. 'So what are you going to do now? Are you going to stay around here?'

'I don't think so.' There was an almost imperceptible shake of her head as Jolie replied. 'I thought if I came back here to the farm it would give me a chance to put my thoughts together. After three years of being whisked along by the steady flow of classes, homework and odd jobs, I feel as if somebody has just put me ashore. I thought coming home would re-orientate myself, but it's only made me more confused. I don't want to take just any job, but I can't keep sponging off my parents either. I've cost them enough.'

'It will all work out.'

'I hope it does . . . for both of us. John?' His gaze that had been turned unseeingly on the landscape reverted to Jolie. 'Is it too much to ask that we still be friends?'

His hand reached out and ruffled her hair in a gesture reminiscent of her teenage days. 'Of course,' he smiled, moving agilely to his feet. She rose to stand silently beside him. 'Don't be so solemn, honey,' tracing the curve of her cheek with his finger. 'It's not as if I'd suddenly discovered you weren't in love with me. I think I would have been more shocked if you were, and a little bit afraid that you were lying.'

Jolie stood on tiptoe and planted a soft kiss on his mouth, her eyes brimming with tears she didn't have any right to shed. 'Aunt Brigitte will have my scalp for letting you go.'

'Don't tell me your neurotically romantic aunt is here,' John laughed.

'Aunt Brigitte is a died-in-the-wool spinster. How can you possible consider her romantic? Mother swears she would be surprised if Aunt Brigitte had ever been kissed.'

'Don't you believe it. There is one woman who knows exactly what love is all about.' That was a puzzling statement to Jolie and one that John was going to let her think about by herself. 'Uncle Ray will be wondering where I am, so I'd better shove off.'

She didn't realize at first that he was leaving until he was already several steps away from her. 'John, I'm . . . I'm sorry,' she called after him.

There was a slight stiffening of his shoulders before he turned and waved. Yet his stride quickly carried him away from her towards his car. Jolie watched him drive off before she walked over to her rotund horse still contentedly stuffing himself with grass.

The screen door slammed behind her as Jolie entered the two-storey, white-framed house. She didn't feel any better or worse than before she had left that morning. Only one thing was definite and that was she would not be looking for a job anywhere near home. It wouldn't be fair to John, not that he was the type to jump off a cliff. Hardly, he was the opposite, the kind who met a problem head on and conquered it.

'Hello! Who is it?' The imperious call came from the sun porch.

'It's me, Aunt Brigitte,' Jolie replied, sticking her head around the door with a wave of her hand. 'Where's Mother?'

'In town getting groceries.' When Jolie would have gone on to her own room, her aunt motioned into the room. 'Come sit with me.'

The iron-grey hair was drawn into a severe bun at the back of her aunt's head. Jolie had always regarded her aunt, who was twelve years her mother's senior, as being stern and practical, but in the light of John's statement, Jolie wondered how correct her assessment was. Her features, which had always possessed the uncompromising lines of age, could quite possibly be attractive when her aunt smiled as she was doing now.

'What have you been doing since you've returned home?' Her Aunt Brigitte's questions always sounded more like a command, but then she had been a teacher for the last thirty years, Jolie mused. On rare weekends her aunt journeyed to her only sister's, Jolie's mother, to spend two uneventful days on the farm. This was one of those rare times.

'Relaxing from the grind of all the finals, mostly and trying to figure out where and what I want to do next.'

'That sounds as if it's a momentous problem.' Jolie saw her aunt's lips quiver, almost breaking into a smile. Brigitte Garson glanced up, noticing the troubled expression on her niece's face. 'It is, isn't it?'

'Yes.' Jolie sighed heavily and turned away from her aunt's searching gaze.

'Where have you been this morning?'

'Out with John.'

'I'm quite sure he had an answer to your dilemma.'

'Yes, he had a suggestion.' Jolie's voice was soft and simultaneously firm. 'I'm not in love with him, Aunt Brigitte.'

It was her aunt's turn to sigh and she did. 'I'm sorry to hear that. Sorry for you as well as for John. He would have been a loving husband and father. You are quite sure about how you feel?'

'What is love?' Jolie asked quietly, turning away from the window to her aunt. 'I'm twenty-one years old and I don't even know what it is.'

'That my dear, is an eternal question that will be asked as long as there are people on earth.' Her aunt's dark grey eyebrows raised significantly. 'At least, I do know you aren't in love with John or you wouldn't ask.'

'Which is a tricky way of avoiding my question.' Depression turned down the corners of her mouth. 'And please don't use Mother's old quote—Love is many things to many people.'

'The kind of love that I believe you're talking about is a rare thing where bells ring,' her aunt answered her quietly. 'Mostly because it's a selfless love and there are few people who can give of their feelings so freely and completely. Others search for it so hard that they never find it. There are only a lucky few who really do find it.'

'Did you, Aunt Brigitte?' The withdrawn expression on her aunt's face drew the whispered question from Jolie's lips.

'Yes, once. A car accident took him away from me.' A melancholy smile lifted the usually stern mouth. 'And that love completely spoiled me for second best, which has made my life very lonely. The type of love you're speaking about can cost very dearly. Perhaps that's why it's so precious.'

'Do you suppose I'll ever find it?'

'Not with that mopey expression on your face. Nobody would be interested in a mourner.' From experience, Brigitte Carson put just enough sharpness in her teasing words to pull Jolie away from the depths of depression.

'Well, I certainly need something to do with myself in the meantime. I'm not looking forward to leaving here and still, I don't want to stay.'

'Sometimes, Jolie, it's difficult to make a decision when you're surrounded by the people you know. You want their suggestions even knowing they're not always helpful. The best thing for you to do would be to take off for a week or two. Go somewhere by yourself, relax, and have a good time. It's surprising how clear everything becomes afterwards.'

'There isn't any place I particularly care to go,' Jolie shrugged.

'Oh, surely there's some place that you've always wanted to see.'

A light shone for a moment in Jolie's eyes as she thought of her long-held childhood wish before she blinked it away.

'Perhaps,' she admitted, 'but it's quite out of the question. What little money I have saved I'll have to use to start out on my own. It wouldn't stretch to include any extravagant whims.'

'It doesn't hurt to talk about it. Where would you like to go—if you could afford it?' the matronly woman persisted.

'I know this must sound awfully strange to you, but I've always wanted to go to Louisiana where my great-grandmother or whatever came from. I remember Grandmother telling Madelaine and myself the stories her mother had told her about the plantation home where she lived.' Jolie glanced over at her aunt, shyness creeping into her voice. 'I can't help wondering if Cameron Hall is still standing.'

'It is rather curious how that one lone ancestor of ours has managed to still be so much a part of our lives.' Dark eyes scrutinized Jolie carefully. 'You were named after her, weren't you? Jolie Antoinette. Somehow all the girls received French names down the years.'

'I don't mind. Jolie is much more romantic than Jane Smith could ever be,' she laughed.

'Perhaps there is a way you can make this trip.'

The wheels were turning almost visibly in her aunt's mind as Jolie watched her set the book from her lap and stand.

'I don't see how.'

'I have a fair amount of money saved and I never have decided what I'm saving it for. I didn't get you a graduation gift because I wanted you to pick it out. It seems you have,' her aunt smiled. 'A trip to Louisiana and the bayou country.'

'That's much too expensive!' Jolie gasped. 'I couldn't possibly let you do it.'

'How could you possibly stop me?'

CHAPTER TWO

Every one of Jolie's arguments was brushed off with logical rebuttals until she found herself sitting down at a desk while her aunt began planning her trip. Jolie's little Volkswagen would need to be checked thoroughly before the journey. A few dresses needed to be added to her wardrobe. Inquiries had to be made as to the accommodation in the town nearest the plantation, Cameron Hall. The amount of funds needed for petrol, meals and lodging had to be estimated. By the time Jolie's mother arrived home from town, her itinerary had been all laid out and it was presented to her mother by Aunt Brigitte as an accomplished fact.

Looking at the total cost of the trip, Jolie moaned, 'You should at least come with me, Aunt Brigitte, and get some enjoyment yourself out of this money.'

'That isn't the object of the trip. The idea is for you to get off by yourself and have fun. Something you certainly couldn't do if you were dragging a spinster aunt along,' her aunt had scolded with mock severity.

No amount of persuasion could alter her aunt's decision. In no time at all Jolie was swept up in the carrying out of the items on the list. Within a week her car was decreed ready for the journey, a reply had been received assuring her of available accommodation, and her suitcases were packed. When she wheeled her cranberry-coloured car on to the highway, Jolie was caught up in the excitement of her journey.

There was only one thing that could put a blight on her journey, Jolie decided, and that was the distinct possibility that Cameron Hall was no longer standing. The letter she had received assuring her that there was accommodation in the town had also stated that they had no knowledge of a plantation called Cameron Hall. Her aunt had been quick to point out that it had been sold shortly after the Civil War for taxes and had very likely been renamed. It was a small hope, but exceedingly logical since renaming of plantations was not an uncommon practice.

Even though she wanted to hurry, Jolie took her time during the long drive, breaking the journey into stages that would spread it over nearly four days. Leisurely she went on the scenic back roads, avoiding the modern roads that were quicker but not nearly as beautiful. Still, when the little red Volkswagen crossed the border into Louisiana, her heart beat a little faster. It was almost as if she were coming home.

It was six o'clock in the evening and Jolie was less than a hundred miles from her final destination. If it hadn't been for her strong desire to see this last portion of her journey during the daylight hours, she would have pushed on. As it was, she reluctantly turned the car into the driveway of a motel, determined that the following morning she would get an early start and allow herself ample time to view the new countryside unhurried by waning daylight.

The following morning the last leg of her journey began, out of the National Forests around Alexandria, down through Opelousas and Lafayette, until finally the turnoff for St. Martinville, the heart of the Evangeline Country, was in front of her. A road marker in the centre of the town beckoned her to visit the Evangeline oak tree, immortalized in the poem by Longfellow, but Jolie steeled herself to pass it by. Almost three full weeks of sightseeing stretched ahead of her, but first she had to have a place to stay, somewhere inexpensive and still comfortable.

She parked the red Volkswagen in front of a restaurant, deciding that an inquiry of one of the local people might direct her to a place where she could rent a place of her own and save the cost of hotel rooms and meals. After ordering coffee, Jolie asked the waitress if she knew of such a place. The young girl offered her a local newspaper, but the small classified section didn't have any listings within Jolie's budget. When the waitress returned with her coffee she handed the paper back.

'I'm afraid there wasn't anything in there that was what I had in mind,' she sighed. 'Do you know where else I might check?'

The young dark-haired girl began to shake her head negatively before putting her hand to her mouth as if some idea had just occurred to her. She glanced towards the counter where a trio of men were sitting, then turned back to Jolie with a wide smile.

'I may know a place. Let me see,' she said.

Jolie watched the waitress walk over to the group of men, tap a dark-haired man on the shoulder, and with a gesture towards Jolie, begin speaking. Seconds later he was excusing himself from the other men and accompanying the waitress to her table. His dark, dark eyes dwelt speculatively on Jolie as the young waitress introduced him.

'Miss, this is Guy LeBlanc. I think he'll be able to help you.' The waitress moved away after Jolie's expression of thanks.

'I'm please to meet you, Miss . . . ?' Jolie knew his wide smile was meant to charm and it did.

'Smith, Jolie Smith,' she supplied, answering his smile with her own.

'Denise, the waitress, said you were looking for a boarding house,' the man prompted.

'Yes, I was hoping for a place where I might have kitchen privileges. I wouldn't be staying more than a few weeks,' Jolie explained, brushing back a feathery wisp of her brown hair and feeling self-conscious under his obvious scrutiny. 'Do you know where I might find something like that?'

'My home,' Guy LeBlanc said calmly, and laughed softly when her eyebrows raised significantly. 'Where my parents also live,' he added reassuringly. 'In the past they've taken in boarders, although we haven't had any for some time.'

'Do you suppose they could be persuaded to let me stay?' Jolie liked the man's drawling voice even while her mind tried to place the difference in his way of speaking that was not like other southern accents she had heard.

'I'm sure, but let me take you there and you may talk to them yourself. You do understand that it will be only a large bedroom and your meals would be taken with the family.' He spoke as he courteously helped Jolie slide her chair back from the table. As she reached in her bag to pay for her coffee, Guy interceded, placing change upon the table and signalling to the waitress that it was for Jolie's coffee. 'My pleasure,' he smiled when Jolie attempted to protest.

As the pair left the restaurant, it was Jolie's turn to inspect the man walking beside her to the Volkswagen. She decided Guy LeBlanc was in his early twenties, a year or two older than herself, perhaps. He was less than six foot tall, but lean and graceful. His hair was brown, but much darker than hers. His features echoed the slenderness of the rest of his body, with darkly arched brows, an aristocratically straight nose, and a finely drawn mouth. But his dark eyes were like burnished coals that gleamed and glittered as they reflected light. He wore dark tan trousers and a brightly printed cotton shirt that was opened at the neckline. He exuded an air of confidence and ease that Jolie knew was part of his charm. She also knew that this young man was fully aware of his looks and made use of them wherever possible. A warning she herself should make note of for the future, especially if she should stay in the same house with him.

His directions were very precise as he instructed Jolie along the route to his house. She had expected him to suggest that he drive her car, but he made it evident that he would rather watch her than the route they were taking.

'The white house on the corner. There's a place to park your car behind the house,' he informed Jolie.

Again she puzzled over the accent in his voice that wasn't quite southern as she followed his instructions, turning into the driveway of the large rambling house and continuing to the rear. She had barely braked the car to a halt when Guy was out of the car and around to her side to open the door. His courtesy was a little overpowering, and Jolie wasn't too sure how to deal with it. Foolishly she reached for the handle of the back door, only to have Guy LeBlanc's hand there before her. She smiled uncomfortably when his other hand offered her entry into his home.

The room he ushered her into was some type of family room with white wicker chairs and sofas scattered about in abundance. Live plants thrived in green profusion. Some were suspended in pots from the high ceiling while other rubber-type plants were in huge tubs on the tiled floor and still others decorated white tabletops. The room had a tropical air, which wasn't unusual considering the heat and humidity that was representative of the Louisiana climate.

'If you would wait here, I'll find my parents.'

Jolie nodded her compliance as he excused himself. She let her gaze stray around the room again, liking what she saw. The immense size of the house told her it was old, but it had been so well cared for that it was impossible to guess its age. Two sets of clicking shoes in the wide hallway leading to the room where Jolie waited signalled Guy LeBlanc's return with one other person.

'Here's the visitor I told you about, Mamma.' At Guy's side was a petite woman, standing barely five feet tall. Her hint of plumpness gave her a very maternal air, as did the escaping wisps of greying dark hair in the bun atop her head. An open, beaming smile accompanied the small hand extended to Jolie.

'My son told me you're looking for a place to stay. Miss Smith, isn't it?'

'Yes,' Jolie nodded, drawn by the friendliness the older woman exhibited that had nothing to do with polite manners.

'She's much more attractive than you told me,' Mrs. LeBlanc admonished her son playfully. 'Is that the reason you're anxious for her to stay with us?'

Jolie couldn't stop the faint blush from filling her cheeks. She did not want this woman thinking that she was interested in her son. But at the sight of Jolie's discomfort, the small woman broke into a tinkling laugh.

'I was making a small joke,' she smiled apologetically. 'My son believes he's quite irresistible to the women. Be warned that he takes delight in new conquests. While you're staying with us, you'd do well to ignore two-thirds of his compliments.'

'Then you do have a room that you're willing to let?' Jolie breathed in relief. Her wide smile hesitated as she realized she hadn't even inquired about the cost. It was difficult giving voice to her question because the woman was treating her as a guest and not a boarder. But the figure named was well within her budget. Jolie now had a place to stay, pleasant surroundings and with pleasant people.

'Tell me, Miss Smith,' Guy inserted himself into the conversation quietly, 'why did you choose St. Martinville as the place to spend your vacation? Why not the more resplendent and exciting New Orleans?'

'Guy!' Mrs. LeBlanc reprimanded her son sharply. 'We have much to offer a visitor, and only minutes away. Our own Acadian House Museum and Craft Shop and the Acadian Heritage Museum in Loreauville. The magnificent Shadows on the Teche antebellum home is in New Iberia. And what about Avery Island and its Bird City and Jungle Gardens? Don't listen to him,' she instructed Jolie. 'There's plenty here for you to do. If you wish to visit New Orleans, it's only a short journey away.'

'I know I'm going to enjoy myself here,' Jolie agreed as she wondered why she was hesitating about confiding the main reason for her journey—to find the plantation home of her great-grandmother. 'There was another reason I came here particularly.' She glanced from mother to son. 'An ancestor of mine once lived on a plantation near here. My namesake, actually, Jolie Antoinette Cameron. The plantation was Cameron Hall. Perhaps you've heard of it?'

She held her breath as the two paused before replying. Guy LeBlanc shrugged his shoulders, accompanying it with a negative shake of his head and a small smile. But his mother didn't give up so quickly.

'Do you know where it is from here?' she asked.

'I only know it was ten or fifteen miles from St. Martinville.'

'That's not much,' the woman added. Her soft voice conveyed a sadness that Jolie didn't want to feel. 'The years didn't treat many of our old homes kindly. What old age, termites and fire didn't destroy fell before the winds of the hurricanes and the creeping hand of progress.'

'You don't think there's much chance that the plantation is still standing?' Jolie inhaled deeply. The lifting of her chin indicated that she wasn't giving up without even trying.

'There are a few old derelicts standing about the countryside,' Guy told her. His perception told him that success with Jolie was linked with her desire to find the mansion.

'What did you say the name was again?' Mrs. LeBlanc asked, a finger resting on the corner of her mouth.

'Cameron Hall.'

'You don't suppose Etienne's old house——' She turned towards her son, then shook her head, 'But no, that was called The Temple, wasn't it? I confused the name of the plantation with his own. Still, he is knowledgeable about such things. We'll ask him if he knows of your place. Now we must make you comfortable in our home. Guy, bring her luggage in while I show Miss Smith—may I call you Jolie?—to her room.'

Jolie passed the car keys to Guy, adding her insistence that they call her Jolie. Only when she began following Mrs. LeBlanc down the wide hallway to the staircase leading upstairs did it dawn on Jolie what the unusual accent was in the LeBlancs' manner of speaking. It was so obvious, she wondered why she hadn't realized it earlier. It was French.

'Have you and your family lived here long?' she asked, her hand holding the carved wooden balustrade.

'In St. Martinville? All our lives, both my husband Emile and myself,' Mrs. LeBlanc replied quickly. 'We bought this house a few years after we were married. My Emile was handy with his hands and even though the house was in terrible shape, he worked and fixed it until it is as you see it today.'

'It's very beautiful,' Jolie agreed. 'Did your family emigrate from France?'

'You don't know of the history of Louisiana?' Mrs. LeBlanc stopped before reaching the top of the stairs, turning to enforce an answer to her gently worded question.

'Just what most people know and what little that was included in the history books,' Jolie flushed, wishing suddenly that she had done some studying before making the journey down here.

'Then you haven't heard the story of the Acadian people?' Jolie shook her head from side to side that she hadn't. 'But you have heard of the Cajuns, haven't you?' Mrs. LeBlanc smiled as Jolie nodded yes.

'Acadians were emigrants from France to Canada where they settled in Nova Scotia. When England claimed the territory of Canada, she feared the large settlement of French people, so she gave them a choice of either returning to France or settling in the American colonies. Over half chose the colonies where they were scattered throughout. Many families and lovers were separated during the journey, some of them searching for years before they found those they had lost. Almost ten years later these Acadians migrated to Louisiana. The fertile land along the Mississippi River had already been grabbed up by the large plantation owners, so the Acadians settled along the bayous. After the United States purchased the Louisiana territory from France, Americans came into their new land and met these Acadian peoples. Somehow they corrupted the name Acadian to "Cajun". So you see Acadians and Cajuns are one in the same. Our families' ancestry goes back to these Acadian settlers. So we are really French–Canadian Americans.'

Mrs. LeBlanc clicked her tongue. 'I didn't mean to recite a history lesson,' she apologized. 'I don't want you to be bored before you've even seen your room. Please follow me.'

'I assure you I wasn't in the least bored. I have a great deal to learn, I can see that,' Jolie smiled, her eyes widening in emphasis. 'What little you told me just now convinces me that I'm going to find it fascinating.'

'I hope you do.' The woman led the way down a hallway almost as wide as the one downstairs. 'The bathroom is at the end of this hall, and here's your room.' After opening a door, she stepped back, allowing Jolie to enter the room first. 'Do you like it?'

'It's so big!'

Jolie didn't know how she could begin to explain that she would have been satisfied with a room half the size. Instead she was standing in a large, high-ceilinged room with two large windows that were nearly floor to ceiling. One corner of the room near the windows held a small desk and chair along with a cushioned armchair and floor lamp. A single bed and large maple dresser were the other pieces of furniture in the room. Throw rugs the colour of a pale blue sky were scattered about the polished wood floors, bringing out the pastel colours in the print material in the bedspread and the cushioned armchair. The whole effect was spacious cosiness.

'This was my eldest daughter's room before she was married,' Mrs. LeBlanc explained. 'It's large enough to give you privacy without making you feel cramped.'

'How many children do you have?' Jolie asked as her landlady revealed the concealed door to the closet, delighting Jolie even more.

'Five. Two of my older girls are married. Claudine is still living with us part of the year. My youngest daughter, Michelle, teaches school here. And of course, our baby of the family, Guy.'

'The little boy who's abominably spoiled,' Guy laughed, poking his head around the door. 'Is it safe to come in? I don't want to interrupt if you were about to begin praising me to Miss Jolie Smith.'

'At least he admits he's spoiled,' Mrs. LeBlanc

winked to Jolie. Her dainty hand waved her son into the room. 'Bring her suitcases in, Guy. Then I'm sure you have some work to do, so our new guest will have time to settle in.'

He placed her suitcases near the bed, his dark eyes dwelling on her with an intentness Jolie knew was supposed to send her heart pounding, but it maintained its steady pace. His exaggerated reluctance to leave was revealed by his long sigh as he promised to see her later. Once Guy had left the room Mrs. LeBlanc turned to Jolie and laughed.

'My son, the lover. I'll leave you to unpack. We'll be having a cold lunch around one o'clock. The dining room is the second door on the right from the stairway.'

CHAPTER THREE

'DON'T you work somewhere, Guy?' Jolie half asked and half demanded.

'Would it be so great a crime if I didn't?' he mocked, firmly tucking her hand under his arm as they strolled down the sidewalk.

'It would be a waste,' she returned brightly.

'And it would disappoint you that I haven't a profession?'

'Why should it disappoint me?'

'Because, from what you've told me, I know that you come from a hard-working family, so therefore a man who lazes about would be considered disreputable. Since I don't want you to think unkind thoughts about me, I'll confess that I'm an accountant with my own very small business.'

Jolie knew her astonishment registered in her face, but she couldn't hide it. Guy LeBlanc was not her idea of an accountant, not with his suavity and good looks. A salesman would have been a more logical profession for him.

'Your expression of disbelief wounds my pride.' His dark eyes looked dutifully hurt. 'It's really very logical. I am self-employed and have no one to answer to for the hours I keep or don't keep but myself. I derive an ample income with little time expended. There are times when I have much to do, but even more times when I have very little to do. And during the times I have very little to do, I can escort attractive young women around town and show them our points of interest. Very convenient, wouldn't you say?'

'I think you're trying to paint yourself as much more of a rogue than you really are.' Jolie's knowing smile carved two very deep dimples in her cheeks.

'Women love rogues. They have a touch of the forbidden fruit about them. Plus women are born reformers. They enjoy trying to make an honest man out of me, and if I should stray——' Guy winked. 'It is, after all, only my nature.'

'And there's safety in numbers,' Jolie agreed.

'For the time being.' He let their pace slacken. 'I have a hunch you could be my undoing.'

'Me?' Jolie laughed incredulously. 'Why?'

'Because you could make a man want to change.' Despite his smile, there was gravity in his gaze.

'After twenty-one years of looking at my reflection in a mirror, I know I don't have the beauty to turn a man's head,' Jolie smiled, 'so your flattery won't get you anywhere with me, Guy LeBlanc.'

'No, I'm speaking the truth. If you were in a room with the most beautiful women in the world, yours is the face a man would remember. It would come back to haunt him with its serene animation. A contradiction, I admit, but it's the only way of describing that combination of pale boyish freckles, dimples and soft brown eyes. A man thinks serious thoughts when he looks at you,' Guy declared firmly.

'The girl you take home to Mother,' Jolie nodded, pleased by his sincere words, but, like all women, wishing she were the type that sent a man's heart racing and his head spinning with thoughts of anything but 'Mother'!

'A girl he would be extraordinarily proud to take home to Mother,' Guy corrected quietly.

'I think you suffer from a lack of competition.' The conversation had become more personal than Jolie wanted. And it called for a change of subject.

'Oh, I have competition, very formidable competition.' The dark-haired man at her side inhaled deeply.

'I must meet him so I can compare notes,' Jolie teased. 'Who is he?'

'No, no, you don't get his name from me,' Guy laughed. 'Besides, he's older and too experienced for you. You're much safer with me.'

'Now, why would you admit that?'

'I'm thinking of my sister who has him all marked out as her personal property, for one thing. And secondly I don't think he'd let your air of innocence deter him. So be warned!' His dark brows raised as he emphasized his air of intrigue.

Jolie merely laughed, the throaty sound rolling out from deep within her. 'How far is it now to the oak tree?'

'Just around the corner. How familiar are you with Longfellow's poem, *Evangeline*?' Guy asked.

'Only the gist of it. I remember Evangeline was separated from her fiancé Gabriel and that she searched until she found him dying in a hospital.'

'Have you heard the story upon which the poem

was based?' When Jolie said no, that she hadn't, Guy continued. 'An orphan girl named Emmeline Labiche was taken in by an Acadian family and raised in their home in Nova Scotia. When she was sixteen she was to marry Louis Arceneaux from the same village. This was during the time when the English were transporting the Acadian families out of Canada. Louis attempted to resist the deportation, was injured and carried away by the English and was thus separated from Emmeline when she was taken to another ship. Emmeline and her foster-family ended up in Maryland, but she had no idea where Louis was. After several years they heard of the settlement of some Acadians in Louisiana and Emmeline accompanied her family here. When she stepped off the boat, her sadness vanished, because under a large oak tree she saw the man for whom she had pined all those long years. There was no happy reunion, however, because Louis had become promised to another woman. The story goes that after that meeting she still talked of him as if he were dead or in some far-off land until she died.'

His step slowed and finally ceased. 'This is said to be the oak tree where Emmeline found and lost again her fiancé, Louis.'

Jolie stared at the spreading oak tree before them, its enormity dwarfing the tiny park that contained it. Beyond were the gleaming waters of a quiet stream, a scene of peaceful melancholy in almost the centre of town. Here was the *Evangeline* oak tree.

'I think it's rather ironic that the building that

houses the Acadian House Museum was the one that Louis Arceneaux and his new wife lived in,' Guy said as Jolie continued gazing at the tree with its large girth and trunk-size limbs. 'We have a monument to each of them.'

'The river on the other side of the tree, that's the one that Emmeline's boat came on?' She slowly made her way across the green grass to the water in question.

'Correction.' Guy followed her. 'That's a bayou, more specifically Bayou Teche.'

'It looks just like a small river to me.' Jolie turned her puzzled brown eyes to the slender man walking beside her. 'I was always under the impression that a bayou was a swamp or, at least, a swampy area.'

'One of the first Frenchmen that saw one called it "sleeping water", because it has no discernible current,' Guy explained patiently. 'The water does flow, but it may change direction and flow one way and for no apparent reason reverse its flow.'

'Just drifting along in leisurely Gallic fashion,' she smiled. ' "Teche" is French, right? What does it mean?'

'Not really. It's a corruption of an Indian word for "Snake" which the French softened to fit their accent.'

Sighing deeply, Jolie turned to Guy. 'I certainly have a lot to learn.'

'Good.'

'Why?' She stared at him with amused astonishment.

'If you have a lot to learn, we may be able to

persuade you to stay longer.' He turned his sexiest smile on her. 'And I'd like that very much.'

'Has anybody ever told you that you come on too strong?' Her teasing question caught Guy off guard, but only for a moment.

'Only girls who haven't been the object of my attention.' This time he made fun of himself.

'Such conceit!' Jolie laughed as Guy could no longer keep a straight face either.

A car pulled up to the curb near the miniature park and honked its horn, drawing both Guy and Jolie's attention. A dark-haired girl waved to them from the driver's seat.

'Now do you believe how popular I am?' His shoulders lifted in a Gallic gesture in which he mockingly resigned himself to the Fates.

'Do you want a ride home?' the girl called out.

Guy turned to Jolie. 'It's a long walk. Would you rather ride?'

'I wouldn't want to cramp your style,' Jolie teased impishly. 'And I wouldn't want to be the object of one of your fans' jealousy.'

'I think I can handle two women at the same time. I didn't tell you I was very adept at juggling,' he returned with the same amount of jest.

'Okay, we'll ride home. I'm dying to see you in action,' she laughed, accepting his guiding arm as he led her to the car.

'You sure took your time making up your mind,' the girl stated as Guy helped Jolie into the front seat, squeezing her in the middle as he joined her. 'Didn't you realize that was a "no parking" zone?'

'We were debating whether we wanted to walk

back,' Guy replied. Jolie flashed him a gleaming smile at the reproving words from their driver. His finesse hadn't impressed this girl very much.

'In this heat! You've got to be kidding! Why, it would sap you of all your energy.' The dark-haired girl quickly changed gears and pulled into the main thoroughfare.

Turning her gaze very briefly from the road ahead, the girl cast a quick, assessing glance over Jolie who did the same. Their driver was fairly attractive with brown hair darker than Jolie's yet not as black as Guy's. Its medium length with a side parting was flipped up at the ends to add fullness to the thin face. A pair of gold-rimmed glasses gave her dark eyes a luminous quality that added something to their childlike roundness.

'Since Guy isn't anxious to introduce us, we might as well do it ourselves,' the girl flashed a quick smile to Jolie. 'I'm his sister Michelle.'

'My name is Jolie Smith,' Jolie replied, casting a sideways glance at Guy's bland expression. 'I've rented a room from your parents for a few weeks.'

'On vacation? Or are you planning to stay?'

'Vacation.'

'And my dearest brother was showing you the sights.' Michelle gave Guy a knowing look which he returned with an amazingly innocent expression. She added with a chuckle. 'How do you always manage to find the attractive ones?'

'I'm a magnet. They find me,' he grinned. 'How were the little brats today?'

'Don't ask!' Michelle raised her eyes heavenward. A mockingly sad look swept over her face as she glanced at Jolie. 'I teach here. Would you believe somebody let the chameleon out of the terrarium today. And it amazingly always managed to pop up on some girl's desk. I've heard enough shrieking today to last a lifetime. I think the little creature was delighted to be returned to his glass world.'

'Don't let her grumbling fool you,' Guy confided to Jolie. 'She likes it as much as boys like girls.'

'You have a one-track mind.' Jolie shook her head sadly.

'You've noticed that, too,' Michelle agreed.

'He led me to believe you were one of his numerous conquests.'

'Okay, you two, stop ganging up on a poor defenceless male,' Guy protested vigorously. 'How is Jolie ever going to appreciate me if you treat me so disrespectfully?'

'The fragile male ego,' Michelle whispered, drawing a laugh from Jolie.

'Didn't Mother teach you that whispering is rude?' Guy asked in false anger. 'Whatever she told you, Jolie, you just ignore it.'

'Someone needs to forewarn her about our "southern gentlemen",' his sister laughed.

Further conversation was halted by their arrival at the LeBlanc home. When Guy would have resumed his baiting with his sister, his mother appeared in the archway of the back door to welcome them. It was an unusual experience for Jolie. She suddenly discovered that she didn't feel the least bit strange or uncomfortable among these people she had only met today. They had opened their hearts as well as their arms, extending that precious gift of friendship.

'Well, what do you think of my sister?' Guy asked as Michelle succumbed to her mother's offer of assistance in carrying her papers into the house.

'She's marvellous,' Jolie smiled. 'I don't know why you warned me about her.'

'Warn you? When did I do that?' His gaze was puzzled as he held the door for her.

'You said she had your competition all staked out as her property,' Jolie reminded him.

'Competition? Who are you talking about?' Michelle asked after overhearing Jolie's reply.

'I wasn't referring to Michelle.' Guy ignored his sister. 'I was talking about Claudine.'

'Ahhh!' Michelle's dark eyes rolled widely towards Jolie. 'Now I know what you were talking about. I'm surprised you were brave enough to mention Steve to Jolie.'

'He didn't . . . at least, not by name.' A wicked gleam lighted her eyes as she surveyed the disgruntled Guy. 'So his name is Steve. I must remember that.'

'I'm glad Claudine isn't here. She'd claw your eyes out for such a statement, even if you are only joking.' The slight seriousness behind his words told Jolie that what he said was true.

'Since Guy refuses to tell me about him, you're going to have to, Michelle.' She couldn't help being intrigued by this unknown Romeo.

'Fire burns, and if you get too near Steve, you get scorched,' Michelle replied cryptically. 'Give me my safe, solid and comfortable Gene any day.'

Guy pounced on her slight change of subject eagerly. 'Can you believe she's fallen for the Ancient History teacher? Socrates and Euripides are her rivals.'

He dodged a playful, flying fist directed at him before the sibling rivalry was set aside by the arrival of their mother in the family room. She carried a tray of glasses and a pitcher of lemonade. No one had to be persuaded to indulge in the refreshment.

'I heard you talking about Claudine. I had a letter from her today,' Mrs. LeBlanc inserted during a lull in the conversation. 'She's coming home this weekend.'

'For how long?' Guy's grim expression revealed more thoroughly than his words his displeasure at the news.

'I imagine until the holidays,' his mother answered.

'She must have an excellent job to be able to take off from work that amount of time,' Jolie commented when the silence started to stretch awkwardly.

'My daughter's an artist, a painter,' Mrs. LeBlanc explained. 'She exhibits in New Orleans during the summer and again during the winter holidays and Mardi Gras. The rest of the year she spends here at home painting new canvases so that she always has an adequate supply.'

'What an exciting profession,' said Jolie, glancing around at Michelle and Guy, expecting them to show the pride that their mother displayed. 'She must be fairly successful.'

'Oh, she is,' the older woman nodded quickly.

'Practically all of the paintings you see here in the house were done by Claudine.'

The two paintings that adorned the walls in her own room sprang quickly to Jolie's mind. They were a pair of matching yet different floral bouquets of white daisies, starburst flowers and baby's breath against a background of palest blue-grey, arranged in identical vases of Chinese design, predominantly coloured in bright blue. If those were Claudine's work, then Jolie decided she was probably a very successful artist. When questioned, Mrs. LeBlanc confirmed that they were her daughter's paintings. She would have continued extolling Claudine's accomplishments, but she was interrupted by the arrival of her husband.

Emile LeBlanc was a man of small stature, standing only five feet six inches in height with a youthfully slender build. His hair had quite likely been as dark as Guy's, but now the sides were silvery white with greying streaks through the rest of his abundant mane. After greeting his family, placing an affectionate kiss on his wife's cheek, he turned to Jolie with an inquisitive smile. She was in no doubt where Guy inherited his charm.

'Who is this lovely young lady gracing our room, Josephine?'

Mrs. LeBlanc immediately explained the circumstances surrounding Jolie's presence as she made the introduction. Mr. LeBlanc's welcome was as generous as the rest of his family and almost as teasingly affectionate as Guy's.

'Jolie Antoinette are very French names to be attached to such a common one as Smith,' he commented.

Jolie went over again her reason for coming to St. Martinville, to try to locate the plantation her namesake once lived in as well as to tour the local sites. Emile LeBlanc drew the same blank as did his wife and son at the mention of Cameron Hall, but he was immediately enthusiastic about the sights to be seen in the area.

'We must draw you an itinerary so that you don't miss anything during your stay with us,' he decreed, looking to his son and daughter to assist with the task.

'There's time enough for that later, Papa,' Mrs. LeBlanc inserted firmly. 'I'm sure Jolie would much rather finish her drink, and take a shower before dinner. She can't possibly be adjusted to our humidity or rested from her long journey. Any planning can be done this evening. We mustn't force our plans on to her anyway.'

'True, true,' he nodded, turning to Jolie with a quick apology.

'I'm completely unfamiliar with this area, Mr. LeBlanc, and I certainly would appreciate any suggestions you would like to make,' she assured him.

'Still, my wife is right. These discussions should wait until after our evening meal.' His arm curled around the older woman. 'What are we having tonight? Have you planned a special treat for our new guest?'

'Not this night. Let her become accustomed to our climate, then our cuisine.'

Jolie tried to express the feeling of guilt possessing her that she was disrupting their life which was one thing she didn't want to do. But her protests fell on deaf ears as Mrs. LeBlanc vehemently denied that Jolie was causing her the least bit of inconvenience. She too much enjoyed the warmth of this family circle to do anything but give in.

CHAPTER FOUR

It was late the following morning before Mrs. LeBlanc was satisfied that Jolie had sufficient food, drink, brochures and directions to enable her to set out on an all-day sightseeing expedition. But at last she was safely behind the wheel of her cranberry Volkswagen and turning it out of the drive.

Despite all the places listed for her to see, Jolie didn't really have any idea where she was going. The day promised to be oppressively warm, so she wasn't particularly interested in walking through museums. Besides, she didn't think her jade green cotton knit slacks with the matching midriff-length top with its peasant-style neckline and sleeves were what should be worn to such places, even if it was acceptable.

Finally she decided to journey along the backroads surrounding St. Martinville and discover what the country was like from other than a major highway. Later, when the coolness of the coming night arrived, she could stop at the Longfellow–Evangeline State Park.

St. Martinville was quickly left behind as Jolie chose a secondary highway leading from the city on the east. Traffic was non-existent and she was able to let the little car toodle along at any pace she chose, slowing down when something caught her eye as it often did, or speeding up so the self-generated wind would blow over her face.

Fields of sugar cane dominated the landscape. Some towered over her car while other younger fields barely reached her window. Scattered along both sides of the road were houses, some no different in appearance than those of her home state. Yet occasionally Jolie caught a glimpse of a large two-storey home setting back from the road with finely groomed lawns and rows of oak trees leading back to it. Then she would slow down, striving to see a sign that might identify it as Cameron Hall. But she was always disappointed.

Yielding to the sense of adventure that had taken over her, Jolie turned off the paved road on to a combination dirt and white rock. At least, she thought it was white rock, only to discover that it wasn't rock at all, but sea shells. More cane fields rose on each side of the car until Jolie felt she was being swallowed up by the grasslike crop. Only the distant branches of trees ahead promised a respite from the unbroken scenery of cane.

Jolie was accustomed to associating trees with dwellings. So when the sugar fields gave way to the trees, she was surprised and delighted to have her first look at the stagnant backwater of a marsh. Dismal cypress trees rose gloomily out of their watery habitat. The trees appeared all the more melancholy because of the Spanish moss draped among their branches. Water hyacinths fought with algae for control of the surface, their clogging green leaves giving way only to the tiny islands of marsh grass and the spiky leaves of the palmetto.

The Volkswagen's pace was slowed to that of a turtle as Jolie tried to catch a glimpse of the wildlife of the marsh. Except for an occasional flutter of wings, she saw none, which was a letdown since she would have loved to see an alligator in the wild. Jolie reconciled herself to the fact that this swamp was very small, really only a backwash, and quite probably too near human civilization to boast an alligator.

A few more feet and the swamp gave way to pasture land. The sight of cattle munching on the thick grasses seemed unnatural to Jolie, especially when they appeared to be crossbred with a Brahman. Here were animals that should be in the wild and woolly section of the western United States, instead they were in Louisiana.

The road made a gentle curve around the pasture and Jolie discovered with some surprise that now on the opposite side of the road was a lazy, meandering thread of water that she immediately realized was a bayou. Sunlight shimmered across its mirror-like surface, letting its becalmed state reflect the serenity of a peaceful scene. A crane was feeding along the rushes on the opposite bank where an oak tree's branches dipped low over the water. The ends of the moss draped over its branches were floating in the water.

Jolie decided it was an idyllic place to eat the picnic Mrs. LeBlanc had packed for her. Obligingly there was a turn-off to a field gate on the opposite side of the road where she could park her car without obstructing traffic. She didn't hesitate using it.

With the picnic basket and rug on one arm and

her purse and the Thermos on the other, Jolie crossed the road towards the bayou. Somehow she managed to jump the water-filled ditch that separated the road from the banks of the bayou without dropping anything or slipping in herself.

But even if she had, Jolie thought, it would have been worth it to have a first hand look at this peaceful, tranquillizing scene. The heavy stillness from the heat of the day hung over everything. Any movement was languid and slow like the stalking crane who in slow motion raised and lowered his stilt legs. The calls of the birds were muted, as if conserving energy. There wasn't even the small sound of water lapping against the bank.

Beads of perspiration collected on her forehead where it matted the wispy fringes of her hair and on her upper lip so that the salty taste was on her lips. Without the benefit of the slight breeze that had been generated by her car's movement, her clothes felt sticky, clinging to her skin and increasing the discomfort of the tropical weather.

Kneeling on the short grass, she spread out the rug and arranged the other items beside it. Inside the picnic basket, Mrs. LeBlanc had placed a washcloth already moistened in a plastic bag. Jolie used its cooling dampness to wipe the perspiration from her face. The relief was immediate as the new moisture evaporated from her skin. She gazed about her, slowly continuing the wiping, but now concentrating on her neck and shoulders. The elastic in the scooped neckline of her peasant midriff blouse had been irritating, so she slipped the short sleeves down until the neckline was a straight line from upper arm to upper arm. Tilting her head back, she squeezed the cloth until droplets of water trickled over her shoulders, some finding their way to the cleavage of her breasts.

Her slow wandering gaze travelled from the view of the opposite bank to cover the surroundings nearest her. Fifteen feet to her left was another oak tree, still just a youngster compared to other giants of the same species she had seen. As her gaze trailed down the upper branches to the trunk and the ground below, her hand ceased its cooling motion with the washcloth as Jolie stared at the man reclining beneath the tree. An embarrassing rush of colour warmed her cheeks, for the man was boldly and openly studying her.

Quickly her hands pulled her sleeves to their former positions, returning the midriff blouse to its more modest neckline. At her acknowledgement of his presence, the man rolled gracefully to his feet, moving out of the shade of the tree to within several paces of her. Unwillingly, Jolie moved backward.

'It seems a pity to cover such attractive shoulders.' His drawling voice had a seductive softness that did little to slow the pace of her heart already beating rapidly in fear.

Jolie's hands moved out to collect her various items. 'I'm . . . I'm sorry,' she stammered. 'I didn't realize anyone was here. I'll . . . I'll find another pl . . . place.'

'There's no need,' he replied. 'I'm quite willing to share this view of the bayou.'

Something in his cultured voice seemed to demand that Jolie raise her eyes to him. She found herself staring into the darkest pair of blue eyes that she had ever seen. They gleamed mischievously at her from the shadows of dark, curling eyelashes. In contrast, his brows and hair were black, as black as a shimmering raven's wing. His skin had tanned to a shade of teak brown and there was not the slightest variance in the shade from his legs, bared by the levi cut-offs he wore, to his arms. The man was tall, but not overpoweringly so, standing perhaps just over six foot. His physique was trim, yet not slender, displaying a sinewy strength in his arms without bulging muscles, with fine wide shoulders, a flat stomach and narrow hips.

Her assessment of his physical attributes were made with the lightning speed of the mind, but it didn't go unnoticed by the stranger. He smiled, showing a flash of pearl-white teeth, and Jolie couldn't avoid observing the grooves that deepened on either side of his mouth.

'I promise I won't pounce on you.' The hint of amusement that lurked behind his words sent another tide of pink into her cheeks.

'It never occurred to me that you would,' Jolie lied, knowing full well it was the first thought that entered her mind.

'It should have, because the thought certainly crossed my mind.' His eyes narrowed wickedly as they travelled over her kneeling form.

Jolie longed to take a deep breath, but knew it would betray her discomfort. Instead she continued gathering her gear together.

'I don't want to intrude on your privacy,' she explained when she finally had the courage to speak again.

'You're not.' The man walked over to his place beneath the tree and resumed his reclining position. 'Your picnic isn't going to disturb my fishing, so you might as well stay.'

Her gaze flicked over to the rod and reel propped up by a stick near the bank's edge. Amidst the taller grass near the edge, she spied a red tackle box.

'This is hardly the time of day to fish. It's too hot.' Her natural candour blurted her opinion out before Jolie had a chance to think.

'Sounds like you've done some fishing,' he drawled, only mild interest evident in his voice.

'Some,' Jolie agreed, ceasing her movements that would hasten her leaving.

'I have a theory about fishing at this time of the day,' turning his smile once again on her. 'Want to hear it?'

'What is it?' She settled back on to the wine-coloured rug, her curiosity aroused in spite of her common sense.

'I believe that the big fish are the intelligent ones that have discovered all the tricks a fisherman uses to lure them to the bait. That means they've probably also figured out that fishermen always go fishing when it's the normal feeding time for fish. Therefore the big fish eat during the times that fishermen aren't about. Then he retreats to the bottom, his stomach full, when the fishermen do come.'

'Has your theory proved out?' A smile widened her mouth, carving the ever-present dimples in her cheeks.

'No,' he admitted with a rueful gleam. 'But my worms are getting some exercise.'

Laughter rolled freely out of her throat at his preposterous assertion, but her laughter was silenced when his rod bent nearly double. With breathless disbelief Jolie watched him grab the pole, give it a quick jerk, then pull the line sharply out of the water well up on to the bank. She had a fleeting glimpse of an object on the end of the line before it disappeared from view in the grass. He reached down to pick it up as she scrambled over for a closer look.

'It's a crawdaddy!' she hooted.

'Down here, we call them crawfish,' he corrected, eluding its pincers as he picked it up and placed it in a small pail.

'That's a crawfish?' Jolie stared at it, wonder creeping into her voice that this common creature, a larger version, was the famed crawfish.

'Have you heard the story of the Cajun people and their migration here from Canada?' he asked.

'Yes.' She glanced up at him curiously, wondering what that had to do with a crawfish.

'Have you heard the legend of the crawfish?'

'No,' Jolie replied, accompanying the shake of her head with a slight sound of amusement.

'When the Acadians, or Cajuns, were forced to leave Canada, their close friend, the lobster, who lived in the icy waters around Nova Scotia, hated to see them leave. Naturally there was no room for the lobster to journey with them on the ships taking the Acadians away, so the lobster had to follow behind. They swam all the way down the Atlantic coast, into the Gulf of Mexico, finally arriving in the bayous of Louisiana where the Acadians had made their new home. But the trip had made its mark. Fatigue reduced the lobsters to a quarter of their previous size.' His deep blue eyes glanced towards her, an eyebrow arching as if saying she could believe it or not. 'So goes the legend of the crawfish.'

'Well, whether it's true or a lot of sentimental nonsense, I like it,' she sighed, a hint of satisfaction in the sound.

'Has my children's tale eased your nervousness enough to persuade you to go ahead and have your picnic here?' The impish twinkle was back in his gaze.

'Yes.' A breathlessness crept into her voice as he held her gaze, but Jolie successfully rid herself of it. 'There's plenty to eat. Would you like to join me?'

'I thought you'd never ask,' he teased.

'I didn't want to distract you from proving your theory. I'd hate to think of myself as the cause for the big fish to slip away,' she returned, laughing as she led the way back to where her picnic basket sat. 'Of course, if the big fish are as smart as you think, they probably heard what you said and are wise to your game.'

She liked the hearty sound of his laughter as he joined in with her. But then there were quite a lot of things about this stranger that appealed to her besides his quite devastating good looks, and not the least was his sense of humour. Yet his air of self-assurance, revealed in the clever way he had set about putting her at ease, told Jolie that she was dealing with someone out of her league in experience. She couldn't allow his roguish charm to go to her head.

Even with her own warning ringing in her ears, she couldn't resist returning his smile as he settled on the rug beside her. She placed the bag of potato chips between them before reaching into the basket to withdraw the rest of the fare. Mounds of sliced roast beef had been sandwiched between a loaf of French bread that had been divided in half to provide two portions. Jolie handed one to him and set the other aside for herself.

'You can have your choice of apples or oranges or both,' she offered. 'There's two of each in here.'

'This is plenty, thanks.'

A mutual silence drifted over them as they ate, letting the savoury food predominate. Jolie was forced to admit she was enjoying it. She was under no pretence to keep a witty conversation going, nor was there any personal delving into her life. For the first time she felt free to be herself and not live up to any expectations belonging to someone else, such as her parents or John.

As she reached for the Thermos of lemon-limeade, Jolie realized there was only one cup. Then she shrugged inwardly that it really didn't matter. She filled the cup and passed it to him with a laughing apology that they would have to share the cup as well as the food.

'Are you an Acadian?' Jolie asked when he had passed the cup back to her after drinking his fill.

'Only by way of believing in their philosophy.'

'Which is?'

'"... it is better to live than exist, better to sing than curse, better to make love than war." Or more simply, an Acadian likes strong coffee, laughter, conversation, singing, dancing, rich foods and most of all women.'

'You left out Acadian women. Is that what they like too?' Jolie teased.

'They would probably include babies and gossip and their husbands.'

'That's unfair!' she protested. 'You just said that Acadian men like women, but the Acadian women are restricted to liking their husbands.'

'You have to consider that the Acadians have certain Gallic tendencies that allow them to appreciate the beauty of every woman regardless of their marital status.' Jolie could tell that he was deliberately being provocative, but still it irritated, even if only slightly.

'Always the great lovers, huh?' she said scornfully.

'Don't you find it exciting and romantic for men to pay you compliments?' He took the orange that was in her hand and began peeling it. 'Frenchmen know that women take on an added glow when they're flattered. For instance, he might tell you that your hair is shiny and thick and he wonders what it would be like to tangle his fingers in its feathery curls. Or that your freckles keep you perpetually young with memories of sun-drenched summer days? And those soft brown eyes remind him of a wary doe wondering if she should dare enter a strange meadow?' Blue eyes dwelt thoughtfully on each feature he mentioned. 'And the soft, rounding curve of your lips promises a yielding sweetness.'

His gaze locked on hers, refusing to let her turn away. Jolie realized she was experiencing the full potency of his magnetism. The peeled orange was in his hand and he tore off a section, carrying it to her lips. Her mouth opened automatically to accept it, leaving Jolie with the feeling that she was eating the forbidden fruit.

From somewhere she drew out the sound of amused laughter, forcing herself to break away from his gaze, and wondering why she felt like crying.

'I'm glad that Frenchman isn't around,' she said, trying for lightness as she busied her hands gathering up the remnants of their meal. 'I would have felt guilty shrugging off his patronizing compliments.'

'Is that what they seemed to you?'

'Let's just say that his poetic embellishments were a little too ... poetic.' An unnatural smile curved her mouth. 'But flattery for its own sake usually is.'

He chuckled in answer, adding, 'You're much too critical of your own attractions.'

'Oh, I'm not so falsely modest that I don't realize I'm attractive in my own way,' Jolie explained, feeling a stab of pain in her chest for no apparent reason she could determine. 'But Helen of Troy I'm not.'

'A man wants to make love to a woman, not war over her. A beautiful woman's attractions wane if you constantly have to fight off rivals to prove your love.'

'That's a profound statement.' An unknown anger darkened her eyes as she secured the lock on the picnic basket and started to rise. 'Is that a reverse compliment? Downgrade beauty and upgrade plainness?'

'No, I was only saying that inner beauty is much more attractive than outer beauty.'

Now on her feet, Jolie began juggling the different parcels into her arms. The man was complimenting her, but for some reason he was only succeeding in making her feel more inadequate. She had always been very confident and well able to hold her own against any man, except this man. He had too much sex appeal, too overpowering a personality, and was much too handsome for her to let herself be drawn into any lighthearted dalliance with him. Jolie knew he would come out unscathed, but she had serious doubts about herself. It was just as well that she flee now.

'I hope you don't think I share my food and run, but I'd really better be on my way,' she smiled, refusing to let the bitter taste in her mouth influence her words of goodbye.

'The afternoon is early.' He, too, was on his feet, looking down on her in such a way to make her want to stay.

'But my vacation is short.' Regret crept into her sigh.

He reached out and removed the picnic basket from her hand. It put a dent in her ego that he gave up his persuasion so easily, standing back waiting for her to lead the way to her car. Once everything was stowed in the back seat, Jolie turned to say goodbye.

'You should paint spots on the car to match your freckles,' a finger brushed her cheek in emphasis. 'Then you would both be ladybirds ready to fly away home.'

'That would be a novelty, wouldn't it?' she agreed, unable to meet his compelling eyes. She slipped behind the wheel. 'Thanks for sharing your fishing hole with me.'

'Thanks for the lunch,' he returned.

'Well, goodbye.' The words sounded artificially bright even to Jolie's ears.

'Not goodbye, au revoir. Till we meet again.'

Not much chance of that, Jolie thought, as she started the car and drove away. How could they possibly meet again? He didn't know her name or where she lived, and vice versa. And that was a depressing thought.

CHAPTER FIVE

Guy and his father were attending a meeting of a local men's club. Mrs. LeBlanc was visiting an older relative who was confined to her home. Michelle was sitting on the green plaid-cushioned wicker sofa, school papers spread around her with more that she was correcting on her lap. The record player had an airy instrumental record on its turntable, filling the room with its lighthearted sound. Jolie was in a matching wicker chair trying to finish the letter she had begun to her aunt Brigitte, but she couldn't match the jubilant enthusiasm in the previous writing.

A strong, tanned face with raven black hair and contrasting deep blue eyes kept springing to the forefront of her thoughts. It was frustrating that a stranger she would never see again kept coming back to haunt her. It wasn't as if she had never been around a man quite as attractive as he, because she had. And while she had admired their looks, she certainly hadn't been sent into the doldrums over them. Why was this one so different? Jolie freely admitted to herself that the stranger had fascinated her with his lore of Louisiana, his ready sense of humour, and the lack of any discernible vanity. He had been confident, but not arrogant, teasing without mocking, and knowing without revealing what he knew.

It was ridiculous to keep dwelling on him, she told herself disgustedly. She wasn't a child any more and she was hardly the type to moon over a man whose name she didn't even know. Jolie didn't realize her heaving sigh had been so loud until Michelle's dark eyes had looked up questioningly from behind the gold-rimmed glasses.

'Writing to the boy back home?'

'If I had an ounce of brains, I would be,' Jolie grimaced. 'But I'm writing to my aunt instead.'

'That illogical answer tells me two things,' Michelle chuckled. 'There is a boy back home and you've evidently split with him.'

'Right on both counts.'

'Miss him?'

'No, except every now and then when I get an attack of conscience,' Jolie admitted, a rueful smile lifting the corners of her mouth for a brief moment.

'He loved you, but you didn't love him. That always makes you feel like a louse.' Michelle tapped the papers in her lap into a neat stack and set them with the others on the other half of the couch.

'John was everything a girl looks for in a man—gentle, loving and good-looking. I cared about him a lot, but nothing happened when he kissed me.' Jolie laughed at herself, realizing how juvenile that statement sounded. 'So I guess I'm still in search of Prince Charming.' Inwardly she shouted at the image of the stranger that jumped to mind, ordering him to go away.

' "Lagniappe",' said Michelle, nodding her head firmly.

'What?'

' "Lagniappe"—"something extra" would be the rough translation. It's a word you see quite often in advertisements of Louisiana,' she explained.

The word suited her feelings perfectly, but it didn't give Jolie any more of a clue to what exactly she was looking for. At the present time, the best solution was to take her aunt's advice and not dwell on the problem, but let the passing of time solve it for her.

'I thought I would drive to Opelousas tomorrow, tour the Jim Bowie museum, then stop in Lafayette,' Jolie decided.

The subject was then diverted to the various sights to be seen in the two cities. Yet later, when Jolie was beneath the covers of her bed, sleep was slow in coming. Despite her attempts to think of her excursion the following morning, her mind kept returning to the day's activities. And very few of her thoughts were conducive to sleep. When it did come, it was a tossing, fitful slumber.

Jolie had set out to exhaust herself mentally and physically on her trip to Opelousas and Lafayette. She had succeeded to the point that she couldn't remember if she had seen that peculiar Steamboat Gothic house with the 'widow's walk' in Opelousas or Lafayette before realizing that it had been neither. The house had been in a smaller town called Washington.

Now, the following morning, she practically had to force herself out of the bed. Her sleep had been heavy and she had awoken with the feeling she was drugged. Her mouth felt dry and cottony. Sleep still clung to her heavy-lidded eyes as she slowly descended the stairs.

'Good morning,' Mrs. LeBlanc's lilting voice rang out cheerfully.

Jolie looked about her blankly, finally finding the source when she saw Mrs. LeBlanc near the kitchen doorway. If she had been drinking the day before, Jolie didn't think she could have felt much worse than she did at the present moment. With leaden movements, she walked to the kitchen.

'There's some fresh squeezed orange juice in the jug,' the woman told her, 'and the glasses are in the right-hand cupboard above the sink. What would you like for breakfast?'

'Just some toast and coffee is good enough,' said Jolie, retrieving a glass from the cupboard. Stifling a yawn, she poured the orange juice in the glass, eager to rid her mouth of its sleep taste.

'What are your plans for today?' Mrs. LeBlanc asked as she set a plate of toast in front of her and returned to the counter for the coffee.

'None, really. I thought maybe I'd go out to the State Park here in St. Martinville,' she replied in between refreshing sips of the citrus drink.

'Good. You remember me speaking about one of our friends who owns an old plantation?'

Jolie struggled for his name. 'Etienne?'

'Yes,' the older woman smiled brightly. 'He telephoned yesterday while you were gone. I mentioned you were staying with us and were anxious to see some of the sights around here, and he very generously offered to show you around his place today.'

'Today?' Jolie echoed. She really didn't know if she was in the mood to spend time with some talkative elderly Frenchman.

'He suggested that you stop out around ten this morning, before the heat of the day. I never thought to ask him, but he might know something about the plantation you're trying to find.'

'Cameron Hall?' Well, that pretty well settled it, Jolie thought to herself. Cameron Hall was the reason she had come down here. It would be foolish to pass up the first opportunity that presented itself to talk to someone who might know about it.

'I told him I was quite sure you'd come. You are, aren't you?' For the first time, Mrs. LeBlanc noticed Jolie's lack of enthusiasm for the invitation.

'Oh, I'd love to.' Jolie managed to shake the sleep away long enough to nod vigorously.

'The Temple, Etienne's plantation, is some miles from town.' Mrs. LeBlanc smiled, reassured that Jolie was interested in her friend's invitation. 'I'll write down the directions how to get there.'

At nine-thirty Jolie set out for Etienne's plantation. Her spirits had still not returned to their previous level of buoyancy. And the imaginary clouds didn't disappear when she discovered that Mrs. LeBlanc's instructions led her in the same direction as the one she had taken the day she met the stranger. She was perversely glad when they finally deviated from her previous course into another section of the countryside. She didn't want to go back to where those blue eyes would haunt her again.

A dirt road branched off to her left bearing the sign 'Private Road—No Trespassing'. This was it,

Jolie sighed, a flicker of interest piercing her boredom now that her destination was near. Mrs. LeBlanc had told her the house would be on her left about a quarter mile from the turn-off on to the dirt road. A dilapidated fence ran parallel with the road. In most places the wire had long since been parted from the posts, but there was little chance that anyone would be able to enter the property that way unless they possessed a machete. A dense growth of vines, shrubbery and spiky palmettoes lay at the feet of a row of pine trees.

No matter how hard Jolie attempted to peer through the tangled growth, all she was able to see was a glimpse of something large and white. It had to be the plantation, but it was invisible from the road. Two crumbling white pillars marked the entrance which was blocked by padlocked iron grillework gates. It was beginning to become obvious to her that prosperity had turned its back on this plantation. She was also beginning to wonder what kind of an eccentric character this Etienne would turn out to be.

Parking her Volkswagen on the side of the narrow lane, Jolie got out and walked over to the gate, looking through the bars trying to see some sign of life. The place looked deserted. Then she spied the bell suspended on the side of one of the pillars. She pulled the rope attached to it and the strident ding-dong rang shrilly in the stillness. That harsh, unmelodic sound had to rouse someone, Jolie thought, walking over to stand in front of the gate.

There was a sudden rustle of brush, followed by a whirlwind sound coming towards her. Suddenly she was staring into the bared, snarling white fangs of a dog, his front feet on the gate until he was eye-level with her. Her heart was in her throat. Her feet were rooted to the ground as she stared at the growling German Shepherd, black as a midnight sky without moon or stars. This was hardly the greeting or greeter that she had anticipated. Although why she should be surprised at anything connected with this derelict plantation, she didn't know.

Mobility finally returned to her as she realized that the dog couldn't get beyond the gate. She didn't intend to stick around to see what Mr. Etienne whoever-he-was was like. She was going back to St. Martinville. Just as she turned towards her car, a voice rang out clear and commanding.

'Black, heel!'

Jolie turned back in time to see the dog's snarling mouth change into a laughing grin as he came down on all fours. With a wagging tale, he reversed his direction and raced towards the man just coming into view. Jolie stared incredulously as he gave the dog a rewarding pat before continuing towards her. It was the stranger from the bayou!

'I hope you'll forgive Black's greeting.' His smile danced out at her, highlighted by the audacious twinkle in his blue eyes. 'He isn't accustomed to strangers, even if they are attractive young ladies.'

'I came . . .' The words stuck in her throat as she continued to gaze at him in a mixture of bewildered astonishment. 'Y-you're . . . You're Etienne?'

'At your service, Miss Jolie Antoinette Smith.' As his head dipped in a bow, his dark hair glistened as blackly as the dog's.

'But how ... I mean ... did you know?' She was stammering like a schoolgirl.

'I was fairly certain I recognized the picnic basket and Josephine's touch with the food. My phone call confirmed it.'

The gate was unlocked and swung open to admit her. Now that the initial surprise had passed, Jolie felt a heady feeling overtake her as she realized that Etienne had sought her out. And her own pleasure at finding him again was revealed in her sparkling brown eyes. She stepped past the barred gate, stopping just inches inside as a question suddenly occurred to her.

'Why didn't you tell Mrs. LeBlanc you'd already met me the day before?'

He had closed the gate behind her and stood so close to her she was almost touching him. His nearness almost took her breath away, especially when she looked into the unfathomable expression in his dancing blue eyes.

'Why didn't you?' he countered smoothly, asking the question in such a way that Jolie felt he already knew the answer.

'I didn't have your advantage of being able to deduce where you were staying.' The faintest blush of pink touched her cheeks before Jolie was able to step away from his disturbing nearness. 'Besides, how would it have sounded if I'd told her about that afternoon?' she laughed hesitantly. 'How could I have said, "Mrs. LeBlanc, I shared my picnic lunch with this man today. He had dark hair, vivid blue eyes, somewhere in his thirties, but I don't know what his name was"? That would have sounded just a little bit strange.'

'Not strange.' He shook his head at her and smiled. 'A bit forward for you, perhaps, which is why I almost didn't call.'

'Didn't call? Why?' Confusion knitted her forehead as Etienne took her arm and began leading her down the narrow path towards the plantation.

'In the past, it's always been my policy to stay away from spirited virgins. They tend to complicate your life ... and your conscience.'

For only a moment did the stabbing hurt flicker in her eyes before Jolie concealed it, damning the look of innocence she had been born with. She knew his gaze was dwelling on her. If he had any doubts about his verdict that she was a virgin, her own reaction had confirmed it.

'Then why did you bother?' she asked stiffly, riveting her gaze on the overgrown path they were walking.

'I haven't decided. It was an impulse, I guess.'

His hand tightened on her arm, checking her stride and bringing her to a halt beside him. Jolie stared down at his polished black shoes and his ivory white slacks. Gathering courage, she raised her eyes past the silk shirt with its large white flowers etched against a background of bright blue that intensified the colour of his eyes gazing into her own. He was every inch the commanding plantation owner.

'But, Jolie,' she couldn't stop the tingle of pleasure tickling the back of her neck at the quiet way he said her name, 'I'm glad that I gave in to that impulse.'

She wanted to say that she was glad, too, but it would have been too revealing of her own budding feelings for this man. To deny that she was would have been an outright lie, and Etienne was much too perceptive not to know. Since nothing she could say would be right, she didn't reply at all.

'Are you sorry you came?' Etienne asked.

With his thoughtful gaze observing every nuance of her expression, she didn't bother to lie. 'I'm not sorry I came,' she replied easily, summoning all her pride to meet his scrutiny without flinching.

A ghost of a smile teased the corners of his mouth. 'You're remarkable. Honesty is not usually a virtue found in women.'

'Nor in men.' Jolie immediately regretted the sharpness that had been in her answering retort.

A throaty chuckle accompanied his full flashing white smile and Jolie felt the warmth flooding her cheeks. She quickly resumed walking, too conscious of the man beside her.

'Your tongue has barbs.' The laughing sound was still in Etienne's voice. 'I think we're going to have a very enjoyable day, Black.'

His teasing words were addressed to the German Shepherd padding contentedly beside him. Jolie's glittering brown eyes cast a venomous look at his confident expression, angered that he was so sure of her attraction to him. His gaze caught the look, his blue eyes deflecting the daggers with amusement. Jolie determinedly looked away from him, forcing her attention ahead of her.

The dense growth had thinned without Jolie being aware of it. Her steps faltered, then ceased altogether as an unobstructed view spread out before her. Dominating the scene rose a mansion of such colossal proportions that it took Jolie's breath away. Immense pillars surrounded the square building, supporting a second floor balcony as well as the heavy cornice crown of the flat roof. Yet its height was so awesome that Jolie couldn't begin to guess how tall it was. Shutters of dark green accented the floor-to-ceiling windows on each floor and complemented the exterior that had weathered to a pale yellow with age, while patches of flaking paint indicated the wooden railings on the upper balcony had once been white.

In spite of the blemishes that had accumulated on the more than century-old structure, there was still that undefinable air of majesty about it. The severity of its heavy Greek architecture gave it an almost regal dignity that carried it through, even in the face of partial deteroriation. Overpowering, palatial, stately, all the adjectives that sprang to Jolie's mind seemed to be inadequate.

Adding to its magnificence, the plantation was surrounded by oak trees of the size and girth that astounded Jolie regardless of how many times she had seen them in her few trips in the area. Their branches were the size of a normal tree trunk and jutted out at right angles with the trunk, here and there dipping so close to the ground that a person could sit on them as if they were a chair. As always, their leafy arms were draped with greenish grey Spanish moss, turning the gnarled giants into picturesque wise old men with flowing grey beards.

Jolie finally tore her gaze away from the impressive scene, her dazzled expression turning towards Etienne. He was smiling at her gently, sympathetically aware of how moving a sight the plantation was.

'The Temple always affects a stranger that way,' he said, when she could still find no words to express herself.

'It is like a temple,' she breathed, shifting her gaze back to the mansion. 'How lucky you are to own it.'

'She owns me.' Etienne smiled ruefully, his gaze following Jolie's as his hand moved to the small of her back and they resumed their walk towards the mansion. 'And she's a much more demanding mistress than any one woman I've ever known. I saw her for the first time four years ago. A year later I gave in and bought her.'

'I thought the Temple was your family's home, that it had been passed down to you through generations,' Jolie glanced at him in slight surprise.

'If it had, I would never have allowed it to get into the state she was in when I bought her. She was being used as a cattle barn.' Jolie didn't have to see his face to know that anger was lurking just below the surface. And she agreed with him, her stomach knotting at such irreverence.

Five steps led to the wooden porch and the enormous double door leading inside. Jolie noticed the new sections of planking that had replaced rotting boards on the porch as Etienne opened one of the doors and waited for her to precede him into the interior of the house. At first the dimness was acute, then her eyes adjusted to the absence of the glaring sunlight. A coolness assailed her as she gazed about her.

'The walls are approximately two feet thick and keep the temperature at about seventy-four degrees year round,' Etienne explained when she shivered slightly at the sudden drop in temperature.

The wide hallway split the house in half with another set of double doors leading outside directly ahead of Jolie. On one side of the hallway there were four doors, and three doors and an oval spiral staircase were on the other side. With the exception of a table in the hallway, the place was barren of any furnishings. Etienne grasped her elbow and guided her further down the hall.

'All the floors in the downstairs had been destroyed by the cattle. I just had them replaced last winter.' His eyes were an even darker shade of blue when he glanced at her. She knew their glittering darkness was for the mistreatment of the house.

Jolie followed silently as he pointed out the butler's pantry, the large room—equivalent to the present day living room, the dining room, the office where the plantation owner directed the day's activities and maintained his records, and a smaller room used as a sitting room-parlour. All the rooms were without furniture and in various stages of re-finishing. Jolie noted the harsh lines about his face as he explained that the carved fireplaces in each room had been vandalized and beyond restoration. New ones were being constructed, but she sensed his indignation that the beauty of the originals were never again to be appreciated by anyone.

'We can be thankful that cattle never showed any inclination for stairs.' Etienne smiled, leading her back to the staircase. 'Because this mansion possesses a magnificent one. A self-supporting oval spiral, the steps are made of cypress and the carved balustrades are mahogany. There are no nails. Each post is individually fitted to the stairs and railing.'

The wood still maintained its lustre and was satiny smooth to the touch. Jolie couldn't resist letting her hand trail along its surface as they climbed the steps to the second floor. Here the fireplaces in the bedrooms were untouched, although they did show signs of neglect, except for one that Etienne had cleaned, re-stained and varnished. There was more furniture, too, but most of it had too many layers of dirt for its beauty to be seen. He showed her an exceptionally old armoire, explaining that clothes were not hung on hangers, but folded and placed in the drawers contained behind the doors of the tall forerunner of the present-day chest of drawers.

Then he led her back into the hallway which was a duplicate of the one downstairs, dividing the second floor into equal parts with double doors at each end leading on to the upper gallery. It was through one of these doors that Jolie was taken and the view was breathtaking. It took her a few minutes to realize that she was at the opposite side from which she had entered the house and looking at the rear lawns. A ribbon of shining water winked at her beyond more clusters of giant oaks and magnolias.

'Is that a pond down there?' She turned excitedly

to Etienne, who was also gazing over his land with a proprietorial air.

'That's Bayou Teche. Roads were practically non-existent in the old days. All plantations were close to one bayou or another since they were the major routes of transportation, just as the first plantations followed the Missisippi River so they would have ready access to transport their products,' he explained. 'The waterways were the roads in early day Louisiana.'

Jolie nodded, realizing the logic of it. She started to look back to the lawns when a thought suddenly occurred to her.

'You didn't show me the kitchens. Where are they?'

'The fear of fire was too great for them to ever be in the main house.' Etienne smiled at her strictly feminine question. 'I found some foundations that I think was probably for the kitchen near the north side, not far from the dining room.'

'Where do you live?' The dancing gleam sprang quickly into his eyes at her impulsive question. It momentarily flustered her. 'I mean, you obviously can't . . . well, live in the house. Not yet, anyway.'

'Come.' He reached out and took her hand, the warmth of his touch sending tremors through her. 'I'll show you where I live.'

CHAPTER SIX

ETIENNE led her back downstairs and out the same door they had entered. Then he turned to the left, instead of taking the path leading to her car. As they rounded the mansion, Jolie spied a petite version of the Temple.

'It's a miniature replica of the house!' she exclaimed in delight.

'Commonly known as a garçonnière where the younger or unmarried male members of the family resided. *Garçon* is the French word for boy.' He released her hand to open the screen door, then brought it back to take her shoulder as he escorted her inside.

It was only one large room with stairs leading to the second floor and a lace grillework partition sectioning off the kitchen area. The furnishings were simple, all functional, and completely masculine. The pressure of his hand guided Jolie further into the room. She felt like a fly being lured by a spider. She was slowly being spun into a web that she couldn't escape.

'Would you like a cold drink?' Etienne's voice had taken on a seductive quality, its caressing softness coming from somewhere near her ear. Or was it only her imagination interpreting it to be so? The hand left her shoulder as Etienne stepped away from her towards the kitchen. Jolie walked hesitantly about the small room, too conscious of their isolation to feel comfortable. It suddenly seemed so terribly improper to be in Etienne's house, which was really ridiculous considering how she had roamed John Talbot's house at will. Yet the feeling of intimacy continued to wrap itself about her.

'Lemonade.' Etienne held out a glass to her.

Warily Jolie glanced up to his eyes that had narrowed at the slight trembling in her hand when she had taken the glass. His dark, curling lashes shadowed the blueness of his eyes.

'Perhaps we should sit outside. You might be more comfortable there.'

Now he mocked her, but Jolie seized the suggestion anyway. Once outside in the lawn chairs, conversation lagged. Etienne seemed content to gaze at the house that dominated the scenery, his eyes occasionally straying about the lawn. Jolie took the opportunity to study him. Since their previous meeting, he had changed. He wasn't quite the same person she had met, or thought she had met.

There was still the same litheness of movement, the instinctive grace of an athlete. The unnaturally dark blue eyes still gleamed with amusement and the smile was just as ready to show the grooves deepening near his mouth. Yet before Etienne had given her the impression of indolence, laziness, a devil-may-care approach to life. And today—today Jolie had seen something else. The purposeful set of his jaw, the finely chiselled, slightly aristocratic nose that could flare with distaste, the blue eyes that flickered with burning anger, and the overwhelming strength that emanated like an aura around him. But she was struck not only by his inborn dignity, but also by his iron-willed determination that indicated he might be quite ruthless if it was required.

'Have you decided whether I can be trusted?' His face was turned away from her. His strong profile was etched against the backdrop of trees. Yet he had been completely aware of her scrutiny.

'I think,' Jolie fought back the briefly rising flush of embarrassment, 'that if you put a gold ring in your ear, you would make an excellent pirate.'

'From some women that might be a compliment.' Now he turned to study her and Jolie avoided meeting his penetrating gaze. 'What a pity I'm only a poor plantation owner.'

'The best things in life are free,' Jolie quipped, seeking a lighter topic.

'Don't you believe it!' The sound that accompanied his derisive words was a combination of laughter and disdain. 'You pay dearly for everything in one way or another.'

'And what is the price for love?' The cynical tone in his voice startled her.

'The most precious thing a man has, his freedom.' His eyes were harsh and piercing as he glanced over at her.

'Are you one of those exasperating men who are determined to be confirmed bachelors?' Jolie laughed, not at all sure just how she should take his remarks.

'Are you one of those exasperating women who believe happiness ends in marriage?' he retorted.

'Yes and no.' Her chin tilted upwards in bright defiance. 'I believe happiness begins in love and continues in marriage, but I'm a died-in-the-wool romantic.'

'You're truthful.' A quirk of his eyebrow revealed his amusement. 'Tell me, what is love?'

Jolie breathed in sharply, then slowly exhaled as she turned her gaze outwards towards the bright sunlight bathing the house in a deeper yellow glow. 'I don't know. I've never been in love. What about you?'

'Many times.' The full force of his magnetic blue eyes were turned on her and she felt the full power of his virility. 'Which is why I don't believe in it.'

'If your freedom is so precious to you, why did you tie yourself down to this plantation? You said yourself that it's more demanding than any woman.'

'You listen to what a man says. That's another rare trait.' His gaze moved over her slowly. 'I was tired of travelling, of not having any roots. And this place bore my name.'

'I don't understand.' She tilted her head questioningly at him.

'I'll show you,' he laughed, sitting his glass on the tiled porch floor of the garçonnière, and Jolie did the same.

His arm slipped around her waist as he assisted her down the narrow steps of the porch. Jolie felt her throat tightening at his easy intimacy that she couldn't match with the same degree of indifference. Etienne puzzled her; he was an enigma. She couldn't help wondering what had happened to him that had made him so wary of women. No, he wasn't wary; he was disillusioned. Of course, a man with his enormous attractiveness would gather women like flies to honey. Perhaps in his case, familiarity bred contempt.

'If you felt the need to settle down, then haven't you ever wished for children of your own?' Jolie asked, finding the silence of their stroll led her thoughts in channels she wasn't prepared to take yet. Besides, the arm around her shoulder was much too disturbing for coherent thought.

Her stomach somersaulted as Etienne looked down on her, his eyes resting on her lips a little too long for her peace of mind. What was worse, Jolie couldn't help wondering what it would be like if he kissed her. She had guessed from the beginning that he would be very experienced in the art of making love.

'Children aren't just a product of marriage.'

There was such wickedness in his smile that Jolie knew he was attempting to shock her.

'It's convenient for the child if it is,' keeping her voice calm, not reacting to his taunt.

'Spoken very properly.'

Etienne halted their strolling pace, his hand squeezing her arm in an unspoken order to remain where she was while he walked to a flowering shrub and broke off one of the large white blooms. He walked back to her, bringing the petals to his nose to sniff the fragrance before offering it to Jolie. As her fingers closed over his hand to take the short stem, he didn't immediately release it, forcing her hand to linger with his.

'Virtue should always be rewarded,' he said in a

husky, drawling voice that enveloped her in his virility. A little rosy hue stole over her face when he finally released it and she tried to hide it in a silent appreciation of the velvet smoothness of the petals.

She stole a glance at his face through the veil of her lashes. A suppressed smile was on his face that was now turned ahead of them. It hurt to discover that her lack of sophistication amused him. His arm was back around her waist, guiding her closer towards the shining mirror of water.

A pillar, ageing and pockmarked, stood forlornly near the water. Its mate lay in a rubble of bricks and stucco in the tall grass. Here along the bayou was the front entrance to the plantation that had once matched the gates Jolie had entered but now had fallen to ruin. Etienne led her to the one standing pillar.

'This is what led to my final decision that the Fates wanted me to buy the house,' he said quietly.

At his curious statement, Jolie followed his solemn gaze to the pillar. Amidst the gouges of time there were fading letters carved into the standing pillar. They were so faint that it took some time for Jolie to make out the word. There was a sudden tightening in her chest as the significance registered.

'Cameron!' she breathed so softly that it was barely audible, blinking hard to make sure the word was not a figment of her imagination. It wasn't. She stared back at the mansion, standing in all its regal glory amidst the giant oaks before turning to Etienne, tears of exultation filling her brown eyes.

'I've found it!' Her voice squeaked with emotion. 'I've found Cameron Hall!'

Her hands reached out for his as her happiness bubbled over. Her delight bewildered him and she managed to control her exuberance long enough to give him the sketchy details. The wonder of her discovery wiped away the reserve that she had erected in defence of his masculinity. When Etienne joined in with her happiness, Jolie found herself slipping quite easily into his arms.

'Can you believe it?' she exclaimed, letting her arms twine around him as they stared at the name etched on the pillar. Her head leaned naturally against his broad chest as she sighed her happiness. 'No one I questioned had ever heard of Cameron Hall. I was afraid I would never find it.' Her voice was husky and emotion-filled. 'And now I find your home is it.'

She raised her head to gaze into his eyes, her face radiant with the thrilling discovery. She sensed more than felt Etienne catch his breath as he looked down upon her, his eyes turning a darker shade of blue. And she became conscious of the pressure of his thighs against her, the muscular hardness of his chest, and the firm caress of his hands on her back and shoulders. Her heart skipped a beat, then accelerated. She felt Etienne's arms tighten about her. The sensuous curve of his lips moved nearer.

Jolie knew she should break her gaze away from the hypnotic darkness of his eyes, but it was impossible. His head had to bend quite a distance to reach her lips and Etienne didn't hurry to close the gap. Jolie felt as if she was on the brink of another discovery. 'Lagniappe'. The word danced in her thoughts.

Then his lips were on hers, soft and gentle like the petals on the flower he had given her. The tenseness that had held Jolie immobilized melted away in the flood of warmth as his lips moved persuasively against hers. There was no thought of resistance, so she simply responded. Her yielding brought an added possessiveness to his kiss that sent tremors quaking through her body. When Etienne dragged his mouth from hers and brought his hands up to cup the face she would have turned away, Jolie felt cheated. That she had just been given something beautiful and it had been taken away. The disappointment was mirrored in her clouded brown eyes.

'I've been wanting to do that from the first moment I saw you.' His face was only inches away from hers.

She had moved her hands from his back to rest against his chest. She intended to disentangle herself from his embrace, but the feel of his heart thudding against her hand stopped her. The roughness of his thumb caressed her lips, parting them slightly before he claimed them again. This time there was no gentle exploration as Jolie's arms wound around his neck in artless abandon, succumbing to the desire to let her fingers curl into his black hair. The flame that blazed within her seemed to be in him too. His arms moved to her back, arching her against him in an attempt to fuse them together.

A moan escaped her lips when his mouth deserted hers to ravage her ear lobe and the pulsating cord in her neck. A curious ringing sound was in her ears as the ache to have his lips on hers became too much to bear. She was crushed so tightly against him that she couldn't breathe, but breath didn't seem to be necessary to life. This was 'lagniappe', the something extra she had been looking for all her life. Then his hands moved to her arms, firmly drawing them from around his neck to hold them tightly against his chest.

Jolie couldn't bring herself to meet his gaze, feeling a spark of shame that she had responded much too openly to his kisses. She stared instead at the darkly tanned hands that clasped hers, experiencing a thrill at the ragged breathing that said Etienne had not been untouched by the passionate embrace.

'Do I thank you or your ancestor for that?' Etienne asked softly.

Peering up at him, Jolie saw his eyes still glittering beneath the partially closed lids. She knew a sudden desire for experience that would have enabled her to make some witty rejoinder. After one embrace, it was idiotic to tell a man you were falling in love with him.

'Both,' she ended up whispering.

'Stay to lunch with me.' His hands tightened on hers as if challenging her to disobey the order.

She had the impression that if she refused he would sweep her into his arms again and kiss her until she relented. She hesitated, wondering whether she didn't want him to do just that.

'Jolie,' Etienne murmured, and she felt his body

straining towards her. Her vulnerability was too great. Another tempestuous embrace like the last and she might agree to anything.

'I'd like to stay.' She swallowed convulsively as she looked into his face.

The very look in his eyes told her she had been right in thinking he would have had his way in one manner or another. She hadn't realized the tenseness that had been between them until Etienne relaxed, bringing one of her hands up to his mouth where he brushed her palm with a kiss.

'At the moment, food is farthest from my mind,' he sighed with a half smile as he turned Jolie until she was nestled under his arm. He held her so closely against him that it made walking difficult, but Jolie didn't mind.

They retraced their steps back towards the plantation. Jolie couldn't help thinking that the big house was looking down at them with satisfaction. She breathed in deeply, drinking in every scent and sound that surrounded this happiest of all moments. Not only had she discovered Cameron Hall, but Etienne as well, and a smile as golden as the sun radiated from her face. When they entered the tiny replica of the plantation, Etienne pulled her again into his arms.

'Is it really necessary that we feed that hunger now?'

Jolie felt the warmth spreading through her loins at the lean hardness of his body against her. Her resolve to remain level-headed was nearly swept away with the fiery desire for his kiss.

'We ... we should, yes.' Her breathy stammer

wasn't too convincing. Blue eyes narrowed on her face that tried to remain composed.

'You're right, of course.' The rueful grimace was meant to appear playful, but Jolie caught the fleeting glimpse of repressed anger.

'Etienne?' Her hand touched his arm to stop him when he moved away from her. He stared down at her puzzled expression that couldn't understand what she had done to upset him.

'Don't look at me like that.' There was no softness in his face. 'I might not win the next battle with my conscience, and you've already destroyed my peace of mind.'

Her question was answered and Jolie was appropriately subdued. She recognized that he was a man who seldom settled for chaste kisses and unless she wanted to deal with the consequences, she had best let him lead the way. Something in her expression must have mirrored her wavering confidence, because Etienne lifted her drooping chin and planted a kiss on her lips.

'I forgot to tell you,' he smiled. His mood changed with quicksilver rapidity. 'You have to help fix lunch.'

'Oh, I'm very good at that.' Jolie adopted his lighter mood quickly. 'I have a diploma in home economics.'

'I'm impressed. We must definitely put that training to use.' Etienne walked to the refrigerator and opened the door. 'What would a home economics graduate make out of lettuce, left-over ham, boiled eggs and tomatoes? Something tasty, I hope, since that's the sum total of my food.'

She laughed easily now. 'If you're able to conjure up some oil and vinegar and some spices, I might be able to make us a chef's salad.'

'That's my speciality,' he assured her. 'Leave the dressing to me.'

Jolie never did discover exactly how Etienne prepared the dressing, since she was busy with her own chores. But one taste of the delicately flavoured dressing had whetted the appetite she didn't think she possessed. Etienne very wisely turned their conversation to his plans for the restoration of the plantation. Although Jolie was interested, every now and then she found herself studying the gleam of his black hair in the sunlight or the sharp contrast his blue eyes made to the darkness of the rest of his features and ended up catching only snatches of his plans. Just looking at his strikingly handsome face and feeling the masculinity that emanated from him sent Jolie reeling, unable to believe that he could be attracted to her.

'... on rainy days, I've been re-finishing the wood on a Victorian sofa and two matching chairs,' he was saying, swirling the white wine that accompanied their meal. 'One more coat of varnish and the sofa will be finished, except for re-upholstering, which I'll have to pay dearly to have done.'

'Upholstery?' Jolie exclaimed. The familiar subject caught her attention. 'It's a hobby of mine.'

Etienne glanced up sharply, causing her to blush. She hadn't meant to force him into a position of asking her to help.

'I'm ... I'm really quite good at it,' she said quickly. 'I used to earn money for college doing it.'

'I don't doubt that you're capable. I remembered you saying you were only here on vacation. It just occurred to me that you would be leaving.'

An inexpressible surge of joy swelled her chest as she realized his tight-lipped expression had nothing to do with upholstering, but her eventual departure. He did care for her.

'I planned to stay for three weeks.' It was hard keeping her voice calm. 'Or until my money ran out.'

'I could pay you for your time.' A dangerous light glittered in his eyes. 'If it would keep you here longer.'

'You might regret that offer,' Jolie laughed tightly, her hands toying with her glass of wine.

Etienne hesitated before replying. 'It would be a shame if you had to leave when you've only just found Cameron Hall.'

'And you? What about you?' Jolie thought silently, wondering why he had chosen his words with such care. He obviously didn't want to commit himself. Just because she felt so sure of her feelings towards him did not make the reverse true. He found her physically attractive, of that he had left her in no doubt. But he was a man, and love was not a necessary emotion to them when it came to making love. Or at least, not to the same degree as it was to a woman. Besides, he had already told her he didn't believe in love.

A nervousness captured her hands. She quickly busied them stacking the dishes to carry them to the porcelain sink. She knew Etienne was watching her intently, but she didn't know what to say. It was beyond her previous experience. She grasped at the one subject that led down the middle road.

'I'm glad Cameron Hall hasn't been restored,' keeping her voice light as she carried the dishes to the sink. 'There's more atmosphere of how it was long ago than if it were filled with priceless antiques. That sounds contradictory, doesn't it?'

She turned to address her question to Etienne, whom she had left sitting at the small table, only to find him standing directly behind her. He was towering over her, making her feel like an insignificant dwarf. The feeling was intensified by the enigmatic expression that had darkened his eyes.

'You're a domestic creature.' His blunt words brought a flicker of pain in her eyes. She couldn't believe his eyes could look so cold. 'Marriage has never been a part of my plans, Jolie.'

'What am I supposed to say to that?' She swallowed at the tears trying to spring forward.

'Nothing.' The retort was sharp and clipped while his gaze burned its cold fire over her face. 'I didn't want any pretence raising its ugly head.'

'However I may look, I'm not a child!' Temper rising quickly to defend her.

A corner of his mouth lifted in a half smile. 'No, you're all woman—I've already discovered that.' That powerful magnetic charm reached out to pull Jolie beneath his spell. She started to move around him, ostensibly to gather the rest of the dishes, but an arm shot out to block the way.

'And in spite of my common sense that tells me to get you out of here before I hurt you, I keep thinking of reasons for you to stay.'

His voice was a caressing whisper against her hair as he moved closer, pinioning her against the sink. Jolie felt her knees weakening and knew that if her hands let go of the counter top they would find their way around his neck. She forced herself to turn around, staring at the dirty dishes in the sink.

'Did you know "Jolie" translates into "pretty" in French?' he asked huskily.

'And Etienne,' she gulped, his closeness cutting off her breath. 'What does it translate to?'

'Steven.' His mouth found the hollow between her shoulder and her neck. Jolie groaned and moved so swiftly away from him that he was unable to check her flight.

'I don't even know your name.' A sudden stab of something akin to fear pierced her heart. Wild panic trembled over her as she remembered Michelle and Guy speaking of a man named Steve.

He was looking at her with puzzled wariness. 'Surely Josep ... Mrs. LeBlanc told you who I am? Cameron, my name is Steve Cameron.'

'She called you Etienne,' Jolie said quietly, realizing there could not be another man that would fit Michelle's adjective phrase—Fire burns and if you get too near Steve you get scorched. The LeBlanc family considered him to be staked out as Claudine LeBlanc's property.

'She's always called me Etienne,' he concluded.

CHAPTER SEVEN

PIECES of the puzzle began to rain on Jolie's head, forming a picture she wasn't sure she could figure out. Guy had referred to Steve as a very formidable opponent. That was an understatement, considering the way her defences had collapsed under his very first advance. Steve Cameron. No wonder the name Cameron on the pillar had persuaded him to buy the plantation!

Through the haze of her racing thoughts, Jolie looked at Etienne who was now Steve Cameron. How could she have been so obtuse not to realize that this extremely masculine male had to be the one Guy and Michelle had described? He was watching her calmly, exhibiting only the slightest interest in her bewilderment.

'I feel very foolish.' An embarrassed laugh accompanied her words. 'Guy and Michelle mentioned you—as Steve, but when Mrs. LeBlanc talked about Etienne, I pictured an elderly man. Even after I met you, I didn't put two and two together until just now.'

'I can understand Guy wanting to protect his claim, but why Michelle?' Although the question was asked, Jolie had the feeling he wasn't the slightest bit interested in the answer as his gaze roved over her thoughtfully.

'Guy has no claim on me.' She hated the knowing smile that sprang to his mouth. He knew that already. 'I merely asked Michelle about you because she was there when Guy mentioned you. She only described you. Not physically, but——'

'Don't tell me Michelle considers me to be a dangerous person?' he chuckled, leaning back against the counter with a complacent expression on his face.

'Not to her,' Jolie said quickly.

'Am I dangerous to you?' The blue eyes darkened with his seductively soft words.

Danger meant harm. Did he have the ability to hurt her? She was so close to falling in love with him without any assurances that he even cared for her as anything other than a female willing to reciprocate his passion. Yes, Steve Cameron was dangerous to her, but that would be revealing too much of her own feelings to admit it.

'Don't be silly. I know you wouldn't physically harm me.' The half truth sprang easily to her lips as she quickly began gathering the rest of the dishes from the table. 'Did ... did Mrs. LeBlanc tell you that Claudine was coming home this Saturday?'

'Yes, she mentioned it,' he replied with marked indifference, taking the dishes from her and placing them in the sink with the others. 'Leave them,' he ordered. 'I want your opinion on the furniture I'm re-finishing.'

Jolie's lips compressed tightly at his adept shifting of the conversation from his personal life. She was no more knowledgeable about his relationship with Claudine than she had been before. 'I may be inexperienced,' Jolie thought determinedly, 'but I'm not a shy, retiring little country girl who can be put off so easily.'

'I understand you and Claudine are quite close?' Defiantly she raised her chin so he could see the glint of determination in her eyes as he led her out of the garçonnière.

If she had expected him to be taken back by her directness, she was mistaken. If anything, Steve Cameron was amused.

'You can thank Claudine for me being here,' he said cryptically.

'What do you mean?'

'I met her in New Orleans and she invited me to visit her parents, which I did—with Claudine along, naturally. It was during that visit that she brought me out here to have a picnic while she did some sketchings of the plantation. Later I bought the place.'

Jolie didn't have the nerve to ask if it was because of Claudine. 'What do you do for a living?'

'I live,' he shrugged, the grooves deepening around his mouth at Jolie's wide-eyed expression. 'I raise sugar cane which brings in enough money to keep the mortgage up to date and make a few improvements in the house. There's a vegetable garden that grows all the year round and I have a milk cow that faithfully gives me a calf to butcher each year. I'm not plagued with any ambitions for power and wealth. Does that disappoint you?'

'No. You just appear to be the type that could succeed at anything. Commanding others would come natural to you.'

Her answer hardened his features, highlighting the hint of ruthlessness around his mouth that had once led her to associate him with the pirates of the old days.

'The furniture is in here.' He adeptly avoided commenting on her statement as he opened the large door of a weatherworn building.

Jolie didn't have the opportunity to pursue the subject further because Steve steered the conversation to the furniture. His technical questions made it quite clear that he was knowledgeable in reupholstering. And Jolie was thankful that she could reply intelligently. It was strange how important it was to her for him to think well of her and her abilities.

When they had strolled out of the small building, Steve had given Jolie the go-ahead to pick out samples of material that they could go over together. Yet, even though she was certain of seeing him again, the intimacy that had encircled them was gone. Steve was urbane and charming, just as he had been the first time she had met him, but there seemed to be nothing personal in his attentions. And despite all this pleasure she felt just being in his company, Jolie wanted to reach out and capture again that which they had had.

No matter where they walked the plantation dominated the scene, rising majestically before them. As Jolie and Steve paused near a low-hanging branch of one of the giant oaks, her gaze was drawn to it again while her restless fingers played with a lacelike bunch of Spanish moss.

'Do you really think they lived as luxuriously

and as grandly as we've heard?' Jolie sighed. 'Were they really wealthy?'

'The life was certainly not all juleps and siestas,' Steve replied. 'Not if the master of the plantation wanted to own it the following year. The men were entrepreneurs who had many facets of their plantations to control and manipulate in order to achieve the lucrative returns from sugar. Two crop failures and he'd be out of business. If he was successful for a couple of seasons, he had himself a little empire.'

'A sugar king,' Jolie mused, a dimpling smile followed the fanciful thought.

'You must remember plantation owners were few. More than two-thirds of the population in Louisiana at that time owned no slaves at all. But the Grand Manner is much more colourful reading than the futile struggles of the poor.'

'You make me feel guilty for admiring the life style of the plantation owners.' She glanced at him, chagrin showing on her face.

'You shouldn't,' he smiled. 'You're young. What's more romantic than imagining the halycon days of the plantations? It was rugged individualists who built their empires, carved them out of this semitropical wilderness. They simply enjoyed the fruits of their labour to the fullest. Slave labour was a common practice in that era all over the world in one guise or another.'

'I guess that's true,' Jolie agreed. 'England had its child abuse and the coalmines. Czarist Russia and Europe had their serfs. And the nobility of other countries had their forms of slavery.'

'We have merely had a harder time absorbing

our former slaves because of the colour distinction.' The blueness of his eyes sparkled down at her. 'Which has led the subject far away from your first question when you wondered whether the plantation owners really did have silver and gold doorknobs and if they tossed silver dollars at the bubbles behind the paddlewheel of a riverboat. That was what you wanted to hear, wasn't it?'

Jolie nodded sheepishly. 'I ... I ... can't help wondering how true they were, especially when you compare them with the hardships of the others.'

'You can rest assured that the stories were true, no matter how extravagant they sound. In one household, it was customary to stop all the clocks when a guest arrived so that while he or she was there time would stand still in the joy of the moment, and they wouldn't be started again until that guest had left, whether it be a day, week or month later. Outdoing each other seemed to be a game to plantation owners, and not just in the opulence of their homes, but in hospitality as well. For instance, when a slave brought the breakfast tray to a female guest in the mornings, a full-bloomed rose was placed on the pillow beside her. If the woman didn't waken then, the servant would draw it gently beneath her nose until she did. Then the woman would be served a *petit noir* of coffee to wake the body. The host believed her spirit had been awakened by the rose.'

'What a beautiful thought!'

'Probably one of the best tales of the extravagance of plantation owners took place near here. Would you like to hear it?' Steve looked down on her indulgently as she nodded eagerly that she would. 'A Monsieur Charles Durand owned a plantation on Bayou Teche a few miles outside of St. Martinville. He was quite a colourful character. His first wife had twelve children before she died. He swore on her grave he would never marry again, but within a year he was wed. He wanted to be completely fair to the woman, so they too had twelve children. Monsieur Durand was an unusual man; therefore when two of his daughters accepted marriage proposals from native Louisiana families, the local people expected him to indulge in his usual opulent creativity for the double wedding. He had his slaves go to the woods near Catahoula, Louisiana and trap large spiders. A few days before the wedding he had them set loose among the avenue of trees leading to the main house. The trees soon became a network of lacy webs and on the morning of the wedding, slaves were sent out with bellows and silver and gold dust which they sprayed upon the webs, turning the avenue into a shimmering gossamer canopy for the bridal parties.'

'Is that true?' A disbelieving laugh escaped her lips.

'I swear.' Steve mockingly crossed his heart to give impetus to the story.

'What if it had rained? Or the wind had blown?' She bit her lip at the thought of such a calamity occurring to destroy the unbelievable decorations!

'On Monsieur Durand's wedding preparations! It wouldn't dare!' He was laughing at her wide-eyed expression, but Jolie didn't mind.

'I'm glad it didn't,' she sighed wistfully, trying

to visualize what the massive oaks surrounding Cameron Hall would look like glittering with silver and gold.

'Do you realize it's after three, almost four o'clock?' he asked gently.

Jolie turned towards him with a start, suddenly feeling gauche and awkward. She could feel the rising warmth spreading up her neck. It didn't seem possible that the time could have gone by so swiftly.

'I'd ... I'd b ... better be g ... going,' she stammered, embarrassment making her fumble for words.

She brushed nervously at her skirt, averting her face from his amused eyes. But when she would have stepped away towards the tangled lane leading to the car, her wrist was caught by him. There was a throaty laugh as he pulled her towards him.

'I don't care if you stay all night.' The fire in his eyes sent her pulse leaping. 'As a matter of fact, I would prefer it. But I wouldn't like to get into Josephine's black book.'

Jolie was more flustered than before. 'I ... I'm sure sh ... she expects me back for dinner this evening.' She couldn't meet that virile gaze. 'I'm glad you reminded me of the time.'

'Are you?' The rhetorical question was accompanied by an enigmatical smile. Steve intertwined his fingers in hers. 'I'll walk you to your car.'

When, minutes later, Steve Cameron had seen her safely installed behind the wheel of her red Volkswagen, he leaned down and brushed her lips in a fleeting kiss.

'This time you can believe me when I say "au

revoir", Jolie.'

Then Steve retreated to the gate where the black German Shepherd sat, ears alert and his bright eyes studying the scene. Jolie raised a hand in farewell and reversed the car into the dirt lane. It was only when she had turned on to the main road that she realized Steve had not said when he would see her again. But that warm, enveloping glow in her heart radiated with his words that he would see her again. Jolie had none of the doubt of their first meeting.

As she walked into the LeBlanc house, the repercussions of her meeting with Steve Cameron, alias Etienne, began to be felt. First Mrs. LeBlanc made her inquiry as to how she had enjoyed her afternoon with Etienne. Guy stood in the doorway, his dark gaze broodingly watching Jolie's reaction. She disguised her elation with the announcement that the Temple, Steve's plantation, was Cameron Hall. Mrs. LeBlanc immediately attributed this discovery as the reason Jolie had tarried longer than she had anticipated. Jolie didn't bother to correct that assumption, excusing herself at the first opportunity to go to her room to freshen up.

'You neglected to tell us your impression of the cavalier Steve Cameron?' Guy had followed her to the staircase. Her hand gripped the banister tightly before she slowly relaxed.

'You could have told me how devastatingly handsome he is,' striving for a light note so that Guy wouldn't guess the impact Steve had made. 'And that Etienne and Steve were one and the same person. I thought I was meeting an elderly French gentleman.'

'And were you?' he asked quietly.

'Was I what?' Jolie frowned, not following his question.

'Devastated.'

Since she hadn't confided that she had met Steve previously, there was no opportunity to admit it now. So Jolie settled for a half truth of her reaction.

'I was stunned. Strangely enough I didn't even connect him at first as being the Steve you mentioned. Of course, I didn't know Etienne was Steve in French either.' The way Guy was watching her mouth was disconcerting, as if he could see the kisses that had started a fire within her.

'Was I right about his experience?' he inserted when Jolie turned to continue her way up the stairs.

His prying questions irritated her and she spun around to face him. 'What do you want, Guy? A blow-by-blow account of his attempt to seduce me?' Her voice trembled with barely controlled anger.

'I never dreamed for one minute that Mother would send you out there to his place!' Guy muttered, his fist pummelling the wooden railing.

'Oh, come on, Guy,' Jolie sighed in exasperation. 'Do you really believe what I just said?'

'No, Steve's too clever to play his hand out the first time,' he sneered. 'But I know he was intrigued by your wholesomeness.'

'I was raised on a farm. I do know a bit about the birds and the bees. And after three years of college I can handle an odd pass or two without being shattered by one measly kiss.' That may have been an outright lie, but Jolie was too angry to care.

'Then I was right—the siege has begun.' His smile

was a cross between sarcasm and smugness.

'But my defences have not been breached,' she retorted. 'And they won't be!'

'Listen, Jolie.' Guy's voice changed to a pleading tone. 'I'm really only trying to warn you so you won't get hurt. I've seen Steve in action before. He just bats those big blue eyes at a girl and smiles and she melts just like that!' He snapped his fingers in emphasis.

'I thought that was you.' Jolie didn't spare the sarcasm.

Besides, it hurt to realize how many other girls had been the recipient of Steve's attentions. Too much had happened today for her to even begin to think clearly. She wished she had never got tangled up in this conversation with Guy. She was only becoming more confused. Inhaling deeply, she tried to control her battered emotions.

'Look, Guy, I understand what you're trying to say and I appreciate it. But I'm an adult and capable of forming my own opinions and judgements. I merely found Steve fascinating.'

She didn't give Guy a chance to reply, turning and walking up the steps immediately. But he was bound to have the last word. And it carried up to her.

'So is a cobra!'

There had been no attempts by Steve to contact her the following day, Friday. Jolie almost despised herself by puttering around St. Martinville with frequent stops at the LeBlanc home in the event that Steve did call. Not that she ever asked outright if he specifically had left any messages. She was much too unsure of her own attraction to him to do that. It was merely a case of being available.

But when Saturday morning dawned, most of her faith that he would contact her vanished with the dark skies of night. No matter how much she wanted to believe that the things Guy had said about him were untrue, they kept hanging about, their pinpricks of doubt deflating her bubble of happiness. Therefore when Guy suggested they spend the day together, Jolie accepted with alacrity. Luckily Guy's plans involved a group of his friends so there were no probing questions, only several rounds of tennis followed by a leisurely afternoon beside a swimming pool.

The physical exertion and subsequent relaxing warmth of the sun eased most of Jolie's tension so that when they returned to the LeBlanc home late that afternoon she was feeling quite refreshed. She hadn't bothered to change out of her red-flowered bikini, deciding instead that her long-sleeved red blouse hid the more revealing aspects of the suit. And Mrs. LeBlanc, who had had her share of girls, didn't appear to think it was at all improper for Jolie to lounge around the sun-porch dressed that way. The whole family was in a festive mood and Jolie was included quite naturally.

Then Michelle dashed upstairs to shower and change for her date with Eugene, her teacher boyfriend. Mr. LeBlanc received a phone call. Mrs. LeBlanc went to check on dinner. And Guy went looking for a newspaper to see what shows were playing in Lafayette so that he and Jolie could select the one they wanted to attend that night. That left Jolie standing alone in the room that had minutes ago been filled with jubilant voices.

She was also the only one to see the car pull up the driveway, coming to a stop near the back door. Idle curiosity drew her to the window to see the new arrival, a girl in slim-fitting white trousers and a red T-shirt that revealed every voluptuous curve, hop out from the driver's side. A yellow flowered band drew the long masses of black hair away from her face and cascaded it down her back. The girl moved with feline grace towards the trunk of the car, her red lips moving with animated happiness although no sound carried into the house.

The colour drained from Jolie's face as Steve stepped from the opposite side of the car and walked to the rear. A memory clicked in her mind. Claudine was coming home today, the same Claudine who considered Steve Cameron her private property. And there he was with her calmly unloading suitcases and packages from the trunk of her car. Feeling like a person just betrayed, Jolie watched the smiling interchange between the two as Claudine began adjusting bags and packages until Steve looked like a hotel bellhop with cases in his hands and under his arms.

Jolie was all ready to turn away from the window so that when they entered the house they would not be aware she had been watching. But the scene had not played itself out yet. She saw Claudine move to stand closer to Steve. She watched the long, artistic fingers spread themselves on his chest, pushing open the tan shirt already half unbuttoned so her hands were resting on the hair-covered skin. Steve was looking down at the girl and although Jolie couldn't see his expression, she knew he wasn't repulsed by Claudine's actions.

A sickening nausea began churning the contents of her stomach as Jolie watched the fingers curl around his neck and pull Steve's head down towards the girl. Like a fool she kept thinking he would break free from the embrace, but he accepted the kiss. Only it wasn't acceptance, because even though his arms were laden, Jolie could see he was returning it. Then she couldn't see any more for the tears that clouded her eyes.

Now she did turn away from the window, hastily wiping her eyes with the back of her hand. She wasn't about to give him the satisfaction of seeing her cry. If he could kiss without feeling then so could she! It was just as well she had witnessed that scene, Jolie told her crying heart. There was little doubt any more as to just how foolish her hopes were. Hadn't she been warned that she was nothing more than an intriguing diversion for Steve?

There was no way she was going to be the lone person in the room when Claudine and Steve walked in the door. Jolie hurried into the hallway. She immediately saw Guy in the dining room bending over the table where the newspaper was lying.

'Did you find anything good?' Jolie forced a brightness and interest in her voice that was a complete contrast to what she was really feeling.

'Come and take a look. See if anything strikes your fancy.'

Jolie was determinedly studying the paper when the sound of laughter and opening doors heralded the arrival of Claudine and Steve. Guy sighed as he straightened, giving Jolie a resigned look.

'The Queen Bee has finally arrived at the hive.' He very reluctantly took Jolie's hand and led her towards the hallway.

If Guy's lack of enthusiasm was noticeable, his parents more than made up for it as they affectionately welcomed their daughter home. Jolie and Guy were standing behind the group. She was grateful for these extra few minutes before she had to meet Steve face to face. The instant Guy had seen Steve with Claudine, his hand had tightened his hold on Jolie's and drawn her closer to him, a situation she was quite satisfied to have occur.

Jolie was sure they had made no sound to draw attention to themselves. Yet, with sort of a sixth sense, Steve turned from the adulation being heaped on Claudine to look behind him. His face seemed devoid of any expression, although there seemed to be a hint of amusement lurking in the depths of his cobalt blue eyes as his gaze flicked over Jolie's hand held so firmly by Guy. A betraying flush of colour crept up her neck, but she boldly returned his glance, daring him to comment. If Steve saw the challenge in her eyes, he ignored it, choosing instead to let his gaze roam over her scanty attire until she felt she was nearly naked.

Before Jolie had an opportunity to exhibit her annoyance at the way Steve's gaze was taking liberties, Emile LeBlanc greeted him in French. His retort was also in French, which continued for several exchanges in the same language. Not once did Steve hesitate for a correct word, proving himself as fluent as the LeBlancs. Jolie grudgingly admired his ability and understood why Mrs. LeBlanc had referred to him by the French equivalent of his name. She refused to allow herself to wonder how he came upon the almost native ease with a foreign tongue.

'Is this your new girl-friend, Guy?'

There was a bite to the question that drew Jolie's gaze sharply from Steve to the girl now facing her. The dark, dark brown eyes were inspecting her with contemptuous thoroughness. Jolie's self-confidence was deflated by the strikingly beautiful Claudine. Here was the personification of all Jolie's dreams of the glamorous looks which she had been denied. Claudine's complexion was a flawless shade of ivory, a perfect contrast to her black hair, raven brows and long curling lashes that owed little to the artifice of cosmetics. Large gold loops hung from delicate ears, giving the girl an exotically gypsy appearance. Claudine was an orchid and Jolie felt like a field daisy standing beside her.

Vaguely she heard Guy explaining her presence as a guest, somehow omitting the fact that she was a paying one. But Guy's attempt to give importance to her status did little to boost Jolie's ego. The sheer futility of attempting to compete with anyone as beautiful as Claudine for Steve's attention was a lead weight on her heart.

That, coupled with the fact that Claudine had turned away from Jolie, dismissing her as unworthy of her attention, to direct herself to Steve, made

Jolie tug at Guy's hand. He looked down on her gently and apologetically.

'I think I'll go and change,' she whispered, noticing out of the corner of her eye the way Steve was listening to Claudine with intense interest.

'We'll eat out somewhere,' Guy said firmly but quietly. Jolie couldn't stop the smile of relief from curving her mouth.

'Are you two going somewhere?' Claudine was suddenly interested in them now that it looked as if part of her audience was leaving.

Jolie let Guy make the explanation and escaped Steve's eyebrow that had raised in her direction.

CHAPTER EIGHT

By the time Guy and Jolie returned late that evening, the house was silent. There was no way of telling whether Claudine was home or out with Steve, and Jolie wasn't about to voice her speculations to Guy. After Sunday morning church, Guy arranged a jaunt with Michelle and her boy-friend for the four of them to drive down to Jean Lafitte's famous pirate stomping grounds, Grand Isle on Barateria Bay. Claudine was still in bed asleep, so there was no reason to suggest that she accompany them.

On Monday, Jolie chose to forsake the area entirely and journeyed to Baton Rouge, taking the interstate highway system that bridged the twenty miles or so of swamps in between on cranelike legs of concrete pilings. On her return to the LeBlanc home that evening, Claudine was missing from the gathering. But Jolie didn't inquire about her whereabouts. She was bound to be with Steve.

After having sleep elude her for much of the night, Jolie wakened late the next morning. She very nearly walked right back out of the kitchen when she saw Claudine seated at the table with her mother. But she had never before allowed envy for another person's looks to stand in her way and she wasn't about to be intimidated by them now. So, helping herself to a cup of coffee, Jolie joined them at the table as nonchalantly as she could.

'Good morning.' She addressed her bright smile to both Claudine and Mrs. LeBlanc. The former barely glanced her way while Mrs. LeBlanc returned the greeting.

'What are your plans for today, Jolie? I was just suggesting to Claudine that she might show you around.'

'There's no need for that,' she replied quickly, noting the bored look on Claudine's face. 'I was thinking of driving to Jefferson Island and touring the gardens there, but I feel too lazy for that today. Besides, I wouldn't want to interfere with Claudine's plans.'

'I was thinking of going into the country today and doing some sketches. The watercolours of Steve's plantation sold quite well.' The vague smile that flitted across the crimson lips said quite plainly that Claudine had more important things to do than act as a tour guide for Jolie. While Jolie couldn't help wondering, a little cattily, how convenient it was that Claudine's work would take her to Steve's home.

'I've seen some of your paintings. I thought they were quite beautiful.' It was difficult quelling the desire to reply with a bit more coldness, but Jolie succeeded in sounding pleasant.

'Most of them are a trifle commercial.' There was that saccharine smile again. 'Few people see my more serious work, but then few people would understand it.'

Jolie felt herself firmly placed in the plebian level of art appreciation. If she had been a dog, her hackles would have been rising about then. As it was, she sipped her coffee and smiled.

'Did I tell you, Claudine,' Mrs. LeBlanc inserted with her usual exuberance, 'Jolie discovered that Etienne's plantation was once owned by one of her ancestors?'

'No, you didn't. How interesting.' Dark eyes turned to Jolie in slow speculation that spoke of re-assessment. 'How did you find that out?'

Something told Jolie that she should tread very softly in her explanation.

'One day last week, Thursday I think, Mr. Cameron,' she secretly thought the formal touch was very clever, 'invited me out to tour his plantation. He showed me the pillars along the bayou with the name Cameron etched on them. My ancestor's name was Cameron and they had called their plantation Cameron Hall.'

'Your ancestor was an American?'

Jolie had already learned that in pre-Civil War Louisiana the landed French considered Americans as uncivilized and barbaric. Doors opened very slowly to 'Yankees' even if they were from south of the Mason–Dixon line. Therefore Claudine's question had a slightly snobbish ring to it.

'As a matter of fact, she was descended from a very old Creole French family. Her father Robert Cameron was the son of Scottish immigrants. He was killed in the Civil War, fighting for the South. A few years after the war was over, her mother remarried, this time to an officer in the Northern Army. Cameron Hall had already been sold for back taxes,' Jolie concluded.

'A very interesting story,' Claudine murmured languidly.

'It really is quite a coincidence that Jolie's Cameron Hall is once again owned by a Cameron, I think,' Mrs. LeBlanc commented brightly.

'Personally, I wish Steve didn't own it.' Her daughter ground out her cigarette in the ashtray. 'He would be much better off if he didn't.'

'How can you say that?' Her mother exclaimed. 'It's a beautiful place.'

'Then let the National Trust remodel it,' Claudine retorted. 'Have you any idea how much it costs to restore that broken-down mansion? Steve could be moderately wealthy if he didn't keep pouring money into that place trying to fix it up to make it partially habitable. The upkeep on such a monstrosity, even if it were like new, would be outrageous!'

'Surely he could open it up to tourists once it's restored,' Jolie suggested quietly, angered by Claudine's cold practicality. 'He could get back some of his costs.'

'Old plantations are two for a penny in the South. The Temple, or Cameron Hall or whatever you want to call it, is hardly more unique than scores of others,' Claudine answered caustically. 'His plantation can't even boast of hoof prints where Union soldiers rode their horses up the stairs.'

'I should think being an artist you'd want to see it restored.' Jolie kept her voice steady and calm as she stirred her coffee, hoping not to show her distaste for such a mercenary attitude.

'I don't care for the cliché life of an artist. Starving in a garret never did appeal to me.' Malicious amusement sparkled wickedly in Claudine's dark eyes. 'A modern home or a beautiful apartment is much more comfortable than a cold and damp, partially restored plantation.'

'Always, she talks like this,' Mrs. LeBlanc protested with a Gallic lift of her hands to the air. 'She lets her head rule her heart.'

'An aspirin can cure a headache, Mama.' Claudine rose from the table and carried her coffee cup to the sink. 'But what is the cure for heartache?'

Jolie was curious to know the answer to that rhetorical question since she just might need the remedy herself if she didn't get Steve Cameron out of her system in a hurry. Claudine's departure from the kitchen brought a sudden bustle of activity from her mother. Jolie finished her own coffee and returned to her room, trying to work up some enthusiasm for the long day spreading before her.

Sunlight flooded the bedroom, spraying golden beams on the sleeping figure. A bird trilled its wake-up call outside the window, causing Jolie to stir slightly, her eyelids tightening against the brilliant glare trying to penetrate her sleep. A strong floral scent teased her nose to wakefulness. She sighed, blinked her eyes and started to snuggle into her pillow for a few extra winks. But those few, barely focused blinks had seen something that shouldn't have been there.

A line creased her forehead as Jolie opened her eyes wide and stared in disbelief at the pillow beside her head. A large, full-blooming rose lay on the white case, its rich pink colour contrasting sharply with the white. Very slowly she inched her hand from beneath the covers, half expecting the rose to disappear before her eyes. But when her fingers touched the stem, Jolie knew it was real. She pushed herself upright, burying her nose in the fuchsia petals.

Two things clicked simultaneously in her mind, Steve's reference to an old plantation custom of awakening guests with a rose and the feeling that she wasn't alone in the room. Her hand reached out to grab the fallen covers and pull them up to hide her skimpy cotton pyjamas even as she turned to look at the dark area near the window. The hands that had been tapping his mouth while Steve studied her with silent concentration fell to the arms of the chair as he pushed himself to his feet.

'How did you get in here?' Jolie breathed, feeling that the wind had just been knocked out of her.

'Through the door.'

He leaned against the bedpost, not showing any remorse for the way he was looking at her or the embarrassing position she was in.

'You shouldn't be here! What if Mrs. LeBlanc finds out?'

'She isn't here. I found a note downstairs for you. It seems she'll be gone all morning.'

'But why are you here?' Jolie was beginning to feel a little ridiculous with the bedcovers clutched around her neck with one hand and the pink rose in the other. The blood was no longer pounding in her temples, but a trembling had taken over her limbs.

'I had the feeling you were trying to avoid me.'

'That's silly.' But Jolie couldn't meet his gaze.

'I'm glad to hear that.' A smile spread across his face with captivating charm. 'You look very desirable first thing in the morning. Did you know that? All rumpled and soft.'

She blushed furiously, not knowing how to reply to such a personal comment. The velvet soft chuckle from Steve didn't help. It angered her that he should find the situation so funny.

'Now that you've determined that I'm not trying to avoid you, I think you should leave my bedroom,' letting him feel a bit of her temper.

'Why? Are you afraid I'll crawl into the bed with you? I admit the idea has some merits.' The blue eyes danced over her.

'You wouldn't dare!' Jolie whispered, hating the betraying leap of her heart.

Steve just smiled and reached out for her robe draped over the end of the bed. Walking to the side of the bed nearest Jolie, he stood looking down at her for an eternity of seconds before finally handing her the robe.

'I'll give you fifteen minutes to meet me in the kitchen, then I'm coming back up to get you.'

While Jolie spluttered indignantly, Steve walked calmly out of the room. She was down in ten minutes, still fuming that he was so sure she would fall in with his wishes and angry with herself because she was. Yet she knew it hadn't been an idle threat by Steve that he would come back to her room to get her. She tried to console her self-respect with that.

'Well, I'm here,' she announced defiantly as she entered the kitchen.

'I poured you some coffee.'

His blue eyes roamed familiarly over her, admiring the blue slacks and the matching polka dot top. But Jolie kept her features frozen, refusing to let the warmth of his gaze melt her defences. It was difficult, especially when her nerves were jumping at the slightest sound.

'Did you find any material you liked?' Steve asked when the silence threatened to last.

'Material?' Jolie forced a frown of false bewilderment on her face.

'To re-cover the sofa and chairs,' he prompted.

'I'd forgotten all about it,' she lied.

'Did you?' His astuteness brought a flash of colour to her cheeks that quickly receded. 'I thought we might do some checking together today. If you're still interested in helping?'

'Claudine would have a much better eye for material than I would.' Jolie lifted her chin a trifle high as she met his gaze with all the coldness she could put into her face. 'Why don't you get her to help you?'

'I asked you.'

'I know,' she retorted sharply and quickly before controlling the desire to resort to sarcasm. 'But that was before Claudine returned.'

'What you're really trying to say is that you don't trespass on other people's property, isn't it?' There was a barely perceptible smile on his face, enough for her to know that Steve was mocking her.

'Something like that,' Jolie replied carefully.

'Just to set the record straight, I belong to no one. Claudine and I have known each other for a long time and we have a lot in common. But I don't run her life and she doesn't run mine. Now do you want to spend the day with me or would you rather persist with your Puritan morals and be alone?'

'Claudine seemed very fond of you and you acted like you liked her. Naturally I assumed you were very close.' Jolie sprang quickly to her own defence. 'I'm not the only one who thinks that way. So does Guy and Michelle.'

'I think you're reading more into Michelle's words than she means. As for Guy, he's merely protecting his flanks.' The knowing gleam was in his eyes as Jolie shifted uncomfortably in her chair. Steve rose and walked around the table. 'Come on, let's go.'

'I haven't said I would go,' she protested as he pulled her chair away from the table. Taking her arm, Steve guided her towards the back door.

'After the fool you've made of yourself, your pride probably won't allow you to give in, so I'll just bully you into accompanying me.' The wide smile as he looked down at her took her breath away. 'What would Guy call it? The masterful touch or the iron hand in the velvet glove?'

'He'd probably call it kidnapping,' Jolie retorted, hearing the door slam behind them.

'Then I'll have you at my mercy all day,' Steve chuckled, opening the door of his station wagon and helping Jolie inside.

'And will you?' she asked quietly when he slipped behind the wheel.

'Will I what?'

'Be merciful,' she replied in a small voice.

Steve paused before turning the key in the ignition, regarding her with intense silence. 'If you promise not to turn the force of those soft brown eyes on me. They can be very unsettling to a man's equilibrium.'

Jolie turned away quickly, wondering if he knew how dangerous his deep blue pools were and how often she had wanted to drown herself in their depths. Still, it was exciting to discover that there was something about her that disturbed him. But was it a weapon or a liability, considering her own weak defences?

When Steve turned in the direction opposite from the downtown business district of St. Martinville, Jolie glanced at him curiously.

'Where are we going?' she asked hesitantly.

'New Iberia.' Steve spared a glance from the road to look reassuringly at her. 'I thought we'd have a bigger selection of upholstery material to choose from as well as take in some of the sights. Have you been there?'

'Just to the plantation called the Shadows on the Teche. I went yesterday,' she replied, remembering how difficult it had been to enjoy the day after her conversation with Claudine in the morning.

'Did you like it?'

'Oh, yes, it was very beautiful especially the lawns and the little gazebo along the bayou.' Jolie was able to admit honestly. She had been too abstracted to take in the beautiful interior furnishing in any detail, but she had wandered the small walled lawn at her leisure, delighting in the chameleons that abounded in the shrubbery. 'I did notice that the front of the house faced the street instead of Bayou Teche.'

'That's because the Old Spanish Trail passed there, which prompted them to reverse the normal procedure,' Steve explained. 'Did you go out to Avery Island?'

'No.' Jolie shook her head.

'We'll drive out there after lunch,' he stated, turning his attention back to the road.

Jolie found herself settling back against the seat in contentment. It seemed natural for Steve to be behind the wheel, his strong hands firmly guiding the car. It was an extremely pleasant sensation sitting there in the seat beside him and knowing she was going to spend the entire day with him at his request. Steve would never know how important the time he spent with her was to Jolie. It was too important, considering the uncertainty of their relationship. The probability that she was nothing more than a passing fancy was too great to be ignored regardless of the depth of her own feelings.

At the second store that they stopped in New Iberia, they found the exact material that Jolie had had in mind for the sofa and chairs. It was a crushed velvet material in a very light shade of moss green, a perfect complement to the dark walnut wood. Unfortunately there wasn't sufficient material on the bolt of fabric to do all three items. The clerk assured them that he could get another shipment of the same material in the same colour.

'I think we should wait until the other bolt comes

in,' Jolie said to Steve in a confidential tone. 'It's quite possible that the material might not be the exact shade.'

'I think you're right,' Steve agreed, turning to the clerk to advise him of their decision.

After determining that the new shipment would arrive in less than a week, Steve escorted Jolie back to the station wagon.

Glancing at his gold wristwatch, he said, 'It's still about an hour before lunchtime, but since you didn't eat any breakfast, why don't we eat now?'

'I am getting hungry,' Jolie admitted.

'Do you like Mexican food? I know a good restaurant that makes some marvellous tacos.'

'Sounds great.'

Rafael's was a small, unpretentious restaurant located on one of the side streets. Its interior decoration was a combination of simplicity and elegance in a classical Mexican–Spanish atmosphere. They had barely seated themselves at a table when a swarthy older man entered the dining area from one of the back rooms. The moment he spied Steve, his face broke into a beaming smile as he strode to their table.

'Esteban!' was the first word uttered, followed by a torrent of Spanish that Jolie's meagre high school course couldn't begin to keep up with. She was able to determine that Steve was Esteban and the man greeting him was Rafael, the owner. The familiarity and gladness in their tones convinced her that Steve was a frequent visitor to Rafael's establishment.

'Raoul, this is Miss Jolie Smith,' Steve presented. 'She's vacationing here in Louisiana.' Turning to

Jolie, he continued, 'I'd like you to meet Rafael Alvarez, a very close friend of mine.'

'*Buenos dias,* Señor Alvarez,' extending her hand to the older man.

'Ah, do you speak Spanish, *señorita*?' The man bowed graciously over her hand.

'Only the "hello", "goodbye", "how are you" variety,' Jolie admitted.

'What a pity!' Señor Alvarez smiled ruefully. 'It is a beautiful language for lovers. You must have Esteban teach you.' Dark eyes danced suggestively at Steve, who was regarding her with speculative amusement. 'He is *mucho hombre.*'

Steve staved off further personal remarks by asking Rafael what he recommended for a light lunch. Jolie didn't pay too much attention to the suggestions offered, letting Steve choose for her as she let her thoughts wander.

'You look in a daze,' Steve said when Rafael left the table. 'What's troubling you?'

'I was . . . just wondering.' Jolie inhaled deeply. 'You speak French fluently and now Spanish. It's not really a common thing.'

'So now you're curious.'

'Yes. I mean, I know that now you own a plantation, but before that . . . ? You must have learned to speak those different languages before you ever moved here. I was wondering what kind of work you did before.'

'I was an officer on a tramp ship for about eleven years,' Steve replied.

'What's a tramp ship?' Mentally Jolie was picturing an old derelict ship.

'She was a very respectable vessel,' Steve insisted with a bit of amusement at her doubtful expression. 'It's a term applied to ships who don't have a regular port of call. They might take a load of grain from New Orleans—for example to, say, Japan and from there they might take cargo to India and so on. It might be two or three years before they ever return to the same port.'

'Which was why and how you learned different languages,' understanding dawning on her.

'Actually I speak four languages besides English. Italian and German as well as French and Spanish.'

'You said eleven years. You must have been very young.' Jolie glanced at him curiously from beneath her lashes. Steve didn't strike her as the type to be very open about his past.

'Seventeen. I was an orphan and had no close relatives. The sea seemed to offer a very romantic and adventurous occupation. At the time I lived in the north, Boston. I dreamed of running away to a South Sea island. I haunted the wharves for months before the captain of this tramp ship took pity on me and agreed to sign me aboard. He became, in a way, a father figure, being without a family himself. I sailed with him until he died nearly five years ago.'

'That's when you came here?'

'I came back to the United States and finally ended up in New Orleans, where I met Claudine. Wandering had lost most of its magic, although the sea life was good to me.' His eyes gleamed at her from across the table. 'Do you want to hear any more about my sordid past?'

'Well, you did omit all the girls in the different ports.' A teasing smile curved the corners of her mouth. 'You must have left a string of broken hearts from one end of the earth to the other.'

'The type of women I met . . .' His face hardened only momentarily before softening with cynical amusement. 'I doubt if their hearts were broken. Respectable women seldom frequented the places where seamen seek their entertainment.'

'At least I was partially right when I thought of you as a buccaneer. You were once a sailor,' Jolie smiled brightly as a waiter approached with their lunch.

'I must remember to give you my gold earring,' Steve joked. 'It would look much better on you than it ever would on me.'

'I don't know. A girl would look peculiar wearing only one earring. Maybe you'd better keep it as a souvenir,' she laughed easily.

'Wouldn't you like a memento of our time together?' Steve asked quietly just as Jolie started to pick up the steaming *taco* from her plate. The question caught her off guard.

'No,' she replied sharply, knowing how vivid her own memory of Steve would be without a tangible reminder. She tried to laugh away her sharpness, but it sounded nervous and false. 'You'd better keep it for another girl who would look good dressed as a gypsy.'

'Whatever you say,' Steve shrugged indifferently, turning his attention to their meal.

CHAPTER NINE

'HAVE you read anything at all about Avery Island?' Steve asked after they had crossed the small bridge over the bayou and paid the toll.

'Not a thing.'

'Being a Yankee Northerner, I don't imagine you've really noticed the flatness of the land here in southern Louisiana, have you?'

'Yes and no. I've noticed it. But do you mean did anything strike me as being strange?' Steve nodded and Jolie answered, 'Then no, it didn't.'

'Hills are so uncommon that they're truly a rarity. In New Orleans at the Audubon park, you'll find probably the only deliberately man-made hill in the world, called Monkey's Hill. Dirt was piled about forty feet high there in the 1930s so New Orleans children could see what a hill looked like.'

'You're kidding!' Jolie laughed.

'No, it's the truth. That's why Avery Island was such a curiosity even in the early days. Its highest point is nearly a hundred and ninety-five feet above the marshes and bayous that surround it. That in itself made it unique, but it didn't make it valuable.'

'What did?' Her attention swung away from the lush foliage on either side of the car back to the driver.

'Salt. It was first discovered in a briny spring in one of the ravines. Boiling it reduced it to a crystal form. But even in the early 1800s, it was still cheaper to get it in bulk from Europe. It wasn't until the War of 1812 when England blockaded the United States that it was recovered in any great quantity through very crude methods of boiling and evaporation. Later, the Civil War and the Union Blockade demanded that the South have its own salt resources. When they tried to deepen the spring, a deposit of rock salt was discovered running for miles at depths they weren't able to determine. It's been mined here ever since. We'll tour the salt mine first,' Steve concluded, ignoring the sign for the Jungle Gardens to drive on past. 'Of course, salt isn't complete without pepper. Avery Island is also the birthplace of tabasco sauce. It's made right here on the island as well.'

Jolie found the mine impressive and interesting. The ceilings towered sixty feet into the air supported by crystal pillars. Yet she couldn't forget that five hundred feet or so above was the surface. Therefore, despite the immensity of the mine, she was just beginning to feel claustrophobic when they started back to the surface.

'Feel better?' Steve asked when Jolie inhaled deeply once outside.

She cast him a startled glance. 'How did you know?' she breathed.

'You were looking a bit pale,' Steve smiled. 'I'll remember that underground places are not your forte the next time.'

'Next time'—those were magic words. Her determination to keep her feet on the ground fled as Jolie floated back to the car with Steve. It was only a short distance back to the turn-off leading to the Jungle Gardens and Bird City.

'Mayward Hill.' Steve pointed to the mansion a few turns in the road past the entrance gate. 'It's the focal point of the Gardens and the former home of the late Edward Avery McIlhenny who was responsible for the creation of the Jungle Gardens and Bird City. I hope you like to walk.' A disarming smile was directed at Jolie.

'The road doesn't end here,' Jolie observed as Steve pulled into one of the laybys. She could see where the narrow road continued on and even branched off into other directions.

'No, it doesn't, but to really appreciate the beauty of the place you should walk. Besides, it's the only way down to Bird City.'

'I enjoy walking.' Jolie asserted quickly as she scrambled out of the car to join Steve. 'I only made the remark because the road continued on.'

'Well, we aren't going to walk through the entire gardens,' Steve smiled taking her hand. 'The size of the place precludes that. There's more than two hundred and fifty acres of gardens. At different points of interest though, there are parking areas and paths to lead you back to a specific place.'

The path they were on led them past giant stands of imported bamboo to culminate with a pier and lookout tower extending over a large lagoon. All types of water-fowl were present in varying numbers. The birds considered the human visitors as commonplace and ignored them while Jolie and

Steve watched. It was such a serene place that Jolie was loath to leave it, but Steve convinced her that there was much more to see and they made their way back to the car.

The road twisted and turned and meandered through the grounds. Magnolia trees and giant oaks sometimes towered on each side to be replaced by lofty stands of bamboo or low, flowering hedges. Azaleas were everywhere. They stopped, walked through the sunken garden and the camellias, saw waterfalls built of old sugar kettles, then drove again with the Petite Answ Bayou on their right and the slender ribbon of a lagoon on their left. A palm-tree-lined road led to another small parking area and a sign directing them to the famous Cleveland Oak used years ago as a survey point for the original grant. This time Jolie needed no invitation to take the walking path leading back to it, stepping out of the car eagerly for a first-hand view of another section of the Gardens.

They paused beneath the giant tree, noting where nature and time had taken their mark with broken limbs and gnarled wounds carved into its moss-green body. Yet the tree itself looked sturdy enough to endure hundreds of years more even with its shroud of grey Spanish moss like an ageing bearded man. But the path didn't end at the Cleveland Oak, but continued on into jungle-like growth.

'Where does it lead?' Jolie wondered aloud.

'Shall we find out?' The knowing look was on his face as he spread out his hand for her to precede him. 'Watch your step, though. This path isn't used very much so it's bound to be overgrown and a little slippery.'

In places the concrete slabs were covered with moss and in others they were chipped and broken. Steve's hand on her elbow helped her over the worst parts, although his touch by itself was unsettling. A tiny streamlike lagoon appeared and bordered one side of the path while tall bamboo canes rose on the other. At a bend in the path, two white swans came into view swimming slowly in the water. Invisible propulsion moved them with regal elegance, causing only the slightest ripple in the mirror-smooth water.

Jolie was so intent on watching the stately birds that she didn't pay attention to the uneven ground ahead of her. Her toe hit a jutting piece of concrete and she stumbled forward with the grace of an awkward duckling. But Steve's arm was there preventing her from falling in an ignominious heap. Breathless embarrassment reddened her cheeks as she stammered her thanks. She tried to slip free of the arm about her waist that held her against the warm hardness of his body, but Steve refused to loosen his hold.

Whispering softly into her hair, he said, 'It was inevitable, you know. You had to end up in my arms one way or another.'

Almost before Jolie could twist around to face him, his lips were clinging to hers in a possessive kiss. All the longing to be in his arms that she had tried to suppress burst free as she gladly gave herself up to his embrace. His mouth all but ravaged hers while his hands explored her body, crushing her against him in the urgency of his ardour. Jolie felt herself being carried to new, dizzying heights of love and desire, surpassing the barely kindled flame of their first kiss. What had once been a glowing warmth of love became a burning, raging fire. And Steve's expert caresses knew exactly how to add more fuel.

The collar of her blouse was pushed away so his mouth could explore the hollows of her shoulder while his fingers raked the waving feathers of her hair. But her sensations were beyond registering pain, for Jolie felt the same frustrating need to explore every inch of Steve's body, too. She was reeling in a kaleidoscope world of bursting lights that sent her rocking at every new touch from him. And while she lacked Steve's experience in making love, she more than made up for it with her desire to please, which left Steve totally in control.

The laughter of children a short distance away finally stilled Steve's kisses before their love making carried them further. Yet he didn't set her away from him, but kept her in the circle of his arms, her head resting against his chest until her thudding heart slowed to a less erratic pace and her breathing was less shaky. Though she still wanted his kisses, Jolie was sensible enough to realize that if it hadn't been for the sound of other people, their embrace had got to the point where she would have allowed Steve to take any liberties he wanted with her. The depth of her love for him gave him unlimited power.

Steve's hand moved to the back of her neck, letting his fingers tangle themselves in her short hair before his thumb moved forward to raise her chin. Jolie didn't make any attempt to dim the radiant lovelight in her eyes. There was no need to hide from Steve what he must already have guessed.

'You start your own fires, don't you?' he muttered hoarsely. The recently banked fires glittered with blue flames out of his eyes as his gaze roamed possessively over her face. 'How have you managed to conceal this passionate side of your nature? Somebody should have snapped you up and married you a long time ago.'

'The lady has to be willing,' Jolie whispered, feeling herself drowning in his gaze.

There was a sharp intake of breath as Steve read between the lines of her words. His arms tightened about her briefly as his eyes darkened and narrowed. A grim smile accompanied a firm slap on her rump.

'That is for playing with fire,' he scolded her with fierce gentleness. 'You say that once too often and some man just might believe you.'

The boldness of her words brought a pair of crimson patches to her cheeks. 'I'm of age,' she retorted defiantly, turning her face away from him.

Steve turned her completely around so that her back was to him, pushing her so that she was forced to continue along the path on legs that were still slightly unsteady. A supporting hand remained on her hips.

'Don't remind me,' he replied as he followed her. 'I'm having enough trouble trying to make sure you don't lose your self-respect, let alone mine for myself.'

Jolie felt properly chastised by his words. What she had said before had only been big talk. She knew she would never be able to convince her conscience that it was all right to go to bed with a man who was other than her husband. Oh, Steve could carry her away all right, but silent recriminations would always rain down on her head from inside. It was very obvious that Steve recognized this. Which didn't leave her in an enviable position since he had stated that his freedom was very precious. Jolie pivoted around abruptly so that Steve nearly ran into her.

'I'm sorry, Steve,' she blinked up at him. 'You were right about what you said.'

His hands were restingly lightly on her hips as he stared grimly down at her. 'Will you stop looking at me with those brown eyes of yours? You make it increasingly difficult to keep my hands off of you.' Jolie could tell the lightness in his voice was forced. 'And I don't think this is the place for a torrid love scene with the Buddha looking on.'

At his peculiar remark, Jolie glanced over her shoulder. On a small hill in a glass-enclosed temple sat a large golden Buddha surrounded by his seven hills, gazing down on a small pool that cast his reflection in the late afternoon sun. She only needed a slight nudge from Steve to continue along the path that brought them closer to the base of the temple.

The Chinese Garden was a popular stop for nearly all the visitors, so that the privacy Steve and Jolie had usually had when touring a special section in this case was not to be. So, after climbing the steps to the temple and getting a closer look at the Buddha that eight hundred years ago had sat in the Shonfa Temple near Peiping, China, they walked back to the car. This time they took the more public narrow road instead of the path, eliminating the opportunity for further shared intimacies.

Under the arched wisteria vines, past the cactus gardens and the camellias, completing the loop at Mayward Hill, they drove on towards the exit gate. The sun was hovering very near the horizon, casting rich golden-orange rays that held off for a time the crimson colours of sunset. Jolie sighed deeply as they passed the stone gates. They, more than the sun, signalled the end of the day, or at least her day with Steve. It was time for him to take her home, and she wanted the day to go on for ever.

'Have dinner with me tonight,' Steve said in that peculiar ordering tone of his that laughed at the question form.

'I'd love to,' Jolie agreed eagerly, pausing long enough to add hesitantly, 'but I'm not dressed for it.'

'Neither am I,' he laughed, glancing down at his white polo shirt and black and white checked slacks. 'But few places around here are that formal.' He looked over at her provocatively. 'About the only way I could imagine you looking any better would be if you were wearing nothing at all.'

The heat spread from her neck all the way up her chin, suffusing her face with colour. She had never realized she could be so embarrassed at the thought of her own nudity, but then it was the words being spoken from Steve's lips that were really the cause.

'I shouldn't make you blush, but you do it so beautifully.' Steve reached across the seat with his free hand and took hold of hers. 'Where would you like to go for dinner? That's a nice safe subject.'

'I don't know anything about the restaurants around here,' she replied, liking the warm, firm grip of his hand. It made her feel she belonged to him.

'Do you like seafood?'

'I haven't eaten any except shrimp and lobster back home.'

'That settles it.' As he shook his head at her in mock pity. 'Seafood it shall be.'

The picturesque restaurant sat next to a bayou, supported by stilts that raised it three feet above the ground. The outer walkway resembled a pier complete with nets draped over the railing and hurricane lamps hanging on the weathered exterior of the building. Inside, paintings of sailing ships in heavy seas and quiet harbour scenes adorned the walls side by side with mounted trophies of swordfish and others of the gamefish species. The dark-panelled walls were illuminated by sconces of modern-style chimney lamps and matching chandeliers hung from the beamed ceiling. The simplicity of life at sea was expressed in the common oilcloths that covered the tabletops, evoking an atmosphere of informality.

Steve excused himself to make a phone call as soon as they had been seated at a table. Jolie studied the menu intently until he returned a few minutes later. He hadn't mentioned who he was calling and Jolie didn't want to appear nosey by asking. The question must have been in her expression when she glanced up at him from behind her menu.

'I called the LeBlancs so they wouldn't be expecting you for dinner tonight,' Steve smiled, picking up his own menu and opening it.

'I should have thought of that. I didn't leave a note or anything to tell them where I'd gone,' she sighed ruefully. 'I hope I didn't put them out.'

'They said it was fine. What have you decided to have tonight?' adeptly changing the subject as he saw the waitress glancing in their direction.

'I can't make up my mind whether to have something safe like shrimp that I know I like, or to experiment with something new that I might not like. Maybe I could go half way. What does boiled shrimp taste like?'

'Try the seafood platter,' Steve suggested, his understanding smile laced with amusement. 'It has a little bit of everything. If you're adventurous enough?'

Jolie agreed, only to doubt her decision later when the heaped plate arrived and she didn't see anything on there that she recognized except french-fried shrimp. One particularly repulsive item had a round body with legs sticking out from it in all directions. For some reason, the only thing she could liken it to was a giant spider, which did little to settle the queasy feeling in her stomach. Steve had ordered the same thing for himself and was quick to notice Jolie's look of confused doubt.

'These are fried oysters.' He indicated three scrunched-up pieces that were crispy brown. Pointing to two small rounded items, he said, 'This is stuffed shrimp and the other is stuffed crab. Over here is the boiled shrimp which looks quite like the shrimp used in cocktails. Usually it's served still in its shell-like covering. Naturally we have fried shrimp and also some catfish, here I believe.' His fork finally stopped at the last item on the platter, the one that first caught Jolie's eyes. 'And this is a soft-shelled crab.'

Jolie started out with the familiar fried shrimp, graduating slowly to the oysters that didn't taste at all like their slimy cousins in oyster stew. The stuffed shrimp and crab were delicious. And the boiled shrimp had a delicate seasoning that was pleasantly spicy. The catfish was not any different from what she had eaten in South Dakota. The only thing left she hadn't tasted was the soft-shelled crab. She forked a small portion out of the soft belly and raised it hesitantly to her mouth. It took her a minute to forget its source and admit that it tasted good. The second bite was better than the first. She was beginning to feel quite proud of herself until Steve spoke.

'On a soft-shelled crab, you eat the legs and all.'

'You're joking!' Jolie stared at him incredulously, then looked down at her plate and added silently, 'Not this girl!'

'I'm not.' Steve's attempt to hide his amusement was not very successful. 'You really do eat them.'

To prove his point, he pulled one of the larger legs off the crab on his plate and popped it into his mouth. Jolie's eyes nearly popped out of her head as she watched him chew it up and swallow. An abrupt laugh came out of her opened mouth when she realized it wasn't a trick and the crab leg wasn't going to reappear by magic.

'Honestly, they're very good. I wouldn't tease you. Try one,' he urged.

This was not the time for her adventurous palate to desert her, especially with Steve looking on. Gathering all her courage, Jolie tore off one of the smaller legs and raised it timidly to her mouth. Before she could have second thoughts, she bit into it. Like everything else, it, too, was good.

'Actually the larger ones, the pincers, are better,' Steve smiled, and returned his gaze to his own plate.

There was very little left on Jolie's platter when the waitress removed it to serve their dessert. Steve had thoughtfully ordered fresh fruit cocktail. Jolie didn't think she could have eaten anything heavier. The cocktail proved to be another surprise as the tastes of the different fruits didn't run together. The watermelon balls didn't taste like canteloupe; the pineapple didn't have the tang of the grapefruit sections; and the strawberries tasted like strawberries. At last she leaned back in her chair, comfortably full.

'That was all delicious,' Jolie sighed as she watched Steve light a cigarette.

'I'm glad you liked it. It's good to eat with a woman who doesn't pick at her food.'

'You don't need to remind me of how much I eat,' Jolie admonished laughingly. 'I guess that's what comes of being raised on a farm.' She sobered slightly. 'Speaking of farms, today you seemed to know what all different kinds of plants were.'

'Yes?' Steve prompted when she hesitated.

'You spent so much time at sea. I was just wondering how you were able to know so much about plants and growing things, like sugar cane and all on your plantation?'

'It didn't take many long days at sea before I discovered reading,' he smiled indulgently. 'Maybe it was because there was so much time that went by when you couldn't see any sign of land that I became fascinated with agriculture, horticulture and geology. Anything connected with the earth interested me. So when I made the decision to buy the plantation, it was a matter of applying what I had taught myself and using common sense. Add a bit of trial and error and here I stand.'

'Farming is hard work.'

'Don't you think I'm capable of hard work?' Steve laughed.

'I was just remembering the first time I met you and you were telling me what a great follower of the carefree Cajun philosophy you were,' Jolie smiled impishly.

'It has its merits. Life can be taken too seriously. Finding the happy medium can be difficult. I do admire their sense of humour and acceptance of things they can't change.'

'You forgot their imagination,' she added. 'Like the legend of the crawfish.'

'They have other fanciful tales, equally romantic,' Steve nodded. 'For instance, there's a story that when Marie Antoinette died on the guillotine, her son and heir to the throne, the Dauphin, was smuggled out of France by Royalist Louisianans.

He ultimately lived here and became one of the United States' more famous persons.'

'Jean LaFitte, I suppose,' she guessed.

'No, John James Audubon, the famous painter of birds.'

'Oh,' Jolie gasped. 'Wasn't he an adopted child?'

'History tells us he was born out of wedlock, although his natural father adopted him legally. But the Acadians would say it was a story fabricated to protect the Dauphin from reprisals of the Revolutionists.' Steve tapped the ash off his cigarette. 'They would have you believe that the records of Audubon's existence before the Dauphin's disappearance were an elaborate foil to keep his true identity from being known.'

'It's kind of exciting, isn't it?' Her fingers trailed around the rim of her coffee cup. 'I mean, if it were true?'

'What are you thinking about now?' Steve asked when a silence stretched across the table and Jolie continued staring at her cup.

'*Lagniappe*.' There was a touch of wistfulness in the smile she gave to him. 'That's the kind of day it's been for me. Something extra.'

'And your escort, was he something extra, too?' She could barely distinguish his features through the haze of cigarette smoke.

'That barbarian!' Jolie teased. 'I guess you could call him that.'

Steve chuckled and ground his cigarette out in the ashtray before letting the fire in his gaze glitter across the table to her.

'You can be glad we're in a restaurant and there's

a table between us.'

The mock threat was accented by the sensuous curve of his mouth, sending her heart racing at the thought of Steve raining kisses of punishment on her. His hand reached out to still her fingers that were playing with her empty coffee cup. In the gentle grasp that was at the same time rough and caressing, she felt the voltage of his nearness shoot through her like electricity, relighting the safely banked glow of desire.

'Have I told you today how very beautiful you are?' he asked softly.

'Freckles and all?' she asked with a shaky laugh. She was too used to regarding herself as only mildly attractive not to jest at such a remark.

'I've seen many beautiful women with freckles, Jolie. And I won't let you slide out of a compliment that I meant very sincerely,' Steve scolded her gently in his husky, caressing voice that sent tremors up her spine. 'If anything, I envy the sun for planting so many kisses on your face so that you'll always shine so radiantly.'

'You make it hard for a girl to keep her head out of the clouds,' shaking her head to free herself of his enveloping spell.

'Turnabout is fair play.' He gently withdrew his hand and signalled for the waitress to bring their check.

'What do you mean?'

'I'm generally the one left with the task of fighting the fires you start, as if you didn't know.' His knowing gaze raked her thoroughly, leaving her in no doubt of exactly what he meant.

CHAPTER TEN

It was pitch black outside when they began their drive home. There was only a sprinkling of stars in the sky and the moon was nowhere in view, although Jolie knew it must be out there somewhere. Wispy fragments of fog lay in grey clouds along the ditches near the road, occasionally sending out gossamer veils that swirled away from passing cars in a dancing mist. To Jolie, the light fog was a part of the ethereal enchantment of the moment as she sat there beside Steve.

Much too soon, Steve stopped the car at the curb in front of the LeBlanc home. Neither spoke as he turned off the ignition. Jolie wasn't in a hurry to go in and Steve wasn't prompting her to leave. He lit a cigarette, the matchlight throwing the carved features of his face into sharp relief. The silence continued to stretch out until the crickets chirping outside sounded unreasonably loud to Jolie's sensitive ears. She shifted uncomfortably in her seat and glanced over at Steve's darkened profile.

'Damn it!' he muttered savagely under his breath. With a vicious movement, he flicked the cigarette out of the opened car window before turning to face Jolie.

'What's the matter?' she whispered, wondering what she had done to make him so angry.

'You.' His hand closed around the back of her neck in a painful grip. 'I've never——'

She never heard what he was going to say because his mouth closed over hers. She would have moved into his arms, but his hand was firmly pinning her against the seat so she could get no closer to him. His kiss was so devastatingly sweet and possessive that the blood roared in her ears until she could hear nothing but the pounding of her own heart. Then Steve dragged his mouth away to nuzzle her neck and ear.

'I don't want you to go in,' he muttered thickly in her hair.

'I don't want to either,' she answered, her voice shaking with the emotion he had aroused.

Her admission served as a brake, halting his caress as he inhaled deeply and moved to his own side of the seat. He stared at her through the dimness of the car.

'You don't know what you're saying. You'd better go in . . . Now,' Steve added with growly emphasis. He raked his fingers through his raven black hair. 'I'll . . . I'll call you tomorrow.'

She opened the car door, the interior light switching on automatically. Glancing over at him before swinging her legs out, Jolie saw the hunger in his eyes as they watched her. She very nearly closed the door again to move into his arms, but discretion and common sense took over and she slid out of the car. She hurried towards the house before her resolve could weaken. Once there, she opened the front door and stood in its shadow to watch Steve drive away.

The house was quiet. Only the muted sound of instrumental music on the record player in the family room indicated anyone else was there. Jolie didn't feel like facing any of the family and recounting the events of the day. She wanted to savour those moments to herself for a little while longer. So she tiptoed up the stairs to her room. Leaving her door open, she crossed her room to switch on the floor lamp. As she turned to go back and shut the door, she saw Claudine standing in the doorway.

Her brunette hair was loose and lying around her shoulders like a black cloud, contrasting perfectly with her milky-white complexion. She was wearing a robe of an exotic blue-green design that reminded Jolie of peacock feathers. Beneath the lined robe was a matching short nightgown. Even from where Jolie was standing she could see that the wispy material peeping through the top of the robe was blatantly transparent. If it wasn't for the fact that the robe was lined, Claudine would have appeared indecently clothed.

'So you're back.' A dark brow was arched at Jolie. 'Did you enjoy your little outing with Steve?'

'I had a very good time,' Jolie replied calmly, refusing to pick up the invisible glove Claudine had thrown.

'I suppose you dragged him around to all those tourist places?'

'As a matter of fact, Steve thought I might enjoy Avery Island. So, at his suggestion, we went there.'

'He's been there so many times, it's a miracle he wasn't bored to death.' Claudine studied her fingernails. It was such a feline gesture that Jolie half expected to hear a miaow when Claudine looked up.

'I don't think Steve was bored,' she replied with a secret smile on her face that lit a fire of anger in Claudine's dark eyes. Jolie turned away to pick up her brush and began brushing her hair. She hoped, futilely, that Claudine would take the hint and discontinue the conversation.

'I hope you don't take his attentions seriously.' Claudine drawled from just behind her. 'An inexperienced girl like you could get hurt.'

'I think I'm old enough to take care of myself.' The brush didn't skip a stroke.

'His masculinity can be overpowering. Older women than you have fallen in the wake of it.'

'Including you?' Jolie blinked innocently at Claudine over her shoulder.

'I have more experience and endurance than most. I stay clear of the undertow. But I think you're out of your depth.'

'That's my problem, isn't it?' Sarcasm gleamed in her eyes and the false smile on Jolie's mouth.

'Of course,' Claudine retorted sharply, contorting her mouth into some semblance of a smile. 'I was just trying to give you a little friendly advice. If all you have in mind is a little harmless flirtation while you're on your holiday, then have it. You won't find a better partner than Steve. But he isn't about to be tied down.'

'That must be very frustrating for you.' Jolie never realized it could be so much fun getting in her little digs at this paragon of a malicious friend. In fact, she was beginning to enjoy their little talk.

'Steve is a man. With a man's appetites.' Smouldering rage burned in Claudine's face. 'I can satisfy his needs.'

'Any woman can satisfy those needs,' Jolie replied calmly.

'Let's get this straight.' The mask was removed now and her hate for Jolie was firmly revealed. 'Right now, your innocence amuses him, but it won't last for long. He'll either seduce you, in which case your innocence will be gone, or he'll grow tired of trying and drop you. You're only a passing fancy and you might as well realize it.'

'You may very well be right.' It was Jolie's turn to unsheath her claws. 'On the other hand, he may be getting tired of "used" merchandise and would prefer to try something brand new so he can mould it to fit his needs.'

Claudine's hand raised threateningly in the air. For a moment Jolie thought she was going to strike her. Instead Claudine turned on her heel and walked to the door. But she didn't leave. She turned, tossing her hair over her shoulder in a defiant gesture and studied Jolie contemptuously.

'You're making a very big mistake,' she said icily.

' "Sticks and stones may break my bones," ' Jolie chanted quietly. She didn't have to finish it as Claudine swirled out of the room.

'Well,' Jolie thought to herself, 'I won the first battle, but now it's war.' Claudine had been the one to drag it out in the open and it just wasn't in Jolie to back down from anyone. Regardless of what the morrow brought, it had been a satisfying day.

And tonight she didn't want to worry about what might happen tomorrow. All she wanted to remember when her head rested on the pillow was the rapturous happiness she had felt in Steve's arms. She wasn't going to let Claudine's spiteful and jealous tongue disturb her dreams.

Jolie was up early the next morning donning her freshly laundered sundress, courtesy of the ever thoughtful Mrs. LeBlanc, of bright oranges and yellow flowers against a background of snowy white. She chose her dressier open-toed white sandals and took special pains applying the light make-up. When she was all done, Jolie, who was usually very critical of her own appearance, couldn't find much fault with her reflection.

Softly humming a gay tune, she skipped lightly down the steps to the kitchen. All Steve had said was that he would call her today. He had made no mention of any plans to go somewhere or, for that matter, what time he would call, morning, noon or night. But Jolie was ready for anything.

Mrs. LeBlanc, Michelle and Guy were seated around the dinette table. Emile LeBlanc had already left and Claudine had not yet risen, which didn't upset Jolie a bit. As always Mrs. LeBlanc was her cheerful self and Jolie's own bubbling happiness matched her bright greeting. Guy's brief nod in her direction was grim and condemning. But she shrugged it off easily as she poured herself a cup of coffee and seated herself in the vacant chair at the end of the table.

'You slipped off to bed last night before you gave us an account of your adventure yesterday.' Michelle's eyes twinkled with a pert gleam from Jolie to her brother.

'Yes, Jolie, tell us where Etienne took you,' Mrs. LeBlanc prompted, while Guy continued staring morosely into his cup.

'We went to Avery Island.' Then she went on to give them some of her impressions of what she saw, carefully avoiding too much emphasis on her companion.

'Oh, you should see the Gardens in March when the azaleas and the camellias are both in bloom!' Mrs. LeBlanc exclaimed with an expressive wave of her hand. 'So many colours! So many flowers everywhere! Everything is so plentiful that it seems almost pagan!'

'The best part about the Jungle Gardens, though, is that the flowers don't have to be in bloom for a person to enjoy the beauty of the place. Of course, there are different flowers blooming all year through,' Jolie remarked. 'I wouldn't have missed seeing it for anything.'

'I'm glad Etienne took you there,' the older woman smiled.

'Claudine isn't,' said Guy, breaking his self-imposed silence.

'Now why should Claudine mind?' With her arms akimbo, Mrs. LeBlanc looked curiously at her son.

'Oh, Mother, surely you don't need to ask.' Guy shook his head hopelessly.

'If you're trying to say that there's something serious between Etienne and Claudine, then you're wrong,' Mrs. LeBlanc stated emphatically. 'How long have they known each other? Four years? Five years? That's a very long time in which to find out if they're serious or not. Too long with a pair as hot-blooded as Etienne and Claudine. No, they're good friends, but nothing more.'

'Mama, you're very old-fashioned,' Guy smiled at her sadly.

'Maybe,' she nodded. 'But when a man puts a ring on a woman's finger, then you know he's serious. Before that he is only fooling around. I think you're upset because it was Jolie who was with Etienne and not because it was your sister's boy-friend who was with Jolie. You regret that it was not yourself who spent the day with her.'

Guy glanced at the uncomfortable look on Jolie's face and shrugged. 'You're probably right about that, Mama.'

It was obvious that Mrs. LeBlanc was prepared to pursue the subject, but luckily the phone in the hallway rang, causing Jolie's heart to skip a beat in anticipation.

'I'll get it.' Guy rose from the table before either his sister or his mother had time to react to the sound.

Jolie couldn't blame him for wanting to escape from the conversation, which although it was slightly embarrassing, was also very enlightening. Michelle glanced up at the clock above the kitchen sink and sighed.

'I almost wish it were the principal calling to say the water main has broken and the school is flooded. I don't feel up to facing those kids today.' Even as she spoke Michelle was gathering her papers together. 'I honestly think teachers look forward to the week-ends more than the students. We're just too outnumbered.'

'Jolie, telephone!' Guy's voice rang clearly in the kitchen.

She mumbled a breathless 'excuse me' before pushing herself awkwardly away from the table. Her heart was tripping away like a jackhammer as she hurried into the hall. Avoiding the condemning glare and bitterly twisted smile on Guy's face, Jolie took the telephone receiver from him.

'Hello,' she answered, knowing there was only one person who could be on the other end of the line.

'Good morning,' Steve replied. His husky voice managed to transmit little tremors that tingled through her. 'Did you sleep well last night?'

'Like a log,' she laughed nervously, wishing Guy would return to the kitchen and stop watching her.

'That's nice. I didn't sleep a wink.' A wry note crept into his voice and it caught at her breath.

'I'm sorry,' she said for want of a more suitable reply.

'Are you?' Steve chuckled. 'That's not much of a comfort.'

'I know.' Jolie turned her back to Guy and twined her fingers in the coiled receiver cord.

'I called to tell you that I'm going to be tied up today,' Steve went on, amusement still tinting his words. 'One of the field tractors broke down yesterday. I'll probably have to go into Lafayette for parts. It might take the better part of the day and night to get it running again.'

'I understand,' Jolie said, trying to hide her disappointment. 'I mean ... there was nothing definitely planned anyway, and the tractor is hardly something you could have known about yesterday.'

Behind her, she heard Guy's footsteps walking towards the kitchen and unwittingly sighed her relief.

'I'm disappointed, too, Jolie.' There was such quiet sincerity in Steve's voice that her heart, which had slowed at the news she wouldn't see him today, set off again at breakneck speed. 'So what will you do with yourself today while I'm slaving trying to get the tractor running?'

'Miss you,' she replied pertly, liking the sound of his laughter on the other end of the phone at her answer.

'Any more comments like that and I'm liable to say to hell with the tractor,' he growled with mock fierceness.

'Promise?' she said boldly, then hurried on before he could take her seriously. 'I take that back. After all, I am a farmer's daughter and I know that broken machinery can't wait for a rainy day.'

'Thanks, ladybird. Maybe tomorrow.'

'Yes, tomorrow.'

After the click of his receiver, Jolie replaced the phone in its cradle, her hand remaining on it for a short time as if she could prolong the contact with Steve. Again there were footsteps in the hall, this time coming nearer instead of retreating. Fixing a smile on her face, Jolie turned. It was Guy entering the hallway. He stared at her, his brown eyes reflecting hurt and uncertainty.

'If you're free this afternoon, we could play some tennis.' The words were said in a defiant manner as if it made no difference to him whether or not she accepted him.

'I'm free,' Jolie answered quietly, wishing the rising compassion would stem the guilt she felt for putting that look in his eyes. But she couldn't control the fact that it was Steve she had fallen in love with and Guy was only a friend.

Guy started to reply, then halted, closing his mouth tightly and nodding as he walked to the front door. Yet neither Guy's depressive mood nor the knowledge that she wouldn't see Steve today could darken Jolie's spirits. The phone call had confirmed her hope that Steve wanted to be with her. Probably not as much as she wanted to be with him, but he had sounded sincerely sorry that he couldn't see her. That in itself had been consolation.

By late afternoon, Guy had shaken free of the sullen mood and Jolie's slight tenseness soon vanished under his carefree demeanour. After two games of tennis with Guy the victor, though not by a large margin, a small group of his friends arrived on the courts. Jolie was no longer the object of Guy's attention as he transferred his allegiance to an attractive blonde. Since Jolie was a competent tennis player, she was a welcome partner choice in mixed and matched doubles. After a particularly blistering game where both couples were equally skilled, Jolie insisted on sitting out and catching her breath. She would have preferred to call it a day and go home, but Guy lingered even when the rest made comments in the same vein. Jolie wanted to remind him that his mother undoubtedly had the evening meal ready, but was afraid she would sound like a wet blanket. She had learned early in her dating that no man wanted to be reminded that momma had supper waiting at home.

Finally the crimson blush of twilight signalled the end of the party and Guy very reluctantly escorted Jolie to the car. He had the grace to murmur an apology which she shrugged off, teasing him about his recuperative abilities.

'I borrowed a page from Steve's book,' Guy replied blandly. 'I heard him taunt Claudine that there was never a woman that another woman couldn't make a man forget in time.'

Did Steve really believe that? Jolie asked herself. Because if he did, then how much did she mean to him? A terrible fear wrapped cold fingers around her heart. Was she reading too much into Steve's attention? In order to believe her love returned, was she reading more into his caresses than he intended? It was frightening to remember that Steve himself had told her that marriage was not a part of his plans. He didn't even believe that love existed. If Steve discovered that she was in love with him, would he smile and tell her that she would get over it?

With the kind of life Steve had known, it was unlikely that he would have ever known a deep abiding love of any kind. Orphaned when he was a baby, spending his early manhood at sea, drifting from port to port, never having a place to call home. No wonder he had been so drawn to Cameron Hall, the plantation that had his name carved on its gates.

But did that help her? Was he in love with her? Or would another woman supplant her memory in his mind? Was she another shipboard romance for him, just another girl in a different port?

As she sat silently in the car beside Guy, Jolie felt afraid, vulnerable and very uncertain.

CHAPTER ELEVEN

WHEN Steve called the following day, Jolie had just left the house to run into town on a personal errand. The message he left with Mrs. LeBlanc had been that he would call Jolie that night. While she regretted missing his call, Jolie still had something to look forward to even if she had a whole day to wait.

Of course, there was always the decision of what to do with the rest of the day. Sitting idle was not something that came easily to her. The minutes passed much too slowly that way. Although the thought of more sightseeing wasn't exciting, it seemed the surest way of making the evening come quicker. About the only place nearby that she hadn't been to was the Rip Van Winkle Gardens west of New Iberia.

The stately English-style gardens seemed cold after the tropical abundance of the Jungle Gardens at Avery Island, but she was minus her companion. Jolie was sure that had a great deal to do with her lack of enthusiasm. The day was extremely hot and humid, so when Jolie drove back through the town of New Iberia, she decided to stop for a cold drink. By accident or a subconscious direction, she had parked her Volkswagen on the same block the store was located where Steve had ordered the material for the sofa and chairs. Obeying an impulse that she knew was foolish, Jolie entered the store. The sales clerk who had waited on them recognized her immediately.

He explained that the shipment had just arrived that very morning and remarked how fortunate it was that Jolie had come when he was about to contact Mr. Cameron. Since it had been prepaid, he inquired if Jolie wanted to take it today. She hesitated briefly, disliking the idea that Steve might think she was being over forward picking up the material before reasoning that she was only saving him a journey to New Iberia.

It took some manoeuvring to get the bulky material into her little car, but it was finally accomplished. Not until Jolie was sitting in the restaurant two stores away did she realize how long she had tarried in the store. After a few sips of lemonade she returned to her car, not wanting to be the cause for the LeBlancs' evening meal being delayed as it had been last night when she and Guy had been late.

Jolie arrived in plenty of time for dinner but too late for Steve's call. Frustrated and angry at herself for being gone so long, she was barely able to eat anything. Did Steve think she was playing a game? He hadn't said he would call again. What if he didn't? All the while she was helping Mrs. LeBlanc carry dishes to the kitchen, Jolie was calling herself fifty kinds of fool. She debated calling him, but the telephone can be a cold communicator. There was only one way, she decided. She would drive out to Cameron Hall that very night no matter how bold and forward it looked. Besides, she had the excellent pretext of delivering the upholstering material.

She didn't tell Mrs. LeBlanc anything except that she was going out and would be back later that evening. Dusk had already given way to night time when Jolie slid behind the wheel of her car. Michelle had just driven in after returning to the schoolhouse for some paper she had left and Jolie was forced to wait until her car was parked and the driveway was clear.

'Are you going out?' Michelle called on her way to the house.

'Yes,' Jolie answered without explaining further.

'The fog is a little thick. Be careful.' Then Michelle waved and entered the house.

Once Jolie left St. Martinville and began her way through the country, Michelle's comment on the fog turned into an understatement. It swirled around her so thickly that her pace was reduced to that of a blind man without a cane. Her headlights could barely reveal the ditch alongside the road, let alone illuminate the road more than a few feet ahead of her. Moisture condensed on the windscreen to add to the difficulty of seeing. It was only by instinct that she found the correct crossroads and put her on the road that would take her to the dirt lane leading to the plantation.

Time inched by as slowly as her Volkswagen. And the more time that went by, the surer Jolie became that she had missed the turn. Her fingers ached from clenching the steering wheel so tightly. A throbbing headache had begun at the back of her neck until her eyes hurt from the strain of peering into the grey shroud that surrounded her. A sob of despair rose in her throat that she had foolishly got herself lost when a small white sign glistened near the side of the road. It was impossible to read it as the fog thickened around it. She stopped the car altogether and stepped out, leaving the motor running while she got a closer look at the sign with the flashlight from the glove compartment.

'Private Road—No Trespassing'. Unwelcome words that brought a sigh of relief. By some miracle, she had made it. The plantation was a quarter of a mile further. The only trouble was the closer she drove to the plantation and the bayou on the opposite side, the denser the fog grew. There was no chance at all that she would be able to see the iron gates of the entrance. The only alternative was for her to guess at the distance and then explore on foot, relying on her flashlight to find them.

Four steps from the car and she could barely make out its peculiar round shape. The fact that it was red helped. Taking two steps forward, Jolie inhaled deeply, knowing that the fog had closed in around the car and hidden it completely from view. She inched her way along the ditch looking for the culvert leading to the gates while she tried to rid herself of the fear that she was only going to end up getting lost in this grey-black cloud.

In the murky darkness, she nearly missed the entrance. As usual it was padlocked. The beam from the flashlight barely penetrated the fog beyond the grillework. Hesitantly she touched the cold, damp bars, giving them a shake to see how sturdy they were. The bell hanging from the pillar didn't seem to have any resonance at all. Jolie decided only a foghorn could pierce this. Still she waited before attempting to climb the iron bars. The last thing she wanted to have happen was for her to meet the black German Shepherd in this weather. But not even the dog appeared to welcome her.

The gate was very easy to climb over, especially for a former tomboy. On the other side, the trees and shrubs loomed ominously on either side of the narrow lane. Any moment she expected the dog to spring from the darkness, white fangs flashing in the night. The only thing her light picked out was the branches of the giant oaks, the Spanish moss taking on ghostly decoration. Jolie couldn't help thinking it was a perfect setting for one of those spooky Gothic novels. A small patch of light winked dimly at her from the garçonnière, and her already jangled nerves were set on edge when a low, rumbling bark sounded from the narrow gallery. Jolie was close enough to make out the light shining from the screen door and the dog standing guard in front of it.

'Steve!' she called out. The dog growled in answer although he didn't come any closer to her. Jolie called again, her voice sounding strange in the ghostly silence. If he were inside the garçonnière, he would have surely heard her.

The dog obviously considered her no threat since he raised no objection when she stepped on to the porch. Still Jolie hesitated to walk past the dog to the door.

'Where's your master, Black?' she asked the dog.

His tail wagged in what seemed a friendly manner and Jolie took a courageous step towards the door. Instantly the dog's lip curled and a threatening growl came from his throat. When she halted, his tail wagged again. Evidently he had decided she could be on the gallery, but the garçonnière was forbidden. She wasn't going to argue with him.

'Is it all right if I wait here for Steve?' It was silly asking the dog since he couldn't reply, but the silence of the fog was beginning to wear on her nerves. The sound of her own voice was a small comfort and at least she wasn't talking to herself.

The muggy dampness had begun to penetrate her clothing, sending its cool fingers into her bones. She shivered and rubbed her arms briskly while she glanced apprehensively around. There was no sign of Steve at all. The thought of finding her way back to the Volkswagen and then back to the LeBlanc home in this fog was frightening.

'What are you doing here?' Steve materialized catlike at the far end of the narrow gallery.

'I came to see you.' Her tongue was jumping about like her heart. 'I'd just decided that you weren't here.'

As Steve walked closer, Jolie could see the anger dancing in his eyes. She had expected surprise, even gladness, but she hadn't thought he would be angry.

'The material for the sofa and chairs arrived today. I was in New Iberia and happened to stop.' She felt compelled to fill the uneasy silence made more uncomfortable by his measuring gaze. 'I left the material out in the car. I didn't have anything special to do tonight, so I thought I'd bring it out.'

'How did you get here?' he demanded.

'I drove,' she answered weakly under his glowering look. 'I didn't realize the fog was so bad until I got out in the country.' She shivered again, but not just from coldness. 'I was practically here by then or I would have turned around. The dampness sure goes right through you.'

'Why didn't you go into the house where it's warm?' he growled, flinging open the screen door and pushing her inside.

'According to your dog, I wasn't allowed any farther than the porch,' Jolie retaliated, hurt by Steve's strange behaviour.

Steve glanced at the dog sitting outside as if he had forgotten it was there. He raked his fingers through his black hair that had begun to curl slightly from the dampness.

'Sit by the fire and warm up while I get the pick-up,' he ordered sharply, gesturing towards the fireplace and the tiny flame licking at a solitary log. 'It has foglights and I can drive your car back in the morning.'

'Thanks for being so overjoyed to see me!' Jolie tossed sarcastically after him as he started for the door. There was a betraying trembling in her chin as the tears burned the back of her eyes.

'What's that supposed to mean?' Steve glared at her.

'Good grief! I drive all the way out here and I don't even get a "hello, how are you" before you're bundling me up and taking me home!' She had to shout or she would cry.

'How are you! How are you! You crazy, mixed-up little idiot!'

With a quaking body, Jolie watched Steve inhale deeply to control his anger. He studied her silently with his hands on his hips.

'I don't understand?' she murmured, finding it harder and harder to meet his accusing eyes.

'That's obvious,' he replied grimly. 'How many cars did you pass on the way here?'

'None.' Jolie felt herself growing smaller.

'That's because anyone with an ounce of sense wouldn't be out in this fog.'

'Michelle had just come home when I left. She didn't seem concerned.'

'You didn't tell her where you were going either, did you?' Steve asked and sighed in exasperation when Jolie shook her head that she hadn't. 'If you had, I'm sure she would have warned you.'

'Well, she didn't, and I'm here! And you needn't be so beastly about it!' She had to cover her mouth to keep that little choking sob from making itself heard.

'You could have run off the road upside down into a ditch or been crunched like an accordion against a telephone pole!' A short angry laugh followed his outburst as he shook his head. 'And I'm not supposed to be in the least upset by such thoughts. What do you think I am?'

'I didn't think you cared,' Jolie whispered.

Steve covered the distance between them in one liquid movement. His fingers dug into the bones of her arms as he lifted her on her tiptoes.

'Cared?' he groaned. His words were muffled by her brown hair.

'You're hurting me,' she protested weakly. His nearness was already dulling her senses of pain where his fingers dug into her flesh.

'You deserve it,' he replied grimly, relaxing his hold enough to reduce the pressure and still retain the grip. 'You can be glad that I can't make up my mind whether to turn you over my knee or to take you in my arms.'

'If you feel that way,' Jolie gazed into his face, thrilling to the fires she saw burning there, 'then why do you want me to leave?'

'Would you rather stay here until the fog lifts? It would be tomorrow morning before it burns off. You can't honestly expect to stay all night with me without "something" happening, can you?'

'No, no, of course not,' Jolie murmured, pulling gently away from him. 'It's just that . . . I haven't seen you for—for so long.' She felt his hands settle on her shoulders, but not so fiercely this time. 'I missed your call this morning . . . and . . . and again this afternoon.' She spun quickly around to face him, the longing for him revealed openly in her eyes. 'I just wanted to see you.'

'I wanted to see you, too.' Was it her imagination or were his hands trembling as he held her? 'But not here!'

'What difference does it make?'

'If I have to explain that to you,' Steve breathed in angrily, 'then you're more innocent than I thought.'

'Damn these freckles and damn my face!' Jolie

cried, flinging herself away from him in a fit of temper. She looked around her desperately for something to throw to relieve her tension and found nothing. 'Why does everyone keep harping on my virtuous nature? Damn my virtue! I don't feel in the least bit virtuous!'

'You don't know what you're talking about!' Steve shouted back.

'What, are you a Boy Scout all of a sudden?' she asked sarcastically, before quicksilver tears sprang from her eyes. 'I can't help the way I feel about you. Don't you see? I just want you to hold me in your arms. I can't help it.'

'You're talking nonsense, Jolie.'

'I'm talking to a brick wall, that's what I'm doing,' she sniffled, wiping the tears of self-pity away from her face and regaining her control.

Before she had an opportunity to apologize for her unwarranted outburst, she was yanked into his arms. Her breath was knocked away as she came to an abrupt halt against his hard chest.

'I wish I were a brick wall,' Steve hissed before covering her mouth with a rough, bruising kiss.

All the checked desire burst forth with the fury of a volcanic explosion as Steve ravaged her mouth, her neck and her face. In the stranglehold of his embrace, Jolie was powerless. She could neither respond nor protest as he brutally forced her to submit to his punishing kisses.

Then he was sweeping her off her feet and lifting her bodily into his arms. The crushing grip about her shoulders prevented her from seeing where he was carrying her. Her head was pushed way back as his mouth continued violating hers while her hands pushed ineffectually against his chest. His stride changed and it took Jolie a moment to realize that he was climbing the stairs. With a great surge of strength she pushed him away from her.

'Where are you taking me?' she asked, gasping for the breath he had denied her.

'The couch is too small and the floor is cold.' His blue eyes gleamed wickedly into her face, their callousness frightening her more than his wrathful kisses. 'My bed will be less restrictive and softer.'

'No,' she whimpered as he twisted her head around for his kiss, not pausing in his flight up the steps. 'Steve, no!'

The savagery of his touch abated with her weak appeal without lessening the strength of his hold. Steve had stopped and was setting her back on her feet. The soft light from the stairs barely illuminated the room they were in, but there was sufficient light for Jolie to see the shining headboard of the brass bed.

'What's the matter?' Steve whispered huskily into her ear as his hands continued their rough fondling of her shoulders and back. 'Don't you want me to make love to you, Jolie?'

An icy-cold numbness spread over her. 'Not this way, Steve,' she sobbed. 'Not this way, please.'

'What way is that?'

'Without any ... any tenderness or ... or affection,' she stammered. 'As if ... if I ... I were just any w-woman.'

The humiliation in her voice brought Steve's head away from his exploration of her neck as he tilted his head upwards towards the ceiling before bringing it slowly back to focus on her tear-stained face that was staring at the floor.

'I want you, Jolie,' he sighed softly, his knuckles tracing the outline of her cheek. 'I won't deny it.'

'Why?' she persisted, needing to know the truth —the depth of his attraction to her.

'Because you're a woman and I'm a man. Is there ever any more to it than that?'

'Yes, Steve, there is,' Jolie answered slowly and firmly, lifting her head up to look into his masked expression. Her own undying love for him proved that.

'You say that because you're young.' There was a faraway smile twisting his mouth. 'You haven't had a chance to discover how fickle humans are.'

'Are you fickle? Will you forget me?'

'Maybe not completely.' The way he was looking at her was as if he were implanting her image on his mind. 'You're a special person. Natural, honest and giving.'

'I suppose I should thank you for that compliment.' There was a bitter taste in her mouth that tainted her quietly spoken words.

'I never really meant to hurt you, Jolie. I'm sorry,' Steve shook his head, his hand tightening momentarily on her shoulder before he released her completely. 'I'll take you home now.'

'Don't be sorry for me, Steve.' A flash of fire flared in her brown eyes. 'My Aunt Brigitte told me once that real love was rare. Few people ever find it because most are too selfish. They are incapable of giving of themselves in more than a superficial way.'

'And you think I'm one of them?' he asked coldly.

No, Jolie admitted to herself, she didn't think he was, although everything he said and did indicated it. Confusion was written on her face.

'Tell me why did you treat me the way you did just now—as if I was a common tramp or something?' she asked, unaware of the pleading tone in her voice.

'The truth?' His eyebrow arched arrogantly at her. 'Because you were so naïvely asking for it.'

'I was not!' Jolie cried indignantly. She would have raised her hand to strike him, but Steve had firmly pinioned her wrists to prevent such an attack.

'Not consciously, no. But if I'd been tender and loving as you said you wanted, we would have been in that bed right now.'

'If you believe that, then why didn't you take advantage of me?' Jolie demanded, her breath coming in short angry gasps.

' "Advantage". What an old-fashioned word!' he chuckled cynically. His dark blue eyes were nearly stripping her of her pride. 'But, in answer to your question, I haven't sunk so low as to be seducing virgins.'

'I don't understand you.' She shook her head in bewilderment. 'One minute you act as if you really care for me and the next you're trying to prove how cold and unfeeling you are.'

His lips compressed into a grim line as he stared at her without answering. The narrowing of his eyes made Jolie aware once again of the length and thickness of his lashes. For a moment she stared hypnotically into the depths of his gaze.

'This isn't the time or the place for the kind of discussion you want,' Steve said, moving past her and walking down the steps. Halfway down, he turned to look up at her. 'Come on, I'll take you home.'

Jolie hesitated. Another thought had just occurred to her. 'Steve,' she called in a fearful voice, 'are you using me to forget . . . to forget Claudine?'

'What put that thought in your head?' he scowled.

'I heard . . .' Then she paused, knowing any reference to Guy would bring a derisive response. 'I heard that men sometimes see other women in order to forget one special woman.'

'Am I going to have to carry you down the stairs as well?' he asked with ominous quietness.

'Is it true . . . that you . . . that men do that?' she persisted, walking to the head of the stairs to look fully into his cold face.

'Yes, it's true, and quite effective. It doesn't happen to apply in this case, although the reverse might be worth considering.'

'Do you mean you want to forget me?' Jolie breathed, a flicker of hope lighting her eyes.

'Especially when you test my patience as you're doing right now. For the last time, I'm taking you home. Now get down here.'

Steve appeared to be encompassed by a strange brooding mood. The savagery of those earlier moments was too easily remembered for Jolie to persist in further conversation when he was making it plain that he wanted none of it. His feelings towards her were so ambivalent that she wondered if even he knew how he felt. She certainly didn't. If anything she had become more uncertain. He was too complex for her limited experience to fathom. And Jolie was sure he knew that, too.

The foglights on the pick-up truck effectively increased the visibility. Although their speed was slower than normal, it was still faster than the snail's pace Jolie had driven on the way out. For all the attention Steve paid her, she could have been an inanimate object in the seat beside him. When they pulled up in front of the LeBlanc house, Steve left the motor running, letting her know there would be no prolonged good nights.

'I'll bring your car back in the morning, probably before you're up.' His harsh words revealed his hurry and Jolie reached for the door latch, but a hand on her arm forestalled her. 'I have to go to New Orleans tomorrow on some business. I'll be gone a couple of days.'

'Why are you telling me?' Jolie knew her question had a belligerent tone, but Steve's coldness had hurt and she wanted to strike back.

'I don't know.' Steve emitted an angry sigh and reached across her to open the door. 'Good night, Jolie.'

CHAPTER TWELVE

'WHERE have you been?'

Jolie had raced all the way into the house and was halfway up the stairs when Claudine's demanding question brought her up short. All Jolie wanted was the seclusion of her room where she could shed some of the tears that were scorching her eyes.

'On an errand, if it's any of your business,' she retorted.

'It must have been a convenient errand since it enabled you to have Steve bring you back,' Claudine jeered. When Jolie would have continued her flight up the stairs, the raven-haired girl went on, her dark eyes flashing like burning coals, 'It's a pity you didn't invite him in. There was something I wanted to talk to him about, but I suppose it will just have to wait until tomorrow.'

'It will have to wait longer than that.' Jolie made her voice sound as quietly sarcastic as Claudine's, although she didn't trust herself to meet the older woman's gaze. 'Steve is going to New Orleans tomorrow. He'll be gone for a couple of days.'

'How unfortunate for you!' Claudine called after her as Jolie scurried up the stairs, the soft complacency in that voice hurting more than the previous sneering words.

The little red Volkswagen was parked in its

former place behind the house the next morning when Jolie arose. She had slept fitfully and the effects were revealed in the drawn look about her face and the dark circles under her eyes. She had tried hard to make herself see how illogical she had been, but there was no room in her heart for logic, only Steve. What did it matter that she had known him less than two weeks? People had fallen in love before in a matter of hours, which never made their love any less potent or lasting.

Physical attraction. Infatuation. Fascination for an older, more experienced man. All of those could be true. Jolie knew they weren't, just as she had known she didn't love John the way a woman should love her husband.

If only she could understand Steve! When she was in his embrace, Jolie was certain he desired her and maybe even more than that. Maybe he even loved her. Then with mercurial swiftness, he would declare that he didn't believe in love—that he would never marry. Was he afraid of love? It was impossible to believe that Steve was afraid of anything, and certainly not something as harmless as love.

Harmless! That was a laugh! Look at what it was doing to her. She was twisted in knots it would take an expert seaman to untangle. Seaman—that's what Steve had been. Had she thought of that analogy because Steve was the reason for her torment? The whole situation seemed so hopeless to her.

And knowing that Steve was in New Orleans made the day stretch ahead of her with incredible emptiness. Even if he were here, it might be just as discouraging. With a bit of wry humour, Jolie remembered the dilemma she had been in before she had come to Louisiana. It seemed such a petty problem now in the face of her monumental love for Steve.

Jolie knew she couldn't wander about the house all day. Mrs. LeBlanc had been very curious about her morose expression at the breakfast table. The thought of visiting any tourist spots failed to interest her. There was one thing she did want to do. It would probably be foolish and a big mistake, one that she would come to regret, but Jolie had wanted to take pictures of Cameron Hall so that when she returned to South Dakota she could show her family what their ancestral home looked like. The very thought of returning home and never seeing Steve again sent her into new depths of despair.

Wandering about the plantation grounds with the ever-watchful German Shepherd at her heels did little to improve her low spirits. It seemed so final to be taking pictures of the place as if she were leaving tomorrow when she had at least another week of her allotted vacation time left. She knew she would never be able to look at the pictures once they were developed without thinking of the present owner of the plantation, of imagining him against the backdrop of flame-pink azaleas and large circular pillars.

Jolie returned to the LeBlanc home late that afternoon, arriving at the same time that Guy and Michelle did. It would have been rude to retreat to her room, although that was what she wanted to do, but Michelle had issued such a friendly invitation to join them for cold drinks that Jolie hadn't been able to refuse. Unfortunately, after only a few minutes of conversation, Michelle was called to the telephone, leaving Jolie with Guy, the one thing she had wanted to avoid.

'Cheer up, Jolie,' Guy said, glancing over at her with a smile that was part amusement and part sympathy.

'What do you mean?' she asked stiffly.

'Your mouth is on the road to a permanent droop. It isn't as if you weren't warned that this would probably happen.'

'I don't know what you're talking about. What would happen?' On the defensive, Jolie rose to her feet and walked over to look out the window, not seeing the red cardinal flitting about the magnolia tree.

'Claudine and Steve, of course.'

'Steve's in New Orleans,' Jolie said absently. Something in Guy's complacent statement made her turn around. 'Isn't he?'

'You don't honestly know, do you?' Guy shook his head in amazement.

'Know what?' A terrible premonition of something bad had a grip on her chest.

'Claudine went to New Orleans with Steve.'

'No!' she breathed. Her head moved from side to side in disbelief. 'No, that's not true!'

A hysterical sob rose in her throat and Jolie stifled it with a clenched hand over her mouth. Now she understood the reasons for some of the things Steve had said last night. He had very tactfully been trying to tell her that he didn't care for her. He had obviously guessed the extent of her feelings and was trying to make her see that he didn't feel the same. He had even made a hint that he might use Claudine to forget Jolie, preparing her for the news that Guy had just given her.

'You really fell for him, didn't you?' Guy had come up behind her and placed his hands gently on her shoulders. She couldn't trust her voice to speak without crying so Jolie nodded agreement. 'You crazy little kid,' he moaned, shaking her gently before drawing her into his arms. 'I told you Claudine would win.'

'She didn't,' Jolie answered in a shaky voice, raising her tear-filled eyes to meet his. 'Don't you see? Steve doesn't care about either one of us. That's what he was trying to tell me last night.'

'Last night? Did you see him last night?' Guy asked in an accusing voice.

'Yes, for a little while.' Not for the world would she tell Guy how Steve had tried to frighten her away with a threatened seducement. If she had felt hurt and humiliated before, it was nothing compared to what she was suffering now. 'What am I going to do, Guy?' she whispered. 'I can't face him again. I just can't!'

'He had no business playing around with you,' Guy declared through gritted teeth.

'It's a little late to be thinking about that now,' saddened and amused by the avenging brother look on Guy's face. 'Besides, it's hardly Steve's fault that I made a fool of myself,' Jolie added soberly as the first wave of shock subsided. 'I think maybe it's time I went home.'

'To South Dakota?'

'Yes. I ran away from one problem there right into another.' Determinedly she wiped her cheeks free from their tears and squared her shoulders. 'If a change of scene was the cure before, it should be effective again.'

'But you planned to stay another week. You told Mother you would be.'

'I know what I planned,' she sighed, 'but . . . but I think it's better that I change those plans.'

Jolie made the announcement to the LeBlanc family that evening at the dinner table. She used the pretext that she had received a letter from her parents, which she had, and that a close relative was ill, which wasn't true, and this had led to her sudden decision. If she packed tonight and loaded the car in the morning, she could be on the road home before Steve and Claudine returned from New Orleans.

But Jolie hadn't counted on the opposition raised by Emile LeBlanc who was insistent that she shouldn't start the long trip until her car had been checked out by a local garage. She tried desperately to assure him that this had been done thoroughly before she had left South Dakota and it was completely unnecessary for it to be done again. He was just as adamant that Jolie, who had become almost a member of his family during her short stay, should not set out on the long trip faced with the possibility of some mechanical failure of her car. Then Mrs. LeBlanc had chimed in that tomorrow was Saturday and the week-end was not a time to be driving. Finally Jolie was forced to agree to have her car checked again, but she refused to wait until Monday. She would leave Sunday morning regardless of the traffic.

By late Saturday afternoon Jolie had all her suitcases packed and ready to load into the car. Guy gave her a lift to the local garage to pick up the Volkswagen which had required only a few minor adjustments. As Jolie settled the bill, she gazed over at the young man who had become her silent supporter.

'When do you think they'll be back?' she asked quietly, knowing she didn't have to spell out that by 'they' she meant Steve and Claudine.

'He probably won't drive after dark because of the fog, so they'll be home any time between now and sundown.'

As it happened when Jolie and Guy returned to the LeBlanc house, it was to learn that Steve had just dropped Claudine off and had left. It was a relief to know that she wasn't going to run into him accidentally. The Fates had been kind to send her to the garage at that time to collect her car, thus saving her further embarrassment. Nor was Claudine about. She was monopolizing the bathroom after a muggy trip from New Orleans, which made Jolie happy since she wouldn't have to suffer the older girl's smirk of triumph.

Jolie and Guy were outside arranging her suitcases in the little Volkswagen when Michelle came to the back door and told Jolie she was wanted on the telephone.

'Who is it?' Jolie asked as she glanced apprehensively at Guy.

'I didn't ask, but it sounds like Steve,' Michelle answered, letting the screen door shut as she walked back into the house.

'Do you want me to tell him you're too busy to come to the phone?' Guy asked.

Jolie brushed her short hair behind her ears and breathed in deeply. 'No,' she said firmly, all the time wondering what kind of fool she was. 'He's not likely to try to change my mind.'

Her words sounded very courageous, but she felt like running as she picked up the telephone receiver lying on the table in the hallway. 'Be brisk,' she told herself.

'Yes?' she said into the receiver. Her voice sounded very cool and businesslike, but her knees were trembling like jelly.

'Hello, it's Steve,' he announced unnecessarily since she would have recognized his voice anywhere. 'Your car was gone when I dropped Claudine off.'

How could he be so offhand about it? Jolie wondered as she made a noncommittal reply. 'I heard you were back from New Orleans.'

'There was a football game, so the traffic was pretty heavy, or we would have been back sooner than we were.'

'Look,' she couldn't stand this small talk, 'I'm glad you phoned. I was going to give you a ring later on,' she lied, 'to let you know I was leaving tomorrow to go back to South Dakota.'

'What?' It was said so quietly that she almost didn't hear it.

'Yes, you see an aunt of mine is in the hospital

and my folks wrote and suggested I return home. It happened rather suddenly, I guess, and she needs this operation.' Why was she rattling on so as if she had to convince him of the sincerity in her reason for leaving?

'It sounds very sudden,' Steve said dryly.

'Yes, well, I wanted to say goodbye before I left, which was why I was going to call you later.'

'I want to talk to you, Jolie.' He spoke slowly and very distinctly.

'I'm sorry. I just have so much to do before I leave—packing and so on—that it's really impossible for me to——'

'Is that Steve on the phone?'

Claudine's voice brought Jolie's hand over the receiver so the voice wouldn't carry through to Steve. Claudine was looking down at her over the stair railing dressed in a green terry cloth robe that stopped short at her knees.

'Yes, it is,' Jolie answered. She asked Steve to hold the line a minute before she turned back to Claudine. 'Was there something you wanted to talk to him about?'

'Yes,' Claudine stated with wide eyes and a theatrical sigh as she walked the rest of the way down the steps. 'I can't find my blue and green peignoir set. I've looked everywhere, but I must have inadvertently packed the nightgown in with Steve's things.'

'Here.' Jolie thrust the phone into Claudine's face. 'You ask him.'

Rigid with anger and jealousy, Jolie remembered the blue-green outfit that had reminded her of peacock feathers in all its see-through glory. Claudine shrugged at Jolie's irate gesture and calmly took the receiver.

'Steve? Claudine.' She smiled sweetly at Jolie, whose feet were rooted to the floor. 'You remember my blue-green gown? I can't find it and I was wondering if it had got mixed up with your things? . . . It did? . . . No, that's not necessary. I can pick it up tomorrow . . . Jolie?'

A perfectly outlined eyebrow arched questioningly at her. Jolie spun around and stalked from the hallway back outdoors.

The closed expression on Jolie's face prevented Guy from making any inquiries as she went about the packing with vengeance. In less than a half an hour she had everything stowed in the car including the maps outlining her route. A purpling dusk was fighting off the dark of night when she locked the car door, everything in readiness for her morning's journey. Guy had gone into the house minutes before to organize refreshments.

As Jolie wiped the perspiration from her forehead, she turned towards the back door to join him. She had only taken a couple of steps when the screen door slammed shut and Jolie glanced up to see a tall figure standing in her path. Pausing, she considered fleeing, but there was nowhere to go. A grim line was drawn across her mouth as she walked towards Steve.

As she drew closer, she could see the lines of tiredness etched on his face, but she refused to allow compassion to weaken her resolve, nor her thudding heart. In the half-light, his eyes seemed even a darker blue as they watched her approach.

'You didn't have to drive all the way in,' she said coolly, stopping when she was within a few feet of him.

'Didn't I?' he jeered.

'We said our goodbyes over the telephone.' Pride made her chin jut out a bit more than normal.

'Our conversation was interrupted,' he reminded her, unnecessarily.

'By that time everything that was important had been said. And Claudine was anxious to talk to you.'

'I returned her missing gown.' His gaze was flicking searchingly over her face.

'That was considerate of you. I'm sure she'll appreciate it, since she was so worried,' Jolie continued to answer him calmly.

'What made you decide to leave so suddenly?' Steve demanded.

'I already explained that my aunt is ill.'

'I don't believe you. Why should the health of an aunt be of such concern to you?' he sneered.

'Aunt Brigitte is a very special person.' Jolie seized the opportunity to strengthen her reasons. 'She financed most of my trip down here. We've always been very close so naturally when she's ill, I just can't shrug it off as unimportant.'

Her genuineness threw him. She could see the struggle in his face to disbelieve her. Here was her chance to leave, to slip away with her dignity intact.

'I have this feeling that there's something you're not saying.' His quiet statement halted the beginnings of her movement.

'I don't know what it would be,' Jolie swallowed, her mind racing wildly to find any loophole in her story. 'I . . . I didn't thank you for showing me all the local colour. It made my trip very special.'

'*Lagniappe?*' A bitter questioning smile caught at her breath. Something extra, the very phrase she had first associated with him. 'I had hoped to make Louisiana come alive for you.'

How could she tell him that he had made her come alive? That she at last recognized the full potential of her emotions as a woman? But of course she could not. So from the depths of her agony, Jolie summoned a smile.

'You were a very romantic escort,' she said, making her trembling leg muscles walk around him to stand on the first step into the house.

'Excellent for shipboard romances,' he added with considerable mockery.

'Yes,' she said quickly, fighting off the pain caused by the vicious thrust of his words. 'It's strange how going home brings a girl's head out of the clouds.'

'No embarrassing scenes. No vows of undying love. It's much better this way.' There was a look of contempt in Steve's eyes that made her glad she had chosen this uncaring attitude. 'Aren't you glad now that you didn't get swept away by your emotions and do something you would live to regret?'

Steve was referring to their previous encounter the night of the fog, but Jolie could only compare it to her silence in not vocally declaring her love for him. She couldn't have stood his pity.

'Yes,' she whispered, grateful the light had faded

and Steve couldn't see the shimmer of tears gathering in her eyes.

'Now you'll be able to gossip with your girl friends about the man you met beside the bayou.' Jolie turned her head away from the flare of his match as Steve lit a cigarette.

'It was really quite a coincidence the way you turned out to be Etienne and Etienne turned out to be Steve Cameron, the owner of Cameron Hall,' she agreed in a tight voice, knowing she would never be able to tell anyone the whole story under the guise of idle gossip.

'I guess you were right when you said there wasn't any more for us to talk about. I was beginning to think I would regret the day I invited myself to your picnic.' Steve sounded as if he was talking to himself, but even in the dark she could tell he was looking at her. 'I guess this is goodbye, then.'

A hand was extended towards her. She hesitated to take it, knowing the touch of his hand would only intensify the desire to throw herself into his arms. Her self-control didn't fail her as Jolie placed her hand in his, feeling the warmness of his firm grip spread up her arm and through her body. But it didn't ease the cold, throbbing ache in her heart that made her chest feel it was about to burst.

'Goodbye, Steve,' she said softly, the words condemning her to a lifetime alone.

' "Ladybird, Ladybird, fly away home," ' Steve murmured sardonically before he released her hand. 'God speed, Jolie.'

The light from inside the house made everything outside appear darker. The trees were cobwebby shapes against the first twinkling stars. Steve's form was a dark shadow before it was lost to the blackness and out of sight.

Only now could Jolie admit why the crack in her heart had not split the rest of the way. She had been hoping against hope that Steve would brush aside her weak story and masterfully sweep her into his arms telling her that he loved her too much to let her go. But, instead, he had just wished her 'God speed'.

Steve was glad to see her go. He wanted to believe her story. He felt better that she had supposedly only regarded him as a romantic escapade. That was the reality—with all the shattering results of a broken heart.

Jolie shivered. She suddenly felt so cold. So terribly cold. And alone. And empty.

CHAPTER THIRTEEN

JOLIE didn't return to her parents' farm. Her destination instead was her Aunt Brigitte's apartment in Sioux Falls. After the strain of the long journey to South Dakota, during which Jolie had refused to give vent to her grief, it was natural that upon the sight of her aunt the floodgates were released and a torrent of tears burst forth.

It was the practical Brigitte Carson who took over, declaring what Jolie had been unable to, that it was impossible for her to return to her parents' home. Within a matter of only a few days Jolie had acquired a position as a dietician at a private nursing home. The salary was minimal, but money had no value to her. She needed to do something to fill in those awful, memory-filled hours.

Her aunt had been insistent that Jolie occupy the second bedroom of the apartment, at least for a while until she could get on her feet, emotionally and financially. It was just as well that Jolie had gone to her aunt since it was Brigitte who made sure she ate, got to work on time, and made the decisions that Jolie was beyond caring about.

The first week set the pattern for the following weeks. Jolie got up in the mornings, went to work, came home, ate the dinner Brigitte prepared, helped with the dishes, read a book or watched television, and went to bed.

At Christmas time Jolie made her first attempt to join in with the holiday spirits and shake off her stupor-like existence. She went to immense efforts to pick out the most appropriate and personal gift for each member of her family. The hardest one was her father, because she found that every time she walked into the men's department of a store she was visualizing what Steve would look like in a particular outfit on display. Aunt Brigitte encouraged her festive mood, indulging in buying sprees for Christmas decorations that she had considered frivolous in previous years since she had usually spent those school vacations at the farm. This year she was staying at the apartment with Jolie, who only had Christmas Day itself off from work.

Several times Jolie appeared completely cheerful. Then she would exchange a look with her aunt which was always followed by a pair of silent sighs. She wasn't kidding herself or her aunt. Steve still occupied the only place in her heart.

There had been a small Christmas party at the nursing home for the patients, all of them elderly, and Jolie had volunteered to stay late and help with the cleaning up. She was feeling more depressed than usual, considering the carols of Christmastide were still ringing in her ears—probably because so many of the patients were without families or had families who conveniently forgot them. It intensified her dread of the future.

Stepping out of the nursing home, Jolie held the collar of her coat around her neck to keep out the biting cold of the north wind. Snow crunched beneath her boots while the flurries in the air promised additional inches before morning. She patted the dashboard of the Volkswagen affectionately as it started with the first turn of the switch. In weather like this, Jolie was glad her aunt's apartment was so close to where she worked.

As always, once away from the demands of her job, her thoughts strayed back to Louisiana and Steve. She had hoped, prayed, that time would lessen the vividness of her memories, but it hadn't. She had only to close her eyes and she could feel again Steve's arms around her and his kisses on her lips. And the betraying race of her pulse and the throbbing ache of her heart would laugh at her foolish wish to forget.

Parking the car in front of the ground floor apartment, Jolie firmly fixed a smile on her face before scampering into the building. It was a game she played to lift her leaden spirits. One day it might become natural and that was as far as she allowed herself to think.

'It's just me!' she called gaily, closing and locking the apartment door behind her, before removing her coat and hanging it in the hall closet. 'I really think we're going to be in for a storm tonight.'

She rubbed her arms briskly to give emphasis to her words as she stepped out of the small foyer into the living room. Her aunt was sitting in her favourite chair just inside the door, her brown eyes dancing mischeviously up at Jolie.

'It's about time you got home,' she said. 'You have a visitor.'

The living room stretched out to Jolie's right. Her questioning eyes followed her aunt's gaze in that direction. Steve stood near a small table holding a recently acquired Nativity scene. A white ribbed pullover sweater complemented the brown suede trousers, but Jolie's eyes were caught by the vivid blue eyes and imprisoned in their depths. The colour drained from her face. He was, if it was possible, even handsomer than she remembered.

'What are you doing here?' she demanded hoarsely, unconscious of her aunt quietly slipping from the room to leave them alone.

'I came to see you,' Steve answered quietly in his drawling velvet voice as he took a step towards her. There was a tenseness, a strain about his face that was more appealing than anything else.

'Get out of here! I don't want to see you!' Her hand came up to her throat to choke away the sobs that were rising.

'There are some things I've got to tell you,' he continued determinedly.

'I don't want to hear them!' She turned swiftly around and would have fled to her bedroom if his hands hadn't closed over her shoulders and stopped her. It was hard to fight the desire to melt in his arms.

'I'm going to say them anyway,' Steve muttered above her ear, the scent of her cologne mixing with his own masculine aroma that was intoxicating. 'And after I've said them, if you still want me to leave, I will.'

'Oh, please, Steve, let me go.' Jolie closed her eyes tightly, hardly able to bear his nearness. 'Words just don't mean anything any more.'

'Not even "I love you"?' She was drawn back against his chest and she felt his lips moving with their caressing roughness in her hair. 'I never meant to fall in love with you. Lord knows I tried not to, just as I tried to forget you. But you haunted me even before you left Louisiana. All those things I said about never marrying and not believing in love were for myself. I was a man protesting too much.'

Waves of pure rapture swept over her, but she refused to give way to them. She had been through too much in these last months. There had been too many tormenting memories. Even as her heart swelled with love for him, her mind fought back.

'Even when you took Claudine to New Orleans with you?' Jolie asked.

Steve twisted her around in his arms so that he was looking into her face. 'I knew you believed that's what I'd done. Maybe I even wanted you to, I don't know. She called me and asked to ride along, but I swear to you, we stayed in separate hotels. And that damned gown she was talking about was an evening gown she picked up at the dry-cleaners the day we left New Orleans. She left it in the car.'

'Why didn't you tell me that?' Jolie whispered. Some of the fight went out of her as she gazed into the face she adored.

'You were so ready to believe the worst,' he smiled ruefully, deepening the grooves near his mouth. 'And so ready to have me believe that I was just a passing fancy to you. A shipboard romance.'

'You were never that,' Jolie admitted shyly.

'Are you sure, Jolie, very sure?' Steve demanded,

the fierceness coming back into his eyes. 'Because these last few months without you have been hell.'

Her arms slid around his neck and pulled his head closer to hers. It was like coming home after a very long time. The need for words had come to an end as Steve took over her initial movement for his kiss, changing it into a hungry embrace that left her in no doubt as to the depth of his feelings. She was quite sure her response was equally revealing.

Much later, they had somehow traversed to the small sofa and Jolie was cradled in his lap where he could kiss and caress her at will. His will was strong and Jolie was willing.

'Do I give you a few minutes or just walk in?' Aunt Brigitte called from just outside the living room door.

Jolie started to struggle upright, but Steve held her in place. 'Come on in,' Steve directed, smiling mischievously at Jolie's flushed cheeks. 'Your niece is behaving very wantonly. I think she's in grave need of a chaperon.'

'A maid of honour might be more appropriate,' Aunt Brigitte commented dryly at the sight of the pair, but with a decided twinkle of happiness and approval in her understanding brown eyes.

'It's something you'd better be thinking about, little Miss Ladybird,' said Steve, planting a firm kiss on her lips as he pushed Jolie on to the sofa beside him. 'Because whether I've asked you or not, we're going to be married just as soon as we can get a licence and a minister. Cameron Hall is in need of another Jolie Antoinette Cameron as mistress, and so is the master.'

'That was a proposal in front of a witness, Mr. Cameron.' Jolie gazed adoringly into his face. 'And in front of a witness, I accept.'

'I don't think Steve intended to give you much of a choice,' her aunt smiled. 'I don't have any champagne for the celebration, but I could make some cocoa.'

'Do you want some help?' Jolie offered, disliking the thought of leaving Steve's side even for a moment. She needn't have worried, because her offer was firmly refused.

'Before I forget,' said Steve, addressing himself to her aunt as he put an arm around Jolie and drew her closer to him, 'Jolie told me that you were responsible for her being able to take that trip to Louisiana. I want to thank you for that, from both of us. If Jolie has no objections, I thought we might name our first girl after you.'

The older woman's eyes became starry bright with tears as she smiled and said, 'Only if I can be her godmother.'

'Consider it done,' Jolie stated, feeling the same tightness in her throat that had been in her aunt's.

'Well, I'd better make that cocoa.' And her aunt hastily left the room.

'Did you mind?' Steve asked, gazing down at her with unbelievable warmth.

'I thought it was wonderful.' A shy blush covered her cheeks. 'We could have boys, though.'

'We'll just have to keep trying until we get it right,' he teased, laughing at her open-mouthed expression. 'Darling, at the moment I don't care if we have two, ten, or twenty children. All I want is you. Anything else will be a bonus, although a boy and a girl would be nice.'

'Oh, Steve, I love you so much,' she said breathlessly, gazing into the face that she had been so afraid she would never see again.

It was an invitation he couldn't resist. And neither could Jolie as she offered her lips to his.

'And I love you,' he whispered against her mouth.

Take
these
4
best-selling
novels
FREE
Harlequin Presents
ANNE MATHER
born out of love
Harlequin Presents
VIOLET WINSPEAR
time of the temptress
Harlequin Presents
CHARLOTTE LAMB
man's world
Harlequin Presents
SALLY WENTWORTH
say hello to yesterday

What readers say about Harlequin romance fiction...

"You're #1."

A.H. Hattiesburg, Missouri*

"Thank you for the many hours of lovely enjoyment you have given me."

M.M., Schaumburg, Illinois

"The books are so good that I have to read them all the way through before being able to go to sleep at night."

N.Q., Newark, California

"Thanks for many happy hours."

M.L., Millville, New Jersey

"Harlequin books are the doorway to pleasure."

E.W., Hawthorne, California

"They are quality books—down-to-earth reading! Don't ever quit!"

G.F., Buffalo, Minnesota

"A pleasant escape from the pressures of this world."

C.T., Hickory, North Carolina

"Keep them coming! They are still the best books."

R.W., Jersey City, New Jersey

**Names available on request*